"Full of twists and turns, with warmth and humor on every page, it doesn't disappoint."
—*Closer*

"A modern fairy tale, it's full of Keyes's self-deprecating wit."
—*Sunday Mirror* (UK)

Praise for Marian Keyes

"Keyes manages to stuff a smorgasbord of genres into one tasty tale. . . . The real joy is in the journey itself; watching Keyes's quirky characters as they change partners, reveal battle scars, and command your attention on every page."
—*People*

"Keyes's witty women . . . humorous writing style, and uplifting tone have become beloved by readers across the globe." —*Chicago Tribune*

"Deeply hilarious and unexpectedly deep. Keyes never falters."
—*Newsweek*

"[A] pleasure to read . . . A sharp and honest exploration of a favorite Keyes theme: resilience." —*Cleveland Plain Dealer*

"Keyes's portrayal of depression is nuanced and authentic. Helen's vibrant voice is spot-on." —*Publishers Weekly*

"A well-crafted novel with engaging characters and a gripping plot."
—*Christian Science Monitor*

"A tasty literary latte." —*USA Today*

"Genuinely human and believable characters within a substantial and gratifying story." —*Booklist*

PENGUIN BOOKS

THE WOMAN WHO STOLE MY LIFE

Marian Keyes is the internationally bestselling author of more than ten novels and two autobiographical works. Several of her novels have been adapted for television and film. She was born in Limerick in 1963 and brought up in Cavan, Cork, Galway, and Dublin. She spent her twenties in London and lives now in Dún Laoghaire with her husband, Tony.

www.mariankeyes.com

@MarianKeyes

MARIAN KEYES

The Woman Who Stole My Life

PENGUIN BOOKS

PENGUIN BOOKS

An imprint of Penguin Random House LLC
375 Hudson Street
New York, New York 10014
penguin.com

First published in Great Britain by Michael Joseph,
an imprint of Penguin Books Ltd.
First published in the United States of America by Viking Penguin,
an imprint of Penguin Random House LLC, 2015
Published in Penguin Books 2016

THE LIBRARY OF CONGRESS HAS CATALOGED THE
HARDCOVER EDITION AS FOLLOWS:
Keyes, Marian.
The woman who stole my life / Marian Keyes.
pages ; cm
ISBN 9780525429258 (hc.)
ISBN 9780143109358 (pbk.)
I. Title.
PR6061.E88W66 2015
823'.914—dc23   2015010571

Printed in the United States of America
1   3   5   7   9   10   8   6   4   2

Set in Fournier MT Std and Avenir LT Std 45 Book

For Tony

The Woman Who Stole My Life

Can I make one thing clear—no matter what you've heard, and I'm sure you've heard plenty—I'm not a full-blown karma denier. It might exist, it might not, like how on earth would I know? All I'm doing is giving my version of events.

However, if karma *does* exist, I'll say one thing for it, it's got a fantastic PR machine. We all know the "story": karma is running a great big ledger in the sky where every good deed done by every human being is recorded and at some later stage—the time to be of karma's choosing (karma is cagey that way, plays its cards close to its chest)—karma will refund that good deed. Maybe even with interest.

So we think if we sponsor youths to climb a hill to raise money for the local hospice, or if we change our niece's nappy when we'd rather stab ourself in the head, that at some point in the future something good will happen to us. And when something good *does* happen to us, we go, Ah, that'll be my old friend karma, paying me back for my erstwhile good deed. "Hey, thanks, karma!"

Karma has got a string of credits the length of the Amazon, when in fact I suspect karma has been doing the conceptual version of lounging around on the couch in its underpants watching Sky Sports.

Let's take a look at karma "in action."

One day, four and a half years ago, I was out driving in my car (a cheapish Hyundai SUV). I was moving along in a steady stream of traffic and up ahead I saw a car trying to get out of a side road. A couple of things told me that this man had been trying to get out of this side road for quite a while. Fact A: the man was bent over his steering wheel in an attitude of weary, imploring frustration. Fact B: he was driving a Range Rover and simply by dint of the fact that he was driving a Range Rover, everyone was going to think, Ah, look at him there, the big, smug, Range Rover driver, I'm not letting him out.

So I thought, Ah, look at him there, the big, smug, Range Rover driver, I'm not letting him out. Then I thought—and all of this was happening quickly, because, like I said, I was moving along in a steady stream of traffic—then I thought, Ah, no, I'll let him out, it'll be—and mark me closely here—it'll be *good karma*.

So I slowed down, flashed my lights to indicate to the big, smug, Range Rover driver that he was free to go, and he gave a tired smile and started moving forward and already I was feeling a warm sort of glow and wondering vaguely what form of lovely cosmic payback I'd be getting, when the car behind, unprepared for me slowing down to let the Range Rover out—on account of it being a Range Rover—went plowing into the back of me, shunting me forward with such force that I went careering into the side of the Range Rover (the technical term for such a maneuver is "T-boning") and suddenly there was a three-car love-in going on. Except there was no love there, of course. Far from it.

For me, the whole thing happened in slow motion. From the second the car behind me began to concertina into mine, time almost stopped. I felt the wheels of my own car beneath me, moving without my say-so, and I was staring into the eyes of the man driving the Range Rover, our gazes locked in horror, united in the strange intimacy of knowing we were about to hurt each other and being entirely powerless to prevent it.

Then came the awful reality as my car really did hit his—the sound of metal crunching and glass shattering and the bone-juddering violence of the impact . . . followed by stillness. Just for a second, but a second that lasted a very long time. Stunned and shocked, the man and I stared at each other. He was only inches away from me—the impact had shifted us so that our cars were almost side by side. His side window had shattered and small chunks of glass glittered in his hair, reflecting a silvery light that was the same color as his eyes. He looked even more weary than when he was waiting to be let out of the side road.

Are you alive? I asked, with my thoughts.

Yes, he replied. *Are you?*

Yes.

My passenger door was wrenched open and the spell was broken. "Are you okay?" someone asked. "Can you get out?"

With shaking limbs, I crawled my way across to the open door and when I was outside and leaning against a wall I saw that Range Rover Man was also free. With relief, I registered that he was standing upright, so his injuries, if any, must be minor.

Out of nowhere a small man hurtled at me and shrieked, "What the hell are you at? That's a brand-new Range Rover!" It was the driver from the third car, the one who'd caused the accident. "This is going to cost me a fortune. It's a new car! He doesn't even have plates on it yet!"

"But, I . . ."

Range Rover Man stepped in and said, "Stop. Calm down. Stop."

"But it's a brand-new car!"

"Shouting about it isn't going to change things."

The yelling quieted down and I said to Range Rover Man, "I was trying to do a good deed, letting you out."

"It's okay."

Suddenly I realized that he was very angry and in an instant I'd got him—one of those good-looking spoiled men, with his expensive car and his well-cut coat and his expectation that life would treat him nicely.

"At least no one was hurt," I said.

Range Rover Man wiped some blood off his forehead. "Yeah. At least no one was hurt . . ."

"I mean, like, not seriously . . ."

"I know." He sighed. "Are you okay?"

"Fine," I said, stiffly. I didn't want his concern.

"I'm sorry if I was . . . you know. It's been a bad day."

"Whatever."

It was mayhem all around us. The traffic was tail-backed in both directions, "helpful" passersby were offering conflicting eye-witness reports and the shouty man started shouting again.

A kind person led me away to sit on a doorstep while we waited for the police and another kind person gave me a bag of sweets. "For your blood sugar," she said. "You've had a shock."

Very quickly the police showed up and started redirecting traffic and taking statements. Shouty Man shouted a lot and kept jabbing his finger at me, and Range Rover Man was talking soothingly, and I watched them both like I was watching a movie. There was my car, I thought, hazily. Banjaxed. A total write-off. It was utterly miraculous that I'd stepped out of it in one piece.

The accident was Shouty Man's fault and his insurance would have to cough up, but I wouldn't get enough to replace my car because insurance companies always underpaid. Ryan would go mad—despite his success we were constantly teetering on the brink of brokeness—but I'd worry about that later. For the moment I was happy enough sitting on this step eating sweets.

Hold on! Range Rover Man was on the move. He strode over to me, his open overcoat flying. "How do you feel now?" he asked.

"Great." Because I did. Shock, adrenaline, one of those things.

"Can I have your phone number?"

I laughed in his face. "No!" What kind of creep was he, that he tried to pick up women at the scene of a traffic accident? "Anyway, I'm married!"

"For the insurance . . ."

"Oh." *God. The shame, the shame.* "Okay."

So let's look at the karmic fallout from my good deed—three cars, all of them damaged, one wounded forehead, much irateness, shouting, raised blood pressure, financial worry and deep, *deep* blush-making humiliation. Bad, bad, all very bad.

ME

Friday, 30 May

14:49

You know, if you glanced up at my window right now, you'd think to yourself, "Look at that woman. Look at the diligent way she's sitting upright at her desk. Look at the assiduous way her hands are poised over her keyboard. She's obviously working very hard . . . hold on . . . is that Stella Sweeney?! Back in Ireland? Writing a new book?! I'd heard she was all washed up!"

Yes, I *am* Stella Sweeney. Yes, I *am* (much to my disappointment, but we won't get into it now) back in Ireland. Yes, I *am* writing a new book. Yes, I *am* all washed up.

But I won't be all washed up for long. No indeed. Because I'm working. You only have to look at me here at my desk! Yes, I'm working.

. . . Except I'm not. Looking like you're working isn't quite the same thing as *actually* working. I haven't typed a single word. I can think of nothing to say.

A small smile plays about my lips, though. Just in case you're looking in. Being in the public eye does that to a person. You have to look smiley and act nice all the time, or else people will say, "The fame went to her head. And it's not like she was any good in the first place."

I'll have to get curtains, I decide. I won't be able to sustain this smiling business. Already my face is hurting and I've only been sitting here for fifteen minutes. Twelve, actually. How *slow* the time is going!

I type one word. "Ass." It doesn't further my case, but it feels nice to write something.

"Begin at the beginning," Phyllis had told me, that terrible day in her office in New York, a few months ago. "Do an introduction. Remind people of who you are."

"Have they forgotten already?"

"Sure."

I'd never liked Phyllis—she was a terrifying little bulldog of a creature. But I wasn't supposed to like her—she was my agent, not my friend.

The first time I'd met her she'd waved my book in the air and said, "We could go a long way with this. Drop ten pounds and you've got yourself an agent."

I'd cut out the carbs and dropped five of the stipulated ten pounds, then there was a sit-down where she was persuaded to settle for seven pounds and me wearing Spanx whenever I was on TV.

And Phyllis was right: we *did* go a long way with that book. A long way up, then a long way sideways, then a long way off the map. So far off the map that I'm sitting here at a desk in my small house in the Dublin suburb of Ferrytown, which I thought I'd escaped forever, trying to write another book.

Okay, I'll write my introduction.

Name: Stella Sweeney.
Age: forty-one and a quarter.
Height: average.
Hair: long, curly and blond-ish.
Recent life events: dramatic.

No, that won't do; it's too bare. It needs to be more chatty, more lyrical. I'll try again.

Hello, there! Stella Sweeney here. Slim, thirty-eight-year-old Stella Sweeney. I know you need no reminding of who I am but, just in case, I wrote the international best-selling inspirational book *One Blink at a Time*. I was on talk shows and everything. They worked me to the bone on several book tours that took in thirty-four U.S. cities (if you count Minneapolis–St. Paul as two places). I flew in a private plane (once). Everything was lovely, absolutely lovely, except for the bits that were horrible. Living the dream, I was! Except for when I wasn't . . . But the wheel of fate has turned again and I find myself in very different, more humbling circumstances. Adjusting to the latest twist my life has taken has been painful but ultimately rewarding. Inspired by my new wisdom, not to mention the fact that I'm skint.

No, bad idea to mention the skintness, I'd better take that out. I hit the delete key until all mention of money has disappeared, then start typing again.

Inspired by my new wisdom, I'm trying to write a new book. I've no idea what it's about but I'm hoping if I throw enough words onto a screen, I'll be able to cobble something together. Something even more inspirational than *One Blink at a Time*!

That's grand. That'll do. Okay, maybe that second-last sentence needs to be tidied up, but, fundamentally, I'm out of the traps. Fair play to me. As a reward, I'll just take a quick look on Twitter . . .

. . . Amazing how you can lose three hours just like *that*. I emerge from my Twitter hole, dazed to find myself still at my desk, still in my tiny "office" (i.e., spare bedroom) in my old house in Ferrytown. In Twitterland we were having a great old chat about summer having finally arrived. Every time it seemed like the discussion might be about to taper off, someone new came in and reignited the whole thing. We discussed fake tan, cos lettuce, shameful feet . . . It was fecking *fantastic*. FANTASTIC!

I'm feeling great! I remember reading somewhere that the chemicals produced in the brain by a lengthy Twitter session are similar to those produced by cocaine.

Abruptly my bubble pops and I'm faced with the fairy-dust-free facts: I wrote ten sentences today. That's not enough.

I will work now. I will, I will, I will. If I don't I'll have to punish myself by disabling the Internet on this computer . . .

Is that Jeffrey I hear?

It is! In he comes, slamming the front door and throwing his wretched yoga mat onto the hall floor. I can sense every move that yoga mat makes. I'm always aware of it, the way you are when you hate something. It hates me too. It's like we're in a battle over ownership of Jeffrey.

I jump up to say hello even though Jeffrey hates me almost as much as his yoga mat does. He's hated me for ages now. About five years, give or take, basically since the moment he hit thirteen.

I'd thought it was girls who were meant to be nightmare teenagers and that boys simply went mute for the duration. But Betsy wasn't bad at all and Jeffrey has been full of . . . well . . . *angst*. In fairness, by dint of having me as his mother, he's had a roller coaster of a time of it, so much so that when he was fifteen he asked to be put up for adoption.

However, I'm delighted that I can stop pretending to work for a little while, and I run down the stairs. "Sweetheart!" I try to act like the hostility between us doesn't exist.

There he is, six feet tall, as thin as a pipe cleaner and with an Adam's apple as big as a muffin. He looks exactly like his father did at that age.

I sense extra animosity from him today.

"What?" I ask.

Without looking at me he says, "Get your hair cut."

"Why?"

"Just do. You're too old to have it that long."

"What's going on?"

"From the back you look . . . different."

I coax the story out of him. It transpires that this morning, he was "down the town" with one of his yoga friends. Outside the Pound Shop the friend had spotted me from the rear and made admiring noises and Jeffrey had said, from bloodless lips, "That's my mom. She's forty-one and a quarter."

I deduce that both of them were badly shaken by the experience.

Maybe I should be flattered, but the thing is I know I'm not too bad from the back. The front, however, is not so good. I'm that strange shape where any weight I put on goes straight to my stomach. Even as a teenager, when the other girls were worried sick about the size of their asses and the width of their thighs, I'd kept an anxious eye on my midsection. I knew it had the potential to go rogue and my life has been one long battle to contain it.

Jeffrey swings a shopping bag of peppers at me, with what can only be called aggression. ("He menaced me with capsicums, Your Honor.") I sigh inwardly. I know what's coming. He wants to cook. Again. This is a fairly new departure and, against all evidence to the contrary, he thinks he's brilliant at it. As he searches for his niche in life, he combines risibly mismatched ingredients and makes me eat the results. Rabbit and mango stew, that's what we had last night.

"I'm cooking dinner." He dead-eyes me as he waits for me to cry.

"Grand," I say, brightly.

That means we'll get fed around midnight. Just as well I have a stash of Jaffa Cakes in my bedroom, so big it almost covers an entire wall.

19:41

I tiptoe into the kitchen, to find Jeffrey staring motionless at a tin of pineapple, as if it were a chessboard and he were a Grand Master, planning his next move.

"Jeffrey . . ."

Tonelessly, he says, "I'm concentrating. Or rather, I was."

"Do I have time to visit Mum and Dad before dinner?" See what I did there? I didn't just say, "What time will I be getting fed?" I made it not about me, but about his grandparents, which hopefully will soften his angry heart.

"I don't know."

"I'm just going out for an hour."

"Dinner will be ready by then."

It won't be. He's keeping me trapped. I'll have to confront this passive-aggressive warfare at some stage, but I'm feeling so defeated by my pointless day and my pointless life that, right now, I'm not able.

"Okay . . ."

"Please don't come in here while I'm working."

I go back upstairs and wish I could tweet "#Working #MyHole" but some of his friends follow me on Twitter. Besides, any time I send a tweet, it reminds people that I'm nobody now and that it's time to unfollow me. That is a true measurable fact which I sometimes test, just in case I'm not feeling like enough of a loser.

In fairness, I was never Lady Gaga with her millions and millions of followers, but, in my own small way, I was once a Twitter presence.

Denied an outlet for my gloom, I remove a brick from my Jaffa Cake wall and lie on my bed and eat many of the little round discs of chocolate-and-orange happiness. So many that I can't tell you because I made a deliberate decision to not count. Plenty, though. Rest assured of that.

Tomorrow will be different, I tell myself. Tomorrow will *have* to be different. There will be lots of writing and lots of productivity and no Jaffa Cakes. I will not be a woman who lies on her bed, her chest covered with spongy crumbs.

An hour and a half later, still a dinner-free woman, I hear a car door slam and feel someone hurrying up our little path. In this cardboard house, you cannot just hear, but you can *feel* everything that happens within a fifty-meter radius.

"Dad's here." There is alarm in Jeffrey's voice. "He looks a bit mental."

The doorbell begins to ring frantically. I hurry down the stairs and open the door and there is Ryan. Jeffrey is right: he *does* look a bit mental.

Ryan pushes past me into the hall and, with zeal that borders on the manic, says, "Stella, Jeffrey, I've got some fantastic news!"

Let me tell you about my ex-husband, Ryan. He might put things differently, which he's welcome to do, but as this is my story, you're getting my version.

We got together when I was nineteen and he was twenty-one and he had notions about being an artist. Because he was very good at drawing dogs and because I knew nothing about art, I thought he was highly talented. He was accepted into art college where, to our mutual dismay, he showed no signs of being the breakout star of his generation. We used to have long talks, late into the night, when he'd tell me all the different ways his tutors were cretins and I'd stroke his hands and agree with him.

After four years he graduated with a mediocre degree and began painting for a living. But no one bought his canvases, so he decided that painting was over. He played around with different media—film, graffiti, dead budgies in formaldehyde—but a year passed and nothing took off. Ultimately a pragmatic man, Ryan faced facts: he didn't like being perpetually penniless. He wasn't cut out for this starving-in-a-garret business that seems to be the stock-in-trade of most artists.

Besides, he had acquired a wife (me) and a young daughter, Betsy. He needed to get a job. But not just any old job. After all, he was, despite everything, an artist.

Around this time, my dad's glamorous sister, Auntie Jeanette, came into a few quid and decided to spend it on something she'd coveted since she was a little girl—a beautiful bathroom. She wanted something—said with an airy wave of her hand—"fabulous." Jeanette's poor husband, Uncle Peter, who had spent the previous twenty years desperately trying to provide the glamour that Jeanette so clearly craved, asked, "What sort of fabulous?" But Jeanette couldn't actually say, "Just, you know, *fabulous*."

Peter (he later admitted this to my dad) had a dreadful moment when he thought he might start sobbing and never stop, then he was saved from such humiliation by a brainwave. "Why don't we ask Stella to ask Ryan?" he said. "He's artistic."

Ryan was mortified to be consulted on such a mundane project and he told me to tell Auntie Jeanette that she could feck off, that he was an artist and that artists didn't "bother their barney" on the placement of washbasins. But I hate confrontation and I was afraid of causing a family rift, so I couched Ryan's refusal in vaguer terms. So vague that an armload of bathroom brochures were dropped off for Ryan's perusal.

They sat on our small kitchen table for over a week. Now and again I'd pick one up and say, "God, that's *gorgeous*," and, "Would you look at that? So imaginative."

You see, I was keeping our little family afloat by working as a beautician, and I'd have been very grateful if Ryan had started bringing in some money. But Ryan refused to take the bait. Until one night he began to leaf through the pages and suddenly he was engaged. He picked up a pencil and some graph paper and within no time he was applying himself with vigor. "She wants fabulous," he muttered. "I'll give her fabulous."

Over the following days and weeks he labored on layout, he spent hours scouring *Buy and Sell* (these were pre-eBay days) and he jumped out of bed in the middle of the night, his artistic head fizzing with artistic ideas.

News of Ryan's diligence began to spread through my family and people were impressed. My dad, who had never been keen on Ryan, reluctantly began to revise his opinion. He stopped saying, "Ryan Sweeney an artist? Piss artist, more like!"

The result—and everyone was agreed on this, even Dad, a skeptical, working-class man—was indeed fabulous: Ryan had created a mini Studio 54. As he'd been born in Dublin in 1971, he'd never had the honor of visiting the iconic nightclub, so he had to base his design on photos and anecdotal evidence. He even wrote to Bianca Jagger. (She didn't reply but, still, it shows the lengths he was prepared to go to.)

As soon as you put a foot into the bathroom, the floor lit up and Donna Summer's "Love to Love You, Baby" began to play softly. Natural light was banished and replaced with an ambient gold glow. The cabinets—and there were plenty of them because Auntie Jeanette had a lot of stuff—were coated with glitter. Andy Warhol's *Marilyn* was recreated in eight thousand tiny mosaic tiles and covered an entire wall. The bath was egg-shaped and black. The toilet was housed in an adorable little black lacquer cubicle. The makeup station had enough theatrical-style lightbulbs to power the whole of Ferrytown (Jeanette had stipulated "brutal" lighting; she was proud of her skill in blending foundations and concealer but she couldn't do it in poor visibility).

When, with a final flourish, Ryan hung a small glitter ball from the ceiling, he knew that the masterpiece was complete.

It could have been tacky, it skirted within a millimeter of being kitsch, but it was—as stipulated in the brief—"fabulous." Auntie Jeanette issued invitations to family and friends for the Grand Opening and the dress code was Disco. As a little joke, Ryan purchased a one-ounce bag of fenugreek from the Ferrytown health-food shop and chopped it into lines on the elegant hand basin. Everyone thought that was a "gas." (Except Dad. "There's nothing funny about drugs. Even pretend ones.")

The mood was festive. Everyone, young and old, in their disco-est of clothes, crowded in and danced on the small flashing floor. I, overjoyed that (a) a family rift had been averted and (b) that Ryan had done some paying work, was probably the happiest person there. I wore a pair of vintage Pucci palazzo pants and a matching tunic that I'd found in the Help the Aged shop and had washed seven times, and my hair was blow-dried into a Farrah flick by a hairdresser pal in exchange for a manicure. "You look beautiful," Ryan told me. "So do you," I replied, perky as you please. I meant it too because, let's face it, suddenly becoming a wage earner would add luster to the most ordinary-looking of men. (Not that Ryan was ordinary-looking. If he'd washed his hair more often, he could have been dangerous.) All in all, it was a very happy day.

Suddenly Ryan had a career. Not the one he'd wanted, no, but one he was very good at. He followed his Studio 54 triumph by going in a different direction—he created a bathroom that was a green-filtered, peaceful, forest-style retreat. Mosaics of trees covered three walls and real ferns climbed the fourth. The window was replaced with green glass and the soundtrack was of birdcalls. For the final reveal to the client Ryan scattered pine cones around the place. (His original plan had been to source a squirrel but, despite Caleb, his electrician, and Drugi, his tiler, spending most of a morning shaking nuts and shouting, "Here, squirrely!" in Crone Woods, they weren't able to catch one.)

Hot on the heels of the forest bathroom came the project that got Ryan his first magazine coverage—the Jewel Box. It was a wonderland of mirrors, Swarovski tiles and claret-colored velvet-effect (but water-resistant) wallpaper. The cabinet knobs were Bohemian crystal, the bath was made of silver-flecked glass and a Murano chandelier hung from the ceiling. The soundtrack (Ryan's music was fast becoming his unique selling point) was the "Dance of the Sugar Plum Fairy" and every time you turned the taps on, a tiny mechanical ballerina rotated gracefully.

Working with a small, trusted team, Ryan Sweeney became the go-to man for amazing bathrooms. He was imaginative, painstaking and ferociously expensive.

Life was good. There was the odd hiccup—when Betsy was three months old, I got pregnant with Jeffrey. But, thanks to Ryan's success, we were able to buy a newly built, three-bedroom house, big enough for the four of us.

Time passed. Ryan made money, he made beautiful bathrooms, he made people—mostly women—happy. At the end of every project, Ryan's client exclaimed, "You're an artist!" They meant it and Ryan knew it, but he was the wrong sort of artist: he wanted to be Damien Hirst. He wanted to be famous and notorious, he wanted people on late-night arty-discussion shows to shout at each other about him, he wanted some people to say he was a fake. Well, he didn't. He wanted everyone to say he was a genius, but the best sort of genius generates controversy so he was prepared to put up with the occasional slagging.

Nevertheless, all was well until one day in 2010, when a tragedy befell him. Strictly speaking, the tragedy was mine. But artists, even unfulfilled ones, have a habit of making everything about themselves. The tragedy, a long-running one, didn't bring everyone together, because life isn't a soap opera. The tragedy ended with Ryan and me splitting up.

Almost immediately, strange, exciting things began to happen to me—which we'll get to. All you need to know for now is that Betsy, Jeffrey and I moved to live in New York.

Ryan stayed in Dublin in the house that we'd bought as an investment in the midnoughties when everyone in Ireland was tying up their futures in second properties. (I got our original starter home in the divorce. Even when I was living in a ten-room duplex on the Upper West Side, I hung on to it—I never trusted that my new circumstances would last. I was always afraid of boomeranging back to poverty.)

Ryan had girlfriends—once he'd started washing his hair more regularly, there was no shortage. He had his work, he had a nice car and a motorbike—he wanted for nothing. But he wanted for everything: he never felt fulfilled. The gnawing pain of incompleteness sometimes went underground but it always returned.

And now here he is, standing wild-eyed in my hall, myself and Jeffrey looking at him in alarm. "It's happened, it's finally happened!" Ryan says. "My big artistic idea!"

"Come in and sit down," I say. "Jeffrey, put the kettle on."

Babbling unstoppably, Ryan follows me into the front room, telling me what has happened. "It started about a year ago . . ."

We sit facing each other while Ryan describes his breakthrough. A stirring had started deep down in him and, over the course of a year, swam its way upward to consciousness. It visited him in vague forms in his dreams, in flashseconds between thoughts, and, this very afternoon, his brilliant idea finally broke the surface. It had taken nearly twenty years of toiling with high-grade Italian sanitaryware for his genius to burst into bloom but finally it had.

"And?" I prompt.

"I'm calling it Project Karma: I'm going to give away everything I own. Every single thing. My CDs, my clothes, all my money. Every television, every grain of rice, every holiday photograph. My car, my motorbike, my house—"

Jeffrey stares in disgust. "You stupid asshole."

All credit to him, Jeffrey seems to hate Ryan as much as he hates me. He's an equal opportunities hater. He could have done that thing that children of separated couples sometimes do, of playing the parents against each other, of pretending to have favorites, but in all honesty you'd have been hard-pressed to know which one of us he hated the most.

"You'll have nowhere to live!" Jeffrey says.

"Wrong!" Ryan's eyes are sparkling (but the wrong sort of sparkling, a scary form). "Karma will see me right."

"But what if it doesn't?" I feel horribly uneasy. I don't trust karma, not any more. Once upon a time, something very bad happened to me. As a direct result of that very bad thing, something very, very good happened. I was a *big* believer in karma at that point. However, as a direct result of that very, very good thing, a very bad thing happened. Then another bad thing. I am currently due an upswing in my karma cycle, but it doesn't seem to be happening. Frankly, I've had it with karma.

And on a more practical level, I am afraid that if Ryan has no money I'll have to give him some and I have almost none myself.

"I will prove that karma exists," Ryan says. "I'm creating Spiritual Art."

"Can I have your house?" Jeffrey asks.

Ryan seems startled. He hasn't considered such a request. "Ah no. No." As he speaks, he becomes more convinced. "Definitely not. If I gave it to you, it might look like I wasn't doing it for real."

"Can I have your car?"

"No."

"Can I have anything?"

"No."

"Fuck you very much."

"Jeffrey, don't," I say.

Ryan is so excited he barely notices Jeffrey's contempt. "I'll blog about it, day by day, second by second. It'll be an artistic triumph."

"I think this sort of thing has already been done." A memory of something, somewhere, is flickering.

"Don't," Ryan says. "Stella, don't undermine me. You've had your fifteen minutes, let me have mine."

"But—"

"No, Stella." He's all but shouting. "It should have been me. I'm the one who's meant to be famous. Not you—me! You're the woman who stole my life!"

This is a familiar conversational theme; Ryan refers to it almost daily.

Jeffrey is clicking away on his phone. "It *has* been done. I'm getting loads here. Listen to this: 'The man who gave away everything he possessed.' Here's another one, 'An Austrian millionaire is planning to give away all his money and possessions.'"

"Ryan," I say, tentatively, keen to avoid triggering another rant from him. "Could you be . . . depressed?"

"Do I seem depressed?"

"You seem insane."

Even before he speaks, I know he's going to say, "I've never been saner." Sure enough, Ryan obliges.

"I need you to help me, Stella," he says. "I need publicity."

"You're never out of the magazines."

"Home decor magazines." Ryan dismisses them with contempt. "They're no good. You're matey with the mainstream media."

"Not anymore."

"Ah, you are. A lot of residual affection for you. Even if it's all gone to shit."

"How are you going to make money from this?" Jeffrey asks.

"Art isn't about making money."

Jeffrey mutters something. I catch the word "knobhead."

After Ryan leaves, Jeffrey and I look at each other.

"Say something," Jeffrey says.

"He won't go through with it."

"You think?"

"I think."

22:00

Jeffrey and I are sitting in front of the telly eating our pepper, pineapple and sausage stew. I'm trying hard to force down a few mouthfuls—these dinners of Jeffrey's count as Cruel and Unusual Punishment—and Jeffrey has his face in his phone. Suddenly he says, "Fuck." It's the first word we've exchanged in a while.

"What?"

"Dad. He's issued a Mission Statement . . . and . . ." Speedy clicking. ". . . his first video blog. And he's started a countdown to Day Zero. It's Monday week, ten days' time."

Project Karma is a go.

Keep breathing.

Extract from *One Blink at a Time*

et me tell you about the tragedy that befell me nearly four years ago. There I was, being thirty-seven and the mother of a fifteen-year-old girl and a fourteen-year-old boy and the wife of a successful but creatively unfulfilled bathroom designer. I was working with my younger sister, Karen (but really *for* my younger sister, Karen), and generally I was being very normal—life was having its ups and downs but nothing to get excited about—when, one evening, the tips of the fingers on my left hand started to tingle. By bedtime, my right hand was also tingling. Maybe it's a sign of how dull everything was that I found it pleasant, like having space dust popping under my skin.

Sometime during the night, I half woke and noticed that now my feet were tingling as well. Lovely, I thought, dreamily, space-dust feet too. Maybe in the morning I'd be tingling everywhere and wouldn't *that* be nice.

When the alarm went off at 7 a.m., I felt knackered, but that was par for the course. I felt knackered every morning—after all, I was very normal. But this particular morning, it was a different sort of tiredness: a bad, heavy, made-of-lead tiredness.

"Get up," I said to Ryan, then I stumbled down the stairs—and in retrospect, I probably really *was* stumbling—and started boiling kettles and throwing boxes of cereal onto the table, then I went upstairs to rouse (i.e., shout at) my children.

I went back downstairs and took a swig of tea, but to my surprise it tasted strange and metallic. I stared accusingly at the stainless-steel kettle—clearly bits of it had infiltrated my tea. It had been such a good friend all these years, why had it suddenly turned on me?

Giving it another wounded look, I started on Jeffrey's special toast, which was simply ordinary toast without the butter—he had a "thing" about butter, he said it was slimy—but my hands felt fumbly and numb, and the enjoyable tingling had stopped.

I took a mouthful of orange juice, then spat it out and yelped.

"What?" Ryan had appeared. He was never good in the mornings. He was never good in the evenings either, come to think of it. He might have been in top form in the middle of the day, but I never got to see him then, so I couldn't comment.

"The orange juice," I said. "It burned me."

"Burned you? It's orange juice; it's cold."

"It burned my tongue. My mouth."

"Why are you talking like that?"

"Like what?"

"Like . . . your tongue is swollen." He grabbed my glass and took a swig, and said, "There's nothing wrong with that orange juice."

I tried another sip. It burned me again.

Jeffrey materialized at my side and said accusingly, "Did you put butter on this toast?"

"No."

We played this game every morning.

"You've put butter on it," he said. "I can't eat it."

"Okay."

He looked at me in surprise.

"Give him some money," I ordered Ryan.

"Why?"

"So he can buy himself something for breakfast."

Startled, Ryan handed over a fiver and, startled, Jeffrey took it.

"I'm off," Ryan said.

"Grand. Bye. Okay, kids, get your stuff." Normally I ran through a checklist as long as my arm for all their extracurricular activities— swimming, hockey, rugby, the school orchestra—but today I didn't bother. Sure enough, about ten minutes into the car journey, Jeffrey said, "I forgot my banjo."

There was no way I was turning around and going back to get it. "You'll be fine," I said. "You can manage without it for one day."

A blanket of stunned silence fell in the car.

At the school gate dozens of privileged, cosmopolitan teenagers were milling in. It was one of the greatest sources of pride in my life that Betsy and Jeffrey were pupils at Quartley Daily, a non-denominational, fee-paying school, which aimed to educate "the whole child." My guilty pleasure was to watch them as they traipsed in, in their uniforms, both of them tall and a little gawky, Betsy's blond curls swinging in a ponytail and Jeffrey's dark hair sticking up in tufts. I always took a moment to watch them merge with the other kids (some of them the offspring of diplomats—the lightbulb of my pride glowed extra bright at that bit, but obviously I kept it to myself; the only person I ever admitted it to was Ryan). But today I didn't hang around. My focus was on home, where I was hoping for a quick lie-down before going to work.

As soon as I let myself into the house, I was overtaken by a wave of weakness so powerful I had to lie down in the hall. With the side of my face pressed against the cold floorboards, I knew I couldn't go to work. This was maybe the first sick day of my life. Even with a hangover I'd always shown up; the work ethic went deep in me.

I rang Karen and my fingers could barely work the phone. "I've the flu," I said.

"You haven't the flu," she said. "Everyone says they've the flu when they just have a cold. Believe me, if you had the flu, you'd know all about it."

"I do know all about it," I said. "I've the flu."

"Are you putting on that funny voice so I'll believe you?"

"Really. I've the flu."

"Tongue flu, is it?"

"I'm sick, Karen, I swear to God. I'll be in tomorrow."

I crawled up the stairs, stumbled gratefully into bed, set my phone for 3 p.m. and fell into a deep sleep.

I woke dry-mouthed and disoriented and when I reached for a swig of water, I couldn't swallow it. I focused hard on waking myself up and swallowing the water, but nothing happened: I really couldn't swallow it. I had to spit it back into the glass.

Then I realized that, even without the water in my mouth, I couldn't swallow. The muscles at the back of my throat just wouldn't work. I concentrated hard on them, trying to ignore the rising panic, but nothing happened. I couldn't swallow. I actually, really, couldn't swallow.

Scared, I rang Ryan. "There's something wrong with me. I can't swallow."

"Have a Strepsil and take some Panadol."

"I don't mean my throat is sore. I mean I can't swallow."

He sounded bemused. "But everyone can swallow."

"I can't. My throat won't work."

"Your voice sounds funny."

"Can you come home?"

"I'm on a site visit. In Carlow. It'll take a couple of hours. Why don't you go to the doctor?"

"Okay. See you later." Then I tried to stand up and my legs wouldn't work.

When Ryan came home and saw the state of me, he was gratifyingly contrite. "I didn't realize . . . Can you walk?"

"No."

"And you still can't swallow? Christ. I think we should ring an ambulance. Should we ring an ambulance?"

"Okay."

"Really? It's that bad?"

"How do I know? It might be."

A while later an ambulance arrived, with men who strapped me to a stretcher. Leaving my bedroom, I had a stab of sudden shocking grief, as if I had a premonition that it would be a long, long time before I saw it again.

Watched by Betsy, Jeffrey and my mum, who were standing at the front door, silent and looking scared, I was loaded into the van.

"We could be gone awhile," Ryan told them. "You know what A&E is like. We'll probably be hanging around for hours."

But I was a priority case. Within an hour of my arrival a doctor appeared and said, "So? Muscular weakness?"

"Yes." My speech had degenerated so much that the word emerged like a slurred grunt.

"Talk properly," Ryan said.

"I'm trying."

"This the best you can do?" The doctor seemed interested.

I tried to nod and found that I couldn't.

"Can you squeeze that?" The doctor gave me a pen.

We all watched as the pen fell from my clumsy fingers.

"How about the other hand? No? Can you raise your arm? Flex your foot? Wriggle your toes? No?"

"Of course you can," Ryan said to me. "She can," he repeated, but the doctor had turned to talk to someone else in a white coat. I caught the occasional phrase: "a fast-moving paralysis," "respiratory function."

"What's wrong with her?" There was panic in Ryan's voice.

"Too soon to say but all of her muscles are shutting down."

"Can't you do something?" Ryan beseeched.

The doctor was gone, being dragged across the room to another crisis.

"Come back!" Ryan ordered. "You can't just say that and then not—"

"Excuse me." A nurse pushing a pole ushered Ryan out of her way. To me, she said, "Just get you on a drip. If you can't swallow, you'll get dehydrated."

Her search for a vein hurt, but not as much as what happened next: a catheter was put into me.

"Why?" I asked.

"Because you can't get to the toilet on your own. And just in case your kidneys stop working."

"Am I . . . going to die?"

"What? What are you saying? No, of course you're not."

"How do you know? Why am I speaking so funny?"

"What?"

Another nurse showed up, wheeling a machine. She put a mask over my face. "Breathe into that, good woman. I just want to measure your . . ." She watched yellow digital figures on the screen. "Breathe, I said."

I was. Well, I was trying to.

To my surprise, the nurse started speaking loudly, almost shouting—numbers and codes—and suddenly I was on the move, being whizzed on a wheely bed through wards and corridors, on my way to intensive care. Everything was happening really fast. I tried to ask what was going on, but no sounds came out. Ryan was running beside me and he was trying to decipher the medical language. "I think it's your lungs," he said. "I think they're shutting down. Breathe, Stella, for God's sake, breathe! Do it for the kids if you won't do it for me!"

Just as my lungs gave up, a hole was cut in my throat—a tracheotomy—and a tube was shoved down into me and attached to a ventilator.

I was put in a bed in the intensive care ward; countless tubes ran in and out of my body. I could see and hear and I knew exactly what was happening to me. But, except for being able to blink my eyes, I couldn't move. I couldn't swallow, or talk, or wee, or breathe. When the last vestiges of movement left my hands, I had no way of communicating.

I was buried alive in my own body.

As tragedies go, it's quite a good one, no?

Saturday, 31 May

06:00

It's Saturday but my alarm goes off at 6 a.m. I have agreed to a writing routine with myself: every day I will "rise" early, "ablute" in cold water and be as disciplined as a monk. Diligence will be my watchword. But I'm knackered. Last night, the news that Ryan really was going ahead with his fool project meant it was gone midnight before I began my Sleep Coaxing Routine.

For most of my adult life, my sleep has been a shy, unpredictable creature, who has to be shown how much it is welcome before it will appear. There are many ways I demonstrate my love—I drink mint tea, eat yogurt, swallow a fistful of Kalms, have a bath in sandalwood oil, spray my pillow with lavender mist, read something very boring and listen to a CD of whales singing.

I was still tossing and turning at 1 a.m. and finally—God knows at what time—I fell asleep and dreamed about Ned Mount, from the telly. We were somewhere sunny and outdoors—it could have been in Wicklow. We were sitting at a wooden picnic table and he was trying to give me a big box containing a water filter. "Please take it," he said. "I've no use for it. I only drink Evian."

I knew it wasn't true about him only drinking Evian; he was just saying it because he wanted me to have the water filter. I was touched by his generosity, even though he'd got the filter for free, from a PR company.

Now it's 6:00 a.m. and I'm supposed to be getting up but I'm too tired, so I go back to sleep and wake again at 8:45.

Down in the kitchen, Jeffrey watches in silent disapproval as I make coffee and throw granola into a bowl. Yes, in my heart I, *too*, know that granola is, in fact, many small pieces of biscuit, with the odd "healthy" cranberry and hazelnut thrown in. But it's an officially designated "Breakfast Food"; therefore, I am entitled to eat it guilt free.

I hurry away upstairs to escape my son's judgment and I grab my iPad, get back into bed and check on Ryan. No more posts from him since last night. Thank Christ. But it's still horrifying.

His video Mission Statement puts me in mind of a suicide-bomber thing—the rehearsed delivery, the zeal; he even sort of *looks* like one, with his brown eyes, dark hair and neat beard. "My name is Ryan Sweeney and I'm a spiritual artist. You and I are about to embark on a unique undertaking. I'm giving away everything I possess. Every single possession! Together we'll watch as the universe provides for me. Project Karma!" He actually raises a clenched fist. I swallow hard. All we're missing is an "Allah Akbar."

I watch it four more times and think, You knob.

But the video has been viewed only twelve times and that was by Jeffrey and me. Nobody else has picked up on this. Maybe Ryan will change his mind. Soon. Before any damage is done. Maybe this video will be taken down in a moment. Maybe the whole thing will just go away . . .

I contemplate ringing him, but, on balance, I'd prefer to live in hope. Until recently I never knew I had such a talent for denial. I take a moment to praise myself: I really am *very gifted* at it. Very!

While I'm here online, I decide to see how things are with Gilda—a couple of clicks is all it will take. Then I manage to force myself to stop and in my head I say the mantra for her: *May you be well, may you be happy, may you be free from suffering.*

Moving on, it's time for my pill—the likelihood of me getting pregnant at the moment is nonexistent, but I'm only forty-one and a quarter and I am still *very much* in the game.

God, I'd better do some work!

I jump out of bed and prepare to ablute—"ablute" sounds so much more admirable than "shower." I don't want to ablute—or, indeed, shower—but standards must be maintained. I can't put clothes on over my unabluted body, I simply can't. It would be the beginning of the end. But until I get curtains I can't sit at my desk in my night attire for any interested passersby to see.

* * *

I ablute in cold water. Because Jeffrey has already had a shower and all the hot water is gone.

For God's sake! My clothes! In one of his many attempts to hurt me, Jeffrey has taken to doing his own laundry—which I have to say isn't at all hurtful—but he's accidentally washed some of my stuff and he's over-dried them to the point where they're as stiff as cardboard. *And* he's shrunk them. I tug on a pair of jeans but I can't close the top button.

I try another pair and it's the same story. I'll just live with it for the moment. My one other pair of jeans is in the wash basket and I'd better make sure Jeffrey doesn't get his hands on them.

I sit at my desk, I fix a small smile to my face and I read the inspirational words I will read every morning until this book is written. They're from Phyllis, my agent, and I'd transcribed them exactly as she'd barked them at me that day in her office two months ago. "You were rich, successful and in love," she'd said. "Now? Your career has tanked and I don't know what's up with that man of yours but it's not looking so good! You've a lot of material there!"

I pause in my reading, to let the words sink in, as you would with a prayer. I'd felt sick then and I feel sick now. Phyllis had shrugged. "You want more? Your teenage son hates you. Your daughter is wasting her life. You're the wrong side of forty. Menopause is racing toward you down the track. How much better does this get?"

I'd moved my lips but no words had come out.

"You were wise once," Phyllis had said. "Whatever you wrote in *One Blink at a Time*, it touched people. Try it again, with these new challenges. Send me the book when it's done." She was on her feet and trying to move me toward the door. "I need you out of here. I've got clients to see."

In desperation, I'd clung to my chair. "Phyllis?" I was pleading. "Do you believe in me?"

"You want self-esteem? Go to a shrink."

I was wise once, I remind myself, my hands hovering over my keyboard, I can be wise again. With vigor, I type the word "Ass."

12:17

I'm distracted from my scribing by my phone ringing. I shouldn't even have it in the room, not if I'm serious about doing uninterrupted work, but it's an imperfect universe we live in, what can we do? I check the caller; it's my sister, Karen.

"Come over to Wolfe Tone Terrace," she says.

"Why?" Wolfe Tone Terrace is where my parents live. "I'm working."

She makes scoffing noises. "You work for yourself. You can stop anytime you like. Who's going to sack you?"

I swear to God, no one has any respect for me. Not for my writing, not for my time, not for my circumstances.

"Okay," I say. "I'll be there in ten minutes."

I throw my phone in my bag and vow, afresh, that I will be disciplined soon. Very soon. Tomorrow.

In the hall I meet Jeffrey.

"Where are you going?" he asks.

"To Granny and Grandad's. Where are *you* going?" Like it isn't obvious, the defiant way he and his yoga mat are staring me down, like a couple on the verge of eloping. *We love each other*, they seem to be saying. *Whataya going to do about it?*

"Yoga? Again?"

He looks at me, all sneery-faced. "Yeah."

"Great. Good . . . er . . ."

I am uneasy. Shouldn't he be going out and getting drunk and into fights like a normal eighteen-year-old boy?

I have failed him as a mother.

Mum and Dad live in a quiet side street in a small terraced house that they bought from the council a long time ago.

Mum opens the front door and greets me by saying, "Why in the name of God are you wearing boots?"

"Aaaahh . . ."

She eyes my jeans. "Aren't you roasting?"

It was early March when I arrived in Ireland and since then I've had the same three pairs of jeans on rotation. There's been so much on my mind that clothes were at the bottom of my list.

But the season has gone ahead and bloody well changed and suddenly I need sandals and floaty pastel garments.

Mum, a short, round creature, has always felt the cold but even she's going about without her cardigan.

"So what's happening here?" I ask.

I can hear a whirring noise, then Karen's eldest child, Clark, bursts past Mum and yells at me, "They got a stairlift! For Grandad's bad back!"

I can see now. A contraption has been fitted to the wall by the stairs and Karen is strapping herself into a seat with three-year-old Mathilde on her lap. Then she lifts a lever and the pair of them start their whirry ascent. A very slow whirry ascent. They wave at Mum, Clark and me and we wave back and the mood is celebratory.

Mum lowers her voice. "He says he won't use it. Go in and sweet-talk him."

I stand at the sitting-room door and stick my head into the tiny room. As always, Dad is sitting in his armchair, with a library book open on his lap. He radiates grumpiness, then he sees that it's me and he becomes a little more cheery. "Ah, Stella, it's you."

"Are you coming for a go on the stairlift?"

"I'm not."

"Ah, Dad."

"Ah, Dad, my eye. I can climb the stairs on my own. I told her not to get it. I'm grand, and we haven't the money."

He summons me closer. "Fear of death, that's her problem. She thinks if she buys yokes like that, they'll keep us alive. But when your number's up, it's up."

"You've another thirty years in you," I say, staunchly. Because he might have. He's only seventy-two and people are living to be ancient. But not necessarily people like my parents.

From the age of sixteen Dad did a physical job, loading and unloading crates, in Ferrytown docks. That wrecks a person, much more than sitting at a desk does. He was twenty-two the first time a disc slipped in his back. He spent a long time—I don't know, maybe eight weeks—immobile in his bed, on strong painkillers. Then he returned to work and eventually banjaxed himself again. He got injured countless times—it seemed to be a feature of my childhood that Dad was "sick again," something that rolled around as regularly as Hallowe'en and Easter—but he was a fighter and he kept on working until he couldn't any longer. At the age of fifty-four, they'd broken him beyond repair and that was the end of his working life. And his money-earning life.

These days, the docks have machines to do the unloading, which would have saved Dad's back but would probably have meant he didn't have a job at all.

"Please, Dad, do it for me. I'm your favorite child."

"I've only got the two. C'mere . . ." He indicates the book on his lap. "Nabokov. *The Original of Laura*, it's called. I'll give it to you when I'm finished."

"Stop trying to change the subject." And please don't make me read it.

It's a curse being Dad's "clever" child. He reads books the way other people take cold showers—they're good for you, but you're not expected to enjoy them. And he's passed that way of thinking on to me: if I have fun with a book, I feel I've wasted my time.

Dad's as thick as thieves with Joan, a woman who works in the local library and who seems to have adopted Dad as her project—no author is too obscure, no text too unreadable.

"It's his final novel," Dad says. "He told his wife to burn it but she didn't. Think of what a loss to literature that would have been. Mind you, he's a right dirty article . . ."

"Let's go on the stairlift." I'm keen to stop talking about Nabokov.

Slowly Dad gets to his feet. He's a small man, short and sinewy. I offer him my arm and he slaps it away.

Out in the hall, Karen has returned to ground level and I study her clothes and hair with interest—in our unadorned states we look very similar so if I copy what she does, I can't go wrong. She seems to be managing this warm-weather-transition thing with ease. Black skinny jeans with zips at the ankle, sky-high wedges and a pale gray T-shirt in some funny shrunken fabric. The whole effect looks like it cost a fortune but it probably didn't because Karen is very clever that way, very good with money. Her nails are perfect nude ovals, her eyes are blue and framed with lush lashes and her blond hair—which in its product-free condition is as wild and curly as mine—has been captured and tamed into a sleek bun. She looks glossy but casual, relaxed but elegant. This is the way I must go.

I grab pretty little Mathilde. "C'mere till I squeezy you!" I say.

But she struggles and says, in high alarm, "Mummy!"

She's a drip, that child. Five-year-old Clark is better. I'd say he probably has ADHD but at least he's a bit of fun.

"Stella!" Karen plants a kiss on each of my cheeks. It's an automatic thing with her. Then she remembers that it's only me. "Sorry!"

Dad actually smiles. He's amused by Karen's aspirational ways and—though he wouldn't admit it—a little bit proud of them. I used to be the success story of this family, but in recent months I've been stripped of my rank and the position has passed to my younger sister.

Karen is a "businesswoman"—she owns a beauty salon—and she looks every inch of it. She's married to Enda, a quiet handsome man from a monied Tipperary family, who's a superintendent in the Gardaí.

Poor Enda. When he started dating Karen, she was so brisk and sassy and pulled together that he mistook her for middle-class. Then, when he'd fallen in love with her and it was too late to back out, he was introduced to her family and discovered that she was an entirely different beast: working-class-made-good.

I'll never forget that day. Poor polite Enda, sitting in my parents' teeny-tiny front room, trying to balance a cup of tea in his giant lap and wondering if he'd ever arrested Dad.

Twelve years later we still laugh about it. Well, Karen and I do. Enda still doesn't find it funny.

"Out of me road, Parvenue," Dad says to Karen.

"Why do you call her 'Parvenue?'" Clark asks. He asks every time but doesn't seem able to retain information.

"A Parvenue," says Dad, "and I'm quoting from a book, is 'A person from a humble background who has rapidly gained wealth or an influential social position; a nouveau riche; an upstart, a social climber.'"

"Shut it!" Mum says, shrill as anything. "She might be a Parvenue but she's the only one in this family with a job at the moment! Now get in that stairlift!"

I take a quick look at Karen, just to check that the Parvenue thing hasn't upset her, but not at all. She's remarkable.

She helps Dad into the seat. "Get in, you old snob."

"How can I be a snob?" he splutters. "I'm part of the underclass."

"You're a reverse snob. A well-balanced working-class man: you've a chip on both shoulders." Then, with a flourish, she lifts the lever and Dad rises up the stairs.

We all clap and shout, "Woohoo!" and I pretend I don't feel sad.

Overcome with the excitement, Clark decides to take all his clothes off and dance, naked, in the street.

Dad returns to his customary position in his armchair, studiously proceeding with his book, and Mum, Karen and I sit in the kitchen and drink tea. Mathilde snuggles on Karen's lap.

"Have a fairy cake." Mum throws a sixteen-pack, cellophane-wrapped slab of buns onto the table. I don't need to look at the ingredients to discover that there's nothing that sounds like food and that the eat-by date is next January.

"I can't believe you eat this shit," Karen says.

"Well, I do."

"Five minutes' walk away, in the middle of Ferrytown, the Saturday Farmers' Market is selling fresh, handmade cupcakes."

"It's far from fresh, handmade things you were reared."

"Grand." Karen is too canny to waste her energy getting into an argument. But she's going to leave soon.

"Have a fairy cake." Mum slides the package at Karen.

"Why don't *you* have a fairy cake?" Karen replies and shoves the package back.

The fairy cakes have suddenly become a battleground. To diffuse the tension, I say, "*I'll* have a fairy cake."

I eat five of them. But I don't enjoy them. And that's the main thing.

To be able to scratch the sole of my foot using the big toe
of the other foot is nothing short of a miracle.

Extract from *One Blink at a Time*

My left hip felt like it was on fire. I could see the clock at the nurses' station—that was one of the perks of being on my left side; when I was on my right side I was just staring at a wall—and it was another twenty-four minutes before someone came to turn me. They rotated me every three hours, so that I wouldn't get bedsores. But the last hour before "the turn" had started to become uncomfortable, then painful, then very painful.

The only way to endure it was to reduce time to bouts of seven seconds. I don't know why I picked seven—perhaps because it was an odd number and it didn't divide into ten or sixty, so it kept things interesting. Sometimes four or five minutes could pass without me noticing and then I got a lovely surprise.

I'd been in ICU for twenty-three days. Twenty-three days since my body had packed up on me and the only muscles that worked were the ones in my eyes and eyelids. The shock had been—was—indescribable.

That first night in hospital, Ryan was sent home by a nurse. "Keep your phone by your bed," she told him.

"I'm not leaving here," he said.

"If she deteriorates further, we'll ring you to come in. You'd better bring the kids too, and her parents. What religion is Stella?"

". . . None."

"You must say something."

"Catholic, I suppose. She went to a Catholic school."

"Okay. We'll organize a priest if one is needed. Go on now. You can't stay. This is the ICU. Go home, get some sleep, keep your phone on."

Eventually, looking like a whipped puppy, he went and I was left alone and I plunged into a surreal horror world where I lived a thousand lifetimes. I was in the grip of the worst fear I've ever known; there was a very real chance I was going to die. I could sense it in the atmosphere around my bed. No one knew what was wrong with me, but it was obvious that all the systems in my body were shutting down. My lungs had given up. What if my liver failed? What if . . . horrifying thought . . . what if my heart stopped?

I concentrated all my efforts on it and urged it to keep beating. *Come on, come on, how hard can it be?*

It had to keep beating because, if it didn't, who would take care of Betsy and Jeffrey? And if it didn't, what would happen to *me*? Where was I going? Suddenly I was staring into the abyss, facing the likelihood that this was where my life ended.

I'd never been religious, I'd never thought about an afterlife, one way or the other. But now that there was a good chance I was on my way there, I discovered, a bit late in the day, that I really was *interested*.

I should have done self-development courses, I berated myself. I should have been kinder to people. I mean, I'd tried my best but I should have done more. I should have gone to Mass and all that holy stuff.

What if the nuns at school were right and there really was a hell? As I added up my sins—sex before marriage, coveting my next-door neighbor's holidays—I realized I was a goner. I was going to meet my maker and then I was going to be cast into the outer darkness.

If I could have whimpered with terror, I would have. I wanted to sob with fear. I desperately wanted a second chance, to go back and fix things.

Please, God, I begged, please don't let me die. Save me and I'll be a better mother, a better wife and a better person.

From listening to the nurses coming and going at my bedside, I gathered that my heart rate was dangerously fast. My fear was making that happen. It was good that my heart was still beating but not so good if I went into cardiac arrest. A decision was made to give me a sedative, but instead of relaxing me it just slowed my thinking down so that I could see my predicament more clearly.

Over and over again, I thought, *This can't be happening.*

The fear alternated with helpless anger: I was outraged by my incapacity. I was so used to doing anything I wanted that I never even thought about it—I could pick up a magazine, I could shift my hair out of my eyes, I could cough. Suddenly I understood that to be able to scratch the sole of my foot using the big toe of the other foot was nothing short of a miracle.

My head kept sending orders to my body—*Move, for the love of God, move!*—but it lay like a plank. It was defiant and disrespectful and . . . yes . . . *cheeky*. I raged and foamed and flailed, but without moving a muscle.

I was afraid to go to sleep in case I died. The lights around me were never switched off and I watched the clock tick away the seconds all through the night. Finally it was morning and I was taken downstairs for a lumbar puncture, then I wished I *could* die—even now the memory of the pain makes me feel faint.

But, very quickly, it produced a diagnosis: I had something called Guillain-Barré syndrome, an astonishingly rare autoimmune disorder, which attacks the peripheral nervous system, stripping the myelin sheaths from the nerves. None of the doctors had ever encountered a case of it before. "You've a higher chance of winning the lottery than contracting this yoke," my consultant, a plump, dapper, silver-haired man called Dr. Montgomery chortled. "How did you manage it!"

No one could say what the trigger had been, but it sometimes "manifested" (medical speak) after a bout of food poisoning. "She was in a car crash about five months ago," I heard Ryan telling him. "Would that have caused it?"

No, he didn't think so.

My prognosis was cautiously optimistic: GBS was rarely fatal. If I didn't get an infection—which I probably would, apparently everyone in the hospitals gets infections; by the sounds of things you had a better chance of living a healthy life drinking seven liters of unfiltered Ganges water every day—I'd eventually recover and be able to move again, to speak and to breathe without a ventilator.

So at least I probably wasn't going to die.

But no one could tell me when I'd get well. Until these myelin sheaths—whatever they were—grew back I faced a lengthy spell, paralyzed and mute, in the intensive care unit.

"For the time being, the name of the game is keeping her alive," Dr. Montgomery told Ryan. "Isn't that right, girls?" he yelled to the nurses, with—in my opinion—rather inappropriate merriment. "Keep her going there, Patsy!

"And come here to me, you!" He grabbed Ryan by the arm. "Don't you be rushing home and Googling things. They write all kinds of codswallop on that Internet and scare the drawers off people and then you'd be coming in here boohoohooing and saying your wife is going to die and be paralyzed forever. I've been a senior consultant in this hospital for fifteen years. I know more than any Internet and I'm telling you she'll be grand. Eventually."

"Are there no drugs to speed up her recovery?" Ryan asked.

"No," Dr. Montgomery said, almost cheerily. "None."

"Could you run tests to get some idea of how bad she is . . . how long before she'll be well?"

"Hasn't the poor woman just had a lumbar puncture?" He glanced over at me. "That was no day at the races, was it?" He turned his attention back to Ryan. "You have to wait this thing out. There's nothing else you can do. Cultivate patience, Mr. Sweeney. Let patience be your watchword. Maybe you could take up fly-fishing?"

Later that day, when they'd finished school, Ryan brought Betsy and Jeffrey to see me. I watched their faces as they noticed all the tubes snaking in and out of me. Betsy's big blue eyes looked terrified but Jeffrey, being a fourteen-year-old boy, with an interest in all things ghoulish, seemed fascinated.

"I brought you some magazines," Betsy said.

But I couldn't hold them. I was desperate for a distraction, but unless someone read to me, I couldn't have it.

Ryan angled my head on my pillow so that I could look at him. "So how are you feeling?"

I stared at him. Paralyzed, that's how I'm feeling. And unable to speak, that's how I'm feeling.

"Sorry," he said. "I don't know how . . ."

"Do that thing," Jeffrey said. "I saw it on TV. Blink your right eye for yes, or your left eye for no."

"We're not in the fecking Boy Scouts!" Ryan said.

"Do you think it's a good idea, Mom?" Jeffrey shoved his face close to mine.

Well, it was the only one we had. I blinked my right eye.

"Score!" Jeffrey exclaimed. "It works. Ask her something!"

Faintly Ryan said, "I can't believe we're doing this. Okay. Stella, are you in pain?"

I blinked my left eye.

"No? That's good so. Are you hungry?"

I blinked my left eye again.

"No. Good . . ."

Ask me if I'm scared. But he didn't because he knew I was and so was he.

Already bored, Jeffrey turned his attention to his phone. Immediately there came the sound of running footsteps. It was a nurse with a face like thunder. "Turn that thing off!" she ordered. "Mobile phones are not allowed in the ICU."

"What?" Jeffrey asked. "Ever?"

"Never."

Jeffrey looked at me with what was, for the first time, compassion. "No phone. Wow . . . Where's your TV? Hey," he called in the direction of the nurses' station. "Where's my mom's TV?"

"Would you *shush*?" Ryan said.

The angry nurse was back. "There's no TV. This is an intensive care unit, not a hotel. And keep the noise down; there are very sick people here."

"Calm down, dear."

"Jeffrey!" Ryan hissed. To the nurse, he said, "I'm sorry. He's sorry. We're all just . . . upset."

"Quiet," Jeffrey said. "I'm thinking." He seemed to be wrestling with some terrible choice. "Okay." He reached a decision. "I'll give you the lend of my iPod. Just for this evening—"

"No iPods!" the nurse shouted from a distance.

"But what are you going to do?" Jeffrey was deeply concerned.

Betsy, who hadn't uttered a word since she arrived, cleared her throat. "Mom, I think . . . I'd like to pray with you."

What the hell?!

My own plight was instantly forgotten and I flashed my eyes at Ryan.

For a while now we'd suspected that Betsy had been dabbling in Christianity, the way many parents fear their teenagers getting into drugs. There was some sort of holy youth club that trawled her school for membership. They preyed on the vulnerability of children who'd been brought up by agnostics and it looked like Betsy might well have fallen into their clutches.

It was okay for me to pray in my own head, but praying—out loud!—with Betsy, like we were Bible-belt Americans, was all wrong. I blinked my left eye—no, no, no—but Betsy took my useless hands and bowed her head. "Dear Lord, look down on this poor miserable sinner, my mom, and forgive her for all the bad things she's done. She's not an evil person, just weak, and pretends she does Zumba when she never goes to class and can be quite bitchy especially when she's with Auntie Karen and Auntie Zoe, who I know isn't my real auntie, just my mom's best friend and they're on the red wine—"

"Betsy, stop!" Ryan said.

Suddenly an alarm started to sound, urgent pulses of noise. It seemed to be coming from about four cubicles away and it triggered the nurses into a frenzy of activity. One of them rushed into my cubicle and said to Ryan, "You all have to leave." But she hurried off to the emergency and my visitors, keen not to miss the show, stayed.

I heard the swish of a cubicle curtain and lots of loud voices giving orders and relaying information. A woman in a doctor's coat clipped briskly to the scene, followed by two younger-looking blokes, their white coats swinging.

Then—and you could feel the change in energy—all the noise and activity stopped. After a few seconds of absolute nothingness I heard, very clearly, someone saying, "Time of death is 17:47."

Within moments a lifeless body was wheeled past us.

"Is he . . . dead?" Betsy stared with saucer eyes.

"A dead person," Jeffrey said. "Cool."

He watched the fast-disappearing gurney, then he turned back to look at me lying motionless in the bed and the light in his eyes died.

14:17

As I walk home from my parents' house in my ill-fitting and weather-inappropriate clothes, I notice I have a missed call. My head goes funny when I see who it's from. And he's left a message.

I shouldn't listen to it. Clean break, didn't I decide?

My fingers are trembling as I hit the keys.

And there's his voice. Just three words. "I miss you . . ."

If I wasn't in the street, I'd double over and howl.

I only realize I'm crying when I notice the interested looks I'm getting from passing car drivers. I hurry toward home and pray that I don't meet anyone I know.

Once I've shut the door safely behind me I do what I've been doing for—I count back—two months, three weeks and two days: I get on with things.

I check on Ryan's video. It hasn't been viewed since I last watched it this morning and nothing new has been added. We could be in the clear here.

Right, I'd better find some summer clothes. Bad and all as I feel, I'm grateful to have a project so that I don't have to try to write. Sitting in front of that screen, with an empty head, would leave too much room for terrible thoughts to rush up.

I dive into my spare wardrobe and start pulling out the warm-weather stuff I'd brought from New York. How nicely and neatly I'd hung them up! There's no evidence at all of the distress I was in when I'd unpacked. I'd have expected hangers to be overloaded and at jingle-jangle angles and for sandals and flip-flops to be in a messy pile on the floor. Instead it looks like an ad for an expensive Italian custom-made wardrobe. I've no memory of arranging everything so tidily but it looks like I'd accepted that I really lived here, that this was now my home, maybe forever.

I'm in a state of shock: I have nothing to wear. None of my New York things fit me. Sometime over the last couple of months, I've put on weight. How much exactly, I couldn't possibly say. There are scales in the bathroom but no way am I standing on them. Anyway, I don't need to. I have my evidence—nothing fits me.

It's my . . . front piece. Whisper it . . . *belly* . . . I can hardly even think the word. Mentally I clear my throat and force myself to confront head-on the unpalatable truth: I have a belly. Full-blown.

And I always knew this day would dawn . . .

After a lifetime of barely containing it, the wretched thing has finally snapped its moorings.

I force myself to stand in front of the only full-length mirror in the house. It's on the inside of the door of the spare wardrobe and I realize that since I got back to Ireland I haven't looked at myself in it. Obviously because I don't have much dealings with my spare clothes.

But that's not the only reason I haven't noticed my expansion. I've been in denial about myself, about my appearance, about my very existence. I've ignored my hair, even though it's clamoring to be cut, and my nails are bitten and broken, even though Karen keeps offering me free manicures.

I've simply got through every twenty-four hours, dealing with the fresh set of challenges that each new day offered to me—money, Jeffrey, the great big hole at the center of me . . .

I've sort of . . . shut down. I had to, in order to survive.

Although I've *eaten* a lot for a shut-down person.

Poor Jeffrey. I'd maligned him by thinking he'd shrunk my clothes, when it was my fault all along.

I flick glances at myself. Tiny ones. I can only digest this unpalatable truth in morsels, in little splintered flashes. Is that me? Is that *me*? I look like an egg on legs. A . . . *belly* . . . on legs.

For the last couple of years I've kept the b-word at bay with near-daily running and Pilates and a high-protein eating plan. But my personal-trainer-private-chef life has disappeared and in its place I've been given this . . . front attachment . . . *thing*. If I don't say the name, maybe it will go away. Maybe all it wants is validation and if I ignore it, it'll eventually slink off and attach itself to another woman who will shower it in attention by grabbing wobbly handfuls and wailing, then immediately dropping to the floor and doing eighteen frantic crunches, then hopping to her feet and Googling How To Get a Flat Tummy in Twenty Minutes.

Yes, I will ignore it. I will carry on as before. I feel calmer now that I have a plan.

Except I still have nothing to wear . . .

This is a worry.

I won't be beaten down by this! I am a positive person! And I'm going shopping!

I come home empty-handed and very concerned. I have stumbled over a shocking fact: there is nothing in the shops for a woman of forty-one and a quarter. They don't make clothes for us. They skip right over my age group. There are sleeveless tops and clingy Lurex dresses for the twelve- to thirty-nine-year-olds. There are washable trousers with elasticated waists for the sixty-plus gang. But for me, nothing. Nothing. Nothing. Nothing.

I followed Karen's lead by trying on ankle-cut skinny jeans and a fancy T-shirt but I looked like an obese schoolboy. Next I went for some tailored linen trousers and looked in the mirror and wondered how Mum had got into the changing room. Then I realized that the person in the mirror was me. Horrors!

No disrespect to Mum. She's a good-looking woman. For seventy-two. But I'm only forty-one and a quarter and this is not on.

Suddenly I understand why designer clothes are so expensive. Because they're better cut. Because the fabrics are of a higher quality. I thought I was just paying that extra money for the laugh, so that I could swank around with a DKNY carrier bag, thinking, "I've made it! And I've just proved it by paying two hundred dollars for a plain black skirt that you could get in Zara for a tenner."

Is this absence of clothing for my generation some sort of plot? To keep us housebound so that our unpalatable aging will be hidden from the eyes of a youth-centric society? Or to make us spend all our money on lipo? I vow to get to the bottom of it.

As I hurried back to the car park, I cut through a newsagent's and was mocked by magazine covers, many of them featuring women who each claimed to be "Fabulous at 40!"

I stopped in front of one of them. I knew the woman smiling brightly at me; I'd been on her talk show in New York, and let me whisper you something: her "Fabulous at 40" spiel is a tissue of lies. Her face is full of injectables, *full* of them. She's mentally ill from chronic hunger. And she's not forty, she's thirty-six—she's cannily aligned herself with the monied forty-plus market, branding herself as a skinny, youthful-looking role model. With her every smile and gesture, she conveys, *I am one of you.* But her army of acolytes will never look like her, no matter how much of her clothing line they buy. It won't stop them trying, though. And it won't stop them blaming themselves when they fail.

When you're going through hell, keep going.

Extract from *One Blink at a Time*

Most people in intensive care are model patients. That's because most of them are in a coma. Also, most people's stay is a short one—either they die or they improve and go to a different ward. But I was in the unusual position of being there for the long haul and the nurses weren't geared up for that. They didn't talk to me because they were out of the habit of talking to any of their patients—and what would be the point, seeing as I couldn't reply?

When they turned me or attached a new feeding bag to the port in my stomach, it was done with the same force as if I were unconscious. If a tube popped out of me, they jammed it back in as if they were shoving a plug into a socket. Sometimes, midmaneuver, they remembered that I knew what was happening and they apologized.

But those were the only times a member of staff spoke to me and I was nearly mad with loneliness.

There was nothing to distract me—no phone, no Facebook, no food, no books, no music, no conversations, nothing. By nature I was a chatty person—if a thought came into my head I immediately blurted it out, but now it had to bounce off the wall of my skull and back into my brain, with all the thousands of other unuttered thoughts.

I was allowed two visits a day, each a paltry fifteen minutes long. The rest of the time I was locked in my own head and I never stopped worrying. There was a rackety routine in place to take care of Betsy and Jeffrey but every day was a challenge: Mum worked shifts in an old people's home, Karen was a workaholic—so was Ryan, come to think of it—and Dad's back could go without a moment's notice.

I was also anxious about money—Ryan earned a lot but our outgoings were massive and we needed what I earned from the salon.

And even though we had health insurance, like all insurance policies it was riddled with cut-off points and caveats and exemptions. When I'd signed up for it I'd tried my best to understand what was covered but my focus had been on insuring the kids, not Ryan and me.

Bigger than my worry about money was my angst about Betsy's and Jeffrey's emotional health—I could see the fear in their eyes every time they tiptoed up to my bed. What would this trauma do to them long term?

Ryan and I tried excruciatingly hard to be good parents, what with the expensive school and all the extracurricular stuff, but this was going to feck them up rightly. How could it not?

Almost as bad was the guilt I felt about Mum and Dad. I was an adult, their job as my parents was done, yet I was breaking their hearts. It was agonizing when they came to visit—Mum held my hand and wept silently and Dad clenched his jaw and stared hard at the floor. The only thing Dad ever said to me was, "When you're going through hell, keep going."

The few breaks I got from worrying were spent marveling at the life I used to live. How lucky I'd been—there I'd be, driving a car and eating raisins that I'd found abandoned in a bag on the floor and giving Betsy a pep talk about her oboe lessons and deciding I couldn't be bothered to go to Zumba—multitasking like no one's business, every muscle group in my body involved.

And now here I was, so paralyzed I couldn't even yawn. I'd have given ten years of my life to be able to put on a pair of socks.

I swore that, if I ever got better, I'd regard every single movement I made as a little miracle.

But would I get better? There were moments—about a million times a day—when I was certain that I'd be locked into my useless body forever.

I kept trying to make my limbs move, I'd concentrate on a particular muscle until I felt my head was going to burst, but nothing ever happened. It was obvious I wasn't getting any better. But at least I wasn't getting any worse—I'd been terrified that my eyes would seize up and my one small way of communicating would be blocked, but they had kept working.

All the same, I was finding it hard to stay hopeful. Ryan did his best to stay positive—he really was heroic —but he knew as little as I did.

When I'd first been diagnosed, my condition generated a lot of excitement among friends and acquaintances. The chance that I might die added extra luster. According to Ryan "everyone" was begging to visit me and dozens of well-wishers sent flowers even though Ryan told them that flowers weren't allowed in ICU. Candles were lit in my honor and I was "kept" in people's prayers . . . but the days passed and I didn't die, and when I was eventually pronounced "stable," my fans deserted me within moments. Even from my hospital bed, I could feel their deflation. "Stable" is nearly the dullest of all medical descriptions—only "comfortable" is worse. What people really like is a good "critical." "Critical" has mothers lingering at the school gates, gleeful with horror, saying sagely, "It could be any of us . . . There but for the grace of God."

But "stable?" It means if you're looking for excitement, you've backed the wrong horse.

Somehow twenty-three days had gone by—I was like a prisoner scraping lines onto the cell wall, where measuring the passing of time was the only bit of control I had.

I looked at the clock again—there were still nineteen minutes to go before I was turned, and my hip was aflame with pain. I couldn't take this. I was going to go mad.

But seven more seconds passed and I didn't lose my mind.

How do you go mad, I wondered. That's a useful life skill that should be taught in schools. It'd be very handy to be able to go out of your wits when everything got a bit much for you.

I could see the call button—it was less than a meter from my face. I willed my head to move along the pillow, I summoned every ounce of strength inside me, so that I could butt it. I could do this. If I wanted it badly enough, I could make it happen. Weren't we forever being told that the human will is the strongest force on the planet? I was thinking of all those stories I'd read in Dad's *Reader's Digest*s when I was a kid— amazing stories of women single-handedly lifting jeeps in order to save their child's life, or men walking forty miles through rugged terrain with their injured wife on their back. All I had to do was head-butt one small call button.

But despite the tumult inside me, nothing happened. Wanting something badly enough was no guarantee that it would happen—I'd been misled by *X-Factor*. Yes, I wanted to move my head. Yes, I was hungry for it. Yes, I was prepared to do whatever it took. But it wasn't enough.

If only one of the nurses passing by my bed would look at me. Surely they'd see by my eyes that I was in agony? But they didn't do random checks; the machines took care of everything and nurses only appeared when something started beeping.

The only person who could get me through this was me. *Hang on, Stella*, I spoke softly to myself, *hang on*.

So I listened to the ventilator and I counted to seven and I counted to seven again and I pretended that my hip didn't belong to me and I stopped looking at the clock and I kept counting and I kept counting and . . . here came two nurses! It was the time! "You take the top end," one of them said. "Careful with the ventilator."

I was being lifted up and suddenly the pain had stopped and the relief flooded me with ecstasy. I felt high, floaty and joyous. I was set down on my right side and the nurses straightened up my tubes. "See you in three hours," one of them said, and looked straight into my eyes. I gazed back at her, pitifully grateful for the human contact.

As soon as they were gone, the fear of dying seized me. It was always at its worst in the few moments after someone left my bedside. I'd been wondering if I should get a priest to cleanse my soul. But even if I'd been able to ask, I suspected that God didn't play by those simple rules. Whatever I had done in my life—and sometimes my misdeeds didn't seem so terrible and sometimes they did—it was too late now to be forgiven.

My biggest fear used to be something awful happening to my kids, but contemplating my own death was—I was surprised by my selfishness—more frightening.

Here came Ryan, Betsy and Jeffrey! One after the other they kissed my forehead, then backed away quickly, bumping into each other, terrified of dislodging my tubes.

Self-consciously, the kids delivered "news" that they'd saved up since their previous visit, the day before.

"Oh my gosh!" Betsy said, with surprise that was badly rehearsed. "You haven't heard? Amber and Logan are on a break!"

Amber was Betsy's best friend, Logan was Amber's boyfriend. But maybe not anymore . . .

Tell me! I tried to push encouraging vibes out from my eyes. *Go on, my sweetie. Any kind of chat is appreciated around here. And I'm so grateful that you've knocked that praying business on the head.*

"Yes! They had like this big talk and Logan said he intuited he was holding Amber back? In her personal development? He didn't want to take a break but he thinks it's the right thing?"

God, they were so serious, this generation of kids, and I wouldn't be so sure about Logan's noble motives.

"Amber is like, devastated? But it's sort of cute that Logan is so mature—"

Jeffrey, clearly not gripped by the Amber–Logan saga, blurted out, "Last night we watched *The Apprentice*! It was cool."

Oh God! What about their study? I put a lot of time and energy into making them knuckle down to their schoolwork and I was terrified that Ryan would let it all slide away to nothingness while I was lying here, powerless.

"They needed a treat." Ryan sounded defensive.

Yes, but . . .

You'd think you wouldn't worry about things like that, small things, when every day you're afraid you might die and go to hell, but there you are.

To deflect attention from his misdeed, Ryan picked up my chart. "It says you had a good night's sleep."

But I hadn't—it was impossible when the lights in ICU blazed twenty-four hours a day, the burning in my hip woke me up every couple of hours and the three-hour turns happened all through the night.

"Amber says the break is a good thing. It will make their bond stronger. But, Mom, can I say something? Does it make me a bad person . . . ?"

Say it! Say it!

". . . I think Logan just wants to get with other girls."

Me too! Remember that business in the summer!

"I'm like remembering . . . that girl, in the summer."

Yes! The girl who worked in the fishing boat?

"It's not cool to call a girl slutty, I know it isn't, Mom, so don't yell at me—oh right, you can't—but she *was* kind of slutty."

Betsy was beautiful, with coltish limbs and a mane of long, wild, blond curls—she'd got the best bits of Ryan and me—but she cultivated a vehemently unsexy look. She dressed in baggy, shin-length pinafores and strange misshapen knitwear that made Karen say, in contempt, "She looks like a nineteenth-century crofter."

"I know Logan said he'd just been helping the slutty girl when she'd got tangled up in the net," Betsy said, "but . . ."

I'd never believed it.

"I sort of thought he was like lying. And last night Amber was like spying on Logan."

Oh my God! This was as good as a soap opera.

"Well, not spying, but . . . watching his house. And she said the slutty girl got out of a car and—"

"Time's up." A nurse was standing at the foot of my bed.

What? Already? No! I needed to hear about the slutty girl! I'd have cried with disappointment if my tear ducts had been working.

"I don't want to go," Jeffrey said, suddenly sounding young and vulnerable.

"You have to," the nurse said. "Patient needs her rest."

"Mom, when will you be better?" Jeffrey asked. "When are you coming home?"

I stared at him. *I'm sorry. I'm sorry. I'm so sorry.*

"Soon," Ryan said, in a fake reassuring voice. "She'll be better soon."

But what if I wasn't? What if I was like this forever?

Ryan bent over me and stroked my hair back from my face. "Hang on," he said quietly, looking steadily into my eyes. "Just hang on. You do it for me and I'll do it for you and we'll both do it for them." We shared a soul moment, then he stepped away. "Okay, kids," he said. "Let's go."

Off they trooped and I was on my own again. I couldn't see the clock but I calculated that it was two hours and forty-one minutes until my next turn.

17:17

I hurry into the house, keen to put my disastrous shopping trip behind me. Jeffrey is at home and my heart leaps to see him. Despite his incessant petulance, I love him with a tenderness that feels almost painful.

"Sorry," I say.

"For what?"

"You didn't shrink my clothes."

He looks at me with fear on his face. "Were you always this insane?"

I straighten my spine, fully set to take umbrage, then my phone rings. It's Zoe. I waver for a moment—I really don't feel able for this—but maybe she's calling to cancel tonight's Bitter Women's Book Club. Also she's my best friend, so *of course* I answer it. "Zoe?"

"You won't believe what that geebag has done now."

There's no need to ask who the geebag is—it's her ex-husband, Brendan.

"He was meant to pick his daughters up at five o'clock and there's no sign of him and—yeah, you're right! What time is it now? Twenty past five! It's one thing to treat me like shit, but to do that to his own flesh and—oh, here he is now, the prick. Christ, you should see what he's wearing! Lemon skinnies! It's like he thinks he's seventeen! Listen, come over early. Come now. I've already started on the wine."

Abruptly she hangs up and I feel hunted, almost afraid.

"Maybe you should get a new best friend," Jeffrey says.

For a sliver of time I'm in wholehearted agreement, then I get with the program.

"Don't be mad," I say. "She's been my best friend since I was six."

Zoe and I had gone to school together. As teenagers, we'd swapped around the same boyfriends—in fact Ryan had been her boyfriend before he was mine—and when we grew up and got married, our husbands had been great friends. We'd had our babies almost simultaneously and we'd often gone on holiday together. Zoe and I would be friends forever.

No matter how difficult I seemed to be finding it these days.

It was all Brendan's fault, I thought, darkly. He and Zoe had been happily married until, about three years ago, he ruined everything by having sex with a girl from work. The fallout had been savage. Zoe said that if he promised to never see the girl again, she'd take him back, but Brendan horrified everyone by saying that if it was all the same, he didn't actually *want* to come back, thank you.

We thought this would be the end of Zoe, that she'd just sag and deflate into a sad shell of her former sunny self. However, we were wrong. Brendan's betrayal brought about a transformation. And not a good one.

You know the way sometimes a very ordinary woman will, out of the blue, take up bodybuilding? All the other women are happy to ponce around with sappy pink hand weights, but this woman starts mixing protein shakes and peels away from the pack. Soon, she's popping steroids and entering competitions and tanning herself mahogany brown. Her body changes entirely—her boobs become pecs and her arms bulk up and pop with veins. She's down at the gym every day, grunting and lifting, giving her life and soul to this new version of herself.

Well, Zoe has done that with her personality. She has rehewn and refashioned herself into someone almost unrecognizable. And she used to be lovely, such fun . . .

"So?" Jeffrey says, in a tone that is almost wry. "Bitter Women's Book Club tonight?"

I chew my lip, I chew and chew and chew as my mind goes down several avenues and finds all of them blocked, then I round on Jeffrey in a sudden fury. "Who has a book club on a Saturday night?" Book clubs are midweek things, so that you have an excuse to drink a bottle of wine on a Tuesday!

"First rule of the Bitter Women's Book Club is that no one talks about the Bitter Women's Book Club," Jeffrey says.

Wrong. First rule of the Bitter Women's Book Club is that everyone drinks red wine and keeps on drinking it until their lips crack and their teeth turn black.

"Second rule," he says. "All men are bastards."

Correct.

"Third rule: All men are bastards."

Also correct.

"So, ah . . .?" I ask. "What did you think of the book?"

"Mom . . ." He shifts awkwardly.

"You haven't read it!" I accuse. "I ask you for nothing! Just to read a bloody book and—"

"Mom, you're the one in the book club, not me. You're meant to enjoy the books—"

"How could anyone enjoy the stuff chosen by the Bitter Women's Book Club?"

"Maybe you shouldn't be in it, then."

I'll have to get pissed tonight. Seriously pissed. I'm not a big drinker but there's no other way I'll get through it. This means that driving is out of the question. But so is public transport—since the split, Zoe has lived far, far away, in a suburb where buses generate the same consternation that eclipses of the sun used to cause in medieval times. (While she was married she was domiciled in the pulsing heart of Ferrytown, adjacent to its many amenities, and her current exile in the furthest reaches of west Dublin is yet another string in her bitterness bow.)

"Dinner with pals?" the taxi driver asks.

"Book club."

"On a Saturday night?"

"I know."

"You'll be partaking of a few jars, so?"

I glance at my bottle of red wine. "Yes."

"What's the book?"

"A French thing. It's called, *She Came to Stay*. Simone de Beauvoir wrote it. I only speed-read it but it was very sad. Autobiographical. Simone de Beauvoir and Jean-Paul Sartre, they were real people, writers—"

"I know who they were." He sounds annoyed. "Existentialists."

"They had an open relationship."

"Dirty articles." He clicks his tongue. "That's the French for you."

"And this other girl, they . . ." How could I phrase a ménage à trois delicately? "They . . . befriended her. And she broke them up."

"That's what you get. There's a lot to be said for playing by the rules. Where on God's earth are we going?"

"Take the next left. And the next right. And the second left." We're in Zoe's enormous estate of identikit houses. "Down to the end here and go left, sharp right, yes, keep going. Second left, left again. Right. Left. Down. Go on, keep going, you're grand."

"My sat-nav doesn't know what's hit it."

"Left. Left at the bottom. One more right and . . . pull in here."

As I pay the driver, he looks anxious. "I might never find my way out of here."

I have a sudden sense of just how deeply I'm gridlocked in this prison of suburbia. I feel like my vision has zoomed in to the top of my head, then shot out, far, far away, past the snarl of small roads, the thick cables of motorways, the viral cluster of Dublin, the coast of Ireland, the landmass of Europe, all the way to outer space. I am tiny and cornered and afraid, and on impulse, I say, "Come back and get me in an hour and a half."

"You can't cut out after an hour and a half." He looks astounded. "Do the decent thing. Two and a quarter hours."

I waver.

"Have some manners."

"Oh, all *right*. Two and a quarter hours. I might be drunk," I feel I should add. "I won't be rowdy but I might be weepy. Please don't mock me."

"Why would I mock you? That's not my way at all. I'll have you know that I'm well regarded in my community. I have a reputation—well earned, I might add—as a courteous person. Animals instinctively flock to me and . . . Oh look, your friend's expecting you."

Zoe has her front door open and by the blackness of her teeth, and the dishevelment of her hair, she's already jarred.

"Welcome," she yells. "To the Bitter Women's Book Club."

I hurry toward her.

"Look at him. The dirty bastard," she says, watching my taxi driver. "Giving me the glad eye. Did you see! And wearing a wedding ring! Dirty dog."

"Am I the first?" I step into her front room.

"You're the only!"

"What?"

"Yeah! Crowd of bee-yatches! All canceled. Deirdre's got a date. With some *man*. Yeah! Cancels on us, just like that!" She tries to click her fingers but it doesn't work. "What a complete See You Next Tuesday."

"And Elsa? Where's she? Have you a glass?" My wine is a screwtop, thank God. I need to get drinking and quickly. I wish I'd started in the taxi.

"Elsa's mammy fell off a ladder and broke her collarbone so Elsa is in—" Zoe pauses and delivers the next phrase with scathing sarcasm— "A&E."

"God, that's terrible." I'm pouring the wine now. I'm pouring it and I'm drinking it and I'm glad.

"Yeah. Pretty. Fucking. Convenient. That her mammy breaks her collarbone on the night of our Bitter Women's Book Club."

"I hardly think her mum broke her collarbone on purpose . . . And where's Belen?"

"Don't say that name under my roof. That bee-yatch is dead to me."

"Why?"

She put her fingers to her lips. "Shssssssh. Secret. Some other time. Any news?"

There is plenty I could tell her—that the Irish economy is displaying signs of modest growth, that scientists have successfully treated bone cancer in mice. I could even tell her about Ryan's mad artistic notion. But the only news Zoe is ever interested in is breakups—

they're food and drink to her. She prefers them to be real, but celebrity stuff will do.

"Not really." I'm apologetic.

"Ryan still single?"

"Yes."

"Not for long, though, right? Not long before some half-wit nineteen-year-old Barbie-brain falls for his tormented-artist shite? So go on. Watcha think of the book?"

"Well." I take a deep breath and try to catch my sinking heart. I'm here. I'm at my book club. I went to the trouble of sort of reading the book so I might as well make the effort. "I know they're French and French people are different to us, they don't get upset about infidelity and that, but it was too sad."

"She was a little c-word, that Xavière one."

I'm inclined to agree, but you can't do that at a book club—you must "discuss" the book. So—a little wearily—I say, "Was it that simple?"

"You tell me! They were happy, Françoise and Pierre. And they invited Xavière in!"

A little startled by Zoe's anger, I ask, "So it was their fault?"

"It was *her* fault. Françoise's."

I swallow hard. "I don't know if it's fair to blame Françoise for Pierre falling in love with Xavière."

Zoe stares hard at me. "It was autobiographical, you know. It really happened."

I'm confused by the undercurrent of rage, but then again Zoe is always like this, it's just worse when she's drunk. "I do know, and—"

"Stella. Stella." Zoe's gripping my arm hard and suddenly it sounds like she's got something terribly important to say. "Stella."

"Yes?" I squeak.

"You know what I'm going to say to you." She fixes me with a look that is both intense and unsteady.

"Ah . . ."

Then an unexpected wave of some new emotion washes over her. "Fuck," she says. "I've got to go to bed."

"What? Now?"

"Yeah." She lurches out of the room and toward the stairs. "I'm really drunk," she says. "These things happen. If you drink a lot." She's clambering up the stairs and into her bedroom. "I'm not going to puke. I'm not going to choke. I'm grand." She's pulling off her dress and crawling under her duvet. "I just want to go to sleep. And preferably never wake up. But I will. Go home, Stella."

I arrange her so she's lying on her side and she mutters, "Wudja stop. I'm not going to puke. Or choke. I told you." She's a strange mixture of extraordinarily drunk and entirely lucid.

She starts to snore softly and I lie beside her and think about how sad things are. Zoe is one of the most tender-hearted people I've ever met, a happy-go-lucky soul who sees the good in everyone. Well, she used to be. But Brendan's betrayal hit every part of her life—she wasn't just publicly humiliated by his leaving, she was heartbroken. She really loved him.

And to make matters worse, Brendan secretly dismantled the contract-cleaning company he ran with Zoe and carved off the big, profitable companies for himself, leaving Zoe to forage for small, unreliable, short-term jobs. She was killing herself trying to make it work.

And Zoe's two daughters, a nineteen-year-old called Sharrie and an eighteen-year-old called Moya, despise her. They were the ones who came up with the Bitter Women's Book Club title and Zoe adopted it in an if-you-can't-beat-them-join-them defiance.

I look down on her slumbering form. Even asleep she looks angry and disappointed. Will this happen to me? Even though my life mightn't have gone the way I'd wanted it to, I don't want to be bitter. But maybe you don't get any say in these things?

When the doorbell rings we both jump.

"Who is it?" Zoe mumbles.

"My taxi driver. I forgot he was coming back. I'll just tell him to go away."

"Don't stay, Stella." She sits up.

"Of course I'll stay."

"Don't. Really. I'm fine. We'll just write tonight off and start everything fresh tomorrow. Okay?"

I waver. "Are you sure?"

"I promise."

I go down the stairs and out into the night. The taxi driver gives me a wary look in the rearview. "Good evening?"

"Great."

"Grand. Home, is it?"

"Yes. Home."

Human touch is as important as water and food
and air and laughter and new shoes.
Extract from *One Blink at a Time*

On my twenty-fourth day in the hospital, a man came into my cubicle. He was carrying a file and to my great alarm I recognized him—not from the hospital staff, but from my old life. It was the narky man whose Range Rover I'd crashed into, the one I'd accused of hitting on me. What was he doing here at my hospital bed? Was it something to do with the insurance claim?

But I'd done everything right—I'd obediently filled in the lengthy forms, then I'd filled in the follow-up forms and I'd rung about it every month, only to be told that they were "seeking clarification" from the other insurance companies involved; basically I'd surrendered myself to the labyrinthine process like any sensible person would.

Surely their man wasn't here to pressure me to hurry it up? Even if I wasn't unable to speak, there was nothing I could do. I was confused and afraid, then utterly *aflame* with the humiliation I'd felt when he'd told me why he wanted my phone number.

"Stella?" He wore a white doctor's coat over a dark suit. His hair was clipped close to his head and his eyes were silvery-gray and weary, just like I remembered. "My name is Mannix Taylor. I'm a neurologist."

I didn't even know what a neurologist was.

"I'll be working on your physical rehabilitation."

This came as news. I thought Dr. Montgomery was in charge of my care. Mind you, as a "stable" patient, I had little to offer by way of excitement and the only time I clapped eyes on him was when he was en route to one of the thrilling "critical" patients in a nearby cubicle. On one occasion he'd actually said, as he'd sailed past, with his retinue, "Ah! You're still here! Keep her going there, Patsy!"

But maybe Dr. Montgomery had sent this narky-man neurologist.

Although I was paralyzed and therefore *extremely* immobile, I ordered myself to lie even more still. Maybe if I made myself totally invisible, Narky Man would leave, looking baffled and telling the nurse there was no patient in bed seven. There was a good chance he wouldn't recognize me—it was nearly six months since I'd driven into his car and I was guessing I looked very different—I hadn't seen a mirror in all my time in the hospital but I'd no makeup on, my hair was a disaster and I'd lost a lot of weight.

"Today we'll do some gentle work on your circulation," he said. "Is that okay?"

No, it wasn't okay.

My sullenness must have leaked into the room because he looked a little surprised, then focused on me in a new way. His face changed. "Have we met?"

I blinked my left eyelid many times, trying to convey, *Go away. Go away and never come back.*

"Yes? No?" His brow was furrowed. "What are you trying to tell me?" It was like an episode of *Skippy the Bush Kangaroo.*

Go away. Go away and never come back.

"The car accident." His face cleared as he remembered. "The crash."

Go away. Go away and never come back.

He watched me closely and he gave a little laugh. "You want me to go away."

Yes, I want you to go away and never come back.

Narky Man—what did he say his name was? Mannix—shrugged. "I've got a job to do."

Go away and never come back.

He laughed, quite meanly. "Christ! When you don't like someone, you *really* don't like them. So!" He took the clipboard from the end of the bed and pulled a chair up to my bedside. "How are you today? I know you can't answer. The nurses' report says you had 'a good night's sleep.' Is that true?"

He watched me carefully. I blinked my left eye. Let him figure out what that meant.

"No? Blinking your left eye means no. So you *didn't* have a good night's sleep?" He sighed. "They say everyone has a good night's sleep. The only time they don't is when a person has been running up and down the ward in the nip yelling that the CIA are spying on them. Then they call it 'a restless night's sleep.'"

He quirked an eyebrow at me, looking for a reaction. "Not even a smile?" He sounded sardonic.

I can't smile and even if I could, I wouldn't. Not for you.

"I know you can't smile," he said. "It was my admittedly crass attempt at humor. Okay. Ten minutes, and I'll be gone. Today I'm going to massage your fingers."

He took my hand in his and, after being deprived of any kind of proper touch for more than three weeks, it was a shock. He began massaging the pad of his thumb around my fingernails, tiny movements that triggered pleasure chemicals in my head. Suddenly I felt giddy, almost high. He took my knuckles and moved them in a circular motion, then he gently pulled my fingers and that triggered a cascade of bliss that sent little thrills of electricity through my whole body. Ryan and the kids kept their distance out of fear of damaging me, but clearly that sort of deprivation wasn't good, if someone just rubbing my hands rocketed me into euphoria.

"How's that?" Mannix Taylor asked.

It felt so intimate that I had to shut my eyes.

"Is it okay?" he asked.

I opened my eyes and blinked the right one.

"Is that yes?" he said. "Blinking the right eye means yes? I've never before worked with someone who couldn't speak. How do you not go mad?"

I'm trying to. I do my best every day to lose my mind.

"Okay, let's do your other hand."

I closed my eyes and surrendered to the sensations and went into a kind of ecstatic trance. I was thinking dreamily of those stories about babies in orphanages, who are never held, and how it impedes their development. Now I could totally understand why. *Totally.* Human touch was important, *very* important, as important as water and food and air and laughter and new shoes and . . . what was going on? Why had he stopped? I opened my eyes; he was shoving his chair back and standing up. "All done." He gave one of his spiteful little laughs. "Now, that wasn't so bad, was it?"

Feck off.

Sunday, 1 June

05:15—in the morning!

Sunday. A day of rest. But not for a failure who's trying to rebuild her life. My alarm is set for six. However, I'm already awake.

Insomnia is an enemy that attacks in many forms. Sometimes it shows up the moment I get into bed and lingers for a couple of hours. Other nights, it stays away until about 5 a.m. and then butts in and hangs around until twenty minutes before the alarm is due to go off. It's a full-time job, battling the fecker.

Today I wake at five fifteen, worrying about many things. I fix on Zoe and text her.

> R u ok? xxx

She replies immediately.

> Sory bout last nite. Wil knock d drinking on d head soon.

I don't know how to respond. She *is* drinking too much but she has a lot to cope with and at what point do you stop feeling sorry for someone and start lecturing them instead?

I worry about this for a good ten to fifteen minutes, then I check on Ryan's project, but mercifully nothing has happened since the last time I looked. With a lighter heart, I watch videos of singing goats and waste time as best I can, until suddenly the itch comes on me, as it does about ninety times a day, to Google Gilda. But I shouldn't, so instead I say the mantra: *May you be well, may you be happy, may you be free from suffering.*

I can't stop myself from remembering back almost two years, to the fateful morning in New York, when I'd bumped into her in Dean & DeLuca. I'd been in the chocolate section, looking for presents to bring home to Mum and Karen, when I reached for a box at the same time as someone else did.

"Sorry." I backed off.

"No, you have them," a woman said.

To my great surprise I realized I knew the voice—it belonged to the lovely woman Gilda, whom I'd met at a dinner party just the previous night. I took a look—it *was* her! Her golden-colored hair was piled messily on her head and she was wearing slouchy workout-style clothes, instead of the chic dress she'd been wearing the previous night, but it was definitely her.

Then she recognized me. "Heyyy!" She looked as pleased as punch and made a move, as if to hug me, then pulled back like she was afraid of being thought "inappropriate." (From what I'd gathered, this was the thing they feared most of all in New York City. More than monsters and career failure and being fat.)

"What a coincidence!" I was full of warm feeling. "Do you live near here?"

"I was working out with clients who live nearby. I took them running in the park."

We smiled at each other and, a little shyly, she asked, "Do you have ten minutes? We could get tea or something?"

I was genuinely regretful. "I'd better go. I'm flying back to Dublin this afternoon."

"How about in a couple of weeks' time when you've properly relocated here?" She pinkened. "I'd like to thank you for the book you wrote." Her blush deepened, making her look as beautiful as a rose. "I hope it's okay, but Bryce gave me a printout. I don't want to embarrass you, but I found it very inspiring. I know I'll read it over and over."

"Thanks," I said awkwardly. "But it's only, you know, a small little thing—"

"Don't! Don't do yourself down. There're plenty of people who'll do that for you."

I thought of the horrible man who'd been at last night's dinner party, and from the look in her eyes, so did she. "Hey." She giggled. "What about that dinner last night?"

"Jesus!" I buried my face in my hands and groaned. "It was awful."

"That Arnold guy with his issues and his angry wife."

"She told me only tourists come here to Dean & DeLuca."

"I'm not a tourist and I adore it—these chocolates make the best gifts. She's just a mean girl."

How lovely this Gilda was!

"When I'm back," I said, "we'll definitely meet for coffee." Then something occurred to me. She was a personal trainer and nutritionist. *Do you drink coffee?*"

"Sometimes. Mostly raspberry tea."

"Are you . . . very healthy?"

"It's a struggle."

This was music to my ears.

"Some days," she said, "it's just too much and I give in and drink caffeine and eat chocolate."

Wheels had started to turn in my head. I'd been told that I needed to lose ten pounds. "I think I need a personal trainer. I don't suppose you . . . ? Sorry. Sorry," I repeated. "You're probably up to your eyeballs."

"I'm pretty busy right now, which is great."

"Of course . . ."

She looked thoughtful. "What are you interested in? Cardio? Strength? A diet do-over?"

"Jesus, I don't know. Being thin. That's all."

"I could probably help. I could take a look at your food and we could run together."

"The only thing is, I'm not sporty. Not one bit." I was afraid now. What had I let myself in for?

"We could try it for . . . say . . . a week? See if we're a good fit."

"A week?" God, they didn't give things much time to bed in around here.

She smiled at me. "Here's my card. Don't look so scared. Everything's going to be fine."

"Is it?"

"Yes, everything's going to be great."

Karen rings. "What are you doing?"

"Working." I sigh. "Listen, Karen, I need new clothes. Nothing fits me. I've put on weight."

"What do you expect, eating all those fairy cakes?"

Stammering, I say, "But . . . but . . . they were disgusting." I realize that I've always thought that if I didn't enjoy a food, then it didn't contain any calories.

"Tell that to the fairy cakes. And all the other carbs you've been scoffing in the last few months."

"Okay." I really do feel quite miserable. "So what should I wear?" Even though Karen is two years younger than me, I've always sought her advice.

"I can take you shopping later."

"Nowhere expensive."

As if. Karen Mulreid is queen of the bargains. At any time, Karen can tell you exactly how much cash she has in her wallet, right down to the copper coins. It's a game we sometimes play. She's like Derren Brown.

"Speaking of money," she says, "how's the writing going?"

"Slow," I say. "Slow and . . . nonexistent." In a burst of fear, I ask, "Karen, what if I can't write another book?"

"Of course you'll write another book! You're a writer!"

But I'm not. I'm simply a beautician who got a rare disease and who got better.

"Chinos?" I say, my voice high with alarm. "I don't think so."

"Well, I do." Karen ushers me to the changing room.

Chinos are for men, those dreadful forty-something rugby fans with boomy voices and no style. I cannot possibly wear chinos!

"Chinos are different now." Karen is adamant. "These are lady chinos. And you've no choice; they're the only things that'll work until you lose the belly."

"Please, Karen." I grasp her arm and fix her with a beseeching look. "Don't say that word. I promise I'll get rid of it, but please don't say it."

After making me try on many, many items, she makes me buy two pairs of navy chinos, some tops and a long, floaty scarf. "I look awful," I say.

"This is the best you can hope for right now," she says. "Wear the scarf always. It'll camouflage your . . . bump."

At the till she haggles me a discount, due to some invisible stain. "Remember," she says, "this is an emergency interim measure. Not a long-term solution. I'll take you home. But first I want to drop in on the salon."

Despite having two children, Karen's business is her best-loved baby and not a day passes that she doesn't check in on it.

"What for?" I ask.

"I like to keep Mella on her toes."

Mella is her manager.

"I thought you trusted Mella."

"You can trust no one, Stella. As you well know."

As we push through the crowds of Sunday afternoon shoppers, making our way back to the car park, I see someone I recognize, a dad from Jeffrey's old school. *Kill me now.* I can't be making small talk, not with this belly. I put my head down and hurry past and I actually think I've got away with it, when I hear him say, "Stella?"

"Oh?" I turn around and do a big fake-surprise face. "Roddy! Roddy . . . !" I can't remember his surname so I trail off. "Ahahaha! Hello, there!"

"Very nice to see you, Stella."

"You too."

I introduce Karen. "Roddy had a son in Jeffrey's class."

"How *is* Jeffrey?" Roddy asks.

"Fine. Great. A nightmare. How is . . .?" What the hell was the son's name?

"Brian. Just finished his leaving cert. Didn't do a tap of work for it. And now him and his mates have colonized the front room. Huge big lummoxy yokes."

"Sounds like Jeffrey," I say, weakly. Apart from the mates.

"They're up half the night playing video games, then they're asleep all day."

Emboldened by perhaps having met a kindred spirit, I ask, "Does he ever . . . cook? Your Brian?"

"Cook? You mean food?" Roddy has a good laugh. "Are you joking me? The junk they eat. I come down in the morning and I can't see the floor for pizza boxes. Whole forests have been cut down to make those containers."

I swallow hard. Jeffrey doesn't order pizzas. What am I doing wrong?

"And he never addresses a civil word to me."

I latch on to this with overwhelming relief. Jeffrey never addresses a civil word to me either. I must be doing *something* right.

"So you're out shopping?" Roddy asks, somewhat superfluously.

"Yes." I try out the sentence: "I've been buying chinos. Lady chinos."

"Lady chinos?" He sounds surprised. "New one on me. Well, er, enjoy them. Take care."

"He'd never heard of lady chinos," I mutter to Karen, as we walk away.

"Course he hadn't; he's a suburban dad. But a man of taste and sophistication would know. I bet—"

"Don't! Don't say it! Don't even say his name."

17:31

Karen pulls up outside Honey Day Spa, parking half on the pavement, half on the yellow lines. "You coming in?"

I feel a bit strange returning to this place which I'd once co-owned with Karen and had worked in for many years.

"Aren't you worried about traffic wardens?" I ask.

"They know me, they know the car. Anyway, I'll only be a minute. Come on."

Karen and I had trained together to be beauticians—I'd stayed at school until I was eighteen but Karen left at sixteen. Coming from our background, we didn't think we had many career options: we could be hairdressers or beauticians or we could work in a shop. Everything around us encouraged us to aim low.

In fairness, Dad had wanted more for me. "You're a bright spark, Stella. Get an education. If I had my time again . . ."

But neither he nor I had enough self-belief to take my education any further. So Mum and Dad borrowed money from the credit union to send Karen and me to beauty school. Within weeks, Karen was doing leg-waxes in her bedroom, generating money from the word go, and when we qualified, we both got jobs in a spa in Sandyford.

Karen often said to me, "This isn't forever. I'm not spending my life, like Mum and Dad, working for other people. We're going to own our own business."

But I was used to being poor.

And with Ryan Sweeney as my boyfriend and eventually my husband, I stayed used to it for a long time.

Karen tried to carry me along with her ambition. She registered us as a limited company and said, "Save your pennies, Stella, save your pennies. We'll need them for when the right premises come along."

But I didn't have any pennies to save—I had Ryan, then Betsy, to support—and I never took Karen seriously. Until the day she rang and said, "I've found the perfect place! In the main street of Ferrytown. Prime location. I've got the keys. Let's go down for a gander."

It was four dingy rooms above a chemist. I looked around in disbelief. "Karen, the place is a kip. You couldn't bring people in here. Are they . . . ?" I ran to a cluster of things growing in a corner. "Are they mushrooms? They *are* mushrooms!"

"Coat of paint, it'll all be fine. Look, our customers, they won't care about fountains and candles. They'll want bald legs and cheap tans. They'll be young, they won't notice the fungus."

I took one final look around and said, "No, Karen. Sorry to rain on your parade, but this isn't the place."

"Too late," she said. "I've bought the lease. Both of our names are on it. And I've handed in your notice at work."

I gazed at her, waiting for the punch line. When there wasn't one, I said, faintly, "I've a three-month-old baby."

"She's doing grand with Auntie Jeanette minding her. This changes nothing."

"Where's the loo? I need to puke."

"Right behind you."

I ran.

"You're a big chicken," she called through the bathroom door.

I dry-heaved, then said, "I'll be too ashamed to bring people into this dump."

She laughed. "You can't afford to be ashamed. Wait till you see how much we have to pay a month."

I heaved again and Karen said, "You're not pregnant, are you?"

"No." Because I couldn't be. We'd taken precautions. It would be the worst thing in the world to be pregnant right now.

But I was.

As soon as we were working for ourselves, Karen moved to warp speed. She'd always been a fast waxer, but now it was as if she were rocket propelled. She powered through every wax, even the delicate stuff, talking nonstop. "This next bit is going to hurt." She'd have grabbed your leg by the ankle and shoved it high in the air and be whipping the strip off your labia before you'd even noticed it had happened. "Bite down," she'd say, with a grim laugh. "The other side is coming. Ouch! Now! Hair all gone, bald as a coot down there, wasn't it worth it?"

No recovery time was allowed. There were no gentle exhortations to "take your time getting dressed, I'll just tiptoe outside." She'd smile down at the poor girl who was splayed on the plinth, shocked and queasy. "Up you get, we need that bed. Next time, take two Solpadine half an hour before your appointment, you'll be grand. If you need to puke, the bathroom's that way. Feel free, there's no judgment here. Stella there, she got sick after her first Hollywood too. Didn't you, Stella?"

Six months after our big opening, I gave birth to Jeffrey, and

Karen—very reluctantly—agreed to me taking four weeks' maternity leave. "This really isn't a good time," she'd said.

When I returned, I was so stunned and exhausted from caring for two infants that I had to use the morning dead zone between ten and twelve to lie on the sunbed and catch up on some sleep. Meanwhile, Karen went out leafleting to generate new business.

She kept abreast of the latest beauty innovations not by reading sales brochures but by studying the pictures in *Hello!*. Every month we featured a shockingly cheap special offer because, as Karen said, "All I need is for someone to come through that door." You wouldn't believe how persuasive she was—people would come in for an eyebrow shape and they'd leave with eyelash extensions, acrylic nails and an entirely bald body.

In Karen's world, the word "no" didn't exist. If someone wanted to go on the sunbed at seven thirty in the morning, she opened up specially for them, and we worked seven days a week, often until nine at night. If someone rang and asked for a treatment she had never heard of she'd say, with great confidence, "That's coming soon. I'll call you back." Then she'd track it down.

She was a ruthless negotiator and established a complex barter system with half of Ferrytown, where she never paid cash for anything.

Nor had she any problem asking for discounts—if she got one, she was blithe and if she didn't get one, she was just as blithe. "Worth a try, eh?"

I was the opposite. I'd rather go barefoot and sleep in a ditch than smile into someone's face and say, "Knock a tenner off that and we'll call ourselves friends!" I was a hopeless haggler and Ryan was just as bad. Which was why, even when he ended up running a successful business, we stayed skint. I suppose everyone has a talent—some people are great at telling jokes and some people are brilliant bakers and some, like Karen, simply never pay the going rate.

Not once, with Honey Day Spa, did Karen take her eye off the ball. When she noticed that our waxing business had decreased, and no spreadsheet analysis was necessary—she knew intuitively—she discovered that it was because everyone had moved to lasering. So it was time for us to move to lasering.

But the laser company wouldn't sell us their equipment until we'd done an expensive training course with them. So Karen did a ton of research and eventually bought a lasering machine, sight unseen, from China and "trained" on her friends and family. In the same way she also mastered two-week manicures, eyebrow tattoos and vajazzling.

When the injectables craze went mainstream, Karen ignored the fact that she wasn't medically qualified and began doing cut-price treatments. As always, she did her training on friends and family. "We live and learn," she'd say, sending Enda off to work with a face that was lopsided and half paralyzed. "Don't worry! They say it lasts three months but you'd be lucky to get six weeks out of it."

Nothing was too much trouble: she gave loyalty discounts, she'd run down to the street to feed a customer's parking meter, and at the weekends the place was always crammed with girls, some with appointments, some with emergencies (like a split nail), some just hanging out.

Honey Beauty Salon became a Ferrytown institution. Many other beauty salons opened and closed their doors during the nineteen years after Karen and I began. Most started their lives saddled with debt from jade tiles and a plinky-plonk sound system, but not our place—which became Honey Day Spa in 1999 (when all that changed was the sign). Apart from the occasional paint job, Karen has never invested a penny in prettifying the premises.

Even though we were joint owners, it was always Karen's salon.

"So are you coming in?" Karen asks impatiently.

"No, I . . ."

. . . don't want to. I don't want to go into that mushroomy place. I thought I'd left all that behind me.

"I'll stay in the car."

"Grand. Something to think about while you're sitting there—you need to start exercising."

"I do exercise."

"You don't."

"I do!" Until recently I was one of those people who, no matter what else was going on in her life, exercised.

"Only saying."

Karen departs and I sit in her car, feeling misunderstood and wounded: I *do* exercise. Well, I used to. And I was *very* disciplined. Very!

Day in, day out, I used to go at it hard. I remembered one particular morning—I don't know why this one stood out because so many of them were almost identical—when Gilda came into my hotel bedroom, turned on the light and said, firmly but kindly, "Stella, sweetie, time to get up."

I'd had no idea what hour it was, the actual numbers on the clock were immaterial; all that mattered was that if I was being told to get up, then it was time to get up.

I remember being very, very tired. I didn't know how many hours' sleep I'd had. It might have been six. It might have been three and a half. But not more than six. It was never more than six.

Gilda handed me a beaker and said, "Drink this."

I hadn't a clue what it was, it might have been green tea, it might have been a kale smoothie. All that mattered was if Gilda told me to drink it, then I drank it.

I gulped it down and Gilda handed me my running gear. She was already in hers. "Okay, let's go."

Outside the hotel, the sun hadn't risen yet. We did our warm-ups and stretches, then we ran through the empty streets. Gilda set the pace and she was fast. I thought I was going to wheeze my lungs right out of my chest, but there was no point asking her to slow down. This was for my own good; this was what I had agreed to.

Sometime later, when we got back to the hotel, we stopped to do our stretches, and she said, "You did really well."

I gasped, "How much did we do?"

"Four miles."

It had felt more like forty.

"We're in Denver," Gilda said. "High altitude. Harder on the lungs."

I had just learned two useful pieces of information!

1) High altitudes make it harder to run fast.

2) I was in Denver.

I'd known it was one of those places—Dallas, Detroit, Des Moines. Definitely one of the Ds. It had been very late when we'd arrived last night from . . . from . . . another place. A city beginning with . . . T? Baltimore, that was it. Okay, it didn't begin with T, but I could be forgiven seeing as I'd been in three cities the day before. I'd woken in Chicago, where I did countless interviews, a midmorning bookshop event, then given the keynote speech at a charity lunch. As soon as that was over, we raced to the airport, where we caught a plane to Baltimore, where I did more media and an evening reading where only fourteen people showed up. Then it was back to the airport for the flight to Denver. I was criss-crossing so many time zones that I'd given up trying to keep track of the hours I was gaining and losing.

But no matter where I was, no matter how few hours' sleep I'd had, I exercised.

For all the good it had done me.

Stay alive. Sometimes there's nothing else
you can do, but you must do it.

Extract from *One Blink at a Time*

The day after he'd first shown up, Narky Range Rover Man breezed into my cubicle. "I'm back."

So you are.

"Mannix Taylor, your neurologist."

I know your name. I know what you do.

"I can see you're delighted." He laughed. He had lovely teeth. Rich person's teeth, I thought contemptuously. *Neurologist's* teeth.

He pulled a chair to my bedside and lifted my chart from the end of the bed. "Let's see how you slept. Oh, an 'excellent' night's sleep, it says here. Not just good, but actually excellent." He looked at me. "Would you agree?"

I looked dumbly at him and refused to blink.

"Not talking to me? Okay, I'll just get on with my job. Ten minutes, same as yesterday." He gave me a sudden sharp look. "Montgomery did *tell* you I'd be coming every day?"

I hadn't seen Dr. Montgomery for almost a week.

I blinked my left eye.

"He didn't tell you? Or he hasn't been to see you? Well, what about that goofy kid who follows him around like a puppy?"

He was referring to Dr. Montgomery's intern, Dr. de Groot, who visited sporadically and who seemed utterly terrified of ICU. His eyes were as big as hard-boiled eggs and he stuttered as he spoke. He always made a point of checking that my ventilator was plugged in, then he ran away. I felt strongly that he'd be more fulfilled in another line of work. Perhaps plug checking.

"He didn't tell you either?" Mannix Taylor closed his eyes and muttered something. "Okay, well, I'll be seeing you five days a week for the moment. Myelin sheaths grow at about half an inch a month. In the meantime we need to keep the circulation on your extremities moving. But you know all this."

I knew nothing. Since I'd been told I'd caught one of the rarest syndromes going, no one had told me anything, except to stay alive. ("Keep her going there, Patsy!") But this Mannix Taylor had just given me my first hard fact—that myelin sheaths grew at half an inch a month. How many inches did they need to grow? Were they growing already?

"Today," Mannix Taylor said, "I'm going to work on your feet."

I almost levitated in shock. *Not the feet! Anything but the feet!*

Thanks to a lifetime of high heels, I had the worst feet in the world—bunions, corns and misshapen toes—and since I'd come into hospital, no one had even cut my toenails.

No, no, no, Mr. Narky Range Rover Man. Back away from the feet.

But he was loosening the blankets and out came my right foot. He sprayed something onto it—some sort of disinfectant, I was hoping for his sake—and then he had taken my foot in his hands, the heel of his thumb pressing into the tender arch. He held it still for a moment, the pressure warm and firm, then he began to move his fingers in slow confident circles, pressing and pulling the tendons beneath the skin in a way that was almost but not quite painful.

I closed my eyes. Thrills of electricity moved through me. My lips felt numb and tingly and my scalp crawled with delight.

Placing the flat of his palm against the sole of my foot, he pressed hard so that every muscle stretched and the bones cracked in joyful relief.

With his thumbnail, he bit little nips of pleasure along the top of my big toe. The movements were tiny, a delicious sort of agony.

I didn't care about my bunions, about my hard skin, about the funny lump on my small toe that might be a chilblain. All I wanted was to stay with these beautiful feelings forever.

I felt myself getting warmer, then I realized that it wasn't me, it was him.

He wiggled his finger between the big toe and the second toe and when it slotted into the space, a jolt of sensation zipped straight to my lady center. In shock, my eyes flew open. He was staring right at me and he looked surprised. He dropped my foot onto the bed with unexpected haste and tucked it back under the blanket. "We'll leave it there for today."

18:11

Karen drops me home. I let myself into the empty house and I'm hit by a slap of agonizing loneliness which my new lady chinos do nothing to assuage.

What can I do to make myself feel better? I could ring Zoe, but I feel sort of poisoned every time I talk to her. I could watch *Nurse Jackie* and eat biscuits, but in my current bellied-up state, I'm going to have to knock off the biscuits. My biscuit days are over. I'll have to go back to that high-protein, carb-free misery, where I ate salmon for breakfast and told myself that donuts were like unicorns: mythical things that only existed in fairy tales.

I was once able to live like that. I should be able for it again. But I had had Gilda to make me do it, to oversee my meals and say encouraging things like, "Delicious cottage cheese! With delicious prawns. Remember, nothing tastes as good as skinny feels!"

I'd depended on her entirely and she'd taken such wonderful care of me; there was no way I could re-create that support on my own.

And maybe I'm too old to be thin. I know forty-one is the new eighteen, but tell that to my metabolism.

I've been brave for the last twelve weeks; I've plowed blindly forward, but, all of a sudden, I feel like giving up.

If only I could talk to him . . . I live in a state of perpetual longing for him—I still feel like nothing has really "happened" until I've told him.

I stare at my phone, trying to hold on to the facts, reminding myself of my reality. Ringing him would achieve nothing. It would probably make me feel worse.

My life is over, I realize. I accept it, but there are still so many years to live. Unless something intervenes, I'll probably live until I'm at least eighty. How am I going to fill the time?

Maybe I should take my cue from the clothes in the shops and disappear for twenty years. I could eat whatever I wanted and watch an endless amount of telly and reemerge when I'm sixty-one. I'd meet some man who'd been a widower for about ten minutes—they go fast, bereaved men, snapped up quickly, according to Zoe—and he could be my boyfriend. We'd go on a mini break to Florence to look at paintings—by then I'd have developed an interest in art (it would kick in around the same time that I started to lose control of my bladder—nature's barter system). Myself and the widower—Clive?—would never have any fights. No sex, either, but that was okay.

Of course, his daughters would hate me. They'd each say, with a hiss, "I'll never call you Mum!" Gently I'd reply, "Your mum was a wonderful woman. I know I can never replace her." Then they'd like me and we would all celebrate Christmas together, but secretly, just to spite the bitchy daughters, I'd whisper to the grandchildren, "I'm your granny now."

I tell myself that someday in my future I'll be happy again. A different sort of happy to the one I've just lost. A far duller sort.

But it's not going to happen for a long time, so I'd better bunker down and get used to the loneliness.

I contemplate having a glass of wine, but it's a bit early for that. Wearily I abandon my new purchases in the hall and climb the stairs and, still in my clothes, get into bed.

I'm a strong person, I tell myself miserably, as I pull the duvet over my head. I've survived hardship—emotional, physical and financial. It's just a question of being positive, of looking forward. Of *never* looking back. Of adjusting to the new normal, the present reality, of riding the roller coaster of life, as I believe I said myself in my first book. Accepting all that is given to me and all that is taken away. Recognizing that even loss and pain are gifts.

Did I *really* write that shit? And people actually believed it? In fact I think I even believed it myself at the time.

I'd always thought that you grew out of heartbreak, that the older you got, the less it hurt, until it entirely stopped having any impact. But I've discovered the hard way that heartbreak is just as bad when you're old. The pain is still awful. *Worse*, if anything, because of—Zoe explained this to me—the accumulator effect: the loss stacks up on every previous one and you feel the full weight of them all.

But wailing and streeling around being heartbroken is a lot less dignified at my age. Once you pass forty, you're expected to be wise, to be philosophical, to calmly settle yourself in your Eileen Fisher co-ordinating separates and say, "Better to have loved and lost than never to have loved at all. Camomile tea, anyone?"

Not everyone can find a cure for cancer. Someone has to make the dinners and sort the socks.

Extract from *One Blink at a Time*

I know you must be blaming yourself for getting this disease," Betsy said, with great earnestness. "Just remember, Mom, you may have done bad things, but that doesn't make you a bad person."

Don't!

"You probably wish you'd never been born. But—" she squeezed my hand fiercely—"you must never think that. Life is a precious gift!"

Er . . .

"I know you and Dad have your issues . . ."

Do we? For a moment I was wildly irritated. It was all so intense and serious with her; everything had to be analyzed and found wanting and eventually resolved.

"But you being paralyzed and him having to drive us to school will bring you closer together." She smiled a horribly euphoric smile. "You simply need to have faith."

She must be going to that holy youth club, she *must* be! I could almost *see* the creepy group leaders, a man and a woman, both in their early twenties—the man would have longish hair and strange flared jeans and the woman would wear a tartan tabard over a white skinny-knit polo-neck jumper. It was only a matter of time before they came in here with their guitars and tambourines and sang "Michael, Row the Boat Ashore" and got me into big trouble with the nurses.

Ryan needed to protect Betsy from these people, but how could I tell him?

I had an uprush of unbearable frustration. Look at the state of Betsy—her school shirt wasn't ironed and her blazer had a strange yellow stain on the lapel. And why was her chin a cluster of spots? Was it simply because she was fifteen? Or because she was living on complete rubbish?

I hadn't a clue what the household was eating—no one told me and I couldn't ask—but there wasn't much chance that Ryan was cooking healthy meals. He could barely open a jar.

It was no good being cross with him; that end of things had always been my responsibility. The unspoken agreement was that Ryan was the talent and I was the second-in-command.

"I'm going to step away now," Betsy said, "and give you and Dad some alone time."

Ryan took the vacated chair and gingerly held my hand. "So . . ." He looked utterly despondent. "Karen will be in tomorrow instead of me," he said. "I've got to fly to the Isle of Man to pitch for a project."

Since my first day in hospital he hadn't missed a single visit, but life had to go on.

"I'm sorry," he said.

It's okay. It's fine.

"I've got to keep working."

I know.

"I'll miss you."

I'll miss you too.

"Oh!" Something just occurred to him. "I can't find my small wheely case. Where do you think—" He stopped when he realized that I wouldn't be able to answer.

Under the stairs. It's under the stairs.

I always packed for his trips. This was the first time he'd had to do it in years.

"Don't worry," he said. "I'll buy a new one, a cheap yoke. It's grand. When you can speak again you can tell me where it is."

"Time!" the nurse called and Ryan jumped to his feet. "Come on, Betsy."

He gave me a quick peck on the forehead. "See you in a couple of days."

There was no soppiness. The circles we moved in, displays of spousal affection were regarded with deep suspicion. The rules were that the men referred to their wives as "the wife" or "Earache," and the women complained that their husbands were lazy cretins who couldn't tie their own shoelaces. On your wedding anniversary you said things like, "Fifteen years? If I'd murdered someone I'd be free by now."

But I knew how strong Ryan and I were. We weren't just a couple;

we were part of a family of four, a tight little unit. Despite how much we all bickered—and of course we did, we were perfectly normal—we knew that without the others we were nothing.

Ryan loved me. I loved him. This was the hardest test we'd had in our eighteen years together, but I knew we'd survive it.

Had it been the mussels in that restaurant in Malahide? Or the prawns in the reduced-price sandwich? They say you should never take chances with shellfish, but it hadn't been out of date, it just had to be eaten that *day*. Which I had.

I was at it again, trying to remember every meal I'd eaten in the weeks before the tingling in my fingers had started, wondering which had contained whatever bacteria had triggered Guillain-Barré in me.

Could it have been the chemicals I worked with in the salon? Or had I had an infection? They often preceded a bout of GBS.

But maybe it wasn't food poisoning or chemicals or infections. Guillain-Barré was so very rare that I had to wonder if the cause was something different, something darker. Maybe—as Betsy had hinted—God was punishing me because I wasn't a good person.

But I *was* a good person. Remember that time I'd scraped a car with my crappy parking in a multistory car park and, after wrestling with my conscience for a good five minutes *and* checking to see if there was CCTV—there wasn't—I'd left my phone number under the windscreen wiper?

(As it happened, the scraped-car person never rang me, so I had the warm glow of knowing I'd done the right thing without incurring any financial hardship.)

Maybe the way I'd been not good was that I hadn't Fulfilled my Truest Potential—that seemed to be an actual crime these days, according to magazines.

But as a mother and a wife and a beautician, I *had*. You don't have to do something dramatic to Fulfill your Truest Potential. Not everyone can find a cure for cancer. *Someone* has to make the dinners and sort the socks.

The burning pain had started in my hip and—I looked at the clock—

I still had forty-two minutes to go. I needed to not think about it. Back to my worrying.

I'd always done my best, I told myself. Even when I made a total shambles of things, like the birthday party where I'd admired a chunky baby girl by saying, "Isn't he yummy! What age is he?" And then compounded matters by saying, "He's the image of you," to a man who wasn't the baby's father but the man whom everyone suspected the child's mother had been having an affair with.

But despite all my rationalization, I *had* done something bad . . .

A crime of omission rather than commission. I'd put it from my mind, but, since I had nothing else to do here in hospital but think, the memory had popped open and the guilt was killing me.

It was a work thing. I'd been doing a Hollywood wax and I thought I'd got it all off, but as Sheryl—see, I still remembered her name—as Sheryl was getting down from the table I saw I'd missed a bit—and I'd said nothing.

In my defense I was knackered that day and Sheryl was in a mad hurry because she was getting ready to go on a third date, ergo a first-ride date. (They treated me like their confessor, my clients, they told me everything.) So I let it go.

And the thing is, it didn't work out with her man—Alan was his name. Sheryl went on the date and herself and Alan did the deed, but he didn't text her again and I always wondered if that little piece of un-waxed hair had unraveled the whole business.

The worry ate away at me until one night when I woke up at a quarter past four and decided that the very next day I was going to track Alan down and beg him to reconsider. My decision felt *absolutely* right, but by the morning my middle-of-the-night resolve had vanished and trying to find Alan seemed like a nuts thing to do.

So I had to live with it. The only way I got peace was to tell myself that everyone does things for which they'll never be absolved. Life isn't about becoming a perfect person; it's accepting that you're a bad person. Not *bad* bad, like Osama Bin Laden or one of those madmen, but humanly flawed, and therefore dangerous—capable of making mistakes that can cause irreversible damage.

I'd managed to forget it—it had been about five years ago—but now the guilt was back and wouldn't leave me alone. What if I'd said, "Hop back up there on the table, Sheryl, I missed a bit?" Would Sheryl be married to Alan and the mother of three children? Had I, with my laziness, altered the course of the lives of two people? Was it my fault that three beautiful children hadn't been born? Were never even conceived?

Or perhaps Sheryl and Alan just weren't compatible? Maybe the fact that they didn't get married had nothing to do with that little clump of hair? Maybe he hadn't even seen it—Jesus, this was dreadful! There was nowhere to go with my thoughts, they went round and round in circles . . .

My hip felt like it was being held over a fire, I couldn't ignore the pain any longer. There were still twenty-one minutes to go and I was starting to feel sick. What if I puked? Was I even able to? What if my stomach could vomit but the muscles in my throat couldn't get it to the surface? Would I choke? Would my throat break?

I gazed beseechingly at the nurses' station. Please look over, please see me, please take me out of this agony.

One, two, three, four, five, six, seven. Panic was coursing through me. I couldn't do this. *One, two, three, four, five, six, seven.* I couldn't endure this. *One, two, three, four, five, six, seven.*

The yellow digital numbers on my heart monitor were getting higher. Maybe when my heart rate got past a certain number an alarm would go off? *One, two, three, four, five, six, seven. One, two, three, four, five, six, seven.*

"Morning." Dr. Flappy-coat Mannix Taylor breezed into my cubicle, then pulled up short. "What's wrong?"

Pain. I flashed with my eyes.

"I can see that," he said. "Where? Oh, for God's sake!"

He was gone. Then he was back with Olive, one of the nurses. "We need to turn her, to take the weight off her left side."

"Dr. Montgomery said the patient is to be turned every three hours," Olive said.

"The patient has a name," Mannix Taylor said. "And Montgomery might be Stella's consultant but I'm her neurologist and I'm telling you she's in severe pain—just look at her!"

Olive set her mouth.

"If you need Montgomery's blessing, ring him," Mannix Taylor said.

Through a haze of pain, I watched this play out. I wasn't sure it was a good thing to have Mannix Taylor as my champion; he seemed to annoy people.

"Although," Mannix said, "he switches his phone off while he's on the golf course."

"Who says he's on the golf course?"

"He's always on the golf course. They're never anywhere else, him and his cronies. They probably sleep in the clubhouse, in their golf bags, all lined up like little pods, like on a spaceship. Come on, Olive, I'll take Stella's top half. You take her legs."

Olive hesitated.

"Blame me," Mannix said. "Say I bullied you into it."

"They'd certainly believe that," Olive said, tightly. "Mind her ventilator."

"Right."

I couldn't believe it was really happening. They lifted me off my hip and rearranged me, so I was lying on my other side. As the pain ebbed away, the relief was blissful.

"Is that better?" Mannix asked me.

Thank you.

"How often do you need to be moved? At what point does the pain start?"

I stared at him mutely.

"For God's sake!" He sounded maddened with frustration. "This is . . ."

It's not my fault I can't talk.

"After one hour?"

I blinked my left eye.

"No? Two hours? Okay. From now on you'll be lifted every two hours."

He put his hand on my forehead. "You're roasting hot." He sounded less irritable. "You must have been in agony."

He was gone again and after a short, angry-sounding exchange with Olive, he was back with a small bowl of water and a washcloth. He wiped cool water onto my burning face and used the little toweling nubbles to massage around my eye sockets, to wipe my eyelids and to circle my mouth. It felt biblical in its mercy.

19:22

There's a noise downstairs—Jeffrey must be home. My heart lifts at the idea of another human being in the house.

I run down the stairs and the sight of my lanky, cranky son fills me with so much love that I want to squeeze him.

For once he isn't carrying his child-bride yoga mat. But he's carrying something else, a shallow wicker basket; it might be called a trug. He's holding it in the crook of his arm and he looks . . . unmanly. He looks, yes, *silly*. He looks like Little Red Riding Hood going to visit her granny.

"What's going on?" I strive for a cheerful tone.

"I've been out foraging."

"Foraging?" Sweet baby Jesus.

"For wild things." He lifts what looks like a handful of weeds out of his Little Red Riding Hood basket. "Wild herbs and plants. Have you any idea how much food there is growing out there? In the hedgerows? Even in the cracks in the pavements?"

I'm going to puke. I am. He's going to make me eat this stuff. My son is a peculiar loner who wants to poison me.

He notices the shopping bags at the bottom of the stairs. "Were you out spending money?" He sounds as outraged as a Victorian patriarch.

"I needed new clothes. I've nothing to wear."

"You've tons of clothes."

"They don't fit me anymore."

"But we've no money!"

I pause, choosing my words carefully. "We don't have 'no money.' " Not yet. "We have enough to live on for a while. A long while," I add hastily. Well, who knew? "And when I finish my new book, we'll be grand." If I got a publisher and anyone bought it. "Don't worry, Jeffrey. I'm sorry you're worried."

"I *am* worried." He sounds like a fussy old woman. No mention of *him* getting a job, I notice. But I say nothing. Fair play to me. There's many a parent who would have.

"While I was out," I say, "I met Brian's dad, Roddy. Remember Brian? Maybe you should give him a shout."

"You want me to have friends?"

"Weeell, our life is here now."

Feck's sake, I feel like saying. It's not like I'm happy about it either, but I'm doing my best to get on with it.

Our standoff is interrupted by my phone. It's Betsy, calling from New York. Earlier this year she'd got engaged to a rich, handsome, thirty-six-year-old lawyer called Chad—a situation that is another one of Gilda's legacies: when Betsy finished high school and couldn't even get a job folding jumpers in Gap, Gilda miraculously swung her an internship in an edgy art gallery on the Lower East Side. One day Chad had come into the gallery, clapped eyes on my daughter and brazenly said he'd buy an installation if she had dinner with him.

Instantly they fell in love and, despite all the money Ryan and I had shelled out on Betsy's education, she immediately gave up "work" and moved into Chad's massive apartment. They're due to get married sometime next year and even though she seems very happy, her lack of ambition terrifies me.

"But don't you get it?" she'd asked. "I don't want to have it all. It looks exhausting. I want to stay home and have babies and learn quilting."

"But you're so young . . ."

"You were only twenty-two when you had me."

"There's a big difference between nineteen and twenty-two."

What worried me was her inability to take care of herself if Chad legged it. And the situation had "Chad legging it" written all over it. He was just the type, hamstrung with too much money and a sense of entitlement. He'd marry her but, in five years or ten, he'd leave her for a younger version and Betsy would be cast adrift.

But maybe she'd be okay. She'd retrain as a real estate agent, that's what they all seemed to do, those ex-trophy wives. They hardened up and came into their own. They bought themselves a zippy little TransAm and went on a lot of sunshine holidays and had younger, freeloading, blandly handsome boyfriends whom you suspected of being secretly gay.

"Betsy!" I say. "Sweetheart!"

Even though we speak nearly every day I'm afraid that she's ringing with bad news—if word of Ryan's idiotic project has reached her, then we have a genuine problem on our hands. Or maybe there was something in today's *New York Times* about Gilda . . . ?

But she just chatters away about the new bag she's bought. "Michael Kors," she says. "And I got three shift dresses from Tory Burch."

In the last six months, Betsy's look, bankrolled by Chad, has undergone a profound transformation.

"I'm going to take my hair down a couple of shades," she says. "I'm going to be totally blond."

"Well . . . great!"

"What if the lighter color doesn't work for me?"

"You can go back to your own color."

"But my hair will be totally damaged."

"You can get treatments."

"I can," she says, chirpily. "Anyhoo! How are things with you?"

"Great, yes, great!" Because that's what you should say when you're a mother.

"Are you sure?"

"Certain, certain! Okay, talk soon, sweetie. And, ah . . . and my regards to Chad."

"Sure." She laughs.

Behind me, I hear the sound of a fork being chinged against a glass.

I turn around. The kitchen table is set with two platefuls of weeds.

"I hope you're feeling hungry!" Jeffrey says. "It's dinnertime!"

I hate my life!" Betsy declared. "And I wish I'd never been born!" She
stomped off away down the ward.

Christ, she'd changed her tune! Was it only yesterday she'd been
telling me what a precious gift life was?

I looked inquiringly at Karen and Jeffrey. *What's happened?*

Jeffrey went beet-red and twisted down from me.

"She got her monthly visitor last night," Karen said. "There were no
tampons in the house. She tried to sneak out to buy some, Ryan stopped
her, so she had to tell him."

I hated myself: I shouldn't be lying in this hospital bed; I should be
at home taking care of my family. That exchange must have been ex-
cruciating for both Betsy and Ryan. Betsy was very private about her
body and Ryan got the man horrors at any reminder that his little girl
had become a woman. You should have seen him the day I'd bought
her her first bra. "She's too young," he'd stuttered.

"But she has breasts," I'd said.

"Don't! Don't." He'd covered his face with his hands. "She hasn't!"

"She was mortified last night," Karen said. "So was Ryan. You can
imagine. But he went out and bought a box of tampons. Wrong brand,
of course . . ." She paused, and added, "But fair play to him. I know I've
always said he's a lazy gobshite. But he's doing well. Cooking and all."

I knew Karen's idea of cooking—if she microwaved a packet of rice
she thought she was a candidate for *Masterchef*.

"I'd better go," she said, standing up. "And get your kids to school.
Mum and Dad will be in for the evening visit. Come on, Jeffrey, let's
find your sister."

And off they went leaving me alone with my thoughts.

Poor Betsy. At her age, everything seemed so important and
dramatic—"I wish I'd never been born!"

Funnily enough, despite the dark places I'd been in over the past
month, not once had I wished I'd never been born.

Maybe it was because death was ever present on this ward—people died in the beds around me, all the time. Sometimes five or six days could go by without any losses and then two might die in a morning.

Every time it happened, I was filled with gratitude that I'd been spared.

Not that my thoughts were always positive—I wished I hadn't got this strange, terrible disease and I wished I could go home to my kids and to Ryan and to my job—God, how precious they seemed! I wished I didn't feel so afraid and lonely, but at no time, even when the pain in my hip was bad, did I wish I'd never been born.

There was some phrase rolling around like a pebble in the back of my mind that my granny used to say: "When you enlist you have to soldier."

You know the way old people always have a litany of awful news—a woman up the road had the tiles stolen off her roof, a traffic light toppled over onto so-and-so's husband, and the man who worked in the post office, his dog had bitten a barrister?

Well, whenever Granny Locke (Dad's mum) came to visit, she'd relate all *manner* of disasters and when she'd finally finished she'd sigh, with a sort of happy gloom, and say, "When you enlist you have to soldier."

She was saying that when you sign up to this life business, you agree to it all, good and bad; there's no opt-out clause for pain. Everyone suffered—I could see it now with startling clarity—even the parents in Betsy and Jeffrey's school. On the surface their lives seemed like one long carousel of fabulous holidays, but you heard things. One of the mums, who was a doctor, was struck off for getting high on her own supply of prescription painkillers.

And another of the mums, one of the more fabulous ones—oh, you should have seen her, she looked like she should be married to a rock star—she wore jeans from the kids' department and was so, so skinny in a way that looked effortless. Well, one day she stood up and broke her thigh bone and it turned out she had osteoporosis—at thirty-five! Life-long anorexia, apparently.

She got hustled off to a psychiatric hospital and I hadn't seen her since. (Does it make me a very bad person—yes, probably—that her story gave me a small bit of relief: my stomach might not be flat but at least I wasn't going around breaking my legs by simply getting out of a chair.)

Everyone suffered. Not just me.

And here came Mannix Taylor. His doctor's coat was flying open—whenever he appeared it was always with a flurry and a flourish.

Button your fecking coat.

He took a chair and said, almost cheerily, "Stella, I know you don't like me."

I blinked my right eye. Yes. I mean, why not? It was obvious. And he didn't like me either.

"But will you work with me on a little project?" He seemed . . . *enthusiastic.*

Er . . . okay . . . Again I blinked my right eye.

"Is that all you can do?" he asked. "Blink?"

I stared at him. In my most sarcastic tone, I thought, *So sorry to disoblige you.*

"All right, I just wanted to be sure. See, I've been thinking about you. You not being able to communicate, it's not on. Have you heard of a book called *The Diving Bell and the Butterfly*?"

I had, actually. Dad had made me read it a few years back.

"Written by a man, who, just like you, was only able to move his eyelids. In fact, he could only use one; he was in an even worse situation than you. What I'm trying to say is, if you can blink, you can talk. So think of something you'd like to say to me." He took a pen from his pocket. With a snarky little smile, he said, "Try and make it polite." He unclipped a page from my bedside chart and turned it over to the blank side. "You won't have the energy to say much," he said. "So make it matter. Have you thought of something?"

I blinked my right eye.

"Okay. First letter. Is it a vowel?"

I blinked my left eye.

"No? So it's a consonant?"

I blinked my right eye.

"A consonant. Is it in the first half of the alphabet, A to M? No? Second half?"

Again, I blinked my right eye.

"Is it N?" he asked.

I blinked my left eye.

"Stop, stop," he said. "You'll be exhausted if you react to every letter. We're going to have to fine-tune this. Okay, if it's not the correct letter, do nothing. I'll watch you; I'll do the heavy lifting. Okay? Is it P?"

I didn't react.

"Q? R? S?"

At S I blinked my right eye.

"It's S? Okay." He wrote it on his page. "Second letter. A vowel? Yes? A? E? I? O? It's O? Okay, next letter. Vowel? No, consonant . . ."

We kept going until I had spelled out the word "SORRY."

He leaned back in his chair and said speculatively, "So what are you sorry about?" He gave a sardonic laugh. "I can hardly *wait* to find out. Do you feel able to keep going?"

Oh yes.

We continued until I'd "said," "SORRY ABOUT YOUR CAR."

"Your first communication for a month and you use it to be sarcastic. Nothing about being too hot, too cold, in pain? Well, it's great to hear that all is so good. And there was me, concerned about you."

Suddenly I was deeply sorry that I'd wasted this valuable opportunity by being snippy. I should have asked if someone would get Jeffrey to wash his hair—I suspected he hadn't done it since I'd come into the hospital—or if Karen would buy *Grazia* and read it aloud to me.

"Anyway." Mannix Taylor bowed his head in a courtly fashion. "Apology accepted."

Now who's being sarcastic?

"Now who's being sarcastic?" he said to himself, then flicked a quick look at me. Almost in alarm, he said, "That's just what you were thinking."

I blinked. No.

He shook his head. "For a woman who can barely move a muscle,

Stella Sweeney, you've a very bad poker face. As it happens, it wasn't *my* car you drove into."

I began blinking. "WHOSE CAR WAS IT?"

Mannix Taylor looked at the page he'd been transcribing my blinks onto, then he looked at me. "Stella . . ." He shook his head and gave a little laugh. "Would you let it go?"

But I wanted to know.

He considered me for so long that I thought he wasn't going to tell me. Then, to my surprise, he said, "It was my brother's."

His brother's?

"Sort of."

Was it or wasn't it?

"Somehow he'd convinced the dealer to let him drive away a brand-new Range Rover without having actually paid for it."

How?

"He's extremely charming, my brother." Mannix gave me a mocking look. "Obviously, there's no family resemblance."

Hey, you're the one who said it . . .

"I was returning it to the dealers but it wasn't insured. It was only a short journey and I have third party, but . . ."

It took me a few moments to join all the dots, then I got the full picture and it wasn't a pretty one—Mannix Taylor had been driving a new car he wasn't insured on so the full cost of replacing it could land on his shoulders.

The irate man who had driven into the back of my car, despite his frenzy of rage, wouldn't necessarily have been liable.

I'd no idea how much a new Range Rover cost but it was bound to be eye watering.

"SORRY."

"Ah, it's okay." Wearily, he rubbed his hand over his face.

I was so hungry for conversation I'd have gladly listened to anything, but this was honest-to-God juicy stuff.

Conveying encouragement with my eyes, I urged Mannix Taylor on.

"He's my older brother. An estate agent. Roland Taylor. You probably know of him. Everyone does. Everyone loves him."

Roland Taylor, yes, I *did* know of him! He was sometimes on talk shows, being vastly overweight and regaling people with funny stories. In fairness, he was very entertaining: Ireland's first celebrity estate agent. One of the many strange things the Celtic Tiger had thrown up, along with celebrity opticians and celebrity water diviners.

Despite his size, Roland Taylor always wore very fashionable clothes and hipster's spectacles but somehow he came across as charming rather than risible. He really was extremely likable—the type of celebrity that you wish was your friend in real life—and he was Mannix Taylor's brother. How unexpected!

"He has . . . problems," Mannix Taylor said. "With money. With spending. It's not his fault; it's . . . ah . . . a family trait. I'll tell you about it someday." He eyed me as if he'd thought better of it. "Or maybe not . . ."

Monday, 2 June

04:14

I awake. I don't mean to but clearly I have not appeased the Sleep Gods with enough offerings. I go to the spare room and switch on my computer. Then I think, What in the name of *Christ* am I doing? It's four in the morning. I promptly switch off the computer and return to bed and rummage in my bedside drawer for some sort of sleep aid. A box of valerian pills presents itself; it recommends two tablets "for peaceful sleep" so I take six because, hey, it's only herbal. My devil-may-care attitude clearly impresses the Sleep Gods because I am rewarded with five more hours of slumber.

09:40

I rise again. Downstairs, there's evidence that Jeffrey has already broken his fast and left the house—a washed mug and bowl are on the draining board, simply *radiating* primness. We have a dishwasher so there's no need for him to hand wash anything but he does anyway, as some strange sort of rebuke to me.

I loiter at the kitchen table and drink tea and muse on what an oddball my son is. He could have poisoned us both with those foraged things last night. Obviously this is just a phase he's going through but the sooner he becomes normal, the sooner I'll like it.

I drink more tea and eat a sizable bowl of granola. Yes, granola: broken biscuits masquerading as healthy food. I know exactly what I'm doing. I'm no longer in denial. But to begin my BARR (Belly Attachment Reducing Regime), I need to buy special horrible food and until then I may as well use up the stuff in the house. After all, it's a crime to waste good food, especially in these straitened times.

I'm seized by sudden horrible fear—the thought of living without carbs is terrifying.

But I've been able for it in the past, I remind myself. Although, in retrospect, I'm astonished at how obedient I was. Again, I remember that day in Denver when Gilda had got me out of bed and made me run four miles in the dark. When we got back to the hotel I'd had a shower and simply awaited further instructions. I was *hopeful* I might get fed but I knew there was no point asking. If I was due food, I'd be given it. If I wasn't, I wouldn't. Simple. No thinking involved. Thinking was Gilda's area.

She was in charge of my diet—a calorie-counted, high-protein, sugar-free plan. Between that and the running, it kept me a size eight. A European size eight, I should stress. Not a U.S. size eight, which is really a size twelve and which nobody admires.

While Gilda had blow-dried my hair—there was very little Gilda couldn't do—she talked me through that day's schedule. "In ten minutes the car will be here to take us to *Good Morning Denver*. You're in the seven thirty-five a.m. slot and you've got four minutes. They're tagging the lunchtime event and flashing the book cover. After that we go to a physical rehab center where you'll meet patients. You'll feed them breakfast. A local news channel will be covering it—"

"What about me?" My anxiety burst out. "Will I be getting any breakfast?"

"Of course," she said.

"Oh yeah, really?"

She laughed. "Don't shoot me. You're going to have some hospital food with the patients."

"Hospital food?"

"Come on," she said encouragingly. "It'll be heartwarming. You'll talk about the memories it brings back of when you were fed through a tube into your stomach. Who wouldn't be moved by a memory like that? I'm feeling teary already."

"And you?" I said. "I guess you'll be getting a big plate of pancakes and syrup."

"Guess I will. But then again, I'm not the star." And we both laughed.

Back in the present, I eat some more granola and consider my morning. Task one: I need to lose half a stone from my b-place. Task two: I need to write a book.

My phone rings. It's Mum.

"Where are you?" She sounds cross.

"Where should I be?"

"Here. Bringing me to the shops. It's Monday."

It's my job to drive Mum to the supermarket every Monday morning. How could I have forgotten?

This means I can put off doing any work for a while. Great!

"I'll be with you in fifteen minutes."

"You should be with me now."

Using my new lady chinos as a fulcrum, I assemble a summer outfit. Luckily my weight gain hasn't affected my feet, so my sandals from last year still fit me.

10:30

I get into my car, the same car that I used to drive Betsy and Jeffrey to school in. The car that I didn't need anymore when my new life started and I moved to New York. I'd asked Karen to sell it for me but she'd held on to it because clearly she didn't have the same faith in my happy ending that I did.

And maybe it was for the best. Because when my happy ending turned out to be an illusion, I needed a car. And this one was waiting to welcome me home, as if I'd never gone away.

As I drive, "Bringing Sexy Back" comes on the radio and I'm thrust right back to the Justin Timberlake gig in Madison Square Garden that Gilda had taken me to. It had been one of the greatest nights of my life. For the millionth time I wonder how she is. But I can't let myself Google her. All I can do is say the mantra: *May you be well, may you be happy, may you be free from suffering.*

10:35

Mum opens her door and she's got her annoyed face on, on account of me having forgotten about the weekly shop, but then she looks me up and down and says, in startled pleasure, "Stella! Did you get new trousers?"

With unexpected pride, I say, "Karen helped me. They're chinos."

"Chinos? Are they not for men?"

"These are *lady* chinos."

"Lady chinos! They must be a new thing. Well!" She is a-puff with admiration. "You look very nice! Go in and show your father."

"Okay. Hello, Dad." I don't just stick my head around the front-room door, I go right in to make sure he gets a proper look at me.

"There you are, Stella," he says. Then he peers at me more closely. "What did you do to yourself? You're looking gameball."

"She's after buying chinos." Mum has come in behind me.

"Chinos?"

"*Lady* chinos," Mum and I say together.

"Did the Parvenue have a hand in this?"

"She did!" we both say.

"Well, credit where it's due," Dad says. "You look gameball."

"Gameball," Mum agrees. "To the max."

Well, what do you know? I look gameball! My lady chinos are a success! My new look works!

12:17

Oh my God, the crap they eat—biscuits, crisps, strange cakes with ten-month eat-by dates. Any combination of trans-fat and sugar is welcome in Hazel Locke's trolley.

Shopping with Mum is always a power struggle—she who controls the trolley, controls what goes into it. This week Mum wins—she told me that I'd better straighten up my parking, then she hopped out of the car, a euro in her hand, and had bagged a trolley before I'd even switched off the engine. When it suits her, Mum can be surprisingly nimble. Also cunning.

We spend a horribly long time in trans-fat central, then I insist we visit the fruit and vegetable aisle. "How about broccoli?" I suggest.

"I hate broccoli," she says, sulkily.

"You've never even tasted it."

"That's right. Because I hate it."

"Come on, Mum. What about some carrots?"

In lackluster fashion, she touches a bag of carrots and then recoils as if it's radioactive. "Organic!"

"Organic is good," I say, like I always do. "It's better for you than the ordinary stuff."

She picks up an organic apple. "How can it be, Stella? Look at the gammy shape of it. It's like an apple from Chernobyl. Anyway," she says gloomily, "at our time of life, let us have our little pleasures."

"You'll die prematurely."

"So what?"

I want to grab her by her shoulders and say earnestly, "You must stop being so old!"

But she can't help it. Mum and Dad, they will never wear white linen and walk barefoot along a beach, smiling and holding hands and glowing with fish-oil-induced health.

Just because you live near a golf course, it doesn't
mean you have to play golf.

Extract from *One Blink at a Time*

Mannix Taylor swung into my cubicle, accompanied by four, no five, of the nurses. What was going on?

"Morning, Stella," he said. "We're going to have a little lesson here. Will you show your nurses the blinking you and I did yesterday?"

Er, okay.

The nurses crowded around my bed in a sullen cluster. *We're very busy*, their vibes said. *We've more than enough to do as it is without having to watch a paralyzed woman blink.*

"Right!" Mannix held a pen over a piece of paper. "What would you like to say, Stella? First letter. A vowel? No? A consonant? First half of the alphabet? Yes? B, C, D, F, G, H? H! Okay! H it is."

He turned to the nurses. "You see how it's done. Who'd like to take over?"

When no one volunteered, he foisted the pen and page onto the nurse nearest to him. "You do it, Olive," he said. "Off you go, Stella."

Almost shyly, I spelled out the word "HELLO."

The nurses stared and eventually one of them said, "Hello back."

"Why are you saying hello to her?" another asked. "She's been here a month."

"But this is Stella's first time to speak to you," Mannix said.

"Aaah. Right. Well, we'd better go."

As they made their way back to the station, I distinctly heard one of them say, "Who the *hell* does he think he is?"

"What time does the husband come in?" Mannix asked Olive.

"Most mornings about eight and again at seven in the evening."

"So we could have been talking all this time?" Ryan, dark and angry, squared up to Mannix Taylor. "She's here for a month before someone lets us know?"

Yes, but . . .

Ryan didn't seem to understand that Mannix had introduced the blinking system specially for me.

"Guillain-Barré is phenomenally rare," Mannix said. "In all my time as a neurologist I've never encountered it. There are no protocols in any hospital in this country to treat it."

"This is bullshit!" Ryan said.

"However, I've put feelers out to experts in the U.S. and—"

"She's been here for a month and she hasn't got any better!"

I was desperately trying to catch Ryan's eye. *Stop shouting*, I wanted to say. *He's helping me. He's stayed late, just so he could explain it to you.*

"Who the hell are you, anyway?" Ryan demanded.

"Like I said, I'm Stella's neurologist."

"What's happened to Dr. Montgomery?"

"Dr. Montgomery is still Stella's consultant. I'm her neurologist. We play different roles. He has overall responsibility for Stella's care."

"Two lots of fees instead of just one?"

I couldn't bear to think of how much I must be costing.

"How come you've taken a month to show up?"

"Stella should have been put under the care of a neurologist the first night she came in, but someone somewhere missed it. An administrative cock-up. I'm sorry the system has let you and Stella down."

"Ah, for fu—"

It was clear that Ryan was at the end of his rope. He'd come straight to the hospital from the airport after his pitch in the Isle of Man, trundling his cheap new wheely case; he looked wrung out and exhausted and miserable beyond belief.

"Stella . . ." he said. "I can't do this tonight. I'll see you in the morning."

He gave Mannix Taylor one final glare, and left.

As his footsteps echoed away Mannix Taylor and I looked at each other.

No good deed goes unpunished.

He gave a little laugh as if he'd understood what I was thinking—maybe he had, maybe he hadn't—then swiveled on his heel and he, too, was gone.

* * *

Dr. Montgomery was late.

After Ryan and Mannix Taylor had clashed, Ryan had demanded a progress report.

"I want answers," Ryan had told me, taut with fury. "I'm sick of watching you rotting in this bed, not getting any better. And I want to know who this Mannix Taylor is."

Ryan had brought Karen along for the meeting; they were standing with Mannix Taylor in an awkward triangle just outside my cubicle and, from the body language, I could tell that Karen didn't like Mannix Taylor any more than Ryan did.

The problem was that Ryan and Karen were angry—angry that I was sick and angry that I wasn't getting better—and their anger had to have a focus.

Note to self, I thought: if someone was angry with me, I shouldn't take it personally, because who knows what's going on for them?

"How much longer is this Dr. Montgomery going to be?" Karen snapped at Mannix Taylor. "I've a job to get to."

"So have I."

Wrong thing to say. Karen bristled and I watched, helpless, from my bed.

Suddenly all the energy in the ward changed—Dr. Montgomery had arrived. Here he came, dapper and smiley, distributing bonhomie on all sides, trailing a retinue of junior doctors. "Good morning, Dr. Montgomery," the nurses called. "Good morning!"

Dr. Montgomery's arrival triggered an outbreak of handshaking, so much so that Ryan and Karen accidentally shook hands with each other.

No one shook my hand. No one even looked at me.

"Dr. Montgomery," Ryan said. "You told me to be patient. I've been patient. But I—we—Stella's family, need an honest update on how she's doing."

"Of course you do, of course you do! Well, my colleague here, Dr. Taylor, is the expert on neurology. Maybe, Mannix, you'd care to share some of your"—sarcastic inflection—"*wisdom.*"

"To put it as simply as possible," Mannix Taylor said, "Guillain-Barré attacks the myelin sheaths on the nerves. They need to grow back before movement returns to the limbs. However—"

Montgomery interrupted smoothly, "You heard the man: the myelin sheaths on Sheila's nerves need to grow back before movement returns to her limbs."

"The patient's name is Stella," Mannix Taylor said. Dr. Montgomery didn't even look at him, just kept his benevolent gaze fixed on Ryan's anxious face.

"But how long will that take?" Ryan asked. "She hasn't changed since the first night she came in. Can you give us some estimate of when she can come home?"

"I know you must be missing her and the home cooking," Dr. Montgomery said. "And I know you know we're all breaking our barncys to get Sheila well as soon as possible. The nurses here on the ward are the best girls in the world."

Mannix Taylor looked pointedly at the nurses' station, where two of the nurses were men.

"Could you give us some sort of time line?" Ryan asked. "Anything at all? A week?"

"Ah, would you catch a grip of yourself." Montgomery gestured to me, prone in the bed. "Shur, look at the cut of her."

"How about a month?"

"It could be," Montgomery said. "Indeed it could. Maybe even sooner."

Really?

Mannix Taylor looked aghast. "Respectfully, if I may—"

Montgomery cut across him, steel in his voice. "However, Sheila's health is our priority and we can't discharge her until she's fully well. You're an educated man, Mr. Sweeney, you know that! So if she's not on her way home a month from today, you're not to be ringing my secretary shouting at her, like you did this morning! Poor Gertie isn't able for it! She's a great oul' warhorse but she's old-school. Hahaha!"

"But a month would be still in the ballpark?" Ryan persisted.

"Without a doubt. Did you take up the fly-fishing?"

"I didn't."

"You should. How about you?" Dr. Montgomery looked at Karen with open admiration. "Do you play golf at all?"

"Um, no."

"You should. Come down to the clubhouse sometime. A lovely girl like you, you'd put a smile on a few faces."

Montgomery looked at his watch, gave a little start, said, "Bless us and save us!" then began distributing business cards, one to Ryan, one to Karen and one to goofy Dr. de Groot, which he promptly retrieved. "Gimme that back, you little scut! I don't want *you* ringing me at home—amn't I sick of the sight of you. Me and my shadow, hahaha!"

To Ryan and Karen, he said, "My home number is on there. Call me. Day or night. Day *or* night. Mrs. Montgomery is well used to it; she's dead to the world after she takes her tablets, hahaha! Any worries at all, just pick up the phone. Now, I'm afraid I must love ye and leave ye, I've an appointment."

"How's your handicap?" Mannix Taylor asked, pointedly.

Dr. Montgomery gave him a look of benign dislike. "D'you know something? You should join us on the fairway sometime, Mannix, it might do you good." He looked around at his audience. "Very serious chap, our Dr. Taylor." Everyone laughed obediently.

"What's that my grandson says?" Montgomery asked. "'Why don't you lighten up!'" And everyone laughed again.

"It's been a pleasure." Dr. Montgomery beamed. "We must do it again soon." Briskly, he shook hands with everyone except Mannix. And me, of course. He declared, "Keep her going there, Patsy!" And off he went, his posse scampering to keep up with him.

"He was a gas," Karen said, watching him go.

Really? Karen was the most canny person I'd ever met—how could she have fallen for Dr. Montgomery's shtick? He had flimflammed everyone when it was clear—to me anyway—that he knew nothing about my condition. And my blood ran cold wondering how much he'd charged for those precious few minutes of face time.

With the departure of Dr. Montgomery, it was like a balloon had burst. All the fun had gone out of things. Then Mannix Taylor started to speak and everything darkened further.

"Look," he said to Ryan and Karen, "I know Dr. Montgomery said Stella might be home in a month, but she won't."

Ryan narrowed his eyes. "Excuse me?"

"There's no way that—"

"Dr. Montgomery got a double first from Trinity," Ryan said. "He's been a senior consultant in this hospital for over fifteen years. Are you saying you know more than your boss?"

"I'm a neurologist. I specialize in disorders of the central nervous system."

"You told me you knew nothing about Guillain-Barré," Ryan said.

"I said I'd never encountered it in a clinical setting. But I've made contact with specialists in the United States and, from what I'm learning, it's better if you manage your expectations."

"So she won't be home in a month?"

"No."

"How can you say that in front of her?" Karen said, hotly. "How can you be so cruel?"

"I'm not intending to be cruel—"

"So when *will* she be home?" Ryan asked.

"It's impossible to say."

"Fantastic," Ryan said, with wild, angry sarcasm. "Just fantastic."

Karen took his arm in an attempt to calm him. "Ryan, listen to me," she said. "We'll go. Let's leave it for the moment."

They each gave me a reluctant kiss on the forehead, then they left and the only person remaining at my bedside was Mannix Taylor.

"Dr. Montgomery *did* get a double first from Trinity," he said. Then he added, "About a thousand years ago."

To my great surprise, in my head I giggled.

"And he *has* been a senior consultant here for donkey's years. It's all true what your husband says."

But it didn't make him a good doctor.

"'Much learning does not teach understanding,'" Mannix said. "I think it was Socrates who said that."

I fluttered my eyelids; it was the signal we'd agreed on for when I wanted to speak. He reached for his pen and paper and I spelled out, "HERACLITUS."

"Heraclitus?" Mannix Taylor was puzzled. "What's a heraclitus?" Suddenly he began to laugh. "Heraclitus! It was *Heraclitus* who said, 'Much learning does not teach understanding.' Not Socrates. You *are* a card, Stella Sweeney. Or may I call you Sheila? How do you know about Greek philosophers and you only a humble hairdresser?"

"BEAU—"

"Beautician. I know. It was a joke."

Jokes are meant to be funny.

"Yeah," he sighed. "Maybe I should give up on the jokes. I don't seem to have the knack of them."

That night, in the long empty hours of my "excellent" sleep, I thought about Mannix Taylor: he was quite a peculiar man. The way he'd slagged off Dr. Montgomery was shockingly unprofessional, even if he was right.

I wondered about Mannix Taylor's life outside the hospital. He wore a wedding ring—of course he did—and he had nice teeth and he worked in a well-paid, respected profession. He would have a perfect wife.

Unless he was gay? But I really wasn't feeling that. No, he definitely had a wife.

I wondered if he was as moody at home as he was at work. I was guessing he wasn't. I'd say his wife took no nonsense from him. "Leave your bad stuff at work," I could hear her saying. "Don't bring it home." I visualized her as a tall, Scandinavian-looking beauty, maybe an ex-model. Very accomplished. She ran her own business. Doing . . . what? Interiors? Yes, interiors. Her type always did that—they faffed around with paint charts and fabric swatches and got paid a fortune. Or she might be a child psychologist—they could sometimes pull something out of the bag and surprise you, those women.

I decided that herself and Mannix had three beautiful, blond children. One of the kids had . . . let's see . . . dyslexia, because no one's life was entirely perfect. But a private tutor came four afternoons a week—he was expensive, but he was worth it and Saoirse was doing very well and keeping up with her year.

Mannix Taylor lived . . . ? Where? Somewhere with electronic gates. Yes, definitely. Probably one of those beautiful houses in Wicklow, near the Druid's Glen golf club. A converted and massively extended barn on a half acre of land. Properly rural, fields all around them, but handy for the N11, so he could whizz up to Dublin in half an hour.

What did he do in his spare time, this Mannix Taylor? Hard to tell, but one thing was for sure, he didn't play golf. Which was a shame, seeing as he lived so near to such a reputable golf club.

16:22

"I hear you've been showing off your lady chinos!" Karen is at my front door, her blond hair blow-dried super sleek.

"Yes!" I stand aside to let her in. "Thank you so much! I must admit I had my doubts—"

"Let me stop you right there." She makes her way to the kitchen. "Is it too early for wine? I suppose it is and, anyway, you can't have any." She flicks on the kettle. "Where was I? Oh, right—don't start thinking you're okay. The chinos are only a temporary solution. A camouflage. You're still going to have to lose ten pounds."

"Not ten!" I cry. "Seven."

"Nine."

"Eight."

"Whatever. Everyone else," she says thoughtfully, "when their life falls apart, they lose weight. How unlucky are you?" She opens and closes a couple of cupboards. "Any normal tea bags? I'm not drinking this herbal shit."

"Neither am I," I say with dignity. "The herbal shit belongs to Jeffrey."

"Christ, he's odd. Mind you, so is my son. Do you think we're carriers for some sort of male oddness? Protein," she said, abruptly. "That's what you need. Lots and lots of protein. Forget carbs even exist."

"Are those your real eyelashes?" I ask, desperate to change the subject.

"These?" Karen blinks the long, spiky lashes at me. "Nothing is my real anything. Everything is fake. Nails." She flicks her hands at me and whips them away again in far less than a second. "Teeth." She opens her jaws in a speedy grrrr. "Brows. Tan. I'll do eyelash extensions for you." She swallows hard and with some effort adds, "For cost."

I shake my head. "I've had eyelash extensions. They're a nightmare to live with. You can't touch them, you can do nothing to upset them. It's like being in a dysfunctional relationship."

Karen stares meaningfully at me.

"It wasn't dysfunctional," I say. "It was functional."

"Until it wasn't."

I'm starting to feel a bit tearful. "Ah, Karen . . . maybe you should go now?" Suddenly I remember something. "I dreamed about Ned Mount again last night."

"What are you doing dreaming about him?"

"We don't get any say in who we dream about! Anyway, I like him." He'd interviewed me on his radio show when *One Blink at a Time* had come out in Ireland. We'd got on great.

"Would you . . . ?"

"No . . . That part of my life is over."

"You're only forty-two."

"Forty-*one*."

"And a half."

"And a quarter. Only a *quarter*."

Karen's gaze roams over my face. "It's about time you got a couple of boosts. Go on. Dr. JinJing will be in on Thursday. My treat."

"Ah, no thanks."

Due to a clampdown in the law, Karen had had to stop administering injectables herself and nowadays a young Chinese doctor came to the salon every second Thursday and jabbed Botox and fillers into a keen clientele. But I'd seen the results of Dr. JinJing's handiwork and it scared me. Heavy-handed would be the best way to describe it and I knew from experience that bad Botox is worse than no Botox.

I'd had a really good person in New York, a doctor who understood subtlety. I was able to move my eyebrows and everything. Then I'd made the money-saving mistake of going to a cheaper person and my forehead turned into a sort of overhanging canopy. I looked like a perpetually disapproving Cro-Magnon lady. The two months while I was waiting for the bad Botox to leave my face had felt like a very long time.

"Are you sure?" Karen asks, impatiently. "I won't charge you. There's an offer you don't get every day."

"Honest to God, Karen, I'm fine right now."

"Did you hear what I said? I said I won't charge you!"

"Thanks. Lovely. Let's just . . . not for now, okay?"

In my hospital bed, everything changed after the advent of the Blinking Code. My initial communication with the family was to ask Karen to wash my hair, and only a person as undauntable as her could have succeeded—because it was a *massive* job involving plastic sheeting, jugs, sponges and countless basins of water. Not to mention the delicate negotiation of all the tubes in and out of me. Mum, Betsy and Jeffrey assisted, running obediently to the bathroom to empty sudsy water and return with fresh stuff, then Karen blow-dried my hair into soft curls and I could have died with cleanliness.

My next request was a solemn promise from Betsy and Jeffrey that they'd stay committed to their schoolwork, and my third wish was for a bit of fun—I was tired of people coming in and staring sadly at me for fifteen minutes, then leaving. I wanted distraction, a laugh, even. I would have given my life for an episode of *Coronation Street* but, as that was out of the question, maybe someone would read magazines to me: I hungered for news of celebrity hook-ups and breakups, of weight gains and weight losses, of new trends in shoes and beauty.

Then things went a bit skew ways. Dad got wind that I'd asked to be read to and he arrived, all excited, with a library book in a plastic bag. "A first novel—" he waved it at me—"American chap. Tom Wolfe called him the most formidable novelist of the twenty-first century. Joan put it by specially for you."

He pulled up a chair and began to read and it was very, very awful. "'Tumbling. Tumbrils. Tombolas. Milkful. Bountyplenty. Creamy flesh in overspill. Abundant cascade.'"

Behind him, Mannix Taylor hoved into view.

"'Flesh. Fleish. A Teutonic truth,'" Dad read on. "'Meat. All that we are and all that we will be. Thin skin-sacks of red water and marbled muscle. Gristle-people—'"

"What's going on?" Mannix Taylor sounded annoyed.

Dad jumped off his chair and turned around.

"Mannix Taylor, Stella's neurologist." Mannix offered his hand.

"Bert Locke, Stella's father." Dad reluctantly accepted the handshake. "And Stella wants to be read to."

"She's not strong. She needs her energy to heal her body. I'm serious. This stuff . . ." Mannix waved his hand at the novel. "It sounds heavy. Too much for her."

Silently, I sighed. He was so high-handed, Mannix Taylor, he made enemies without even breaking a sweat.

"So what *should* I read to her?" Dad asked, sarcastically. "*Harry Potter?*"

I was chopping an onion. Even if I do say so myself, I was utterly brilliant, like a chef in one of those shows. My nimble fingers were flying along, wielding my very expensive Japanese knife, flashing blue steel through the air. There were people all around me; their faces were blurry but they were oohing and aahing in extreme admiration. With great confidence I shifted my onion ninety degrees and commenced another flurry of chopping, almost too fast for the human eye to see, then I put down my very expensive Japanese knife.

Now for the money shot. My hands were cupped around the onion, almost in prayer. I gently moved them apart as if they had taken flight and—voilà!—the onion just collapsed, chopped into tiny, perfect pieces. Everyone clapped.

Then suddenly I was awake. And in my hospital bed, in my immobile body where my fingers were completely useless.

Something had woken me.

Some*one*. Mannix Taylor. Standing at the bottom of my bed, watching me.

He was silent for so long I wondered if he'd been struck dumb, making a pair of us. Finally he spoke, "Do you ever think, 'Why me?' "

I looked at him with contempt. What was up with him? Was Saoirse, his imaginary dyslexic daughter, not performing in the top five percentile, despite the extra tuition?

"I'm not talking about me," Mannix Taylor said. "I'm talking about you." He gestured around at all the hospital paraphernalia. "You contracted this extraordinary disease. You can't imagine how rare it is. And it's a cruel one . . . Being unable to speak, being unable to move, it's most people's worst nightmare. So. What I'm asking is, do you ever think, 'Why me?' "

I took a moment and I blinked. No. I thought lots of things, but not that.

Mannix Taylor reached into the sterilizer beside my bed and took out a pen and a notebook, which someone—maybe him?—had brought in.

"Really no?" he asked. "Why not?"

"WHY NOT ME?"

"Go on." He seemed genuinely interested.

"WHY AM I SO SPECIAL? TRAGEDIES HAVE TO HAPPEN. A CERTAIN NUMBER HAVE TO HAPPEN EVERY DAY. IT'S LIKE RAINFALL. I GOT RAINED ON."

"Jesus," he said. "You're a better person than me."

I wasn't. It was down to my dad—when I was growing up, he'd totally disabled my self-pity app. Any time I'd tried it, he'd given me a clip on the ear and said, "Stop it. Think about someone else."

"Ow!" I'd howl, and he'd say, "Be kind, for everyone you meet is fighting a hard battle. Plato said that. Greek chap."

Then I'd say, "Well, *you* aren't very kind, giving me a clip on the ear!"

"While I remember . . ." Mannix Taylor produced a book from the pocket of his white coat. "I asked my wife to recommend something. She says it's light, but well written." He placed the book into the sterilizer and flicked me a tongue-in-cheek look. "See what your dad thinks."

Ah, don't make fun of my dad.

"Sorry," he said, though I hadn't actually spoken.

"Anyway," he said. "I've been in contact with two neurologists in Texas who've worked directly with Guillain-Barré and I've information. When your nerve coverings start growing back—and we don't know when that will be—you may be itchy or tingly or you could be in pain, which might be acute. In which case we'll look at pain management." He paused and said, sounding exasperated, "By that, I mean, we'll give you drugs. I don't know why we just can't say that . . . Anyway. When your movement returns, your muscles will have atrophied from lack of use, so you'll have to do intensive physical therapy. But your energy will be low so you'll be able for only small amounts every day. It will take several months before your body and your life feel normal again. Your sister said I was cruel to tell you the truth. I think *not* telling you the truth is cruel.

"One other thing," he said. "There's a test called an EMG that can tell us how badly damaged the sheaths are. It would give a real measure of how long your recovery will take. But the machine in this hospital is broken. I do clinics in another hospital which has a working machine."

Hope jumped in me.

"But," he said, "because you're in ICU you can't be taken to another hospital—bureaucracy, insurance, the usual. They won't discharge you from here, even for a couple of hours. And no other hospital will take responsibility for you."

A great wail of anguish rose up in me, but it had no place to go so it got shoved back down into my cells. I'd always heard about how crap the medical system was but it was only now that I was caught up in it that I realized how true it was.

"I'm seeing what I can do," he said. "But you need to know that an EMG is nasty. Not dangerous, but painful. A series of electric shocks are sent along your nerve lines to measure your responses. From a medical point of view, the pain is a positive; it shows your nervous system is functioning."

Okay . . .

"Do you want me to keep trying?"

I blinked my right eye.

"You understand it'll be painful? You can't be given painkillers beforehand because they'll compromise precisely what we're trying to measure. You understand?"

Yes! Feck's sake, yes! I understand.

"You understand?"

I shut my eyes because now he was just being a smartass.

"Come out," he said. "Talk to me. I was just joking."

I opened my eyes and glared at him.

"Is there anything you want to ask me?"

I should be using my precious energy to ask him more about the test or about my illness but for the moment I was sick of the whole business. I bit the bullet and blinked something I'd been curious about since he'd first mentioned his brother. "TELL ME ABOUT YOUR FAMILY."

He hesitated.

"PLEASE."

"Okay. Seeing as you asked so nicely." He took a deep breath. "Well, looking at it from the outside, my upbringing was . . ." Tone of heavy sarcasm. "*Gilded*. My father was a doctor, my mother was a looker. Sociable types, both of them, they were always going to parties and to the races—especially the races—and being in the papers. I've one brother—Roland, whom you know about, who got the burden of Dad's expectations. Dad wanted him to be a doctor, like he was himself, but Roland didn't get the grades. I wanted to be a doctor but I also hoped it would take the burden off my brother. But it hasn't worked. Roland's always felt like a failure."

I thought of the man I'd seen on the telly, being so nice and funny, and I felt sad for him.

"I've two younger sisters," Mannix Taylor said. "Rosa and Hero, they're twins. We all went to posh schools and we lived in a big house in Rathfarnham. Sometimes the electricity would be cut off but we weren't allowed to tell anybody."

What! I hadn't seen that one coming.

"There was money . . . weirdness. One day I opened a drawer and there was a fat bundle of cash in it, like thousands. I said nothing and a day later it was gone. Or people would come to the door and you'd hear these tense muffled conversations being held outside on the gravel."

This was utterly *riveting*.

"People think it's glamorous, going to the races and putting ten grand on a horse."

I didn't. The very thought made me feel sick with anxiety.

"But if the horse doesn't win . . ."

Exactly!

"Stuff was always arriving into the house, then disappearing." He stopped, deep in thought, then continued. "One Christmas Eve my parents came home with a massive painting. They'd been at an auction and they burst in, full of excitement. They couldn't stop talking about the bidding and how they'd held their nerve and how they'd won. 'Never show fear, son,' Dad said. 'That's the key.' They said it was a genuine Jack Yeats and maybe it was . . . They cleared a place and hung it above the living-room mantelpiece. Two days later a van drew up outside the house and a couple of silent men came and took it away. It was never mentioned again."

Cripes. Well . . .

"They live in Nice now, my parents. The south of France. Less glamorous than it sounds but they make the most of it. They're a blast."

More sarcasm?

"Ah no, they *are* a blast," he said. "They love a party. A word of advice—never accept a gin and tonic made by my mum: it'll kill you."

18:49

I'm in my office, on Twitter, when Jeffrey arrives home with some "mates"—three young men who won't look me in the eye. They go to Jeffrey's room. The door closes firmly in my face and I know instinctively that they're looking at online pornography and that soon they'll be ringing for pizzas. It's only a matter of time before the floor is littered with massive pizza boxes.

We are acting like normal people! I am immensely cheered!

Nevertheless, in the event of being offered some of their pizza, I cannot permit myself to eat it. It would be an excellent bonding exercise, but after Karen's earlier cheerleading visit, I went out and purchased enough for a fridge full of high-protein food. I am committed to losing weight. As yet, I haven't been able to throw my beloved Jaffa Cakes in the bin, but I'm working up to it. Soon, I will do it soon.

As I sit at my desk, I become aware of a low droney noise. Wasps, I think, suddenly fearful. Or bees, perhaps. A nest of bees. A hive . . . whatever they're called. Please God, don't let me have a bees' nest in my attic.

The noise dies away and I tell myself I imagined it.

Then the droning starts again, louder this time. It sounds like they're massing for an attack. Maybe the nest is attached to the outside wall; gingerly I open the window and stick my head out. I see no sign of any bees, but I can still hear the noise. They must be in the attic. I stare fearfully at the ceiling.

Who can I ask for help? Ryan is useless, and so is Jeffrey. Enda Mulreid would probably squeeze the life out of a bees' nest with his bare hands, but I limit my interactions with Enda. He's a good man, but I never know what to say to him.

However, there are some young men in the house right now—perhaps some of the "mates" are braver than Jeffrey. I should ask them to help. Yes, I will!

I step out onto the landing and hover outside Jeffrey's room—I don't want to barge in while they're looking at the pornography. I'll knock, I decide, then wait five seconds, then knock again. Yes, this is the best way to proceed.

But as I stand at Jeffrey's door, I realize something dreadful—the droney noise is coming from in there. Maybe the bees had arrived because they heard pizza was on the way? Do bees like pizza? Or pornography?

Then I admit the dreadful truth—there are no bees in that room. Jeffrey and his mates are the ones making the noise. At a guess, I'd say they're meditating.

This is a blow.

A bad blow.

A very bad blow.

No one ever said life was fair.

Extract from One Blink at a Time

S o if you look here," Ryan positioned the bill in front of my face and
jabbed with his finger, "it says we're €1.91 in credit. What's going on
there? And what am I meant to pay them?"

How could I explain that we paid a monthly standing order to our
gas supplier to avoid being hit with big bills during the winter?

I'd always done the family finances, but as my time in hospital had
mounted up—I was now into my seventh week—Ryan was having to
wrestle with them.

I started blinking, trying to spell out "standing order."

"First letter?" Ryan said. "Vowel? No? Consonant? First half of the
alphabet? No? P? Q? R? S?"

I blinked but he didn't notice.

"T? V? W?"

Stop, stop!

I fluttered my lashes wildly to get his attention.

"It's T?"

No!

"I missed it?" He sighed heavily. "Okay, back to the start. Is it P?
Q? R? S? Yes, S. Okay." He wrote it down. "Second letter. Vowel? No?
Consonant? First half of the alphabet? No. Is it P? Q? R? S? T?"

I blinked and he missed it.

"V? W? X? Y? Z?" He stared accusingly at me. "It must be one of
them, Stella! Jesus *Christ*. You can tell your Mannix Taylor that this is
one shitty system. You know what?" He crumpled up the bill and threw
it on the floor. "Who cares? Let them cut us off."

I couldn't see the nurses sniggering but I *felt* them at it.

Poor Ryan. He was frustrated and confused and sick of it all. He'd
had to go to the Isle of Man four times in the past two weeks, pitching for
this new project, and he was exhausted.

"I'm sorry." He took a breath. "I apologize. Jeffrey, pick that up and
put it in the bin."

"Pick it up yourself. You threw it, you pick it up. Consequences, Dad, consequences."

"I'll consequence you! Pick it the feck *up*!"

Another wave of nurse-sniggering moved across the ward. The Sweeney Family Show was proving quite a hit.

"I'll get it," Betsy said.

"I told *him* to do it," Ryan said.

God, it was so embarrassing.

Jeffrey and Ryan locked themselves into a long stare-off and eventually Jeffrey broke. "Ooookay."

He picked up the crumpled ball of paper, threw it at the nurses' station and yelped, "Catch!"

Several nurses leaped back in exaggerated alarm, and startled cries and tut-tuts reached me. I was mortified.

Jeffrey was getting worse; he was becoming more defiant and it was my fault. I'd abandoned him by getting sick and I needed to get home and be a proper mother to him.

As if I weren't already feeling deeply despondent, Ryan produced another piece of paper. "I've been looking at our bank statement. Why are we paying a tenner a month to Oxfam?"

I don't know. To build wells in Ghana?

"We could do with that money," he said. "Especially now. How do I stop it?"

I didn't think he could. As far as I remembered it, too, was a standing order; it had been set up for a year. But I hadn't the energy to even try to explain.

"She doesn't know," Jeffrey said, dismissively. "My turn now. Mom, do you know where my hockey socks are?"

But how would I know? I haven't been at home in seven weeks.

"Dad can't find them," he said. "I thought you might know."

But . . . but how could I? Even though it was mad, I felt guilty, because I *should* know. They could be in his drawer, in the washing machine, the tumble dryer, his kit bag, his locker at school, they could have got jumbled up with Betsy's laundry. But I couldn't blink all that—it would take the entire day.

"Can I talk now, please?" Betsy said, haughtily. "Mom, where's my bunny rabbit onesie?"

I don't fecking well know. Where did you last see it?

"I need it," she said. "We're going for a sleepover in Birgitte's house and we made a pinky-promise that we'd all wear our onesies."

Who was this Birgitte that she was going for a sleepover with? I'd never heard of her before. Had Ryan spoken to the parents? Had he checked that everything was—

"And another thing," Ryan said. "The tenants in Sandycove have given notice."

My heart sank. Our investment property was proving to be an absolute curse. We needed to rent it out so we could cover the mortgage payments but no one ever stayed longer than six months. I seemed to spend my life doing inventories and changing bank details and—toughest of all—trying to find tenants who wouldn't trash the place.

"What am I to do about it?" Ryan asked.

Surely visiting time was up? But I'd noticed that the nurses had taken to letting my visitors stay for longer than the recommended fifteen minutes. I suspected that they were delighted that Mannix Taylor's Blinking Code was proving to be such a burden to me.

Finally Ryan and the kids left and I was on my own once more. The funny thing, I thought, was that people paid fortunes to go on retreats where they weren't allowed to speak or read or watch telly. They had to spend the whole time trapped with their thoughts and feelings, no matter how uncomfortable.

It was remarkably similar to what I was doing right here in my hospital bed and it really was a *colossal* pity that I'd never been interested in any of those soul-searchy kinds of things.

I was jolted out of my thoughts by the sight of Mannix Taylor walking toward me. What was he doing here? We'd already had our daily session.

He got the pen and notebook from the sterilizer and he pulled up a chair.

"Hello." He looked at me, lying motionless on my side, and said,

"You know, the gas thing is that people *pay* for this kind of lark—silence, sensory deprivation . . ." He waved his hand dismissively. "They do it to get to know themselves."

"I WAS JUST THINKING THAT."

"And is it working? Are you, Stella Sweeney, getting to know yourself?"

"I DON'T NEED TO KNOW MYSELF. I KNOW ENOUGH PEOPLE."

He laughed. There was something about him—he was skittish, almost giddy. Something good must have happened.

"It's not very fair, though, is it?" he said.

"WHOEVER SAID LIFE WAS FAIR?"

I was getting much better at the blinking, or maybe he was getting better at reading me. He often guessed the whole word from the first letter. It meant I didn't get tired so quickly and I could say more.

He noticed the book his wife had given me. "How are you getting on with this?"

Fantastic, as it happened. We were nearly at the end.

When Dad had first seen it, he'd started twitching with suspicion. "I'm not reading you anything till it has Joan's imprimatur." He'd taken it away in his plastic bag and he'd returned with Joan's blessing. "She says it's well written."

Then, of course, I assumed it would be dreadful.

But, to my great surprise, the book from Mannix Taylor's wife was fun. It was a biography of an upper-class British woman who had caused a big scandal in the thirties by leaving her husband and running away to Kenya and having all manner of high jinks. Both Dad and I were gripped and entertained. "I feel sort of . . . *wrong*," Dad had said. "For enjoying it so much. But if Joan says it's okay . . ."

I blinked to Mannix Taylor, "BRING ANOTHER."

"Another what? Book? Okay, I'll ask Georgie to pick out a few more for you."

Georgie. So that was her name: Georgie Taylor. The Scandinavian-looking interior-decorator-stroke-child-psychologist. I'd been wondering what she was called.

"Anyway!" He really *did* seem in sparkling good form this afternoon. "Ask me what I'm doing here!"

As I began to blink, he said, hastily, "No, don't! Figure of speech. Well, Stella Sweeney? How do you fancy a day out?"

What did he mean?

"We've got the go-ahead for the EMG! This crowd will let you out and the other crowd will let you in!"

Oh!

"How did I manage it? I won't bore you with the details. There's a clause . . . Ah no, I'm not getting into it, the tedium would kill you and I'm bound by the Hippocratic oath to try to keep you alive. It doesn't matter. All that matters is that it's a go. Your husband will have to sign no end of insurance papers, but basically we're on."

Hope rushed up through me. Finally I'd get some idea of how much longer this hell would last.

Suddenly Mannix Taylor became serious. "You remember what I said? It'll hurt. As I told you, it's actually better if it does; it shows you're getting better."

I had a memory of the lumbar puncture and I was filled with fear.

"But it'll be okay!" He sounded like he was trying to cheer up a child. "We'll go in an ambulance. We'll put the blue light and the siren on and we'll speed through the streets. We can pretend to be foreign dignitaries. We'll have a great time. What nationality do you want to be?"

Easy. "ITA—"

"Oh no," he said. "Italian is too . . . Everyone wants to be Italian. Have a bit of imagination."

The neck of the man! Every time I started to like him, he went and ruined it. I wanted to be Italian. I *was* Italian. I was Giuliana from Milan. I worked for Gucci. I got free things.

Mutinously, I glared at him. *I'm Italian, I'm Italian, I'm Italian.*

Then, with an unexpected change of heart, I decided I wanted to be Brazilian. What had I been thinking? Brazil was where it was at. I lived in Rio and was a brilliant dancer and had a big bum but it didn't matter.

"BRAZ—"

"Brazilian! Now you're talking. And what about me? I'll be . . . Let's see. I think I'd like to be Argentinian."

Fine with me.

"You don't think it's a waste that we've both picked the same continent?" he asked, suddenly anxious. "When we have the whole world to choose from? No," he said, firmly. "I definitely want to be Argentinian. I'm a gaucho from the pampas."

With feeling, he added, "God, I fecking wish I was. I'd spend every day riding my faithful horse, rounding up cattle, no one to answer to, and at the weekends I'd go into town and dance the tango. With other gauchos," he said, his mood darkening. "Because there aren't enough women. We have to dance with each other and sometimes when we're doing the flicky leg moves, we accidentally get each other in the balls." He sighed. "But we don't hold it against each other. We make the best of things."

"YOU'RE A NUTTER."

"Believe me," he said. "That isn't news."

Tuesday, 3 June

09:22
My breakfast is 100g of salmon. I'd have been happier having nothing.
I am not a protein person. I am very much a carb person.

10:09
Despite my joyless breakfast, I commence work. Today will be a good writing day. Of this I am certain.

10:11
I need coffee.

10:21
I recommence work. I feel inspired, invigorated . . . Is that the post?

10:24
I get into bed with the newly delivered Boden catalogue and I peruse the pages with great concentration, assessing every item of clothing for its belly-reducing qualities.

13:17
The front door opens and slams shut. Jeffrey shouts, "Mom," and starts pounding up the stairs. I leap out of bed and try to look like a person who has been working diligently all morning. Jeffrey bursts into my bedroom, in a state of high agitation. He looks at my rumpled duvet and says, suspiciously, "What are you doing?"

"Nothing! Writing. What's up?"

"Where's your iPad?" He holds up his phone. "It's Dad's karma project. It's happening."

I start clicking and together Jeffrey and I check things out. Ryan has uploaded sixty-three pictures of things to be given away, including his house, his car and his motorbike. Feeling sick, I scroll through the images of his beautiful furniture, his lamps, his many televisions.

"Hey!" I feel a surge of possessiveness as I recognize something of mine. "That's *my* Jesus Christ figurine!" A neighbor of Mum's had given it to me when I was sick. It's super creepy. I hadn't wanted it when Ryan and I separated, but now that it's about to be given away to some random stranger, I do.

Ryan's video has been watched eighty-nine times. Ninety. Ninety-one. Ninety-seven. One hundred and thirty-four. The numbers are mushrooming right before our eyes. It's like watching a natural disaster unfold.

"Why is he doing this?" I ask.

"Because he's a prick?" Jeffrey says.

"Seriously?"

"Maybe he wants to be famous."

Fame. It's what everyone thinks they want. The good fame, of course. Not the bad fame, where you throw a cat into a wheely bin and you get caught on CCTV and it goes viral on YouTube and you become an international pariah.

But the good sort of fame, that's not so great either, certainly not as nice as it sounds. I'll tell you about it sometime.

13:28

I ring Ryan. It goes straight to voice mail.

13:31

I ring Ryan. It goes straight to voice mail.

13:33

I ring Ryan. It goes straight to voice mail.

13:34

Jeffrey rings Ryan. It goes straight to voice mail.

13:36

Jeffrey rings Ryan. It goes straight to voice mail.

13:38

Jeffrey rings Ryan. It goes straight to voice mail.

13:40–13:43

I eat eleven Jaffa Cakes.

14:24

A new photo appears on Ryan's site—his Nespresso machine.

14:25

Another new photo appears on the site; this time it's a blender . . . Followed by three cans of tomatoes. A bread board. Five tea towels.

"He's doing his kitchen," Jeffrey whispers. We're frozen in horror as we watch the screen.

Here comes a frying pan . . . and . . . another frying pan . . . and half a jar of curry paste. Who would want half a jar of curry paste? The man's a lunatic.

This is my fault. I should never have got a publishing deal and moved to New York. It should have been obvious that, at some stage, Ryan would do something to reassert himself as the true creative person of the two of us.

More and more photos of his possessions are appearing with each passing second—a salad spinner, a toasted sandwich maker, a collection of forks, a packet of Custard Creams.

"Custard Creams?" Jeffrey sounds dazed. "Who eats Custard Creams in this day and age?"

Ryan's video has now been viewed 2,564 times. 2,577. 2,609 . . .

"Should we go over there and stop him?" Jeffrey asks.

"Let me think."

14:44

I lurch at my handbag, unzip the secret inner pocket, locate my one emergency Xanax and take half of it.

"What's that?" Jeffrey asks.

"Ah . . . a Xanax."

"A tranquillizer? Where did you get it?"

"Karen. She says every woman should keep a Xanax in the secret zippy pocket of her handbag. In case of emergency. This is an emergency."

14:48

Karen rings. "Listen," she says. "There's some weird shit going down with Ryan—"

"I know."

"Has he lost his reason?"

"It looks that way."

"What are you going to do about it? You'll have to get him sectioned."

"How would I do that?"

"I'll ask Enda. I'll call you back."

14:49

"Enda's going to find out how to get Ryan sectioned," I tell Jeffrey.

"Okay. Good."

"Yes. Good. That's right. Good. We'll get him nice and sectioned and everything will be grand."

But I have a niggly suspicion that getting a person sectioned isn't as easy as it sounds. And that once they're sectioned it may be hard to get them unsectioned.

I take the other half of the Xanax.

15:01

"Let's go over to his house and try to reason with him," I decide.

Ryan lives only a couple of miles away and both Jeffrey and I have keys.

"How? You're going to drive? You've just taken two tranquillizers."

"One tranquillizer," I correct him. "One. In two halves."

But he's right. I can't drive, having just taken a Xanax. Something bad might happen.

"Very well," I say with hauteur. "We'll walk."

"And you'll fall into a ditch. And I'll have to pull you out."

"This is an urban area, there *are* no ditches." But my voice is starting to sound a little slurred. I might not fall into a ditch but ten minutes into the walk I might decide it would be delightfully pleasant to lie down on the pavement and smile beatifically at passing pedestrians.

"Why must you take drugs?" Jeffrey sounds angry.

"I don't 'take drugs.' This is a medicine! Prescribed by a doctor!"

"It wasn't *your* doctor."

"A technicality, Jeffrey. A mere technicality."

"We need to talk to somebody sensible."

We eye each other and even in my rapidly burgeoning Xanax cocoon, I feel pain. I know what Jeffrey is going to say.

"No," I say.

"But—"

"No, he's not part of our lives any longer."

"But—"

"No."

The sound of my phone ringing makes me jump. "It's Ryan!"

"Give it to me." Jeffrey grabs it. "Dad. Dad! Have you gone totally nuts?"

After a short conversation, all on Ryan's side, Jeffrey hangs up. He looks crestfallen. "He says it's his stuff and he can do what he likes with it."

Overwhelmed by my own incapacity, I eat three more Jaffa Cakes. No, four. No, five. No—

"Stop." Jeffrey pulls the box away from me.

"They're my Jaffa Cakes!" I sound a bit wild.

He holds the box above his head. "Can't you find some other way of dealing with things? Instead of drugging yourself with Xanax or sugar?"

"No, not right now, no."

"I'm going to meditate."

"Okay, well, I'm just going to . . ."

. . . lie on my bed and feel floaty. And retrieve another box of Jaffa Cakes from my "wall."

How do you eat an elephant? One bite at a time.

Extract from *One Blink at a Time*

I was in a blissful floaty place, a white happy nothing-land. Every time I began to eddy to the surface, where hard-edged reality awaited, something happened and I tumbled back down to the pain-free paradise.

But not this time. I was coming up; I was rising and rising and rising until I popped through the surface and I was awake and in my hospital bed.

Dad was sitting on a chair, reading a book. "Ah, Stella, there you are! You've been in the land of nod for the last two days."

My head was fuzzy.

"You had your EMG test," Dad said.

I did?

"It took it out of you," Dad said. "They gave you drugs so you'd sleep."

The horrible details started coming back to me. First there had been stuff to do with the legal responsibility of me: I'd had to be temporarily discharged by Dr. Montgomery from this hospital into Ryan's care—which went okay. But then Ryan was supposed to sign me over to Mannix Taylor until I reached the other hospital, and Ryan was bristling with hostility. And when Mannix Taylor said, "I'll take good care of her," it had only made things worse. Ryan compressed his mouth into a tight line and I'd been afraid that he was actually going to refuse to sign.

After about ten tense seconds, he scribbled something on the consent form and off we'd set. Four orderlies were required to get me from the ward into the ambulance. I'd been disconnected from my heart monitor and catheter—"Special treat," Mannix Taylor had said—but I still had one porter wheeling my ventilator, another maneuvering my drip and two more pushing my bed. Everyone had to move at exactly the same speed, in case the ventilator man went too fast and whipped the tube out of my throat and I suffocated.

Also in my posse was a nurse and Mannix Taylor.

The day before the test, Mannix had brought a printout into the ward. "Would you like a Brazilian name for tomorrow? I've a list here: Julia, Isabella, Sophia, Manuela, Maria Eduarda, Giovanna, Alice, Laura, Luiza . . ."

I blinked: Luiza it was!

"And what about me?" he asked. "I need an Argentinian name. Santiago, Benjamin, Lautaro, Alvarez." He looked at me. "Alvarez," he repeated. "That's a good one. It means 'noble guardian,' which is appropriate, I thought."

I didn't respond, so he kept on reading the list. ". . . Joaquin, Santino, Valentino, Thiago—"

I blinked. I liked Thiago.

"How about Alvarez?" he said. "I like Alvarez."

"TH—"

"Thiago? Really? Not Alvarez? Alvarez means 'noble guardian.'"

"SO YOU SAID. YOU'RE THIAGO."

I was incensed. I mean, why had he read out the other names if he'd already decided?

"Alvarez," he said.

Thiago.

He stared me down, then lowered his eyes in submission. "Thiago it is. You've a will of iron."

God, he was a fine one to talk.

In the ambulance he said, "So, Luiza, you live in Rio, a city of constant sunshine, and you're a star in a telenovela. After work every day you go to the beach. You buy your clothes from . . . well, wherever you like—you fill in the details. But listen to me, if the test gets too much, pretend you're Luiza, not Stella. And," he added, "if it really gets too much, we can just stop."

No. We wouldn't be stopping. This was my one chance to find out when I'd be getting better and I wasn't wasting it.

"Think Brazil," he reiterated. "Right." He looked out through the little window. "We're here."

At the new hospital, I was unloaded with great care from the ambulance onto the tarmac, but we didn't go in. We seemed to be waiting for someone.

"Where the hell is he?" I heard Mannix mutter.

A pair of shiny black shoes came striding toward our little party. There was something about them that told me their owner was aquiver with rage.

As the shoes got closer I realized they belonged to this new hospital's version of Dr. Montgomery—he had the same godlike air and the same collection of awestruck young doctors.

"You're unbelievable," he said to Mannix, in a shrill, angry voice. "The insurance headache you've created . . . Where's the thing to be signed?" Some craven helper person stuck a clipboard under his nose and he tore an angry signature onto it.

"Right," Mannix said, "we're in."

With my small army of helpers, we proceeded down corridors, up in a lift, down more corridors and into a room. The mood, which had been almost festive, suddenly dipped. The orderlies and the nurse hastily withdrew and Mannix introduced me to Corinne, the technician who'd be carrying out the tests.

"Thank you, Dr. Taylor," she said. "I'll page you when we're done."

"I'll stay," he said.

"Oh, right . . ." She seemed surprised.

"If Stella needs to tell us anything . . ."

"Oh. Okay . . ."

She turned her attention to me. "Stella, I'm going to attach an electrode to a nerve point on your right leg and send electricity through it," she said. "Your response will send information to the machine. I'll move the electrode to various nerve points on your body until adequate data has been accumulated to inform us of the functionality of your central nervous system. Ready?"

Afraid, actually.

"Ready?" she repeated.

Ready.

When the first electric shock went through me, I knew immediately that I couldn't do this. The pain was far worse than I'd expected. I wasn't able to shriek, but my body jerked from the force.

"Okay?" Corinne asked.

I was reeling. I understood now what Mannix Taylor had been trying to tell me: this was really painful. So painful that I'd have to go to another place in my head to survive it. I tried to remember what he'd been saying in the ambulance—I was Luiza. I was Brazilian. I had a starring role in a telenovela.

"Okay?" Corinne repeated.

Okay.

. . . I lived in a city with constant sunshine and—Jesus! Jesus, Jesus, Jesus!

I looked at Mannix; he was so white he was almost green. "What do you need to ask?" He had his pen and paper out.

"HOW MA—?"

"How many do you think you'll need?" Mannix asked Corinne.

She consulted her screen and said, "Ten. Maybe more."

Jesus. Well, I'd done two. I'd do one more. And after that, I'd do one more.

Corinne was remarkably nonplussed. Presumably she had to face this sort of thing all the time. I supposed it was like when I had to laser a person's hairy legs—in order to do my job properly, I had to disconnect from their pain.

"Would you like to stop?" After every bout she gave me the option of ending it.

No.

"Would you like to stop?"

No.

"Would you like to stop?"

No.

I focused on everything that Mannix Taylor had done, on all the red tape he'd battled, to make this happen. I didn't want to let him down.

It was hard, though. Each shock ate into my endurance, and on the seventh one the force lifted me off the table.

"Stop!" Mannix was on his feet. "That's enough."

He was right. I couldn't take this. It wasn't worth it and I didn't care anymore.

Then I had a flash of Dr. Montgomery and his mockery if I bailed on this. Keep-Her-Going-There-Patsy and all his underlings would have a great old laugh, as would the shrill, angry consultant at this hospital. The nurses on ICU would probably break out a celebratory tin of Roses, because everyone wanted Mannix Taylor to fail, even my own husband.

"NO."

"She wants to keep going," Corinne said.

"Her name is Stella."

"Dr. Taylor, perhaps you should step outside for the duration . . . ?"

"I'm staying."

Corinne had eventually settled for twelve readings and, as I returned in the ambulance to my own hospital, I felt extremely strange. The oddest chemicals were flooding my brain, a mixture of elation and horror, like I'd gone a little crazy.

It was a blessed relief when Mannix Taylor asked the nurse to sedate me.

"You need to sleep and sleep," he said. "Your body has been through hell. You need to recover, probably for a couple of days."

Now I was awake, and looking at my dad and still feeling a bit dazed.

"That Taylor chap was in looking for you," Dad said. "He'll be back. He says it was hard going for you, Dolly, but you were very brave. Will I read to you?"

Er . . . grand.

Our current book was another hit from Georgie Taylor. It was about an imaginary despot in an imaginary country in the Middle East and told from the point of view of his wife. Dad was so impressed that, every couple of lines, he had to stop reading to marvel at how great it was. "Your man is one cool customer, isn't he, Stella? Ordering all of them executions and then just calmly eating his couscous . . ."

He orated another half page for me, then put the book down to deliver a few more comments. "You'd nearly feel *sorry* for the man. There he is with a fine-looking wife, who seems like a decent woman, but he's neglecting her for the job. Overseeing that torture when he's meant to be taking her out for her birthday. But could you blame him? His so-called allies plotting and scheming against him . . . One slip-up and he's a goner."

He read on, but it wasn't long before he felt compelled, once again, to pause the narrative. "Ah, dear, dear . . ." he said sadly. "Heavy is the head that wears the crown."

A click-click of high heels announced the arrival of Karen. Her hair looked freshly done and her handbag was new. "How is she?" she asked Dad.

"Grand, I think. We're waiting for the Mannix chap to come and give us news."

"Howya, Stella." Karen pulled up a chair. "You look a bit fucked, if I'm to be honest. I heard it was awful, but fair play to you. So tell us how you are." She took the pen and notebook from the sterilizer. "Go on. First letter."

I blinked, trying to say, "Tired," but it got all messed up, I didn't have the energy and Karen didn't have the patience.

"Ah, feck it," Karen said. "Leave it, it's too hard." She tossed the pen and pad back into the sterilizer and snapped it shut. "I'll read to you instead."

Dad twitched, all set to start again with the book.

"No, Dad!" Karen was firm. "I've *Grazia* here. Put away that shit you're reading her."

"It's far from shit—"

"Hello, there." Mannix had arrived.

Dad jumped up off his chair. "Dr. Taylor," he said with a mixture of innate humility and I'm-as-good-as-you chippiness.

"Mr. Locke." Mannix Taylor nodded.

"Bert, Bert, call me Bert!"

"Karen," Mannix said. "Nice to see you again."

"Nice to see you too." Karen managed to wrap her hostility in a veneer of civility.

Dad blurted, "We're reading another one of the books your wife sent in. She has excellent taste."

Mannix Taylor gave a little smile. "Except in husbands."

"Not at all," Dad blustered. "Aren't you a great chap? Sorting out the test for Stella and everything."

"How do you feel?" Mannix had automatically produced the pen and notepad.

"Tired."

"Doesn't surprise me. But you did good."

"So did you," I blinked back.

In wonderment, Dad and Karen watched our exchange—me blinking and Mannix writing down the words.

"God almighty," Karen said, the strangest expression on her face.

"You're very quick, the pair of you," Dad said.

"Very quick," Karen echoed. "It's nearly like a normal conversation." She narrowed her eyes at Mannix. "How are you so good at it?"

"I don't know," Mannix said, evenly. "Practice? Anyway, I've the results of the EMG." He waved a sheaf of printouts at me. "I'll give you the boring details when you're stronger, but here's the gist: at the rate your myelin sheaths are growing, you can expect movement to start returning in about six weeks' time."

I was stunned. I wanted to shriek and cry with joy.

Really? Really? Really?

"You're going to get better," he said. "But remember what I keep telling you. It'll be a big job. You need to stay patient. Can you do it?"

Of course I could. I could do anything if I knew the end was in sight.

"I'll do a road map for you. I'll tell you what you can expect, but it'll be approximate. And we're still looking at several months. It's going to be a long, tough recovery. It's going to ask a lot of you."

"How do you eat an elephant?" I blinked at him.

"How?"

"One bite at a time."

17:14

I'm lying on my bed, like a starfish, eddying on a Xanax and Jaffa Cake cloud and, in all honesty, things don't seem *that* insurmountable. I am a strong woman. Yes. A strong, strong woman and . . . my phone rings and my heart almost jumps out of my throat. Very loud! Really, unnecessarily loud! Going around scaring relaxed people . . .

Then I see who's calling and my fear increases. It's Enda Mulreid! Even though he's my sister's husband, he will always be a policeman to me.

Quickly I sit up and clear my throat and try to sound together. "Ah, hello there, Enda!"

"Stella. I trust you're well. I'll 'cut' to the 'chase.' " I can almost see him doing the inverted-commas thing with his fingers. I will admit that the alliance between himself and my sister has always been a mystery to me. They are *so* different.

"I hear," he says, "that you wish to involuntarily detain your ex-husband Ryan Sweeney under Section 8 of the Mental Health Act 2001."

Oh my God. When he puts it like that . . . "Enda, I'm just worried about Ryan. He wants to give away all his possessions."

"Are they his to give away? He's not, for example, harboring stolen goods? Or profiting from criminal activities?"

"Enda! You know Ryan. How could you even think that?"

"Is that a no?"

"It's a no."

"Well, then."

"Yes, but—"

"As there is not a serious likelihood that the subject in question may cause serious and immediate harm to himself or others, there is no legal basis for invoking the act."

"I see. Yes, you're quite right, Enda. No need to, er, *invoke* the act.

Thank you, you're very good to take the time. Yes, thank you, good-bye now, good-bye." I hang up. I'm sweating. Enda Mulreid always does this to me.

Jeffrey comes thundering into the room. "What? Who was that?"

"Enda Mulreid. Uncle Enda. Whatever name you have for him. Look, Jeffrey. Let's try to put it from our minds that we considered getting Dad sectioned . . ."

"It's a no-go?"

"It's a no-go."

18:59

My Xanax fog has finally lifted and I decide to ring Betsy.

"Mom?" she answers.

"Sweetie. Something weird is going on with your dad." I explain everything and she takes it calmly.

"I'm looking it up," she says. "Found it. Oh my gosh. Twelve thousand hits! I see what you mean."

"I just wanted to keep you in the loop." But if I'm honest, I think I rang her for advice.

"It looks like he's having a psychotic episode. It happens."

"Really?" How does she know? How is she so wise? "It happened to a couple of guys Chad works with."

"Karen told me I should get him sectioned."

"Oh, Mom, no," she says, softly. "That would be so bad. It would cause such bad feeling. And it would always be part of his story; he'd never be able to shake it off. But I do think you should talk with a doctor. Fast."

19:11

It's gone seven o'clock, so it's too late to try to get hold of a doctor this evening, but I have the brainwave of ringing a mental-health help-line.

A woman with a gentle, kind voice answers.

"Hello," I say. "My ex-husband . . . I don't really know how to put this, but I'm worried about him."

"I see . . ."

"He's behaving strangely."

"I see, I see . . ."

"He says he's going to give away everything he owns."

"I see, I see . . ."

"All his money, everything, even his house."

The voice of the anonymous woman becomes animated. "You mean Ryan Sweeney? I just saw him on YouTube."

"Oh . . . you did? Well, do you think he's, you know, ill, mad, insane?"

"I see, I see . . ."

"Well, do you?"

"I see, I see . . . But it's not for me to say. I'm not a doctor. I couldn't diagnose him."

"So what are you there for?"

"To be sympathetic. Say if you were feeling depressed and you rang me, I'd listen and say, 'I see, I see, I see.'"

"I see." Tearful rage rises in me. "Thank you for your help."

23:05–02:07

Sleep eludes me. My whales, normally so friendly, sound sinister tonight. As if, within their high-pitched cries and songs, there are coded threats.

Sometimes you get what you want and sometimes you get
what you need and sometimes you get what you get.

Extract from *One Blink at a Time*

I was thinking about sex. The way you do when you're lying in a hospital, entirely paralyzed.

Ryan and I, we never had sex—I mean, we'd been together eighteen years, be *reasonable*. No one had sex, well, none of the couples I knew anyway. Everyone thought everyone else was at it hammer and tongs, but once you got people drunk enough they'd admit the truth.

I say Ryan and I *never* had sex, but of course we did—once in a while, when we'd been out for the evening and had a fair bit of drink on board. And you know what? It was grand. We had three different versions to choose from and it was always quick and efficient and it suited both of us just fine—with a job and two children, who had time and energy to devote to elaborate sexual shenanigans?

But this was the wrong attitude, the magazines told me: you're supposed to "work at your marriage." Even before *Fifty Shades of Grey* came along, I felt under pressure to go way outside my "sexual comfort zone."

"Should we . . . try stuff?" I'd asked Ryan.

"Like what?"

"I don't know. We could . . ." It was such a dreadful word I didn't know if I could say it. "We could . . . spank each other."

"With what?"

". . . A table-tennis bat?"

"Where would we get a table-tennis bat?"

". . . Elverys Sports?"

"No," he said. The discussion was closed and I was relieved. I'd been thinking of buying those little chrome balls, the ones you insert into your ding-dong and leave there for the day. Now I didn't have to, and with the money I'd saved myself I'd buy a nice pair of shoes instead.

Karen, being Karen, was more determined to keep her sex life zinging, so herself and Enda did some role play where they pretended to be strangers who pick each other up in a bar. She even wore a wig, a black bob. But they couldn't carry it off.

"Did you laugh?" I'd asked.

"No." Karen had seemed uncharacteristically depressed. "It wasn't funny. It was just cringy. In fact," she said, "seeing him across that bar . . . Tell me, Stella, were his ears always that big? In normal life, I practically never look at him. And to get a proper gawk at him after so long, well . . . there was a moment when I felt horrified that I was married to him, to be honest with you . . ."

I wondered if Mannix Taylor and his Scando-type wife had lots of sex. Maybe they did. Maybe *that* was his hobby, seeing as he didn't play golf.

Yes, him and his fabulous wife would be the type to put the rest of us to shame.

Georgie Taylor would come home from a hard day of color swatching to find her house silent and lit only by candles. Before she had time to be alarmed, a man (Mannix Taylor, of course) would step up behind her, press his body hard against hers and say with quiet authority, "Don't scream." A silk blindfold would cover her eyes and she'd be led to a candlelit bedroom, where he'd strip her of her clothes and bind her arms and legs to the bedposts.

He'd brush her nipples with feathers and, agonizingly slowly, drop by drop, trail fragrant oil between her breasts and down to her stomach and further . . .

Naked, he'd straddle her and toy with her for a long time before finally he entered her and her body burst into orgasm after orgasm.

Well, lucky Mrs. Taylor.

"Tell me more about your family." I blinked out the words to Mannix Taylor.

"Oh . . . okay. I'll tell you about my sisters. They're twins. Rosa and Hero. Hero was called that because she almost died when she was born; she spent six weeks in an incubator. They're not identical—Rosa is dark and Hero is fair—but they sound alike and all the big things in their lives happened at the same time. They had a double wedding.

Rosa is married to Jean-Marc, a Frenchman who's lived in Ireland for . . . God, twenty-five years? They've two sons. Hero is married to a man called Harry and they also have two sons, almost the same age as Rosa and Jean-Marc's. It's absolutely spooky how their lives mirror each other's."

"But tell me about *your* kids."

A strange expression flickered across his face. He looked wounded and almost ashamed. "We don't have kids."

That was a huge surprise. I'd spent so much time in my head and in the imaginary life I'd created for him that I'd really believed he had three children.

"Today," he said. "I'm going to do a run-through of your reflexes, to see if there's any response. Okay?"

"Okay."

"We're trying for a baby, Georgie and I."

Oh?

"We've been trying for a long time. It's not going so well."

God! I didn't know how to reply.

"We're doing IVF," he said. "It's a secret. Georgie doesn't want anyone knowing until it's all okay. She doesn't want everyone's eyes on her, wondering if this time it's worked. She doesn't want anyone's pity."

I could understand that.

"So I haven't been able to tell anyone."

But he was telling me. Then again, did it matter, seeing as I couldn't speak and I'd never meet his wife?

"Well, I've told Roland, obviously."

What was obvious about it?

"Because he's my best friend."

That surprised me a little and Mannix bristled. "Roland is a lot more than someone who buys cars he can't afford," he said. "He'd do anything for anyone and he's the best company you could ever have."

Right, that was me told.

After a short tense silence, Mannix began talking again. It was as if he couldn't stop. "We've had two rounds of IVF already. Both times the embryo implanted and both times Georgie miscarried. I knew the stats weren't in our favor, but still, when we lost them, it knocked us sideways."

I was shocked by this tragic story; it was so unexpected. I managed to blink, "I'm very sad for you."

Mannix shrugged and studied his hands. "It's far tougher for Georgie—all the hormones she has to be injected with. Then she tries so hard to hold on to the embryo and I can do nothing to help. I feel like a big, useless eejit. At the moment we're on round three and Georgie is PUPO—Pregnant Until Proven Otherwise. We're holding our breath."

Desperately trying to convey encouragement, I blinked out, "Good luck." Sometimes language was so useless. Even if I'd been able to speak I couldn't have communicated how much I hoped this would work for him and his wife.

He kept talking. "I was forty last year, Georgie this year, and suddenly everything seemed meaningless if we didn't have kids. We should have started trying earlier, but we were . . . stupid, delusional. We thought we had more time than we did." He lapsed into silence. After a few moments he spoke again.

"I'd love a big family," he said. "Both of us would. Not just one or two but five or six. It would be fun, right?"

"Hard work."

"I know. And right now I'd be more than grateful with just the one."

"I hope it happens for you."

"What's that thing you once said?" he asked thoughtfully. " 'Sometimes you get what you want and sometimes you get what you need and sometimes you get what you get.' "

Three days later, he arrived into my cubicle and said, "Morning, Stella."

Immediately I knew that his wife had lost their baby.

I'm sorry.

"How do you know?"

I just do. "I'm very sorry."

"We're going to take a break from trying for a while. It's so hard on Georgie."

"It must be hard on you too."

He looked absolutely heartbroken, but all he said was, "It's much harder for her."

Something moved at the edge of my vision—about two meters away was a man.

They say that television cameras add ten pounds to everyone; but Roland Taylor—for it was him—was the first person I'd ever seen who was actually fatter in real life. He was decked out in a fashionable jacket and his trademark trendy glasses, and even though Karen was always going on about how fat people were fat because they were bitter and angry, this man radiated kindness.

He gathered Mannix into a bear hug and I heard him say, "I was talking to Georgie. I'm sorry."

He held Mannix for a long time, in a solid embrace, and I would have cried if I'd been able.

Then Mannix's pager beeped, and they broke apart.

"Hang on." Mannix read whatever was written on his pager. "Don't leave. I won't be long."

Mannix disappeared and Roland lingered, looking like he didn't know where to go. I exerted every ounce of my will to pull him in my direction.

He turned toward me and looked at my face. "Sorry," he said, awkwardly. "For interrupting like that."

I blinked my eyes several times and an expression moved across his face, some sort of recognition.

He leaned over to read from the chart at the foot of my bed. "Your name is Stella?"

I blinked my right eye.

"I'm Roland, Mannix's brother."

I blinked my right eye to show that I knew.

"Mannix has mentioned you to me," he said.

That took me aback.

Looking suddenly horrified, Roland said, "Not by name! Don't worry, he entirely respects doctor-patient confidentiality. All he mentioned was your condition and how you communicate by blinking."

Well, that was okay and I tried to convey that through my eyes.

"Hold on." He fumbled around in his Mulberry man bag and produced a pen and a piece of paper, probably a receipt, and I blinked out the words, "LOVELY TO MEET YOU."

"That's amazing!" Roland smiled in delight. "*You're* amazing." Buried in his face, he had the exact same eyes as Mannix. "You've just communicated a whole sentence with your eyelids."

Ah, thanks . . .

He glanced, a little anxiously, down the ward. "I don't know where he's gone. He should be back soon."

"SIT DOWN."

"Should I? I'm not intruding?"

Was he mad? At the best of times I was desperate for company and I wasn't passing up the chance of a few minutes with arch raconteur Roland Taylor.

"TELL ME A STORY."

"Are you sure?" Slowly he lowered himself into a chair. "I could tell you about a time I met a famous person? Cher? Michael Bublé? Madonna?"

I blinked my right eye.

"Madonna? Excellent choice, Stella!" He settled himself in his chair. "Well, she's an absolute goddess. *Obviously.* But sort of . . . *tricky* . . . We got off to a bad start when I sat on her cowboy hat and rendered it *hors de combat* . . ."

As he chatted away about Madonna's high-handedness, he was more than a little camp. I was guessing he was gay, not that it mattered one way or the other.

Wednesday, 4 June

06:00

I awake from a lovely dream—Ned Mount was in it. Again! He was saying, "There are new cakes on the market. They're made entirely from protein. You can eat as many as you like."

I spend a few moments nestling in the rosy afterglow, then, seized by horrible anxiety, I remember everything and I lurch for my iPad: Ryan's video has now been viewed over twenty thousand times.

I can hear Jeffrey loitering on the landing and I call him to come in.

"You saw?" He nods at my iPad. "It's a lot but it's not, like, hundreds of thousands. It could be worse. And there are no new photos."

"I'm going to see old Dr. Quinn today," I say. "See if he has any advice about Ryan."

Dr. Quinn has been the family GP for donkey's years. He knows Ryan and he might be able to help.

"I'm off to yoga," Jeffrey says.

"Okay."

I ablute in a halfhearted fashion, then I eat 100g of salmon—I'm back on track after yesterday's Jaffa Cake debacle. I sit in front of the computer, affix my fake smile to my visage and type "Ass."

09:01

I ring the Ferrytown Medical Center and ask for an appointment with Dr. Quinn today. The receptionist gives me short shrift until—just testing things—I say my name and suddenly she sounds impressed and a little bit flustered. I'm given an appointment for later this morning: one of the boons of being an ex-celebrity. I may not be able to swing a table at Noma, but if I'm ever in urgent need of antibiotics, it's nice to know I'll be taken care of.

11:49

What will I wear? Well, it's all so simple—my new lady chinos, or . . . my new lady chinos.

There was a time when my clothes were so complicated that they were given their own spreadsheet. All thanks to Gilda.

She'd arrived one afternoon at my New York apartment for our daily run and found me on the verge of hyperventilating. "I can't exercise today," I said.

"What's up?"

"This." I gave her my iPad, which contained the proposed schedule for my first book tour. "Look at it." I was gasping for breath. "Twenty-three days, criss-crossing the country. It'll be snowing in Chicago, it'll be roasting in Florida and it'll be pissing rain in Seattle. I have to visit hospitals and be on telly and attend charity dinners, and I have to have the right clothes for every single event. There's no time off and I'm never in one place for longer than a day so I can't get any laundry done. I'll need a suitcase the size of an articulated truck."

Gilda scrolled through the plan.

"And why is it so illogical?" I asked. "The order of the places I'm visiting? I keep having to double back on myself. Why is it Texas one day and Oregon the next and then Missouri, which is practically beside Texas? Why don't I do Texas, Missouri and *then* Oregon? Or here's another mad one—South Carolina, Seattle, then Florida. Wouldn't it make far more sense to go to Florida straight after South Carolina, they're so near to each other, and *then* on to Seattle?"

"Because," Gilda said, gently, "you're not Deepak Chopra or Eckhart Tolle. Not *yet*."

"How do you mean?"

"This is how it is in the beginning for any writer on tour. With the big names, they call the shots; they announce that they're in town on a particular date and the residents flock to see them. But with a newbie like you, your publisher has to start with the local event, then match you to it. So see here—" she tapped the screen—"the ladies of Forth Worth, Texas, are having their annual charity lunch on March the fourteenth, so that's when they want you. You're no good to them on the fifteenth, right? Because the lunch is over. Then this new book-shop opening in Oregon on March the sixteenth? Local media are lined up to cover it so there's no point you coming to cut the ribbon three days later when they're up and running. And the Readers' Day in Missouri on March the seventeenth? That was firmed up maybe six months ago. For now you've got to fit yourself around what the world wants. But that will change."

Okay, I got what she was saying: there were an awful lot of self-help writers in the world, jostling for the same spot on the telly, the radio and the charity circuit.

"You're lucky," she said. "You may not feel it, but you are. Book tours are expensive. Big money has to be spent on plane tickets and hotel bills and car services and local publicists. Every writer wants a chance to tour their book and you're one of the few, the chosen few."

"Oh?" Suddenly discovering I was one of the chosen few put a different perspective on things. But I still had the problem of my clothes.

"We're going out to run now," Gilda said.

"No, I—"

"Yes! You need to burn off this toxic energy. And when we come back, you show me your wardrobe. I'm sure you've already got a lot of stuff that will work. But, to fill the gaps, I'll call clothes in for you—I know a few people."

"People?"

"Designers. Up-and-coming. Not too expensive. And personal shoppers with very rich clients who order next season's collection from a catalogue. They pay up front, but by the time the pieces arrive in the store, they've lost interest and often don't take delivery of them. Those clothes have to go somewhere, right?"

"What do you mean?"

"I mean, the clothes are sold on for next to nothing if you ask nicely. And if you know who to ask."

I was utterly amazed—at all of it. That people paid for clothes but never claimed them. And that it was possible for ordinary people to benefit.

"There's nothing bad about this," Gilda said. "The store has already been paid. So what if the personal shopper gets a little backhander? It's all good."

Gilda was true to her word: two days later, she came to the apartment with armloads of designer clothes and I spent the entire afternoon trying stuff on, while she assessed me with brutal honesty.

"That color kills you. Discard. Okay, this is better. Boat-line necks are good on you. Try it with the dark skirt and the boots. That's a go. What about this tunic? Too small. Discard. This dress? Is it day wear? Is it cocktail hour? It doesn't know what it is. Discard."

"But I love it!"

"Too bad. Every single piece has to work super hard. Nothing makes it into your luggage unless it *performs*. Over and over."

She drew up a grid of every event I was due to attend on the tour and everything I should wear, right down to shoes, underwear, accessories and even nail lacquer.

"How are you so good at this?" I asked, in wonder. "You're incredible."

She laughed lightly. "I was a stylist in another life."

"How many lives have you *had*?"

12:05

In the Ferrytown Medical Center, I'm shown into old Dr. Quinn's office. "Stella," he says, seeming a little uncomfortable, "I heard you were . . . er . . . back in Ireland."

"Yes. Yes, indeed, hahaha."

"So how can I help you?"

"Right. Well, you know Ryan, my ex-husband?"

"Yes . . ."

"He's gone a bit . . ."

I launch into the whole Project Karma story and as soon as Dr. Quinn realizes why I'm there, he clams up. "I can't diagnose someone else."

"But I'm worried about him."

"I can't diagnose someone else." He's quite adamant.

"Can't you give me an off-the-record opinion? Please?"

"Weeeeelll, he does sound a bit manic."

"That's bipolar, is it?"

Very quickly Dr. Quinn says, "I'm not saying he *is* bipolar!"

"Could he be having a midlife crisis?"

"There's no such thing . . . but he *is* in the correct age range. Has he taken up cycling? I mean, obsessively? Buying a lot of Lycra?"

I shake my head.

"Doesn't he have someone else to worry about him? Does he have a partner?"

"No."

"A girlfriend, then, if we're allowed to say the word 'girlfriend' these days without inciting the wrath of someone? What's that thing they say instead?" He stares into the middle distance for a moment. "Fuck buddies, that's the one."

"Er . . . 'girlfriends' is grand with me. But he doesn't have one."

"And him with a good job." Dr. Quinn marvels.

"Don't get me wrong, he often has a girlfriend, but they're always about twenty-five and after eight weeks they dump him for being immature and self-obsessed. The latest one departed about a month ago."

"I see. That's . . . unfortunate. Could you talk to his parents?"

"I could if you had a medium handy."

"I remember now. Deceased."

Ryan's mother had died six years ago and his dad had followed within four months.

"Any siblings?"

"Just one sister. And she lives in New Zealand."

Dr. Quinn looks almost awed. "That's a long way away. Mind you, they say it's very scenic. Mrs. Quinn would like to go but I don't know if I'd be able for the flight. Even with the special thrombosis socks."

"It's a long one, right enough."

"So the sister isn't going to be very hands-on in talking sense into Ryan?"

"No," I say gloomily.

"And he has no other siblings? No? That's very small for an Irish family from that generation."

"There're only two in my family also."

"That's right. Yourself and Karen. How *is* Karen?"

"Fine."

"Great girl, Karen. Great girl. Great . . . *vim* in her. Full of beans. She sorted out Mrs. Quinn's whiteheads."

"Is that right . . . ?" I know *all about* Mrs. Quinn's whiteheads but there's an unspoken vow of confidentiality between beauticians and their clients. How would a woman like to go to a dinner party and discover it was common knowledge that she had a hairy stomach?

"You could try getting Karen to talk to Ryan." Dr. Quinn looks unexpectedly hopeful. "If anyone could sort him out, she could."

"It's not really up to her . . ."

"I see."

We sit in downcast silence, then Dr. Quinn rallies.

"And how are you doing, Stella?" he asks. "With all the . . . er . . . changes in your life? I don't mean Ryan, I mean—"

"I'm fine."

"You're coping okay?"

"I'm fine."

"Well, fair play to you. Anyone else, they'd be in here begging for antidepressants and whatnot—"

"I'm fine."

I don't want his pity and I don't want his antidepressants.

"Mind you," he says, "you're looking well. Nice . . . ah . . ." He nods at my chinos.

"Chinos," I say. "Yes. Lady chinos."

"Lady chinos? Who would have thought? So anything else I can do for you as you're here?"

"Nothing, thanks."

"I could take your blood pressure," he says, almost wheedlingly.

"Okay." I sigh and begin rolling up my sleeve.

I sit patiently while the cuff on my upper arm tightens and Dr. Quinn watches the numbers. "It's a bit high," he concludes.

"Is it any wonder?"

Trust your intuition.

Extract from *One Blink at a Time*

"W ell?" Mannix Taylor asked. "What's the Wisdom of the Day today?"

He'd taken to saying this to me every morning and initially I'd thought he had a bit of a cheek: after all, *I* was the one paying *him*.

"You're full of wise stuff," he'd said. "About eating elephants and going through hell and getting rained on."

I'd quickly realized that he wasn't asking for him, but to give me something to think about. And in general I *did* think about it. It was nice to have a project, it made the time go faster, and some of the things I'd come up with so far were: "Disaster isn't just for 'other' people"; "Be grateful for the smallest of kindnesses"; "When is a yawn not a yawn? When it's a miracle."

Some were better than others, obviously. I was quite proud of the yawn one.

I'd told him my golf-course one—"Just because you live near a golf course, it doesn't mean you have to play golf."

To my surprise, he'd countered with, "But there's another way of looking at things. How about, 'If you find yourself living near a golf course, you might as well take up golf.' "

"Are we having a philosophical discussion?" I'd asked.

"Christ," he'd said thoughtfully. "We might be. I mean, why would someone choose to live near a golf course if they weren't secretly inter-ested in playing golf?"

This morning, however, Mannix Taylor wasn't just humoring me, he really *was* looking for some wisdom. "I'm worried about Roland."

Oh?

"I've mentioned to you that he has problems with money. Well, re-member that day, the day . . . we . . . of the car crash? I'd just discov-ered that Roland had taken the deposit on a house sale but spent it before he'd paid it to the vendor."

Oh my God. How much?

"Thirty grand. Then when I started going through his documents I found out he has all these credit cards and he owed—owes—money. A lot. That day, I was sitting at his desk, in the horrors, then I looked out of the window and noticed the brand-new Range Rover sitting in his parking space . . ."

Cripes.

Suddenly his eyes lit up in alarm. "I shouldn't be telling you this."

"I'm ringing the papers right now."

That made him laugh and for a moment he looked trouble free.

"Roland's trying really hard to rein in his spending and repay what he owes. He's deeply ashamed. But he keeps lapsing—it seems like he can't help it, like he has no control over it—and I think he needs to go to rehab for compulsive overspending. But . . . well, he doesn't want to go, obviously. My parents and sisters, they don't want him to go either. They say he's fine—because they're all bad with money too."

He paused, deep in thought. He looked vulnerable, guilty and very upset. "So, Stella, what's the Wisdom of the Day?"

I was stymied. This wasn't really my area of expertise. "Er . . . trust your intuition."

"Trust my intuition?" he said, scornfully. "That's a bit fortune cookie. You're usually better than that."

Ah, feck off.

However, the following day, when Mannix arrived on the ward, he said, "This is going to sound . . . weird."

Really?

"Roland? I mentioned his problems with money? And me thinking he should go to rehab?"

Right . . .

"He was wondering if he could ask your advice on it?"

"Why . . . ?"

"He liked you." Mannix amended this to, "He *really* liked you. He was blown away by your attitude. He says he'll trust whatever you have to say."

I was extremely startled at my new incarnation as the wise, paralyzed woman of Ferrytown. What is it about differently abled people, that we attribute noble characteristics to them? It's the way everyone thinks blind people are really nice. But they're not, not always. They're just like the rest of us. There was one time I tried to help a blind man through the crowds of Grafton Street and he hit me with his stick—a sharp crack on my shin, really painful. He pretended it was an accident but it wasn't.

Also, it was impossible for me to be neutral on the question of debt. The thought of anyone owing tens of thousands of euros filled me with terror, even if the person wasn't me.

Zoe once said that the only way she'd truly be happy was if everyone in the world was coupled up in a happy relationship. I, on the other hand, felt that a huge weight would lift off me if every debt in the world was canceled. I had a terrible fear of owing money and I projected it onto the whole of mankind.

"But I don't know the first thing about Roland," I said.

"You do! He said you clicked."

And actually, I had to agree with that.

"Just let him talk to you," Mannix said. "I know this is inappropriate. Unprofessional, even. But—"

He didn't have to say it—he knew it, I knew it: lying in this hospital bed, I was bored beyond endurance and I was grateful for any piece of drama.

"Okay." I blinked out the letters. "He can come in."

"This afternoon?"

"Okay."

Later that day, Mannix led Roland to my bedside. Mannix loitered in the background while Roland looked sheepish and anxious. "Stella, you are kindness itself to give me your time and wisdom."

Er, not at all . . .

He sat down and got the notebook and pen out.

"My story in a nutshell, Stella—I owe money and instead of paying it back, I . . . ah . . . borrow more and go on sprees where I do things like buy four Alexander McQueen jackets in one go. And then I hate myself. And—of course—owe even more money."

Jesus. My heart rate was increasing just hearing about this.

"I want to stop. But I can't . . . Mannix wants me to go to rehab to sort myself out. What do you think I should do?"

"WHAT DO YOU THINK?"

"I think I should go. But I'm afraid."

"IT'S NORMAL TO BE AFRAID OF REHAB."

He considered that. "Are you afraid? Being in the hospital, like this?"

"YES."

"Okay." He had a think. "If you can live like this, day after day, surely I can do six weeks in rehab?"

"IT MIGHT HELP YOU."

"Might it?" That seemed like a novel idea to him.

"IT MIGHT NOT BE A PUNISHMENT."

"Riiiight." A cloud seemed to lift from him. "I'd been sort of thinking that they'd whack me with birch branches while reading out my credit card statements over a tannoy. You know—'Eighty quid on a Paul Smith tie.' Whack! 'Nine hundred quid on a Loewe messenger bag.' Whack! 'Two thousand quid on a fancy bicycle'—which I never used. Whack!"

I was starting to feel sick. Did he really spend all that money on those things?

"YOU WONT BE WHACKED," I said. Of that I was certain. Almost.

"Of course I won't. What have I been thinking? You know something?" he said. "You are profoundly inspirational. You have such courage."

But I hadn't done anything.

"You're a lovely woman. Thank you."

The following morning, when Mannix arrived, he greeted me with, "Guess what? Roland's gone to rehab."

Well, great!

"Thank you."

There was no reason to thank me: Roland had talked himself into it. His mind had already been made up; he simply wasn't fully ready to acknowledge it.

"My sisters are furious with me," Mannix said. "So are my parents. I'm the most hated person in my family." He gave a lopsided smile. "But, hey, it's nice to be the best at something . . ."

12:44

I emerge, heavyhearted, from Dr. Quinn's clinic into the street. A newsagent's, full to the brim with chocolate, beckons me and it takes every ounce of my self-restraint to stop myself from going in and buying five Twirls.

I decide to have one final go at bringing Ryan to his senses. He answers his mobile by saying, "I'm not backing down."

"Where are you?" I ask.

"In the office."

This is a rarity. He's always out at meetings or having to go to sites to shout at useless plumbers.

In the distance I see a bus shimmering into view. "Don't move," I say. "I'm on my way."

I hop on the 46A—I have the correct change in my purse, which I take as a good omen—and prepare for a journey of several days, as this has always been my experience of the 46A route in the past. But something strange happens—perhaps we pass through a hole in space and time—because in thirty-nine minutes I'm in the city center outside Ryan Sweeney Bathrooms.

It has its HQ on the first floor of a Georgian house in South William Street and when I arrive five staff are working with great concentration at screens, their faces aglow with computer light. In the center of the room Ryan is sitting on a swivel chair, swinging from left to right and right to left, and smiling into space in such an inane fashion that I'm really alarmed. I nod hellos to the diligent workers and pick my way between towers of sample tiles and brochures.

Ryan has seen me. "Stella!" He smiles like he's stoned and he keeps on swiveling.

"Stop that!" I say, and mercifully he does.

I gesture around at all of Ryan's drawing boards and computers and technical wizardry.

"So," I say, "where does all of this fit into your karma . . . thing?" Don't call it Project Karma, I beseech myself. Don't legitimize it by naming it.

"I'm giving the business away."

Now I'm really shocked. Shocked and afraid. "But . . . but this is your livelihood . . ." I stammer. "What about your children? Ryan, you have responsibilities."

"My kids are adults—"

"Jeffrey isn't."

"He is. It's not my fault he doesn't act it. My daughter is getting married. I brought them up, paid for their education, gave them everything they needed and everything they wanted. I'm still there for them and there's money set aside for Jeffrey's last year of school, but financially my job is done."

"Well, what about your staff? They'll be out of a job."

"They won't. I'm giving the business as a going concern. Clarissa will own it."

I whip my head around to glare at Clarissa. She's been Ryan's second-in-command for a long time and I've never taken to her; she isn't what you might call friendly. She's tall and slender and always wears black leggings and workman's boots and frayed jumpers and chunky silver jewelry—most of it in her eyebrows –and she does that thing of having her sleeves too long, in a little-girl-lost way, which makes me itch to smack her.

She makes steady eye contact and gives a small, enigmatic—triumphant?—smile. Big smacky-rage rises up in me and I'm the first to look away. I always am. I'm one of life's weaklings. I turn my back on her and I face Ryan. "Can we speak privately?"

We step into the corridor. "Ryan, it's obvious you're having a mid-life crisis." I speak gently. "And you will really regret this. Can't you just train for a triathlon like every other man of your age? We'll help. Jeffrey could go swimming with you."

"Jeffrey hates me."

"He does," I agree. "He does. But he hates me too. You mustn't take it personally. So if he does the swimming, I'll go running with you." With my current belly crisis I'll have to do some sort of exercise, and a commitment to Ryan would be a good thing. "And we'll find someone to do the cycling. Maybe Enda."

"I'm not going on bike rides with Enda Mulreid," Ryan says mutinously. "He's got guard's thighs. Built for endurance"

"Someone else, then. It doesn't have to be Enda."

But Ryan is deep, deep inside his project, too far away to be reached. "Stella—" he places his hands on my shoulders and looks at me with fervor—"I'm doing something important here. This is Spiritual Art. I'm proving that karma exists."

For a moment I'm caught up in Ryan's zeal. Maybe he *is* doing a good thing. Maybe it'll be okay. But . . . "What if it all goes wrong, Ryan? What then?"

He laughs gently. "You'll never stop being that working-class girl who's terrified of poverty, will you?"

I splutter, "I'm practical. Someone has to be! Would you go to see Dr. Quinn? Just to check that you're not . . . you know . . . unwell. Like, in the head."

"I'm not."

Miserably, I stare at him. I don't know what to do. Should I go back into the office and try to reason with Clarissa? But I know her game; she'll give me a mysterious smile and say in her precise, annoying way that Ryan can do what he likes. And even if Clarissa decides not to take the business, Ryan will simply offer it to someone else and eventually someone will accept it and refuse to give it back.

Ryan is the one I have to keep working on.

"I've got to go," he says. "I want to go back in and swivel in my chair."

"You do?"

"It feels . . . nice. I feel swingy and free."

" 'Swingy and free?' "

Abruptly he changes the subject matter, the way mad people do. "You know something, Stella." He gazes into my eyes. "You're looking *very* well. There's something new about you."

"Extreme fear?"

"No, no, no. You've always been afraid. Is it . . . ?" He looks me up and down and eventually points to my legs. "It's those things."

Almost shyly, I say, "They're chinos. Lady chinos."

"They're great." And even though I know he's not in his right mind, his praise warms me.

Some people can make their ears move—it's their party trick. Don't feel bad if you can't do it. Just find yourself another party trick.

Extract from One Blink at a Time

H is anus stared at her like a steady, unblinking eye . . .'" Dad read. Yikes! This book from Georgie Taylor was a bit racy. It was about a bored woman who was married to a respectable company director but lived a secret life as a prostitute.

"'She cupped her hands around his ball sac and —' Ah, here! I'm not reading this." Dad closed the book with a snap. "I don't care what prizes it's after winning. I'm not saying it's not literature. Some of the world's greatest books are jammers with dirt birds. But you're my daughter, and this isn't right. What else is there?"

He consulted the small pile of Georgie Taylor's books. "*Jane Eyre?*" He sounded shocked. "But that's only for schoolgirls. The slippery slope. What would it be next? *Bridget Jones's Diary? Dick and Jane Go to the Seaside?*"

Oh dear. Without ever having met her, Dad had developed a little crush on Georgie Taylor. One day he'd actually brought in a bunch of garage flowers and given it to Mannix Taylor to give to her. Now it seemed his faith in her impeccable taste was shaken.

"What else is here?" Dad picked up another book. "*Rebecca?* So we've got *Jane Eyre*, a book about a mad first wife in the attic. And we've *Rebecca*, about a second wife being haunted by the memory of the first one." He stared hard at me. "What's that all about?"

I didn't know and it was hard to give it my full attention because I was turning over a thrilling little secret: it was six weeks to the day since Mannix Taylor had told me that movement would start returning to my muscles. I'd been counting down the time, ticking off each twenty-four hours as they passed, and finally day zero had arrived.

I was wondering which part of my body would be the first to wake up. It might be my hands, it might be my neck muscles, it might—best of all—be my voice box. It was hard to know where life would blossom because I was still as motionless as a sack of sand, but something would definitely happen today. Because Mannix had said it would.

Mind you, he didn't seem to remember having said it; he'd certainly made no mention of it on his routine visit this morning. Well, he had a lot on his mind . . .

"Look, Dolly, I'll hit the road." Dad got up to leave. "I can't read you any of these books, they're just Gothic chick lit." He shook his head regretfully. "I'll get something decent from Joan. Maybe it's time to read Norman Mailer again."

I was relieved to see him go. I wanted to concentrate on my body, to beam my attention like a spotlight, systematically moving from muscle to muscle, ready to pounce on any stirring.

Nostrils, tongue, lips, neck, chest, arms, fingers . . . Starting from the other end—toes, feet, ankles, calves, knees . . . eyebrows, ears . . . No, that was stupid. Even when I'd been in the whole of my health I hadn't been able to move my ears. Some people could, it was their party trick, but not me. Forehead, jaw, neck, shoulders, elbows . . . Nothing yet.

My plan was to have some movement to show to Ryan when he came to visit this evening. He needed a shot of hope.

But the day passed and nothing had happened by the time he arrived, looking slightly grimy and neglected.

"Well?" Wearily he sank into a chair and, even more wearily, got the pen and notebook from the sterilizer.

I'd been about to tell him to get his hair cut, then abruptly I decided against it. "ALL FINE," I blinked.

"Lucky you," he said. "I wouldn't mind a few days in bed myself."

Aghast, I tried blinking compassionate words at him, but we couldn't get a rhythm going.

"Stop," he said, after we'd got four letters wrong. "I'm too tired for this."

Okay. It's okay. I pushed soothing thoughts out through my eyes. *Let's just sit here and be together.*

"It's a bit pointless, when we've nothing to say." He stood up. He'd only been here for five minutes.

Stay.

"Somebody will be in to see you tomorrow. I can't remember who. Somebody."

Maybe. Visitors no longer arrived mob handed. They came one by one, and sometimes they didn't come at all. It was early December, and the build-up to Christmas was in full swing. The kids' lives were even busier than usual, Ryan was working like the clappers to complete a project before the end of the year, Karen was frantic in the salon and Mum was working extra shifts at the care home.

I was being left behind in everyone's slipstream. The extreme closeness Ryan and I had shared in the early days of my illness was eroding beneath the relentless grind of his life. I'd really want to start getting better soon.

"Anyway, your man Mannix Taylor will visit you."

Was Ryan being snide? I didn't think so; he was making a simple statement of fact—Mannix Taylor *would* visit me. He was my neurologist and he came every weekday. Because he was paid to.

"Bye. See you soon." Ryan left and I felt depressed—good, plain, old-fashioned depressed. Nothing to do with being paralyzed. Nothing to do with the fear of going to hell. Just depressed.

Ryan wasn't able for this and I didn't blame him. Everything would be okay in the end, I told myself. But it was tough going while it was happening.

For once, the day had rattled by and, all too soon, night fell. The day was over and none of my muscles had even flickered.

I tried to be reasonable: it wasn't fair to have taken Mannix Taylor so literally. It was a very approximate timescale he'd given me. But, as I drifted off to sleep, I felt unsettled and sad.

At some point I was woken by the nurses turning me. There was the usual to-do with my tubes and sensors, and just before I was set on my right side to face the wall I caught a glimpse of the clock; it was seven minutes to midnight.

The nurses squeaked away on their rubber-soled shoes and I settled back into stillness. Sleep began to steal over me again, and, at the very moment I tumbled down into the darkness, my left knee twitched.

The next morning Mannix Taylor arrived almost an hour earlier than usual. And I realized I'd been completely wrong to think he'd forgotten the six-week promise. Hope and hunger were stamped all over his face. He wasn't even pretending to assume a professional veneer.

I looked at him and, with my eyes, smugly messaged the word "Yes."

He almost jumped onto the bed. "Where?"

"Kn—"

"Which one?" He whipped my blanket back.

"L—"

"Do it for me." He put his hand on my left knee and I concentrated every ounce of will I had into getting the muscle to twitch. Nothing happened. But I'd felt it last night. I swore I'd felt it.

Or had I? Maybe, because I'd wanted it so badly, I'd conned myself into believing it.

I looked at him apologetically. *Sorry*.

Then, beneath his hand, my knee pulsed.

In one fluid movement he rolled off the bed and leaped to his feet. "No fucking way!"

On the inside I was screaming with joy.

"Do it again!" he commanded. "If you do it again, I'll believe it's real."

He stole back onto the bed and put his hand on my knee and warily we watched each other, wondering if anything would happen. He was holding his breath but my leg lay like a plank of wood.

"Go on," he said impatiently.

I'm trying.

"Go on."

I'm fecking *trying*.

"Okay," he sighed. "We'll leave it for today—"

Beneath his hand my knee twitched.

"Ha!" He gave a shout of laughter. "Drag things out, why don't you?"

Once again, the muscle in my knee fluttered. It was the oddest sensation, a little like when Ryan used to put his hand on my stomach when I was pregnant with Betsy and Jeffrey.

"*Now* I believe you," Mannix said. "It's real! It's happening! You're getting better."

"You told me I would."

"I didn't mean it. Not this fast. Mind you—" his tone was a mix of admiration and exasperation—"with you, I should have known better."

15:17

At home, Jeffrey is at the kitchen table, crouched over his phone. "Dad's video has had ninety thousand hits. It's speeding up. And . . . he's trending on Twitter."

I feel myself go pale. Not Twitter, my beloved Twitter. *I've* never trended on Twitter. I'm angry and afraid and . . . yes . . . *jealous*.

"Don't worry," Jeffrey says. "It's only in the blogosphere."

I nod tentatively. There is nothing "only" about Twitter. Not in my book.

"Only in the blogosphere," Jeffrey repeats soothingly. "It's not in the real world. It'll never be in the real world."

At that very moment, my phone rings. Caller unknown. And yet I answer it. Am I insane?

"Stella Sweeney?" a woman's voice asks.

"Who's calling?"

"My name is Kirsty Gaw. I work for the *Southside Zinger*."

The *Southside Zinger* is a neighborhood free sheet, which once featured a front-page headline: "Local Boy Breaks Plate." Parochial would be the kindest way to describe it.

"I'm calling about your husband, Ryan Sweeney." My heart sinks— someone in the *Zinger* must have made the connection between Ryan and me.

"*Ex*," I say, anxiously and very firmly. "He's my ex-husband."

"So you're Stella?" She sounds friendly.

My media training kicks in. "No, no, I'm not. Wrong number. Thank you. Thank you very much. Good-bye now." I end the call, as politely as is possible.

The awful thing about being sort of famous, I reflect, as I scream into my hands, is that you have to be constantly pleasant. Things are difficult enough without people going around saying, "That Stella Sweeney. Seems so nice. But she's a right snotty cow!"

"What?" Jeffrey asks.

I stare at him with hollow eyes. "The *Southside Zinger*. Fuck! Oh fuck!"

"Please don't swear, Mom. Anyway, it's only the *Southside* 'Local Lady Loses Eyelash' *Zinger*."

I look at him with almost admiration—that was quite funny, for Jeffrey.

My phone goes again. Kirsty Gaw must be ringing back. But she's not. This is another newspaper, a *real* one: the *Herald*. The name flashes up on my screen and I hold it out to show Jeffrey.

"They know," I whisper. "Real people know."

"Fuck," he says.

"Now you're at it!" Despite everything, I'm pleased to have the moral high ground. "You're swearing."

"Not swear*ing*. Just once. I swore just once."

"Whatevs."

" 'Whatevs,' " he mimics. "Listen to yourself."

My phone rings again—it's the *Mail*. Then the landline starts ringing. It's the *Independent*. Then both phones are ringing together. It's almost like the old days. Voices are leaving messages, and as soon as they hang up the phone starts ringing again. I switch off my mobile and pull the landline connection from the wall.

"What if they come to the house?" Jeffrey asks.

"They won't."

But they might. They had, once before, two years ago . . .

I lean against the sink and let the present dissolve into wobbly, vertical lines as I disappear down memory lane . . .

. . . to an otherwise ordinary day in late August. I'd finished work and had popped home to pick up the kids; we were going to Dundrum to buy stuff for their new school year, which was starting the following week.

"Come on." I stood at the front door and shook my keys. "Let's go."

"Have you seen this?" Betsy asked warily.

It was *People* magazine. I read dozens of magazines because we got them in the salon, but we didn't get the U.S. ones, because we didn't know the people in them—celebrity crash-and-burns were only really interesting when you knew who the celebrity was.

"Have I seen what?" I asked.

Betsy slid the magazine in front of me: there was a picture of Annabeth Browning. I hadn't much interest in American politics but I knew who she was. The wife of the U.S. vice president, she'd created a big stir a few months back, when she'd been arrested for "driving erratically" and was found to be banjoed out of her head on prescription medication. The state troopers didn't realize who she was and the press had got hold of it before the White House had time to cover it up.

A media storm had followed. Naturally Annabeth had had to put on a big public display of remorse by going immediately to rehab. Everyone expected she'd do her twenty-eight days and then snap straight back into her public duties, perky as anything, followed by a glassy-eyed photo shoot of her with her husband and two children, and an interview with Barbara Walters, in which she described her arrest as "the best thing that ever happened to me."

But instead of returning to public life, she went to live in a local convent. Her approval ratings, which had been going steadily upward, dropped dramatically. This was going way off script. She'd had her twenty-eight days, what more did she want?

This picture in front of me was a fuzzy shot of Annabeth sitting in a garden—I was guessing it was the convent garden, it looked sort of convent-y—sitting on a bench, reading a book. The headline shouted: "WHAT'S ANNABETH READING?" I studied the photo—Annabeth was letting the blonde grow out of her hair and it suited her.

"She's looking well," I said. "She was too bouffy before. Natural suits her better."

"Forget her hair!" Betsy sounded agitated. "Look!" She tapped a circular close-up of Annabeth's hand. "That's your book."

I stared and stared until my eyes started to go funny, but Betsy was right—it *was* my book.

"How did she get it?" I was suddenly extremely uneasy. My little book was a personal, privately published thing. And Annabeth Browning wasn't exactly popular. An unpopular woman publicly reading what I'd written? It couldn't end well for me.

My brain started working overtime, trying to connect some dots. There were only fifty copies of my book in existence; it had never been for sale; the only people who had it were my friends and family. I tried coming at the issue from the other end—Annabeth was in a convent. Nuns lived in convents. Did *I* know any nuns? Who might have had access to my book?

"What's going on?" Jeffrey had come into the hall.

"Look at this." I thrust the page at him. "Do we know any nuns?"

"Doesn't your uncle Peter have a sister who's a nun . . . ? Hey, look, it's your book!"

"I know. How did Annabeth Browning get it?"

"I dunno. Ring your uncle Peter?"

"Okay." I shut the front door—I didn't think we'd be going to Dundrum just yet—and reached for my phone. "Uncle Peter? Hello, yes, grand, grand, except, you know my book, with my little sayings in it from my time in the hospital, like 'When is a yawn not a yawn?' "

" 'When it's a miracle,' " Peter finished. "I do know it. Yessss." Was it my imagination or did he sound shifty?

"Have you still got it?" I asked. "I mean, is there any chance that your sister, the nun—is her name Sister Michael? Could she have it?"

There was a long, long pause. "I'm sorry, Stella," Peter whispered.

"What?"

"We had it in a lovely spot in the cabinet but she was always light-fingered."

"Who? Sister Michael? She's a nun!"

"How many normal nuns do you know?"

I remembered the ones who'd taught me at school. Psychopaths, for the most part.

"She just can't resist nice things," Peter said, miserably. "She puts herself through hell afterward, acts of penance and all sorts, but she doesn't seem able to stop."

"Peter, would you be able to find out if she actually took it?"

Peter exhaled heavily. "I can ask her. But she lies a lot. Especially if she's in the wrong."

"I see. Okay. Listen, what brand of nun is she?"

"Why? You're not going to ring her?"

"I need to check something. My book is after turning up in the U.S. In a convent. In . . ." I skim the piece in the magazine. "In the Daughters of Chastity."

"That's her bunch, all right," Peter said.

"How would the book have got to the U.S.? Has Sister Michael been there?"

"No. But . . ."

"What?"

"In May, she had a visitor from one of the U.S. convents. A younger nun. Sister Gudrun. They got caught shoplifting in Boots. They had twenty-one Bourjois blushers on them. Twenty-one! It was almost like they wanted to be caught! I had to go down and bail them out. The only reason the shop didn't press charges was that Sister Gudrun was a U.S. citizen and Sister Michael cried her eyes out and said she'd never do it again. I think the store detectives thought Gudrun had led Michael astray, but I'd say they were as bad as each other."

"Do you think this Gudrun could have taken my book back to the U.S.?"

"From the carry-on I saw, I'd say anything is possible."

"Can you remember what branch, convent, whatever the word is, Sister Gudrun was from?"

"Of course I remember. Didn't I have to fill out a thousand forms putting her address on them? She's from Washington, D.C."

"Thanks. Er, sorry, Peter." What a life he had, between glamorous Auntie Jeanette and a sister who was a shoplifting nun.

I felt vulnerable and afraid. Those words I'd said in private were now out there in the world. People would judge me. I'd get blamed for Annabeth Browning no longer being perky and not going on *Barbara Walters*.

Just then the landline rang. Jeffrey, Betsy and I looked at it, then looked at each other. We had an inkling this call was about to change our lives.

I picked up.

"Stella Sweeney?"

Lie, lie. But I stammered, "S . . . speaking."

"The Stella Sweeney who wrote *One Blink at a Time*?"

"Yes, but—"

"Hold for Phyllis Teerlinck."

After a click, a new voice spoke. "Phyllis Teerlinck, literary agent. I'm offering to represent you."

A million thoughts zipped through my head and I settled on, "Why? You haven't even seen the book."

"I visited Annabeth. She's lent it to me for twenty-four hours. Look, you're having a moment. Right now you might be the most influential woman in the world, but in six days' time a new *People* will be on the stands. This is your window and it's closing shortly. I'll call back in one hour. Google me. I'm real."

I hung up the phone. Immediately it rang again. I let it go to answerphone. And immediately it rang again. And again. And again.

If it is made with love, the imperfect becomes perfect.

Extract from *One Blink at a Time*

Y ou have to leave now," Nurse Salome said to Mum and Dad. She had my food bag, ready to connect to the port in my stomach.

"Any chance there's a turkey leg in that?" Dad nodded at the bag. "It's not Christmas without a bit of turkey."

Salome ignored him. There were only two nurses on duty in ICU on Christmas Day and she clearly wasn't happy to be one of them.

"You'd hardly know it was Christmas at all, round here." Dad gave Salome a look full of blame. "No tree, no decorations, not even," he said meaningfully, "a bit of tinsel."

About a week earlier, Betsy had brought in some tinsel and wrapped it around the bars of my bed, but it had caused a right commotion. "This is ICU! People are grievously ill. Tinsel could harbor bacteria."

"We'll go, so," Mum said. "Happy Christmas, Stella." She was in tears. She cried at every visit. I felt so guilty that sometimes I wished she wouldn't come. Then I felt even more guilty.

"Enjoy your Christmas dinner, Dolly." Dad threw another dark look at Salome.

About an hour later Ryan came in with Betsy and Jeffrey.

"Happy Christmas, Mom, happy Christmas," Betsy squealed. She was wearing a pair of antlers on her head. "Thank you for the voucher."

I'm sorry it's . . .

"A little impersonal, yeah?" she said. "But we'll go shopping together when you're better. Then it'll be totally personal."

"It'll be out of date by then," Jeffrey said.

"Stop it!" Betsy cried. To me, she said, "He's just peed off because Santa gave him the wrong upgrade."

Before I could stop myself, I looked at Ryan in a blaming kind of way.

"We'll change it tomorrow," he said tightly.

"You think it's that simple?" Jeffrey said, equally tightly.

This was a horrible Christmas, totally different from any other. In previous years I'd always gone a bit mad—buying a real tree, covering the house with lights, hand making the decorations, spending a fortune on gifts and wrapping everything elaborately. Even though Betsy and Jeffrey had long stopped believing in Santa, I still put stockings at the end of their beds and filled them with trinkets and chocolate.

For me, Christmas was all about the kids and it was important to make it magical. Not being able to do anything this year made me terribly sad. It was the hardest thing so far about being sick.

I'd made sure Ryan had done the basics—he'd put up a tree and he bought Betsy her voucher and Jeffrey his phone upgrade—but I hadn't dared to ask him to do more. He was stretched way too thin as it was.

I'd tried to get Mum to organize stockings for the kids, but blinking really only worked with simple requests; even then I had to know in advance exactly what I planned to say and I had to use the least number of letters possible. If things went off piste in the middle of a word, it was hard to find my way back to the right path. It was exhausting and the only person who was any good at it was Mannix Taylor.

"Open my gift to you," Betsy said. "Open my gift!" She thrust a small chunky parcel at me. "I totally know you can't but I'm acting 'inclusive,' right?" She tore off a little of the paper. "What can it be?"

I could see a brown ceramic foot. My hopes weren't high.

She kept tearing off the paper until she'd revealed a lopsided dog. "I made it in pottery class! Not so perfect, I know, but made with love. Because we all know how much you'd love a dog."

At that moment, I welled up with so much love for her I thought my heart would burst. She was so sweet and I loved my crooked little dog.

"I guess I'll have to take it away." She threw an unforgiving look at the nurses' station; she still wasn't over Tinsel-gate. "But it'll be there when you come home."

"In ten years' time," Jeffrey said sullenly. "Here's my gift. I'll unwrap it, shall I?"

Sarcastic little feck.

Unceremoniously he ripped off the wrapping paper . . . and revealed a tuning fork. I didn't know what to read into it. A tuning fork? But . . . *why?*

Ryan had nothing for me. "I'm sorry," he said. "Just with everything . . ."

Of course. And what could he give me anyway?

But I had a gift for him, a voucher for Samphire, a restaurant he'd often said he wanted to go to. I'd got Karen to buy it and what I'd really been trying to do was to give Ryan the gift of hope: the day would come when I'd be better and we'd be able to go there together. I started blinking it out for him, but we got bogged down in the wrong letters. "I know," he said. "It's okay. Thank you. I really appreciate it." He held it against his heart.

"Time!" Salome yelled, and they leaped to their feet and scampered away, as if they'd been let out of school early.

The hospital settled down into stillness. All but the acute cases had been sent home for Christmas. No operations had been scheduled, so no one was recovering from surgery. There was only one other patient in intensive care—an older man, a heart attack victim. I could hear his family whispering and weeping around his bed, then they had to leave and it was just him and me.

The whole place felt echoey and empty. I couldn't even see the nurses. Maybe they were in some back room drinking Malibu and eating sausage rolls, and who could blame them?

Time always went slowly in here but today it was almost at a standstill. I watched the clock dragging away the seconds, taking its own sweet time about it. I just wanted it to not be Christmas Day anymore. It was too sad being away from my kids and husband and family. Any other day I was prepared to be brave, but this was too hard.

To pass the time I played with my muscles. By now I could lift my head a centimeter from the pillow and slightly flex my knees. My right ankle could be rotated a little and both my shoulders would twitch on command. Life in my muscles was returning but it was random; there seemed to be no pattern to it.

The big-ticket items would be my voice box or my fingers, but while I was waiting for them to fire up, I exercised the muscles that did work and paid beady-eyed attention to every other one, poised to swoop on any response, no matter how small.

But it was scary how fast I ran out of energy—if twisting my ankle half an inch exhausted me this much, how would I ever walk again?

By eight o'clock I'd used up all of my distractions. Maybe I could go to sleep and when I woke up it would be tomorrow and Christmas Day would be over. I closed my eyes and willed myself into unconsciousness, and then I heard footsteps, coming from far away, from the entrance to the ward.

They were very loud in the silence.

I recognized the sound. But what was he doing here on Christmas night?

The footsteps got closer and here he was, Mannix Taylor. "Happy Christmas." Automatically he got out the pen and notebook.

I started to blink, "What are you doing here?"

By the time I was two letters in, he said, "I thought you might be lonely."

I didn't know what to say.

"Nice day?" I asked.

"Grand," he said. "Were your family in?"

"Earlier. You get nice presents?"

"No. You?"

"A pottery dog and a tuning fork."

"A tuning fork? From your husband?"

"Jeffrey."

"Maybe that's not so bad; he *is* a teenage boy . . . Was the dog from your husband?"

"Betsy."

"What did your husband give you?"

I didn't want to say. I was ashamed.

And this was just too weird. Why was Mannix Taylor here?

"I went in to see Roland today," he said.

"How is he?" I took a proprietorial interest in him.

"Great. Positive. Getting out soon. He said to send his love and undying gratitude to you."

Well, that was nice.

Something flickered at the edge of my vision—there was a woman standing at the empty nurses' station. It was so unexpected that I wondered if I was hallucinating. She was watching us and my instinct told me she'd been there for a while.

Her hair was long and dark and her eyebrows were fabulous and she wore a narrow-cut black top and—God!—skinny vinyl jeans.

She was so brooding and still and out of place, I felt she was being beamed in direct from a horror film.

Next thing, she was moving toward me and I was afraid. Mannix looked over his shoulder and when he saw her he tensed up tight.

She crossed the ward in a way I can only describe as aggressively slinky and she looked hard at me, lying helpless on my bed, then she looked at Mannix. "Really?" she said. "I mean, *really*?"

I wanted to yelp: You're not seeing me at my best! If my hair was blow-dried like yours and if I had my makeup on and if I didn't have a life-threatening illness, you might take me seriously. I may never win Miss World but . . . No, just leave it at that. I may never win Miss World.

Then she stalked away—and yes, it was a right stalk, a right proper angry, prowly sort of thing—on her long legs.

A strange silence followed.

Eventually Mannix spoke. "That was my wife."

Really?

But your wife is meant to be cool and calm and Scando looking. She's not supposed to be dark-haired and dark-eyed, with magnificent eyebrows and—for the love of God!—vinyl jeans!

"I'd better go," he said. And he went.

Thursday, 5 June

07:03

I'm awoken by the sound of my doorbell being rung again and again.

I take a sneaky look out of an upstairs window, terrified that it might be a journalist. But it's Karen, already fully made-up and wearing very high, red, patent-leather shoes that look oddly sinister.

I go down and open the door and she thrusts a newspaper at me. "You'd better see this."

It's the *Daily Mail* and Ryan's face is on the front of it.

"Where's Jeffrey?" Karen looks around, almost fearfully.

"In bed!" his muffled voice shouts.

We go into the kitchen, where, with a dry mouth and a thumping head, I read hungrily. It describes Ryan as "sexy" and "talented" and says his house is a €2 million "luxury home," which it so isn't.

"You're in it too," Karen says. "It says you're a self-help writer."

"A 'failed' self-help writer?"

"No. Because you're not. Not really. Not yet."

"Does it say why I'm in Ireland?" How much of my personal circumstances are out there in the public domain?

"No, all fairly neutral stuff. But I've only read this one and he's in all the other papers too," she said. "Well, the Irish ones. But I wasn't wasting my money buying them; you can read them online. He's looking well, I must say." She studies his picture from various angles. "I suppose he was always good-looking, with the dark hair and the dark eyes . . . It was just that his terrible eejitry canceled it out. Now, tell me, what are you going to do about him?"

"What can I do? Enda says I can't section him. Dr. Quinn was no help—he was asking for you, by the way, says you did a great job on Mrs. Quinn's whiteheads. It's pointless talking to Ryan; there's no way he's going to change his mind. And I've no legal redress because we're getting divorced."

"But where's he going to live when it all goes wrong?" Karen asks.

"I don't know."

"He can't live here."

"Maybe it won't go wrong," I say. "Maybe he's right and the universe *will* provide."

Karen flashes me a witheringly skeptical bat of her eyelids. "The universe helps those who help themselves. Ryan Sweeney will end up sleeping on your couch. Unless, of course, he ends up sleeping in your bed."

"What do you mean by that?"

She starts jingling car keys, the international signal for imminent departure. "I'm off. Nippers to wash and dress."

She sweeps her bag onto her shoulder and click-clacks down the hall in her terrifying red shoes. I follow in her perfumed wake. "Karen, what did you mean?"

"I mean, you're a soft touch."

"I'm not. I'm stubborn. And proud."

"You are if someone has really wounded you. But you're a sucker for a hard-luck story. You're the first person Ryan will come to when he finds himself homeless. You'd better have your resistance ready."

And with that she breezes out through the front door.

I go online and read the coverage about Ryan. I'm bloody terrified of what people might have written about me—I'd tried to keep my ignominious return to Ireland as low-key as possible. I wanted to keep people from finding out how badly things had gone wrong in order to buy some time in which to fix them. But Ryan and his fool project have started dragging me reluctantly back into the limelight, where there's every chance my threadbare truth will be mercilessly spotlit.

Every article mentions me. "He was married to self-help writer Stella Sweeney, with whom he has two children." "His ex-wife is the writer Stella Sweeney, who enjoyed international success with her inspirational book *One Blink at a Time*."

But nothing too revealing is said. For the moment. This might all wind down and go away.

Very tentatively I switch on my phone—I've twenty-six missed calls. Instantly it starts ringing. I hold it away from me and, with one eye closed, I look at the screen—it's Mum.

"What?" I ask. "Is it shopping day again?" I could have sworn we'd gone very recently.

"Your father wants to talk to you."

There's some scuffling and static as the phone is handed over, then Dad's voice says, "He's on the telly."

"Who?"

"That eejit, Ryan Sweeney. He's says he's giving all his stuff away. He's on *Ireland AM*."

I grab the remote and, to my horror, Ryan is indeed on *Ireland AM*. He's standing outside his house and chatting enthusiastically. "Because of the legalities some of my bigger possessions will be gifted in advance of Day Zero," he's saying. "The house you see here behind me, I've given it to a homeless charity. The paperwork's being done by solicitors right now."

"Very worthy," the interviewer says. But she's trying to hide a smirk. She thinks Ryan's a nutter. "Now back to the studio."

"Don't let it get to you, Dolly," Dad says. "He's a tool. Always was, always will be. Do you want to come over and go up and down on the stairlift a few times?"

08:56

Jeffrey appears. "I'm going out," he says. "I'm going dancing."

"Dancing? Really?" How . . . well . . . normal! How bizarrely normal!

Then I realize that this is not normal at all. That, in fact, this is an extremely strange time of day to be going out dancing. Under my anxious interrogation, Jeffrey tells me he is not planning to go to a nightclub and drink until he falls over. No. He's going to something called a "dance workshop." Where he will "work out" emotions.

I gaze at him. I have an almost uncontrollable urge to snigger. I have to suck my tongue to hold it back. It takes every ounce of my strength.

10:10

My doorbell rings. I flatten myself against the bedroom wall and take a sneaky look, like a cowboy in a shoot-out. It's not a journalist, it's Ryan, and I'm happy to welcome him in because I'm prepared to bet that all this media coverage has shocked him back into sanity.

"Come in, come in!"

"I need to talk to you," he says. "I've had a call from *Saturday Night In*."

Saturday Night In is an Irish institution: a chat show that has been presented since the Stone Age by televisual dinosaur Maurice McNice— real name Maurice McNiece, but everyone called him Maurice McNice, even though I'd always found him to be spiteful and patronizing. But two short months ago, Maurice McNice keeled over and passed into the great green room in the sky, and the battle between Irish broadcasters to replace him was a hard-fought and bitter one. The microphone of power had eventually been won by the inhabitor of my dreams, Ned Mount.

"And—" I ask, cautiously.

"The thing is, they want both of us on the show. You and me together."

"For what? For why?"

"Because we have a story. Both of us. You and your books and me and my art."

"Ryan, we're separated, we're getting divorced—there *is* no story."

"You could do with some publicity."

"I couldn't! I have nothing to promote. I'm trying to keep a low profile. I'm trying to put my life back together. The last thing I want is to go on national telly and tell everyone how bad it all is. And look at my belly!" I'm practically shrieking. "How could anyone go on telly with this belly?"

"They don't want me on my own," he said. "I need you to do it."

I take a deep, deep breath. "Read my lips, Ryan." I enunciate the words clearly. "There is no way *on earth* I'm going on *Saturday Night In*."

"That was a long, complicated sentence," he says. "It's a good job I'm not deaf because I wouldn't have had a clue what you were saying."

"Yes, but you're not deaf. You heard what I said. I'm not doing it."

"You are incredibly selfish." He shakes his head, the way a very bad actor would, to convey contempt. "And judgmental. Totally rigid. You know what happens to the person who doesn't bend, Stella? They *break*. And you wonder why your life has fallen apart? Well, you made it happen; you brought it all on yourself."

Holding his back ramrod straight, he says, "I'll see myself out."

And even though I'm very, very upset, I reflect on the fact that I've never before heard a person say those words in real life.

11:17

I eat 100g of cottage cheese. It doesn't uplift me the way, for example, 100g of milk chocolate would.

12:09

I sit at my keyboard and type the word "Ass."

12:19–15:57

I cease typing and start meditating upon my life. Am I as judgmental and rigid as Ryan says? Are my current circumstances all my own fault? Or could I have done things differently?

I don't know . . . I try to not think about what happened because it's simply too painful. At the time I'd decided on a clean break because I knew it was the only way I'd survive. I didn't want doubts stirred up about whether I'd done the right thing. I did what I did at the time because I had no other choice.

But what if it had been the wrong thing . . . ?

Oh, feck Ryan for opening this can of worms in my head!

15:59

I decide to go for a jog. Just a small one. To ease me back into exercise.

16:17

I find I am still sitting at my keyboard.

But I've made a decision: I'm giving up on this book business. I can't do it. I have nothing to say and I can't bear the publicity end of things. However, I need a job. I need to earn money somehow. Is there anything I can do? Anything at all . . . ?

Well, I *am* a trained beautician.

There! That's the solution: I'm going back into the beauty game! You never forget those skills. It's like riding a bike, right?

17:28

It's *not* like riding a bike.

I ring Karen and tell her of my plans and she says, "Umm-hmmm. I seeeee. You can thread lady sideburns?"

"Well, no . . ."

"You're trained in medical pedicures?"

"Well, no . . ."

"You can do microneedling? Mesotherapy?"

"No." I don't even know what those last two are. "But I can wax, Karen, I can wax for Ireland."

"Waxing! Waxing went out with mullets. Here's the truth, Stella. I wouldn't give you a job. And I'm your sister. You stepped off the beauty treadmill—vol-un-tar-ily, I might add—and it's going too fast for you to ever get back on."

17:37–19:53

I sit with my head in my hands.

19:59

I gather up all the Jaffa Cakes and granola and other nice carby stuff in the house and throw it in the brown wheely bin, in the front garden. Then I bring out a bottle of washing-up liquid to squirt over it all so that there can be no possible temptation to retrieve anything. Mrs. Next-Door-Who-Has-Never-Liked-Me appears out of nowhere. She thinks I'm jumped up. I *am* jumped up—it's called social mobility.

"The brown bin is only for food," she says. "You can't put the packaging in the brown bin. That goes in the green bin."

I restrain myself from squirting the bottle of washing-up liquid all over her. I stomp back into the kitchen and come out in a pair of Marigolds, and grimly I put the packaging into the correct bin.

"Happy now?" I ask.

"No," she says. "I'm never happy."

20:11

At what time is it acceptable to go to bed? I suspect nothing short of 10 p.m. will do. Okay, I can wait until 10 p.m.

20:14

I go to bed. I am my own person. I can do as I please. I am not hidebound by the silly, bourgeois rules of our society.

20:20–03:10

I can't sleep. I toss and turn for almost seven hours.

03:11

I go to sleep. I dream about Ned Mount. We're on a train and we're singing "Who Let the Dogs Out?" I have an unexpectedly melodic voice and he's very good at doing the barking.

> Getting better is easier if you actually want to get better.
>
> Extract from *One Blink at a Time*

S tella?" a voice asked. "Stella?"

I opened my eyes. A woman was standing over me and smiling. "Hi, there. Sorry to wake you. I'm Rosemary Rozelaar."

And?

"I'm your new neurologist."

I felt as if I'd had a hammer blow to my heart.

Rosemary Rozelaar smiled again. "I've taken over from Dr. Taylor."

Locked into my motionless body I stared at this woman with her bland, pleasant smile.

I hadn't seen Mannix Taylor for ten days—not since that strange visit on Christmas night, when his wife had materialized.

In theory, I shouldn't have expected to see him—all but the most routine hospital care had been suspended until the first Monday in January. But he'd taken such a personal interest in my case that I felt the normal rules didn't apply. And that business with his wife showing up on the ward was too weird. Everything felt strange, made ragged by the abrupt way he'd legged it, and some sort of explanation was needed.

Each day in the dead zone between Christmas and New Year I'd been tense and expectant, and the more time that passed without Mannix Taylor appearing, the angrier I became. I spent long hours in my head practicing all the different ways I'd ignore him when he eventually *did* show up.

But he didn't come. And now this woman was telling me that he wouldn't be coming again.

"What's happened?" I began blinking frantically.

"Hold on," Rosemary said. "Dr. Taylor has told me how you communicate by blinking. If you just bear with me, I'll find something to write on."

She twisted around, looking for a piece of paper. She didn't even know about the notebook in the sterilizer, and I couldn't help but think that Mannix and I would already be six sentences in at this stage.

My head was racing. Maybe Mannix had cut down on his hours? Maybe he'd had some tragedy and had to give up work entirely?

But even then I knew.

Rosemary had finally located a piece of paper and a pen and, with tortuous slowness, I managed to ask the question "WHY HAS HE GONE?"

"Caseload," she said. But there was something shifty in her eyes. She wasn't exactly lying because she didn't know the full story. But she wasn't exactly telling the truth either.

"I'm a highly experienced neurologist," she said. "I share a practice with Dr. Taylor. I can assure you, you'll get the same quality of care from me as you did from him."

I wouldn't. He had gone above and beyond the call of duty.

"I NEED TO SPEAK TO HIM," I spelled out.

"I'll convey that to him." And, again, there was that look in her eyes, almost of pity: *You haven't gone and got a great big crush on our Mannix Taylor, have you?*

She turned her attention to a computer printout. "So I see that movement is returning to several of your muscle groups," she read. "Why don't you show me what you can do and we can use that as a platform to build on."

I shut my eyes and folded myself deep inside my head.

"Stella. Stella? Can you hear me?"

Not today.

I was incredibly depressed. I couldn't figure out exactly what had gone on with Mannix Taylor and me, but I felt rejected and humiliated on an epic scale.

Days passed and Rosemary Rozelaar dutifully visited, but she never mentioned Mannix and I resolved to never ask about him again.

Soon Rosemary began to express dismay at how my recovery had slowed down. "On your chart it shows you were doing very well before Christmas."

Was I?

"You're going to have to work at this, Stella," she said, quite sternly.

Am I?

"Is there anything you'd like to ask me, Stella?" She had her pen poised over a sheet of paper but I refused to blink. There was only one question I wanted the answer to; I'd already asked it of her and I wasn't going to mortify myself by asking again.

Later that day, Karen came to visit. "*Wait* till you see who's in *RSVP*!" She shoved a magazine in front of my face and there was a photo of Mannix Taylor (41) and his lovely wife, Georgie (38), at some New Year's Eve ball.

Mannix was wearing a black dicky bow and looked like a man facing a firing squad.

"Happy little bunny, isn't he?" Karen said. "You never told me his wife was Georgie Taylor."

That's because:

A) I am mute,

B) I didn't know Georgie Taylor was "someone."

Karen had never actually met Georgie Taylor but she knew everything about anyone worth knowing and, to my shame, I was ravenous for information.

"She owns Tilt," Karen said.

Tilt was a boutique specializing in those odd asymmetrical Belgian designers. I'd gone there once and tried on an enormous, cripplingly expensive, lopsided coat made of gray carpet underlay. The sleeves had been attached with giant staples. I'd stared at myself in the mirror, desperately trying to love the coat, but I'd looked like an extra from a medieval drama that featured lots of stumpy-looking peasants who had walked long distances on bad roads.

"Fabulous looking, isn't she?" Karen ran her professional eye over the photo. "Eye lift, jaw lift, Botox round the eyes, fillers in the marionette lines. Not much. A natural beauty. No kids," she added, meaningfully.

I already knew that.

"They're that type, you know," she said. "Kids would interfere with their skiing in Val d'Isère and their last-minute weekends in Marrakech."

I said nothing. Because obviously I was unable to. But it struck me how little we know about people. How we so often buy the surface story they sell us.

"And she's not thirty-eight, she's forty."

I knew that but how on God's earth did Karen?

"Enda's sister works in the passport office. She saw Georgie's application for her new passport. Saw that she's really forty even though she's going round town telling everyone she's thirty-eight. Fair enough, we all lie about our age."

I managed to ask Karen how long the Taylors had been married.

"I don't exactly know," she said, turning information over in her head. "A good while. It's not a recent thing. Seven years? Eight? At a guess, I'd say eight." Suddenly she narrowed her eyes. "Why do you want to know?"

Just making conversation . . .

Her face cleared, then she looked almost angry. "You fancy him."

I don't.

"You'd better not," she said. "You've got a good husband who's killing himself to keep everything going. You know he went out to buy tampons for Betsy?"

Christ. Would I never hear the end of how Ryan had gone out to buy tampons for Betsy? It had become like a tale from Irish mythology. Great deeds done by Irish men: Brian Boru fighting the Battle of Clontarf; Padraig Pearse reading the Proclamation of Irish Independence on the steps of the GPO; Ryan Sweeney buying tampons for his daughter, Betsy.

And here came the mythological hero himself.

"Hi, Ryan," Karen said. "Here, have my chair. I'll go now."

Ryan sat down. "Fecking January. It's freezing out there. You're lucky to be here in the warm all the time."

Lucky? Am I?

"So you'll be wanting news, I suppose," he said. "Well, the tiles for the hotel in Carlow still haven't left Italy. Can you believe it? Oh," he said, suddenly remembering something. "I went to that place last night."

What place?

"You know, Samphire, the restaurant you gave me the voucher for. I went with Clarissa. A quick bite after work. God, talk about overrated."

Anger roiled in my gut. You selfish prick, I thought. You selfish, selfish prick.

Friday, 6 June

06:01

I wake up and I want to die—I'm in carb withdrawal. I've been here before and it's horrible. I have no energy and I have no hope. Down in the kitchen is 100g of cottage cheese that I am entitled to for my breakfast but I can't be bothered.

Instead, I pick up my iPad and peruse the Ryan situation. He's posted hundreds of items for his giveaway and his four video blogs have been watched hundreds of thousands of times. The media coverage is worldwide and every piece is positive. There's talk of "the New Altruism" and "Altruism in a time of Austerity."

09:28

I'm in the kitchen, gazing at a small bowl of cottage cheese and trying to muster the will to eat it, when the doorbell rings.

I tiptoe into the front room and take my sneaky cowboy-in-a-shoot-out look out of the window and almost collapse when I see that it's Ned Mount. From the telly. From *Saturday Night In*. Ryan must have put him up to this!

And yet I open the door. Because I think warmly of him. He'd interviewed me on the radio when *One Blink at a Time* came out and he was generous and kind. And he'd given me a water filter. Although, actually, I'd only dreamed that, hadn't I . . . ?

"Hello," I say.

"Ned Mount." He sticks out his hand.

"I know."

"I wasn't sure you'd remember me."

"Of course I remember you." I have a wobbly moment when I fear I'm going to tell him about my dreams. "Come in."

"Would that be okay?" He's twinkly-eyed and smiley. Because that's his job, I remind myself.

In the kitchen, I make a pot of tea. "I'd offer you a biscuit," I say.

"But I'm doing a carb-free thing and I had to clear the house of nice stuff. Would you like some cottage cheese?"

"I don't know . . . Would I?"

"No," I admit. "You wouldn't."

"So you're back living in Dublin," he says. "I thought we'd lost you to the States."

"Well." I squirm. "Between one thing and another . . . Anyway, I'm guessing you haven't just dropped in for a bowl of cottage cheese."

"That's right." He nods, almost regretfully. "Stella . . ." His look is sincere. "What can I do to persuade you to come on the show with Ryan tomorrow night?"

"Nothing," I say. "Please. I can't do it. I can't go on telly. Everything's too—"

"Too?" he prompts, his eyes kind.

"I can't sit there and pretend everything is good . . . when everything is bad."

I've said too much. Ned Mount's antennae are on the alert and I'm on the verge of tears.

"Look." I try to regain control. "I don't think Ryan is doing the right thing. I'm worried about him. I think he's having a breakdown or something."

"So come on the show and say that."

I take a moment to reflect on how utterly shameless they are, media people. No matter what way you try to wriggle off the hook, they always manage to shove you back on it again.

"You'd get your say," he says. "I'm sure lots of people would agree with you."

"They wouldn't. I'd be the most hated person in Ireland. Ned, I just want a quiet life."

"Until the next time you have a book to promote?"

"I'm sorry," I say. "I really am."

I'm distracted by a strange lurching sound in the hall. It's Jeffrey. He bursts into the kitchen, looking wildly disheveled. His gaze flicks from me to Ned Mount but he doesn't seem to be actually registering either of us. "I danced nonstop for twenty-two hours." His voice is hoarse. "I saw the face of God."

"Go on." Ned Mount leans forward with interest. "And what was it like?"

"Hairy. Really hairy. I'm going to bed." Jeffrey departs.

"Who was that?" Ned Mount asks.

"No one." I feel intensely protective of Jeffrey.

"Really?"

"Really."

We stare each other out.

"Okay." I give in. "He's my son. He's Ryan's son. But, please, Ned, don't try to make him go on the telly. He's only young and a bit . . ."

"A bit . . . ?"

"A bit, well, into yoga and . . . vulnerable. Just leave him alone. Please."

13:22

In its weekly online poll, *Stellar* magazine has voted Ryan Sweeney the sexiest man in Ireland. There's a photo of him looking like Tom Ford's less handsome brother. Interestingly, in at number nine, also a new entry, is Ned Mount.

You can flirt with danger but you can pull back from the brink.

Extract from *One Blink at a Time*

Mannix Taylor never came back and I stayed horribly angry with him. He was the one who had complained about the hospital system being inhumane, but he'd abandoned me. He hadn't even said good-bye.

As the days went by, Rosemary Rozelaar was in despair at how my progress had stalled. Eventually my condition became such a worry that even the elusive Dr. Montgomery visited to deliver a rousing speech. "What did I say the first day I saw you?" he demanded of me. "I said, 'Keep her going there, Patsy.' Come on! Don't fall at the final hurdle! Keep her going there, Patsy!" He swept his arm out to encompass his retinue and the nurses and Ryan, who happened to be visiting. "Come on, lads. Say it with me. 'Keep her going there, Patsy.'"

Dr. Montgomery and goofy Dr. de Groot and all the ICU nurses chanted, "Keep her going there, Patsy."

"Louder," Dr. Montgomery said. "Come on, Mr. Sweeney, you've to say it too."

"Keep her going there, Patsy!"

Dr. Montgomery cupped a hand around his ear. "I can't hear ye."

"Keep her going there, Patsy!"

"Louder!"

"KEEP HER GOING THERE, PATSY!"

"Once more for luck!"

"KEEP HER GOING THERE, PATSY!"

"Good." Dr. Montgomery beamed. "Good. That should do the trick. Lord, would you look at the time. The fairway beckons! God bless!"

I turned my gaze inward. My name was not Patsy and I would not be keeping anything going. Not here, not there, not anywhere.

On 15 February everything changed: I suddenly decided to get better. Ryan had given me nothing for Valentine's Day, not even a card, and I saw, with chilling clarity, how my life was slipping away. Ryan was bored with me being sick and so were the kids, and, if I didn't rally soon, there would be nothing left to return to.

And there was something else—I wanted to get out of the hospital, away from the system and the illness that had made me vulnerable to whatever strange stuff had gone on with Mannix Taylor. I knew that when I was better he would no longer have any power over me.

I took charge of my recovery and, almost overnight, my improvement began. I started blinking instructions all day long and my new steeliness must have been evident because everyone obeyed me. I requested and got strong painkillers when my freshly covered nerves started itching and burning. I alerted Rosemary Rozelaar to each new twitch in my muscles and insisted that a physiotherapist come every afternoon to help me to exercise. In the evenings, when the physio left, I kept at it, flexing and squeezing my muscles until they gave up with exhaustion.

The hospital staff had no other case to compare me against but, still, I knew they were amazed by my sudden steep recovery arc.

By early April, the muscles of my ribs and chest were strong enough for me to be taken off the ventilator, first for five seconds at a time, then ten seconds, then whole minutes. Within three weeks I was breathing unaided and I was moved from intensive care to a regular ward.

In May, I stood up and walked a step. Soon I was moving around, first in a wheelchair, then with a frame, then with a single crutch.

Another massive milestone was the return of my voice. "Imagine if you started talking all posh," Karen said. "Like the way people's hair grows back totally differently after chemo? What if you sounded like something out of *Downton Abbey*. Wouldn't that be a gas?"

The last muscles to recover were the ones in my fingers, and the first text I sent felt like a miracle.

By late July, I was deemed well enough to go home and a small army of staff turned up to wave me off—Dr. Montgomery, Dr. de Groot, Rosemary Rozelaar and countless nurses, porters and aides. I scanned the faces, wondering if he might appear. There was no sign of him, but by then I'd made peace with it.

Something weird had happened between us, I was able to acknowledge. There had been some connection—in fact there had been ever since the car crash. In the aftermath of the collision, we'd had a few seconds of communicating almost psychically.

It was natural that I'd got a little crush on him—I was vulnerable and he was my noble guardian. As for him, he was carrying some heavy burdens and the project of curing me had given him a focus.

He'd done the right thing by cutting me dead. I was committed to Ryan and my family, and clearly Mannix was committed to his wife.

Things in life, relationships, they don't "just happen." You can flirt with danger, you can test the edge of your marriage, and you can pull back from the brink. You get a choice; he'd made that choice and I respected him for it.

On 28 July, almost eleven months since the tingling had first begun, I saw my bedroom again. I'd missed a whole academic year in my children's life, but I resolved to not be sad. The only way to do this was to slot back as quickly as possible into my life, to be the best wife and mother and beautician that I could be. So I did, and I forgot all about Mannix Taylor.

Monday, 9 June

07:38

I wake up and I can hear the telly on in the sitting room. Jeffrey must be up. Assailed with dread, I go downstairs and sit beside him on the couch.

"It's started already," he says, tonelessly.

Ireland AM is on and Alan Hughes is reporting from Ryan's street.

"I'm live from Ryan Sweeney's Day Zero." Alan Hughes is almost shouting with excitement.

Day Zero actually started last night—a few early birds came in vans and slept overnight outside Ryan's house. It's like the first day of the sales.

Alan is interviewing some of the hopefuls and asking what they have their eye on. "His kitchen table," one woman says. Another says, "His clothes. He's the same size as my boyfriend. He's up in court a lot for petty crime, so he could do with some nice suits."

In the background is a cordon of police in high-viz jackets. After Ryan's dazzling appearance on *Saturday Night In*—yes, in the end the interview went ahead without me—the authorities realized that this thing had the potential to turn into a stampede. So ground rules have been laid down: people will be admitted in batches of ten, they will be permitted to stay in the house for a mere fifteen minutes and allowed to take only what they can physically carry.

"The atmosphere here is very festive!" Behind Alan Hughes's head, three men are passing, a king-size mattress hoisted onto their shoulders. "Hello there, gentlemen. I see you got yourselves a bed."

"We did, we did!" The men lean in to talk into Alan's microphone. But the mattress is heavy and wobbly and, because the men have ceased their steady forward propulsion, it starts flipping and flopping and then topples to one side, knocking Alan Hughes over and pinning him to the ground.

That bit is funny.

07:45

"I'm Alan Hughes, reporting live from under Ryan Sweeney's mattress."

We can hear him, but we can't see him.

"This is horrific." Jeffrey makes a low moaning noise.

"One, two, three, HEAVE!" Several men work together to lift the mattress up onto its side and to free Alan Hughes and his microphone.

Alan Hughes gets to his feet, looking tousle-haired but in good form. "That was a gas," he says. "Has anyone a comb?"

"Jeffrey," I say, "I had a very difficult labor with you."

Jeffrey is silent, but his mouth goes tight.

"It was agony, so it was."

"What do you want?"

"It was long; it was twenty-nine hours—"

"And they wouldn't give you an epidural," he says. "I *know*. What do you want?"

"Go to the Spar and buy me some Jaffa Cakes."

I will start my protein thing again tomorrow. But today? Today is impossible.

08:03–17:01

Jeffrey and I keep vigil as, all day long, various radio and TV stations cross live to Project Karma. Now and again, Ryan himself appears, full of smiles and saying how delighted he is with how it's all going. Sometimes the interviewers praise him; sometimes they can barely hide how insane they think he is.

It is mortifying, depressing and actually very boring. And gets more boring as the day goes on and people emerge with smaller and crappier things: tarnished spoons; decommissioned mobile phones; keys to garden sheds that no longer exist.

A sense is building that the end is in sight. At about five in the evening, a young woman comes out of the house and holds up a jar of olives to the camera. "This is the very last thing. The eat-by date is two years ago."

"Hold on," Jeffrey says. "Dad's coming out."

And sure enough, here's Ryan. He stands in the street outside the house that is no longer his.

"Look at him," Jeffrey says. "The prick. I bet he's going to do a speech or something."

Ryan savors his moment. He spreads his arms wide and announces to the media of the world, "I stand here before you with nothing."

People applaud and Ryan does an aw-shucks smile and gives a humble little namaste bow, and I am filled with *enormous* smacky rage for him.

Then someone calls out, "You're still wearing your shoes."

Ryan looks slightly disconcerted.

"That's right," another voice comes from the audience. "You're still wearing your shoes."

"Okay," Ryan says, expansively. "Fair point." He takes off his shoes and they promptly disappear into the crowd.

"And his clothes," someone else says.

"And your clothes," a louder voice calls. "You can't say you have nothing while you're still wearing clothes."

Ryan hesitates. Clearly he hadn't expected this.

"Go on," someone shouts. "The clothes."

Ryan is starting to look a little rabbit-in-the-headlights, but he's come this far, he has no choice but to go to the very end. He unbuttons his shirt and flings it toward his audience with a certain amount of pizzazz.

"Keep going!"

Ryan's hands go to his waistband.

"God, no," I whisper.

Ryan unzips his jeans and shimmies out of them, then whips his socks off and casts them toward the mob.

All that remains are his black underpants. Ryan pauses. The people are holding their collective breath. Surely he won't . . .?

"He won't," Jeffrey pleads.

I stuff another Jaffa Cake into my mouth. He won't. I swallow down the Jaffa Cake and shove in another one. My fear is extreme. He won't.

He will! In a teasing fashion, Ryan begins to roll his underpants down, revealing his pubic hair. A good half of his penis has appeared before an onlooker cries, "Breach of the peace!"

To be accurate, it's public indecency, and the coppers are on top of Ryan before his testicles appear.

Jeffrey is howling in distress and Ryan is being led away, covered in a police blanket. Immediately, pixelated images of his penis are zipping around the world. People in Cairo, in Buenos Aires, in Shanghai, in Ulan Bator, you name it, they're all getting a look at my ex-husband's penis. (But not in Turkmenistan, the voiceover tells us. Apparently they're not allowed to look at penises on the telly there.)

17:45
Ryan spends the night in a police cell and is let off with a warning. A thoughtful member of the public delivers his shoes and clothes to the station.

Tuesday, 10 June

07:07

In the bright, early morning air, Ryan stands in the street outside the police station and waits for the universe to provide.

But it doesn't.

HIM

You know the way when celebrities split up with someone and two seconds later they're going out with someone else but they're super keen to let everyone know that there was no overlap? Yes?

Well, they're probably lying . . .

It was one night in March, almost eight months since I'd come home from hospital. Ryan and I had gone to bed around eleven and I'd tumbled down into a deep sleep; I was back at work full-time and I was always bone-tired.

Sometime, in the darkness of the night, I woke up. I glanced at the alarm clock—03:04. Obviously my insomnia was paying a visit and I prepared myself for a couple of sleepless hours, then I realized that what had woken me was a small, sharp, cracking noise. I listened hard, all my muscles tensed, wondering if I'd imagined it.

Ryan was still sound asleep and I began to settle back into slumber when I heard the noise again. It came from the bedroom window, and Ryan bolted awake. "What was that?"

"I don't know," I whispered. "I've heard it a couple of times."

I reached to turn the light on. "Don't," Ryan said urgently.

"Why not?"

"Because if someone's breaking in, I'm going to surprise them."

Oh God, no. I didn't want Ryan to be a have-a-go hero. It would end badly.

He leaped out of bed and went to the window and looked out into the dark front garden.

"There's someone down there!" He narrowed his eyes. A small amount of light was coming from a street lamp.

"Should we ring the police?" I asked.

"It's Tyler!" Ryan gasped in outrage. "What the hell's he doing here at this hour?"

Tyler was Betsy's boyfriend. She was in the throes of her first proper love affair, and Ryan and I thought it was sweet. Well, at least until tonight, we did.

Another crack sounded.

"He's throwing stones," Ryan said.

"What have we done?" Clearly I watched too many dramas about wrongly accused pedophiles being hounded out of villages.

"Ssssh," Ryan said. "Sssssh. Listen."

Then I heard it: the sound of Betsy giggling. "Come up," she said, her voice carrying on the cold still air.

I tiptoed to the window and watched in disbelief as Tyler took a determined run at the house and got several feet up the wall before falling back to the ground.

"Fuck this!" Ryan began stomping about, looking for clothes to put on.

"I'll handle it." I hated being seen without my makeup—even a bit of mascara would have helped—but Ryan was too much of a hothead for this.

I swept down the stairs in my robe and opened the front door. "Hi, Tyler."

"Oh, hi, Mrs. Sweeney."

I was watching for signs—was he drunk, was he stoned? But he seemed his usual self-possessed, handsome self.

"Can I help you?" I asked, mildly sarcastically.

"I just wanted to say hey to Betsy."

I looked up at Betsy's bedroom, just in time to see her hurriedly closing her window.

"Will you come in for a cup of tea?" I asked.

He smiled. "Aw, hey, it's a bit late."

"That's right," I said firmly. "It *is* late. Would you like me to drop you home?"

"It's okay, Mrs. Sweeney, I've got my car." He indicated with his thumb over his shoulder. And despite how farcical this all was, I couldn't help a ping of pride that my daughter's boyfriend had his own car.

"Okay. Well. Please go home. School tomorrow. Betsy will see you then. Goodnight, Tyler."

"Night, Mrs. Sweeney."

I raced up the stairs and into Betsy's room, where she was pretending to be asleep.

"I know you're faking," I said. "And this isn't over."

Back in our bedroom, Ryan was furious. "Standing down there like fecking Romeo. And then trying to climb up the side of the house like . . . like . . . Spiderman!"

I was desperate to go back to sleep. I was always so tired. "We'll deal with this in the morning."

"You'd better talk to her," Ryan said. "I mean, about contraception. I don't want her coming home saying she's up the duff."

As advised by the experts I had regular "chats" with Betsy, where I tried to discover if she was sexually active. But she'd held on primly to her virginity—she and her girlfriends used words like "skanky" and "slutty" about any of their classmates who were putting it about; I was often glad I hadn't known them when *I* was seventeen.

Every time we had "the talk" I impressed on Betsy that when she really "cared" about the boy, she needed to go on the pill. But I realized now that, because she'd been prudey for so long, I'd thought she would always be that way.

"Could we do it together? Both of us?" I asked Ryan.

"Have you *any* idea the pressure I'm under? *You* have the talk. I've a job. I'm busy."

"Okay. Sorry." I had a job too but guilt had colored everything I'd done since I'd come home from hospital.

Next morning, I was awoken by Ryan, fully dressed, leaning over me. "You make sure you have that chat with Betsy," he said. "Unless you want to be a granny before you're forty."

Then he thumped down the stairs and slammed the front door with such force that the house nearly fell apart.

I dragged myself out of bed and knocked on Betsy's door. "Can I come in, honey?"

She looked up warily.

"You and Tyler." I sat beside her on her bed. "It's great to see you so happy. But your dad and I, we just want to make sure you're keeping yourself safe."

"Safe?" Comprehension dawned. "You mean, like . . . ?"

I shrugged. "Contraception of some sort."

She looked luminous with revulsion.

"If you like," I said tentatively, "we can go to Dr. Quinn—"

"Mom, you're disgusting." She shoved the heels of her hands into her eyes and shrieked. "You and Dad have been talking about this?"

I nodded.

"That. Is. Super. Gross." She sat up in the bed and said, "I need you to leave my room."

"But, Betsy, we're only trying to help—"

"You're in my space!"

"But—"

"Out!" she screeched.

"I'm sorry." I'd try again later, when she wasn't so emotional. I scuttled out and bumped into Jeffrey.

"Good job!" he said. "Uncle Jeffrey has a nice ring to it. And do you want to be Grandma Stella? Or just Granny?"

"There was a time," I said to him, "when you loved me so much you wanted to marry me."

I went downstairs and sat in the kitchen and shakily sipped a cup of tea.

Our small house crackled with tension and I was trying to remember if it had always been so combative. Perhaps this amount of family narkiness was normal? Maybe during those months I'd spent in the hospital I'd idealized our life?

But in my heart I knew the truth: they didn't even know it themselves, but Ryan, Betsy and Jeffrey were angry with me for all that time I'd been sick. Jeffrey held the worst grudge; he seethed with a variety of unpleasant emotions. Now Betsy was acting out and I had to admit that Ryan and I weren't doing so well either.

In the past I used to joke that we never had sex, but now we *really* never had sex. Shortly after I came home from the hospital we'd done it once; that was more than seven months ago and there had been no action since.

Sitting at my kitchen table, I had a moment of real cold fear. Something had to be done. Somehow I had to seize control and fix things.

Date Night was the answer. Ryan and I needed a few hours away from the kids and their fluctuating emotions. Nothing elaborate. None of that stuff that Karen and Enda had done, with the wigs and the false identities. Just reconnecting over a nice dinner and a few drinks. I might even buy new knickers . . .

Fired with desperate hope, I asked Karen if she'd babysit, then I got onto the Powerscourt Hotel because that's where everyone went on Date Night. I booked a room for Thursday, two days away. No point in dithering. Things needed to get back on track and fast.

I rang Ryan, who answered by saying, "What now?"

Trying to sound minxy, I said, "I hope you haven't got plans for Thursday night."

"Why? Who wants me to do what?"

"You and I, Ryan Sweeney, are going on Date Night."

"We haven't got money for Date Night."

Financially we were in poor shape—my year off work had knocked a big dent in things and two months ago the most recent tenants had given notice on the house in Sandycove and we hadn't yet found replacements.

"Sometimes you have to prioritize," I said.

"Date Night is too cheesy."

"We're going on Date Night," I said, grim and defiant. "And we're going to have a great time."

On Thursday afternoon, I got my hair blow-dried and I packed a little bag with a nice dress and high heels and—yes—some new knickers. Karen arrived and we had a glass of wine in the kitchen while I waited for Ryan to pick me up.

Jeffrey eyed my hair and my overnight bag and said, with a sneer, "You're pathetic."

"If you were my child," Karen said, "and you spoke to me that way, I'd give you such a clout, you'd be seeing stars for a week."

"You would?" Jeffrey seemed slightly in awe.

"I would and it wouldn't do you any harm. Might teach you a bit of respect."

"But you can't," Jeffrey said. "There are laws."

"More's the pity."

My phone rang. Ryan. I stood up and reached for my case. "It's Ryan. He's probably outside."

I hit answer. "I'm on my way out."

"No. Wait. I'm delayed. You drive down yourself and I'll be with you as soon as I can."

"When will that be?" A slide of disappointment began.

"I don't know. As soon as we sort out this problem with the bath. It's too big to get through the doorway. Someone fucked up on the measurements and—"

"Okay." I didn't need to hear any more. During my marriage to Ryan I had heard every Great Bathroom Disaster story there was. They had lost their power to enchant.

"Okay, Karen," I said. "I'm off. Thanks for doing this. Don't let Betsy out. Don't let Tyler in. If the chance comes up, talk birth control to Betsy—"

"A good clout is what she needs too. And that Tyler. I'd clout the lot of them if I had my way. They'd all be seeing stars."

As I drove the half-hour journey to Powerscourt I repeated over and over in my head, I am cheerful. I am cheerful. I am cheerful. I am on my way to a date with a sexy man.

It was actually better that I was driving myself, I decided. We would arrive separately, as if we barely knew each other.

I checked into the hotel and rattled around the lovely room, feeling like a bit of a fool. I sat on the bed, I admired the view, I looked at the cost of the Pringles in the minibar and wished someone was with me to share my outrage at the hefty price.

After a while, I decided to go to the Jacuzzi and told myself that when I got back, Ryan would have arrived.

But my time in the Jacuzzi was an anxious one, not just because I was afraid my freshly blow-dried hair would get splashed, but because I really wasn't a fan of water—and when I returned to the room, Ryan still wasn't there. Tired from waiting, I lay down on the bed, and the next thing I knew, Ryan was standing in the room. I'd fallen asleep.

"What time is it?" I asked, groggily.

"Ten past nine."

"Oh. Oh, we've missed our dinner." I sat up and tried to be awake. I reached for the phone. "We can still go. Hold on."

"Ah, no, don't. We'll just get room service."

"Really? But the restaurant is so nice—"

"It's too late, I'm too tired."

To be honest, I was too tired also, so we ordered BLTs and a bottle of wine and ate in silence.

"The chips are nice," Ryan said.

"The chips *are* nice." I seized on this conversational gem.

"Check with Karen, would you? Make sure Tyler hasn't sneaked in and isn't impregnating our daughter as we speak."

"Let's leave it for tonight."

"I can't relax, thinking about it."

I swallowed a sigh and rang Karen.

"Everything okay?"

"Grand."

But I'd picked up something in her tone. "What?"

"Well, I had a chat with Betsy. And she *is* doing the business with your man Tyler."

"Jesus Christ." I mean, I'd known but I hadn't wanted to.

"They're using condoms."

Oh. I felt like crying. My little girl.

"I've told her she needs to be on the pill. She said she'll go to the Well Woman, but not with you."

"Why not?"

"Because all teenage girls are little bitches. She says she'll come with me. I'll bring her next week."

"Oh. All right." This was a lot to process and I was trying to not take it personally. "And how's Jeffrey?"

"Jeffrey? Jeffrey is a little bitch too."

I hung up, sick at heart, and turned to give Ryan the news, only to discover that he'd crawled under the duvet and was fast asleep.

Okay. I was very tired myself. But tomorrow morning, come hell or high water, we'd have high jinks.

We had breakfast in bed. We sat in white towelling robes, eating fresh pineapple and sipping coffee.

"This is nice," Ryan said, demolishing a Danish pastry. "Almond, is it? Are you eating your one?"

"Ah no, you have it."

"Thanks. And what's this? Some sort of muffin?" He ate his way steadily through the pastry basket, then groaned, "God, I'm full." He lay down and rubbed his stomach and I snuggled closer and began to untie the knot on his robe.

He tensed and leaped out of bed. "It's too fakey! I can't relax. I'd rather be at work."

"Ryan—"

He hurried toward the bathroom and, in an instant, he was in the shower. Within seconds he was back out and pulling on his clothes.

"You don't have to leave," he said. "We have the room till twelve, right? Have a massage or something. But I'm going to work."

The door slammed behind him. I waited for a few minutes, then slowly I began packing up my stuff and I went to work too.

When I arrived, Karen was at the computer. "I thought you weren't coming in until this afternoon?"

"Date Night ended early."

"Oh. Anyway," she said, in a strange, clipped way, "you know who has a new boyfriend?"

"Who?"

"Georgie Dawson."

"Who?"

"You might know her better as Georgie Taylor."

After a silence I asked, "What are you telling me?"

"That Mannix Taylor and his wife are separated. They're getting divorced."

"*Why* are you telling me?"

Her face was unfriendly. "I don't know. I'm wondering if you knew about it."

"Are you insane? I haven't seen him in . . ." I counted back. "More than a year. Fifteen months."

Karen did a couple of angry clicks with her mouse. "That nutter Mary Carr is coming in this afternoon for a growler wax."

"There was nothing between me and him," I said.

"Why the woman with the hairiest growler in Ireland has to pick us for a wax . . ." she muttered. "There was, Stella." The planes of her face were hard in the light cast by the screen. "I don't know what, exactly. But there was." She looked concerned. "You know that in real life you'd never be suited?"

"I know." I'd never confess to a crush. Or whatever it had been.

"He's posh and cranky . . ."

"Ryan's pretty cranky too."

"Ryan is great."

"He is," I said. "Did you know that while I was in hospital, he went out one night and bought tampons for Betsy?"

"Yeah, I did—Oh, haahaa," she said, sarcastically. "You're a gas."

"Tell me, how am I fixed today? Have I lots of appointments? Have I time to see Dr. Quinn?"

"What do you want to see him for?"

"Because I'm always tired."

"Everyone is always tired."

"You're not. Anyway, I just want to check I'm okay. That the Guillain-Barré thing isn't coming back."

"It's not coming back. It's so rare it's a total freak that you got it in the first place. But," she said, "it's a slow day. Go ahead."

Dr. Quinn took bloods. "You might be anemic," he said. "But maybe you should have a checkup with your consultant in the hospital. Make the appointment today because it'll be ages before you get a slot. That's consultants for you," he said, wistfully. "They work about half an hour a week. The rest of the time they're out playing golf."

I swallowed. "Who should I see? The overall consultant? Or the neurologist?"

"I don't know. The overall lad, I suppose."

"Not the neurologist? Seeing as it was a neurological thing I had?"

"You're right. The neurologist."

I went out to the street to make the call. As soon as the number started ringing, I hung up. My heart was racing and my hands were sweaty. Fuck. What was I at?

I rang again and this time I waited until a woman answered.

"I need to make an appointment," I said.

"With Dr. Taylor or Dr. Rozelaar?"

"Okay . . . well . . . I was a patient of Dr. Taylor's first, then I was transferred to Dr. Rozelaar. I think the best thing is if you ask Dr. Taylor."

"I can't bother Dr. Taylor with an admin question—"

I interrupted. "Really. I think it's best if you ask him and he decides."

Something in my tone had an effect. "Give me your name," she said. "But be warned he has a long waiting list. I'll call you when I know."

I stood in the street, in the cold March afternoon, and went into suspended animation. About ten minutes later, the woman rang back. She sounded a little bemused. "I spoke to Dr. Taylor. He says it's him you should see. Unexpectedly, he has an opening today."

"Today?"

Okay.

It was easy to get off work. All I had to do was tell Karen that Dr. Quinn was concerned about a recurrence of Guillain-Barré and she was rushing me out through the door. She didn't want me getting sick again. It had been very inconvenient last time round.

I told Karen my appointment was with "the consultant" and she assumed I meant Dr. Montgomery because she smiled and said, "Say hello from me."

I didn't feel the need to set her straight.

The appointment was for four o'clock and I drove to Blackrock Clinic and parked and waited for myself to get out of the car. But I didn't.

I was astonished at what I was contemplating. But what exactly *was* I contemplating? And what was Mannix Taylor at?

Maybe he'd given me the speedy appointment out of professional concern. That was the most likely explanation.

But what if he hadn't?

What if there was more than that?

There was a good chance I was being delusional. I knew how life worked—people ended up with partners with the same "rating" as them: people from the same socioeconomic group, with the same education level and the same type of good-lookingness. Mannix Taylor and I were from different worlds. I was considered pretty in an unremarkable, regular-featured sort of way, whereas he wasn't conventionally handsome but he was . . . sexy. Yes, there, I'd admitted it to myself for the first time: he was sexy.

Or at least he had been the last time I'd seen him, fifteen months ago.

When I had been very sick and therefore probably not the most reliable of witnesses.

It was five to four now, I needed to get moving. I looked up at the building. He was in there somewhere. Waiting for me.

Even thinking those words sent a shiver through me.

He was waiting for me.

And if I got out of this car and went in there, what would happen? Nothing, maybe.

Maybe Mannix Taylor wasn't looking for anything. Or perhaps, when I met him again, I wouldn't find him so . . .

But what if I did?

Then what?

I'd never cheated on Ryan. I'd never even been close. I mean, I'd had the occasional moment when a man reminded me that I was a woman. A few weeks ago, at a petrol station, a nice-looking man had engaged me in chat about my car—a dull-as-ditchwater Toyota—and when I realized that he was hitting on me, I'd driven away a bit flustered and pleased.

At the monthly-ish book club I was a member of, I joined in as enthusiastically as everyone else, raving about who we'd ride if we got a one-night pass from our marriage. In fact, that was *all* we did at the book club—none of us read the books, we just drank wine and talked about holidays we couldn't afford and wondered if Bradley Cooper was a "hammer" man or a "soft and gentle" boy.

And had Ryan ever cheated on me?

I didn't know. And I didn't want to know. Certainly he'd had plenty of chances, a lot more than me. He was often away from home and there were times when I'd wondered how he'd managed his sexual impulses while I'd been in hospital . . . and how he was managing them now, seeing as he didn't want to have sex with me anymore.

For a moment I saw my life from the outside and I went cold with fear. Seven months without sex was a long time in a marriage. A relationship of twenty years, you don't expect that you'd still be ripping the clothes off each other, day and night. Everyone went through dry spells but, still, seven months was a long time.

Maybe Ryan was having an affair? There were times when I wondered about him and Clarissa. But Ryan seemed too bad-tempered—if he was cheating on me, wouldn't he be feeling guilty and sporadically showering me with flowers and affection?

At the moment my radar with Ryan was way off. I'd tried with our crappy date night and it had been an epic fail.

And here I was, still sitting in my car, and it was one minute past four. I should get moving, but I was paralyzed with fear.

There was a chance that if I got out of my car and walked into that building, I'd be walking into another life. Or at least away from the one I had.

I let myself imagine being with Mannix Taylor, being the significant other of a neurologist and living somewhere beautiful and getting full custody of Betsy and Jeffrey and them loving Mannix and Mannix loving them and Ryan not minding any of it and all of us being friends.

I'd have to deal with Mannix's mad-spendy sisters and the gambling parents, of course, and maybe Georgie would be tricky, but no one's life is perfect, right?

But what if I went in there, to Mannix Taylor's office, and there was some sort of spark between us and we ended up having a fling that lasted about three weeks—short enough to mean nothing but long enough to totally destroy my family? That wouldn't be so good.

It was seven minutes past four. I was late now, properly late. He'd be starting to think that I wasn't coming.

I had to wonder what was wrong with me—was I bored? Did other women go through something like this in their marriages? Where they want to try out being someone else?

One thing I knew for sure: you only get one life. I remembered that occurring to me during my first night in the hospital, when I'd thought I was going to die: you only get one life and you should live it as happily as you can.

But sometimes your life isn't your own. I had responsibilities. I was married and I had two children.

I loved Ryan. Probably. And even if I didn't, I couldn't break up my home. Betsy and Jeffrey had gone through a horrible, scary time while I'd been in the hospital. In the ledger of life, I was in the red with them. Maybe forever.

I'd have to find some other way of filling the gap that seemed to be hankering after Mannix Taylor. I'd have to . . . get an interest. Maybe I'd do a course in Buddhism. Or meditation. Or perhaps give crochet a try.

I watched the entrance to the clinic and imagined Mannix coming out through the door and running toward my car and telling me that I had to be with him. Then I thought, Why would someone like him want to be with someone like you?

Fifteen minutes past four now. I made a bargain with myself—I'd count to seven and if Mannix didn't appear, I'd leave.

So I counted to seven and even though plenty of people exited the building—it was Friday afternoon, lots of the staff were heading home—none of them was Mannix Taylor.

I'd give it one more go of counting to seven, I decided. But he still didn't appear. Okay, one more go. On my eighth or maybe my ninth round of counting, I turned the key in the ignition and I started my car and I drove home.

The house was empty. Jeffrey was away on a school rugby trip. Betsy was at a sleepover with Amber, and she really *was* at a sleepover with Amber, and not off riding Tyler, because I'd checked with Amber's mum.

And where was Ryan? I hadn't heard from him all day, so I could only assume he was at work.

I opened a bottle of wine and tried to read but I couldn't concentrate. I thought about ringing Karen or Zoe, but I didn't know how to put my peculiar feelings into words.

It was nearly ten when Ryan came home and went straight up the stairs. I heard him thumping about, then came the sound of the shower running. Eventually he came down and into the front room. "Any wine?" he asked, staring at his phone in his hand.

I gave him a glass and said, "How was your day?"

"My day," he said, still looking at the phone, "was fucking shite."

"Was it?"

Clicking out a text he said, "All my days are fucking shite. I fucking hate my life."

A slow prickle lifted the hairs at the nape of my neck. "What do you hate?"

"Everything. I hate my job. I hate having to do fucking bathrooms. I hate the gobshites I have to deal with. I hate the suppliers who extort money from me. I hate my stupid clients with their stunted ideas. I hate—" His phone rang and he looked at the number. "Fuck off," he said, scornfully. "I'm not fucking talking to you." He threw the phone onto the couch and the ringing stopped after a while.

Ryan's rant about his job was a familiar one, but today was different because today I'd relinquished my imaginary life with Mannix Taylor in order to stay with him.

Suddenly I was light-headed—a lot of feelings had been stirred up by my visit to the Blackrock Clinic car park. I thought they'd been parceled away, but Ryan's sourness had set them free again.

"What about the kids?" I heard myself ask Ryan. "Do they make you happy?"

He looked at me properly for the first time since he'd come home. He seemed amazed. "Are you mad? Jeffrey's so narky. And Betsy's so fucking . . . *chirpy*. Well, she was until this bullshit carry-on with Tyler started. I mean, I love them, but they don't make me happy."

Then I said it. "What about me?"

A sudden wariness entered his eyes. "What about you?"

"Do I make you happy?"

"Course."

"No, do I? Do I really make you happy? Sit down, Ryan." I touched the couch. "And before you answer, can I say something? You only get one life."

He nodded, a little tentatively. "How do you mean?"

"I mean, you might as well be happy. So, I'm asking you, Ryan, do I make you happy?"

After a long, long pause he said, "When you put it like that . . . no. You don't make me happy. I mean," he added quickly, "you don't make me *un*happy. I don't mind you."

"Right."

"You shouldn't have got sick," he said, in a sudden burst of anger. "That's what's put the kibosh on things."

"Maybe."

"Definitely."

This was the most honest we'd been with each other in years.

"I know you haven't asked," I said. "But you don't make me happy either."

"I don't?" He seemed amazed. "Why not?"

"You just don't."

"But . . ."

"I know. You're great. And the way you stood by me all that time I was in the hospital . . . You're great, Ryan." I didn't even know if I was being sincere. I was, in a way.

"And—" he said.

"I know. The way you went out and bought tampons for Betsy. Not many men would do that."

Some empty moments ticked by and he said, "So what are we going to do?"

I could hardly believe the words even while I was saying them. "I think we're going to split up."

He swallowed. "That seems a bit . . . like . . . extreme."

"Ryan, we don't have sex. We're like friends . . . who aren't very nice to each other."

"I'm nice to you."

"You're not."

"Jesus, I don't know about this, Stella. Couldn't we go for counseling?"

"Do you want to go for counseling?"

"No."

"Well, then."

"But won't I be lonely?"

"You'll meet someone else. You're good-looking, you've a good job; you're a catch."

A strange energy hopped up between us and this was the moment to ask if he'd ever cheated on me. But I didn't want to know. It no longer mattered.

"I'm forty-one," he said.

"Forty-one is young these days."

"And I need a certain type of woman," he said. "Someone who knows I'm an artist. I don't mean to sound like it's all about me, but . . ."

"Don't worry. There are millions of suitable women out there."

"What about the kids?"

I fell silent. This was my biggest worry. "They'll be very upset. Or maybe they won't." Then I started to rethink things. "Maybe we should wait? Until they're a bit older? Until Jeffrey is eighteen?"

"More than two more years? Ah no, Stella. They say it does as much damage to children to be brought up in a loveless marriage as to come from a broken home."

Loveless? We were moving further and further into uncharted territory.

"Who gets custody?" he asked.

"We'll share it, I suppose. Unless you want full custody?"

He exclaimed. "Are you joking me?" In a calmer voice he said, "No, no, we'll share it. I can't believe we're talking about this." He looked around the room. "Is this really happening?"

"I know what you mean. I feel like I'm dreaming. But I know it's real."

"When I woke up this morning in the hotel, I had no idea that this evening . . . I thought we were grand. Well," he qualified, "I never thought about it at all. How will we manage for money?"

"I don't know. I don't have all the answers. We've only just decided this. But we're luckier than lots of people. We've got the place in Sandycove." Suddenly the fact that we hadn't been able to get new tenants seemed like divine endorsement for our separation.

"When you say we're splitting up?" he asked. "Do you mean we're getting divorced?"

"I suppose."

"Fuuuuck." He exhaled heavily. "Like, this isn't a trial thing?"

"It can be if you want."

He thought about it. "Ah no, we might as well go for it. No point in messing. I mean, everyone's at it." It was true that in our circle of friends, several couples had started divorce proceedings in recent months. "Like the way everyone was buying a holiday apartment in Bulgaria a few years ago. Sort of a zeitgeisty thing, yeah?"

"Maybe." For God's sake.

"Fair play to us for being so civilized," he said. "Not like Zoe and Brendan." Zoe and Brendan's separation was continuing to be very bitter.

"You don't seem sad." Ryan sounded accusatory.

"I'm in shock." Perhaps. "The grief will come. Are you sad?"

"A bit. Should I sleep on the couch tonight?"

"There's no need."

"Will we watch Graham Norton?"

"Okay."

We watched a bit of telly and around eleven thirty we both went to bed. Ryan undressed himself very prudishly, taking care to hide his nudity.

When we were both under the duvet he said, "Should we have sex for old times' sake?"

"I'd prefer if we didn't."

"Okay. Me too. But we'll have a snuggle, will we?"

"Okay."

The next morning, he said, as soon as we woke up, "Did I dream it? Are we really getting divorced?"

"If you want."

"Okay. Will I move out?"

"One of us will have to."

"I suppose it'd better be me. I'll move into the other house."

"Okay. Today?"

"Jesus, I haven't even had my first cup of coffee. And how come you're so calm?"

"Because it's been over for a long time."

"Why didn't we know?"

I thought about it. "You know the way we can see the light from the stars even though they're long dead? That's us."

"That's very poetic for you, Stella. Long dead? That bad. Wow." He rolled over onto his back and said, "Well, at least I'm a star."

Monday morning, first thing, Karen and I were getting set for our day when we heard a person coming up the stairs to the salon.

"Already?" I said. "Someone's in a hurry."

Karen saw the visitor before I did and her face became hard and unfriendly. "Can I help you?"

It was him. Mannix Taylor. Not in his hospital clothes but in the gray expensive-looking coat that he'd been wearing the very first time I'd seen him, when I'd driven my car into his.

"Can I see Stella?" he said.

"No," Karen said.

"I'm here," I said.

He saw me and the shock of our eye contact made me dizzy.

"What happened to you on Friday?" he asked.

"I . . . well . . ."

"I waited until nine o'clock."

"Oh." I should have rung. "I'm sorry."

"Can we talk?"

"I'm at work."

"Do you get a lunch break?"

"Have it now." Karen sounded angry. "Go and have your talk. But remember, mister," she stepped between Mannix Taylor and me, "she's married."

"Actually," I said, apologetically, "Ryan and I have separated."

Karen's face blazed white with shock. Never before had she been so wrong-footed. "What? When?"

"Over the weekend. He moved out last night."

"And you didn't tell me?"

"I was just about to."

She rallied with aplomb. "Just remember." She narrowed her eyes at

Mannix, then me, then Mannix again. "You two, and your little hospital romance—it's all in your heads and in real life you'd never be suited."

Out in the cold, blue March morning, I suggested we go to the pier. We sat on a bench and stared at the boats and I asked, "What's going on? Why did you show up at my work?"

"Why did you make an appointment with me on Friday? And then not come?"

"I heard that you and your wife have split up—"

"It's true."

"I'm sorry."

"It's okay."

"I wanted to see you. But then I was too scared."

"Right." After a pause he said, "Isn't it strange to be actually talking to each other in words and not blinks?"

"Yes." It had just dawned on me that we were communicating with our voices. "We were very good at the blinking." Suddenly I was exasperated by all our pussyfooting. "Just tell me," I said. "What happened? With us. In the hospital. I didn't imagine it, did I?"

"Nope."

"So explain it."

Staring out to sea, he was silent for a long while, then he said, "There was some sort of connection. I don't know how it happened but you became . . . the person I liked the most. Seeing you, it was the bright shiny part of my day, and when our appointment finished, all the sparkle went."

Oookay . . .

"On the home front, Georgie and I, we'd been trying so hard for a baby . . . babies. The IVF wasn't working, but even without kids I wanted to give me and Georgie my best shot. But I couldn't be fully with her while I was thinking about you. So I had to stop seeing you. I'm sorry I didn't explain. If I'd tried, it would have opened up too much stuff; it would have made it worse."

"And then what happened?"

"In the end we did six rounds of IVF and none of them worked," he said. "And Georgie and I, we just fell apart. I moved out about five months ago. We've applied for a divorce. She's seeing someone else now; she seems to like him."

"And is it shouty and bitter and all that?"

He laughed. "No. That's how over it is. No shouting or anything. I suppose we're . . . friends."

"Really? That's good."

"We've known each other since we were kids, our parents hung out together. I think we'll always be friends. What about you and Ryan?"

"He's moved out and we've told the kids. But it's all a bit freaky. Very freaky."

"Do you still love him?"

"No. And he doesn't love me. But it's okay." I stood up. "I'd better get back to work. Thanks for coming. Thanks for explaining. It was nice to see you."

"Nice?"

"Not nice. Really weird."

"Stella, sit down for a minute, please. Can we see each other again?"

I sat gingerly on the edge of the bench and, almost angrily, I asked, "What do you want from me?"

"What do *you* want from *me*?" he asked.

Startled, I studied him. I wanted to smell his neck, I realized. I wanted to touch his hair. I wanted to lick his . . .

"Answer me something," I said. "And please be honest. I'm not your type, am I?"

"I don't have a 'type.' "

I stared him down.

"No," he admitted. "I guess you're not."

"So the connection we had in the hospital—"

"And at the car crash," he said. "Even then, we were communicating without words."

"But the state of me while I was in hospital, with tubes in and out of me and my hair not washed and no makeup on and all, it wasn't like you fancied me?"

"No."

Oh.

"It's worse," he said. "I think I fell in love with you."

I hopped off the bench and put a bit of distance between myself and Mannix Taylor. I was shocked, then thrilled, then, very quickly, I began to wonder if he was mentally ill. I mean, what did I know about him, *really*? He could suffer from delusions or . . . episodes, or whatever it was that mad people got.

"I'm going back to work," I said.

"But—"

"No!"

"Please—"

"No!"

"Meet me later?"

"No!"

"For lunch tomorrow?"

"No!"

"I'll be here at one o'clock. I'll bring sandwiches."

I hurried back to the salon, where Karen fell on me like a hungry dog. "I rang Ryan." She spoke rapidly. "He says you really have split up. I didn't tell him Mannix Taylor had shown up here because why upset him with something that's not going to happen again? So what's going on?"

Around six o'clock the previous night, Ryan and I had had the historic talk around the kitchen table that sundered our little family. We'd given each other the nod, then asked Betsy and Jeffrey to turn off their electronic devices and sit with us, and they obviously sensed something serious was in the air because they complied without resistance.

I kicked off by saying, "Your dad and I, we love you both very much."

"But . . ." Ryan said. I waited for him to continue but he didn't, so it was up to me.

"Your dad and I have decided to separate, to . . ." It was hard to say because it was so momentous. "To split up."

Silence fell. Jeffrey looked sick with shock, but Betsy took it calmly. "I knew things weren't right," she said.

"Really? How?" Then I remembered the pep talks she used to give me when I was in the hospital, about how my illness would bring Ryan and me closer together.

"This is your fault," Jeffrey yelled at me. "You shouldn't have got that disease thing."

"That's what I said!" Ryan chimed in.

"It wasn't right long before the hospital," Betsy said. "Mom never got a chance to self-actualize. This marriage has always been about Dad. Sorry, Dad. I love you, but Mom was always playing backup."

I was amazed. Only a few days ago, Betsy had been a little girl who wouldn't discuss contraception, and now she'd morphed into a mature young woman with a greater understanding of my marriage than I had.

"Are you getting divorced?" Betsy said.

"It takes a long time, five years. But we're going to start the process."

"Are you getting lawyers?" Jeffrey demanded.

"It'll be very friendly."

"Is Dad moving out?" Jeffrey asked.

I looked at Ryan; he looked at me. Was this really happening?

"Yes," I managed to say. "He's going to stay in the house in Sandy-cove."

"And who do I live with?"

"Who do you want to live with?"

"You're not supposed to ask me questions like that. You're supposed to *tell* me. You're the parents!" He sounded tearful "I don't want to live with either of you. I hate you both. Especially you, Mom." He shoved his chair back and made for the door.

In a flash I decided to stay with Ryan. I was horribly frightened at what we'd unleashed. We couldn't do this to our children.

"Please, Jeffrey. Wait. Let's see. We can rethink things."

Ryan was starting to look a little sweaty.

"No," Jeffrey said. "You've said it now. You can't pretend it's okay when it's not."

"Exactly," Ryan said, a bit too quickly. "I know this is hard for you, mate, but life is full of hard lessons."

Slowly, Jeffrey sat down again.

"Mom and I are splitting up," Ryan said. "But it's really important that you know we love you."

"When are you moving out?" Jeffrey demanded of Ryan.

"Well, tonight. But it doesn't have to be. I can wait until you're ready."

"If you're going, you might as well go now." Jeffrey sounded like he was getting his lines from a soap opera. "Do you have a girlfriend?"

I watched Ryan closely. This was a question I, too, was interested in. "No."

"Are you going to marry her and have other children and forget all about us?"

"No! You'll see me as often as you see me now."

"Which is practically never."

In fairness, Jeffrey had a point.

"We're still a family," I said. "A loving family. You and Betsy are the most important people to us and that will never change. We're always here for you, no matter what."

"Exactly. Always here for you, no matter what. Well, there we are!" Ryan had the air of someone bringing an overrun meeting to a close. "Sad news, but we'll get through this, right?"

He stood up; our family roundtable had clearly come to an end.

"So . . . ah," Ryan said to me. "Will you help me get a few bits together . . . ?"

I packed his wheely case with enough clothes to get him through the next few days. The plan was that he'd gradually remove his stuff over several weeks. There would be no dramatic arrival of a removal van, we'd decided.

As he left, it nearly felt as if he were just going on a work trip and that everything was the same as it had ever been, that there hadn't been a seismic shift in all of our lives.

Jeffrey went straight to bed and I could hear him sobbing, but when I knocked on his door he yelled, his voice thick with tears, for me to go away.

Eventually I went to bed, but I couldn't sleep.

I'd had countless nights in that bed on my own while Ryan had been away on business; in theory, tonight shouldn't be any different. But everything had changed and I was overwhelmed with sadness. I remembered the girl I'd been when I first met Ryan—I was seventeen, the age that Betsy was now. Ryan and I had milled around in the same gang for a long time and even though I'd had a couple of boyfriends and he'd had a fair few girlfriends, I'd always fancied him. It wasn't just that he was good-looking, he was talented too, and when he started in art college I thought I'd lost him forever to those cool college girls.

But it didn't happen that way. He stayed in touch with his old friends and eventually he and I gravitated to each other and it hit us both hard. It was different from any other romance we'd had: it was real, it was serious, it was grown-up.

I'd been mad about him, absolutely wildly in love, and as I remembered how much I'd meant my marriage vows, I cried and cried.

At around 1 a.m. my phone rang; it was Ryan. "Are you okay?" he asked.

"Sad, you know . . ."

"I just wanted to check something," he said. "We loved each other once, didn't we?"

"We really loved each other."

"And we still love each other now? Sort of? Just in a different way?"

"Yes." I was choking with tears. "Just in a different way."

We hung up and I cried even harder.

"Mom?" Betsy was at my bedroom door.

She tiptoed across the floor and got into bed beside me and snuggled her body into mine, and sometime late into the night I fell asleep.

O n Tuesday morning, I checked my appointments: I had nobody in at one o'clock.

"Is it okay if I go to lunch at one?" I asked Karen.

"Are you mad? That's our busiest time."

"Grand," I said, mildly. We'd see.

While I was waiting for my ten o'clock appointment, I decided to give myself a pedicure. As I exfoliated my feet with vigor, Karen watched me with narrowed eyes. "You're putting a lot of work into that. You make sure you charge yourself for it."

"I'm equal owner of this salon, Karen. I know our system."

"It's all going to go horribly wrong, you know."

"What is?"

"Whatever is going on with you and Mannix Taylor."

"Nothing's going on."

"You've lost your mind. Splitting up with Ryan."

"It's been over for a long time with Ryan."

"Things were grand before Friday. Until you heard Mannix Taylor was single."

"What color should I do my toes?"

She clicked her tongue and left the room.

By one fifteen, no walk-ins had appeared, so I grabbed my coat and said to Karen, "I'm going out." Then I belted down the stairs before she could stop me, wondering if he'd still be there.

When I saw him sitting on the bench, staring out to sea, I felt like I'd had a blow to my chest. I was as breathless as if I were fourteen and this was my first-ever date. It was dreadful.

At the sound of my footsteps, he looked up. Gratitude seemed to wash over him.

"You came," he said.

"You waited," I replied.

"I've already waited a long time for you," he said, "what's another half hour?"

"Don't say things like that." I perched on the edge of the bench. "It's too . . . slick."

"I've brought sandwiches." He indicated a brown paper bag. "Let's play a game."

Startled, we looked each other in the eye. We both swallowed hard.

I cleared my throat and asked, "What's the game?"

"If I've managed to bring your favorite sandwich, you meet me again tomorrow."

"I like cheese," I said cautiously. I was afraid of him producing turkey and cranberry, my most hated.

"What kind of cheese?" he asked.

"Any kind."

"Go on. Be specific."

"Mozzarella."

"I got you mozzarella and tomato."

"That's my favorite," I said, almost fearfully. "How did you know?"

"Because I know you," he said. "I *know* you."

"Jesus Christ," I muttered, pressing my hand over my eyes. This was way too heavy.

"And," he added, almost breezily, "I bought eight sandwiches. One was bound to be something you like . . . but just because I made sure I was right doesn't mean it wasn't meant to be. Either way, it means you've got to meet me again tomorrow."

"Why? What do you want from me?" I felt on the edge of tears. Five days ago, I'd been a long-term happily married woman.

"I want . . ." He looked into my eyes. "You. I want, you know . . . The usual."

"The usual!"

"I want to lay you down on a bed of rose petals. I want to cover you with kisses."

That silenced me for a while. "Is that from a song or something?"

"I think it might be Bon Jovi. But I'd still like to do it."

"What if you're a weirdo who only likes me mute and paralyzed?"

"We'll soon find out."

"But what if I've started to like you?" It was already way too late for that. "In all seriousness, do you do this sort of thing a lot?"

"What? Fall in love with my patients? No."

"*Are* you a weirdo?"

After a pause, he said, "I don't know if this counts, but I'm on anti-depressants."

"For what?"

"Gout."

He laughed and I stared at him.

"Depression," he said. "Mild depression."

"This isn't funny. What sort of depression? Manic?"

"Just the ordinary kind. The kind that everyone has."

"I don't."

"And maybe that's why I like you."

"I have to go back to work."

"Take a sandwich for your sister. I've got six spares. Go on." He showed me the inside of the paper bag, which was indeed rammed with sandwiches. I took a beef and horseradish and put it in my bag along with my own uneaten one.

"See you tomorrow," he said.

"You won't."

Back at the salon, Karen greeted me sourly. "How's Mannix Taylor?"

"He sent you a present." I smirked into her baleful face and handed over the sandwich.

"I never eat carbs."

"But if you did, beef and horseradish would be your favorite."

"How did he know?" She was interested, despite herself.

"That's the kind of man he is." I shrugged, like it was no big deal.

He wants to lay me down on a bed of rose petals and cover me with kisses, I told myself. In which case I'd want to get busy. I went at my bikini area with the laser, then did a full agonizing half hour of the anti-cellulite machine on my thighs, then—disregarding all safety regulations—immediately gave myself a full-body spray tan.

Wednesday was another dry, bright-blue day, very unusual weather for Ireland. Cold, though, bitterly cold. But I couldn't feel it even though I'd worn my not-warm, show-off coat that I only ever wore from car to restaurant, just long enough for everyone to say, "God, your coat is gorgeous!"

Once again I was almost thirty minutes late, and yet there he was, sitting on the bench, staring out to sea, waiting for me.

"I have your sandwich," he said.

I accepted it without enthusiasm. There was no point; I couldn't eat it. I'd barely been able to swallow a mouthful since Monday.

"Can I ask you things?" I said. "Like, where do you live now?"

"Stepaside. A rented flat. Georgie has the house. Until we sort out all the . . . you know, legal stuff."

"Where's the house?"

"Leeson Street."

Almost in the city center. Not in a rural retreat near the Druid's Glen, like I'd imagined. All that detail I'd put into the life I'd invented for him . . .

"No one else talked to me in the hospital," I realized. "You were the only one who treated me like an actual person." Then I remembered something. "Apart from Roland. How is he?"

"Doing really well. Working. Paying off his debts. Not buying twelve pairs of shoes in one go. He often mentions you."

Lovely Roland. "Tell him I said hello."

But as I remembered how frightened I'd been through those long weeks and months I'd been in the hospital, I began to feel irrationally angry with Mannix. "I was like a prisoner, wasn't I?"

He looked surprised and I replied for him. "I was!"

"But . . ."

"And you were like my jailer, the good-cop one who shoves pieces of bread under the door." My anger grew. "I was vulnerable. And you took advantage of that. I want to go now."

I was on my feet and he stood up too, anxiety all over his face.

"Tomorrow?" he asked.

"No. Definitely not. Maybe. I don't know." I hurried away and immediately became entangled with a number of gangly, untucked schoolboys who were clearly on the mitch.

On Thursday morning, I said to Karen, "I won't be going out today at all."

"Good," she said, with satisfaction.

"You can take the day off, I'll cover everything."

"I'm not taking the day off, you eejit. Paul Rolles is booked in for a back, sack and crack wax at one o'clock."

Brightly, I said, "I'll do that."

"He's my client," Karen said. "He's decent, tips big and he trusts me."

"Let me do him today. You can have the tip anyway."

"Okay."

At one o'clock I welcomed Paul in and got his clothes off and got him up on the bed and started whipping strips off his back, and as I thought of Mannix sitting on the pier, waiting with my sandwich, I felt very pleased with myself and my iron willpower.

I was chatting away with Paul, a cat lover, and I was doing the automatic-pilot thing that counts as beautician talk: "Go on." "Did she?" "Climbed the curtains all by herself?" "God, that's a gas." "She sounds like a right mad yoke!"

But my head was elsewhere. This Paul was a big bloke and even though I was going at warp speed, waxing him was taking a long time. As I painted on molten wax and pressed down the fabric strips, then whipped them off, I was like a wire that was stretching tighter and tighter. "Stick your bum up, good man. I'll just get in between your—" Paint, press, whip. Paint, press, whip. PaintPressWhip. PaintPressWhip.

It was about ten to two when, coming at Paul's testicles from the rear, the wire inside me snapped. "I'm really sorry, Paul, but I'm going to ask my sister to step in to finish you off."

"What—" Paul sat up on his elbows, his bare bum in the air, looking very vulnerable.

"Karen?"

She was on her stool, at the desk.

"Karen." My voice was high and wobbly, "Would you mind stepping in and tidying up Paul? All done except the . . . you know, last bit. I've suddenly remembered that I need to pop out."

Her eyes blazed with rage but she couldn't berate me in front of a customer.

"Of course," she said, through lips that didn't move.

I was already pulling on my coat. I hurried down the stairs, trying to put on lip gloss as I ran.

It was almost two o'clock and he was still there.

"So?" he said.

"So I'm here." I sighed and buried my face in my hands. "I wasn't going to come. I can't do my job. I'm going to vomit. This is horrible."

He nodded.

"It's not horrible for you!" I said.

"How do you think I've felt sitting here, thinking you weren't going to come?"

"*Don't* make me feel guilty."

"Sorry. I'm sorry." He touched my hair and said, "It's so pretty."

"Really? I just washed it this morning and put the GHD through it."

"GHD?"

"I'm a beautician," I said, defiantly. "Welcome to my world."

On Friday morning, Karen said, "Will you be meeting him today?"

"Nothing happens," I said defensively. "We just sit and talk."

"How long can that go on for?"

"Forever."

But it couldn't. When I arrived at our bench, Mannix said, "Can you believe the weather?"

"We're talking about the weather?" I was almost contemptuous. But I looked up at the sky—it was still freakishly bright blue and cloud free, like God was conspiring to bring Mannix and me together.

"One day soon it'll rain," Mannix said.

"And . . . ?"

The meaningful look in his eye made me scoot along the bench, away from him.

He too scooted along the bench and he grabbed my wrist. "We'll have to meet in another place."

"And . . . ?"

"Exactly," he said. "And . . . think about it."

I looked at my lap, then gave him a sideways glance. He meant the bed of rose petals and everything that went with it.

Then my attention snapped to something else entirely—I'd just seen someone I knew. It was so unlikely that I had to be imagining it. But I looked again and it was definitely him: Jeffrey.

Horrified, my gaze locked with his.

I stammered, "You . . . you should be at school."

Jeffrey looked from Mannix Taylor to me and yelled, "And you should be a proper mom. I'm telling on you!"

"I haven't done anything!"

Jeffrey ran off and, wild-eyed, I said to Mannix, "I have to go."

I chased after Jeffrey and he must have heard me because he stopped and whirled around.

"They saw you," he shouted. "The guys in my class."

What guys? Then I remembered the gang of schoolboys I'd bumped into the other day, and I could have wept. They'd been in Jeffrey's class? How about that for awful luck? With a sinking heart, I realized that my bad deeds would always be found out.

Shame washed over me. Shame and sorrow for Jeffrey. "Sweetheart, I'm sorry, please—"

"Get away from me. You whore!"

All hell broke loose. A deputation showed up at the house to shout at me—Ryan, Mum, Dad, Karen and—of course—Jeffrey. Even Betsy turned on me. The gist of their complaint was that Ryan had stood by me during a lengthy illness and I had repaid his loyalty by starting a thing with my neurologist.

It was no good trying to remind anyone—including Ryan—that Ryan no longer loved me. He was the one who had done the "Standing By." A very visible thing, "Standing By." They'd all seen him—juggling everything, working himself into the ground, gray in the face from exhaustion and worry. And don't forget he'd bought tampons for Betsy. Imagine! A man! Buying tampons! For his daughter!

"You lied to me." Ryan had high patches of color on his cheeks. "You tried to make out that we just don't love each other."

"We don't."

"But, all along, you had someone else."

"I didn't. I haven't."

"Jeffrey told us what he saw."

I checked that the kids weren't in earshot and I muttered, "Nothing has happened."

"Yet!" Karen exclaimed. "Nothing has happened *yet*!"

I was distracted by thumping noises coming from upstairs. Jeffrey and Betsy were up there—what the hell were they doing?

"We couldn't cope with this Taylor chap in our lives," Mum said.

"You don't have to!"

"We like to laugh at people," Dad said. "We're well able to mock Ryan here—no offense, son, but we make fun of you all the time. And Karen's Enda, even though he's a copper, he's comical, in his way. But this Taylor chap is a different prospect. He has . . . *gravitas*."

"Is that the same as 'cojones?'" Mum asked, in a quiet aside.

"It's not." Dad sounded exasperated. "Cojones is different."

"Although he has them too," Ryan said. "Putting the moves on my sick wife. On my *paralyzed* wife."

"He *didn't*!""

"The thing is," Mum explained, anxiously. "We'd have to invite him into our house. And it's too small!"

"For what?" I asked. "What are you planning to do? Hold a dance for him?"

"Your mother and I have discussed this," Dad said. "The only way we could avoid inviting him over is to burn the house down."

"You live in a terrace," Jeffrey said, walking past them, trundling a suitcase. "You couldn't do it to your neighbors. Is the car open, Dad?"

"Here, take the remote." Ryan handed Jeffrey the key fob.

Betsy appeared. She too was rolling a suitcase.

"What's going on?" I cried out.

"We're going to live with Dad," Betsy said. "We're leaving you."

And off they went, every single one of them, leaving me all alone.

All alone, and upset and confused and ashamed and defiant.

All alone with smooth, callous-free feet. And a bald bikini area. And a gleaming golden tan.

I'd done nothing wrong, and yet everyone was judging me—damned if I do; damned if I don't.

So I might as well "do."

"Mannix, I want to see you."

"Okay. Where? Do you want to go for a drink?"

"No." I was rooting through my underwear drawer. "I've had enough of this bullshit."

"What bullshit is that?"

"Come on, Mannix."

"Okay. I've had enough of this bullshit too."

I dressed in the underwear I'd bought for my date night with Ryan. No point in being sentimental, they were the only sexy things I had. I covered myself in gleamy body lotion and shoved my feet into a pair of very high shoes, then took a quick glance in the full-length mirror.

Right. I'd had two children, I'd been with Ryan for a long time and I'd let things slip. I was thirty-nine and even at my best I'd never have passed for a model.

I was seized with knuckle-gnawing regret that I hadn't done daily Pilates for the past twenty years. Christ, how hard would it have been? A mere thirty minutes a day would have kept the wolf from the door. And yet I hadn't bothered, and now I was paying the price.

I forced myself to stop agonizing about my stomach and my age and all the chances I'd wasted to be Elle Macpherson. Mannix had seen me with tubes coming out of most of my orifices so anything I offered him tonight had to be an improvement.

I put on my blue Vivienne Westwood dress that covered my knees and that draped flatteringly across my stomach—I knew Karen thought I was a fool, but that dress had been worth every penny.

The decision between stockings or tights threatened to trigger another head melt, so I decided to dispense with both. Quickly, like it was no big deal, I slipped off my wedding ring and engagement ring and let them fall into a drawer, then, before I could talk myself out of it, I ran down the stairs and into the cold night.

Mrs. Next-Door-Who-Has-Never-Liked-Me was standing in her front garden, in the dark. "What's going on?" she asked. She must have seen the drama earlier, with Betsy and Jeffrey leaving with their suitcases. "I should tell you, Stella, that your clothes are completely unsuitable for this weather."

"It's okay," I said, opening my car door. "I don't plan on wearing them for very long."

Mannix's flat was on the second floor in a massive new development. I had to walk down a cruelly bright, undecorated corridor, in my crippling shoes, for what seemed like miles.

Finally I got to 228. I knocked on the bland fiberboard door and he opened it immediately. He wore a loose shirt and faded jeans and his hair was messy.

"I feel like a prostitute," I said. "And not in a good way."

"Is there a good way?" He handed me a glass of wine and shut the door behind me.

I glanced anxiously over my shoulder. "Make me feel trapped, why don't you?"

"I . . ."

"Karen says there *is* a good way, about the prostitute thing." I couldn't stop talking. "Role play, you know?"

"How about we just be ourselves for tonight?" He took me by the hand and tried to lead me forward. "I didn't have time to get the rose petals. I wasn't expecting this—"

"Never mind the rose petals." I choked down a massive slug of wine. "Where's the bedroom?"

"You're keen."

"I'm not," I said. "What I am is scared. I'm scared out of my wits." My voice was getting faster. "It's twenty years since I've been with someone else. This is a big deal for me. I'm this close to losing my nerve."

I stood in the hall and glanced into the kitchen, the bathroom and the front room, all furnished in nothing-y neutrals. There was a bare, unfinished look about them, as if he'd never bothered to fully move in.

"Is this the bedroom?" Tentatively, I pushed open a door.

Mannix glanced in at the bed, an anonymous affair covered with a white duvet. "Yes."

"It's too bright in there. What's the story with the lights? Is there a dimmer switch?"

"No . . . Look, Stella, please, come in, sit down in the front room. Take a few breaths."

"We'll have to do it in the dark."

He shook his head. "I'm not doing it in the dark."

"Have you a lamp? Get a lamp. There must be a lamp." I'd noticed one in the front room. "There's one. Go on. Get it."

While he unplugged the table lamp and moved it into the bedroom, I stood in the hall, drinking my wine and tapping my foot. When Mannix switched on the lamp and turned off the overhead bulb, the bedroom hummed with rosy, forgiving light.

"That's better." I handed him my empty glass. "Any more?"

"Yes, of course. I'll just . . ." He went into the kitchen and when he came out again, I was in the bedroom, perched anxiously on the bed.

He gave me my glass and asked, "Are you sure about this?"

"Are you?"

"Yes."

"Then let's go." I took a massive mouthful of wine. "By the way," I said, lying myself on the bed, still wearing my shoes, "I'm not a big drinker. Don't let me get too drunk."

"Okay." He removed the glass from my hand and set it on the floor. Quickly, I reached down and took another swig, then handed the glass to him and lay down again. "The first time is bound to be the worst." I looked up at him for reassurance. "Right?"

"It's not meant to be unpleasant," he said.

"I know, I know. That's not what I meant. Just, I need you to be the way you were in the hospital."

"And you're the one who's worried that I'll only fancy you if you're mute and paralyzed?"

"I just mean, I need you to take control."

After a beat, he asked, softly, "You want me to take control?"

I nodded.

Slowly he began to unbutton his shirt. "You mean like this?"

Jesus. Mannix Taylor was unbuttoning his shirt in front of me. I was about to have sex with Mannix Taylor.

He shrugged off the shirt in a rustle of cotton and I reached up and touched his skin, stroking my hand from his neck to his collar bone. "You have shoulders," I said in wonderment. And he had hard pecs and an enviably flat stomach.

I wanted to lighten the mood by saying, "Not bad for a forty-something." But I couldn't speak.

"Now you." He was removing my shoes.

"No," I said anxiously. "They need to stay on. To create the illusion of elongating my legs."

"Shhh." He took my right foot in his hands and placed it in his lap and pressed both thumbs into the arch. He held them still for a moment, the pressure a strangely pleasurable sort of pain, then he began to slide his hands along the length of my foot, stretching the tendons beneath the skin. I closed my eyes as thrills moved through me.

"Remember this?" I heard him say.

I did remember—the one and only time he'd worked on my feet when he'd been my doctor. Something powerful had happened between us on that day long ago and he'd never done it again.

As he pressed and kneaded, my lips began to tingle and my nipples tightened and hardened.

With his thumbnail, he made little nips of bliss along the top of my big toe. The movements were tiny bites of delight. He placed his middle finger between my big toe and my second toe, wiggling until they began to spread, then he slid his finger into the space and a pulse of desire zipped straight to my lady center.

My eyes flew open and he was staring right at me. "I knew it," he said. "You felt it too? Back then?"

I nodded. "Jesus Christ," I whispered. I was absolutely on fire and we hadn't even kissed.

And then we did. I bent my right leg and reached up to him and pulled him down and we kissed for a long time. My foot was still in his lap and it was pressed up against something very hard. I pushed my foot even harder against it and he took a sharp breath.

"Is that . . . ?" I asked.

He nodded.

"Show me," I said.

He stood up. He opened the top button of his jeans and slowly unzipped himself until his erection burst out.

Naked, he stood before me, not a bit shy. "Now you show *me*," he said.

I began moving my dress up my thighs. "Are you sure we can't turn the light off?"

"Oh, I've never been more sure of anything." His eyes were a-gleam. "I have waited so long for this."

As I wriggled out of my dress he watched me like a hawk. The look on his face was so brazen and appreciative, and his lopsided smile so hot, that by the time I took off my bra I'd lost all self-consciousness.

He'd told me that he wanted to cover me with kisses and he did. Every part of me—my neck, my nipples, the backs of my knees, the insides of my wrists and where it mattered most. Every nerve in my body was lit up. A thought floated into my head—I was like the switchboard in *Jerry Maguire*—then floated away again.

"It's time for the condom," I whispered.

"Okay," he said, his breath hot against my ear.

Efficiently he snapped one on, and as soon as he entered me, I orgasmed. I clutched his buttocks and pressed his weight into me, almost unable for the intensity of the pleasure. I'd forgotten how fabulous sex could be.

"Oh God," I choked. "Oh my God."

"This is only the beginning," he said.

He slowed things down to a delicious agony. He was supporting himself on his arms, carefully moving in and out of me, watching me with those gray eyes of his.

I was in awe of his control. This was not a man who'd been deprived of sex for several months. But I wasn't going to think about that now.

Without taking his eyes from mine, he moved in and out of me until he'd brought me to another peak, even more powerful than the previous. Then again, and again.

"I can't take any more." I was drenched with sweat. "I think I'll die."

He picked up speed, moving faster and faster, until finally, thrashing and moaning, he came.

He lay on top of me, until his gasps had slowed down to regular breaths, then he rolled off and gathered me in his arms, my head on his chest. Immediately, he fell asleep. I lay still, stunned by wonder. Me and Mannix Taylor, in bed together. Who would have thought it?

After about half an hour he woke, still adorably sleepy. "Stella." He sounded amazed. "Stella Sweeney?" He yawned. "What time is it?"

There was an alarm clock on the floor. "Just gone midnight," I said. "Would you like me to call you a taxi?"

"What?" I hopped out of bed.

"I thought . . . you might like to go home."

I picked up my shoe and threw it at him.

"Jesus!" he said.

Jerkily I retrieved my shoe, then the other one and, mortified, I stepped into my knickers and dress. I shoved my bra in my handbag.

"I thought, with your kids and all," he said.

"Grand." I opened the front door, carrying my shoes in my hand. I wasn't going to wear those crippling fucking things.

I was still waiting for him to stop me, but he didn't, and as I made my way down the anonymous, sodium-lit corridor toward the lifts, I really *did* feel like a prostitute.

I fumbled in my bag for my phone and, almost in tears, I rang Zoe. "Are you awake?" I asked.

"Yeah. The kids are with Brendan and his bitch and I'm sitting here with my box set and my bottle of wine."

Twenty minutes later I was with her.

She took me in her arms. "Stella, your marriage has broken up, you're bound to feel lost and—"

I broke free of her embrace. "Zoe, can I ask you what the rules on dating are these days?"

"Same as they ever were. They fuck you once, then they never ring you again."

Shit.

"But it's a bit early to be worrying about that, yourself and Ryan have only just decided. I mean, you might even get back together . . ."

I was shaking my head. "No. No, Zoe. You know Mannix Taylor?"

"The doctor?"

"He came to see me in work on Monday."

"Monday just gone? Monday less than five days ago? And you didn't tell me?"

"Sorry, Zoe, it's all been a bit weird—"

She was quickly putting the pieces together in her head. "And you let him fuck you? Tonight? Oh my God."

"And then, after . . . he asked if he should call me a taxi."

Her face was a picture of compassion. "I'm sorry, Stella, that's how men are. You've been out of the game too long. You weren't to know."

My phone rang and I looked at the screen. "It's him."

"Don't answer it," she said. "He's just looking for another fuck."

"So soon?"

"He's the sort who'd be able to get it up four times a night. Mr. High Achiever. Mr. Alpha. Switch your phone off. Please, Stella."

"Okay."

Zoe did her best but she couldn't provide much comfort so I went home to my empty house and faced the facts: my marriage was gone, my kids were traumatized and everyone hated me. This was *exactly* my worst-case scenario. I hadn't even got three weeks out of it; I'd got one night.

I'd known in my heart that Mannix Taylor would humiliate me. Everyone had known it, that's why they'd all objected to him.

Wearily I wondered about myself and Ryan. Could we patch things up and carry on? It hadn't been a bad life; he wasn't a bad man, just selfish and, well, self-obsessed. But there was the small fact that I didn't remotely fancy him anymore. Even if I'd been able to fool myself up till now, my night with Mannix had ruined sex with Ryan forever.

Then again there was more to a marriage than sex. And maybe, if I got Ryan to wear a latex mask to look like Mannix . . .

It took me most of the night to fall asleep. It was probably gone six before I finally shifted into a strange, uneasy dreamland, and I was awake again by nine. Immediately I switched my phone on, because I couldn't not. Anyway, I had a legitimate reason: the kids needed to be able to contact me.

There were no calls from either of them, however there were eight missed calls from Mannix. Zoe would have deleted the messages without letting me listen to them, but Zoe wasn't there.

"Stella." In his first message, Mannix sounded touchingly contrite. "I called it wrong. You have kids and I was trying to let you know that I'm okay with it. Please get in touch."

His second message said, "I'm really sorry. Can we talk about it? Will you call me?"

His third message said, "I messed up. I'm very sorry. Please call." Then, "It's me again. I'm starting to feel like your stalker."

And, "I'm sorry for getting things so wrong. You know where I am."

The final three were hang-ups with no message. The most recent had been seven hours ago and I knew in my heart he wouldn't ring again. He wasn't the sort to prostrate himself; he'd done his bit, he'd decided. Then my phone rang and my heart nearly jumped out of my mouth.

It was Karen. "I was talking to Zoe," she said. "She told me what happened."

"Are you calling to gloat?"

"Not gloat exactly. But, Stella, get a grip. He's not for you. This is the man who was married to Georgie Dawson. *Georgie Dawson*. Do you hear me? Compared to her, you're just . . . you know." Earnestly she said, "I'm not putting you down, Stella, but she'd know about art and that stuff. She can probably speak Italian. She can probably stuff quails. What can you do? Apart from waxing growlers?"

"I read books," I said, hotly.

"Only because Dad makes you. You're not a natural. Georgie Dawson is a natural."

She sighed.

"Here's how it is, Stella: you've fecked things up royally. I was talking to Ryan and he won't take you back—"

The cheek of her!

"But you've got Zoe, right? The pair of you can hang out together. Let yourselves go. Wear flat shoes. Give up on your stomachs. Think of all the cake you can eat . . ." For a moment she sounded wistful. "And hear me on this, Stella." She was utterly sincere. "I know your kids hate you now but they *will* forgive you. Come on," she cajoled, "no one could take Ryan full time. Okay?"

She hung up and I called Betsy. The phone rang twice, then went abruptly to message—she'd rejected my call. Then I rang Jeffrey and the same thing happened. It cut like a knife.

I forced myself to ring them both again and I left faltering, abject messages. "I'm sorry for all the upheaval I've caused. But I'm here for you, day or night, no matter what."

After I finished speaking I decided to put a wash on, but when I went to the laundry basket I found it almost empty—only my clothes were in it. The kids and Ryan had taken their dirty clothes with them. With a pulse of shock, I realized that now there was nothing for me to do. I *never* had nothing to do. But there was no washing and ironing to be done and no chauffeuring Betsy and Jeffrey around to their various weekend commitments. Under normal circumstances, it was a constant battle to keep on top of the massive mountain of jobs that had to be done in a day. Without Ryan and the kids, my life seemed to have no scaffolding.

I went back downstairs and lay on the couch and contemplated: as Karen said, I really *had* fecked things up royally.

But maybe, in the bigger scheme of things, everything that had happened was meant to have happened. Maybe Mannix Taylor was just a catalyst, a cosmic device to show me that I didn't love Ryan anymore. Sometimes things fall apart so that better things can fall together— Marilyn Monroe had said that. Mind you, look at how she'd ended up . . .

And maybe I was wasting my time trying to make sense of things: sometimes things don't happen for a reason, sometimes things just happen.

It felt like forever since I'd had this much time alone. It reminded me of when I'd been in the hospital and my thoughts had had to race around and around in my head, with no way out, like rats in a run.

At some stage I rang Zoe, who answered after one ring. "You haven't rung him?"

"No."

"Listen to me—no drive-bys, no texting, no sexting, no calling and no tweeting. You *cannot* get drunk. That's when you'll be at your weakest."

But there was no chance any of those things would happen. I had pride, a lot of it.

The day was over and it was already dark when the doorbell rang. For a long time I thought about just staying on the couch and ignoring it, then it rang again. Reluctantly I hauled myself to my feet, and when I found Mum and Dad on my doorstep I refused to acknowledge the wash of disappointment.

"'Ask not for whom the bell tolls,'" Dad said. "'It tolls for thee.'"

"We brought bagels," Mum said.

"Bagels?"

"Isn't that what they do in films to show they care?"

"Thank you." I surprised myself by bursting into tears.

"Ah, come on now." Dad put his arms around me. "You're gameball, you're gameball, you're gameball."

"Come into the kitchen." Mum switched lights on and led the way down the hall. "We'll have tea and bagels."

"How do you eat them?" Dad asked.

"You toast them," Mum said. "Don't you, Stella?"

"You don't have to." I tore off two sheets of kitchen paper and convulsed into them.

"But they'd be nicer?" Mum said. "They would, they'd be nicer. Warm is always nicer. We're here to say we're sorry, Stella. I'm sorry, your father's sorry, we're both sorry."

Dad was at the toaster. "They're too fat. They won't fit."

"You've to slice them first," Mum said. "To halve them, like."

"Is there a knife?"

"In the drawer," I said, thickly.

"I'm on your side," Mum said. "So is Dad. We just got a fright. All of us."

"It was a shock," Dad said, jamming bagels into the toaster. "And we let you down. Your mother let you down."

"And your father let you down."

"And we're both sorry."

"Everything will be grand," Mum said. "The kids will get over it. Ryan will get over it."

"In the fullness of time, everything will be gameball."

"Is Mannix Taylor your boyfriend?" Mum asked.

"No." A thin stream of evil-looking black smoke began to issue from the toaster.

"Will you get back with Ryan?"

"No." The black smoke was starting to billow.

"Well, no matter what happens, we love you."

A high-pitched, ear-piercing noise started up: the fire alarm was going off.

"We're your parents," Mum said.

"And I think we've broken your toaster, but we love you."

Despite invitations from Zoe, Karen and Mum and Dad, I spent Sunday entirely alone. I decided the house needed to be cleaned—properly cleaned, in the way it hadn't been in over a decade—and I seized on the job with relief. Zealously, I scrubbed the kitchen cupboards and tore at the oven and went at the grouting in the bathroom with such vigor that the knuckles on my hands reddened, then cracked. Despite the pain, I kept scouring, and the more my raw hands burned, the better I felt.

I knew what I was doing: I might as well have taken the scouring pad and bleach to myself.

It was just gone seven when Betsy called. I pounced on the phone. "Sweetie?"

"Mom, there are no clean clothes for school in the morning."

"Why not?"

"I don't really know."

Casting around for solutions, I asked, "Is it because nobody washed any?"

"I guess."

"So just wash some."

"We don't know how to work the machine."

"Ask your dad."

"He doesn't know either. He said to ask you."

"Oh? Put him on."

"He says he's never speaking to you again. Can you come here and do a wash?"

"Okay." I mean, I might as well, what else was I doing?

Fifteen minutes later, Betsy opened the door to me. Nervously, I stepped into the hall, braced for the wrath of Jeffrey and Ryan.

"They've gone out," Betsy said. "I have to call them when you've left."

I swallowed back the hurt. "Okay. Come into the utility room and I'll explain everything."

In under thirty seconds Betsy had grasped the workings of the washing machine and dryer, which were identical to the ones at home.

"It's really that easy?" she said, suspiciously. "Huh. Well, who knew?"

Something was troubling me. "If none of you know how to do this, how did you manage all the time I was in the hospital?"

Betsy thought about it. "I guess it was Auntie Karen and Grandma and Auntie Zoe who did the laundry."

But Ryan had got the credit. And now the gaps in his skill set were being exposed. And there was a shameful little part of me that was glad. Maybe Jeffrey and Betsy would see that I had *some* uses.

"So, Mom, you'd better go."

"Right." Then I flung myself at her and began to cry and said, "I'm so sorry," over and over again. "Call me if you need anything. Yes? Promise?"

I got into my car and headed for home, and in the light cast by a street lamp I saw Ryan and Jeffrey standing on a corner, their faces baleful. I knew I was being fanciful, I knew there was no way they were *actually* holding burning pitchforks and shaking their fists as they watched me leave, but that was the impression I got.

On Monday morning, I awoke to a silent house. I ached for the noise and fuss of a regular morning, getting Betsy and Jeffrey ready for school, getting myself ready for work. But there was nothing I could do, except wait things out.

I picked up my phone and stared at it. Nothing. No missed calls, no texts, nothing. I couldn't help thinking that Mannix Taylor might have tried a *bit* harder.

It was a relief to go to work, and for once I was in before Karen.

"Jesus!" She drew up short at the sight of me. "You're keen!"

"That's me."

"That delivery from SkinTastic had better come this morning," she said, and before she'd even finished speaking, the buzzer rang. "There it is. I'll go!" She raced away down the stairs. Karen would never pay for gym membership but she kept skinny by moving constantly. She considered it a sign of personal weakness to remain seated for more than seven minutes.

She reappeared, huffing and puffing up the stairs, carrying a large cardboard box. "Feck's sake!" She was struggling under the weight. "Lazy fecker courier fecked off. Just left this at the door, and it weighs an effing ton."

She dumped it on the desk and attacked the Sellotape with a Stanley knife. I waited for the litany of complaints that usually accompanied a delivery—according to Karen, the suppliers always sent the wrong quantities of the wrong products: they were cretins, gobshites, morons and fools.

"What the hell's this?" she demanded.

Obviously they'd got it really wrong this time. I feared for the rep who would feel the sharp side of her tongue.

"Look, Stella!" She was holding up a book, a small hardback. It looked like a prayer book or maybe a little collection of poetry. The cover was decked out in rose-gold and bronze swirls and it gave the impression of being expensive and beautiful.

"There's a load more in here, all of them the same." She did a quick count. "Looks like fifty of them. They must have been sent by mistake. But the box is addressed to you."

I took one of the little books and opened it at random. The paper was heavy and sheeny and sitting in the middle of a page, in graceful curlicues, were the words:

> *I'd give ten years of my life to be able to put on a pair of socks.*

"What's this?" I asked.

The next page said:

> *Instead of thinking, 'Why me?' I think, "Why not me?'*

I flipped to look at the cover, something I should have done straight away. The name of the book was *One Blink at a Time* and it was written by someone called Stella Sweeney.

"Me?" I was startled. "I wrote this? When?"

"What? You wrote a book? You kept that to yourself."

"But I didn't. Write a book, that is. Go to the front. See if there's information."

"There's an introduction."

Karen and I read it together.

> On 2 September 2010, Stella Sweeney, a mother of two, was admitted to a hospital, experiencing fast-moving muscle paralysis. She was diagnosed with Guillain-Barré syndrome, a rare autoimmune disorder that attacks and disables the central nervous system. As every muscle group in her body, including her respiratory system, failed, she came close to death.
>
> A tracheotomy and a ventilator saved her life. However,

for several months, the only way she could communicate was by blinking her eyelids. She was lonely, frightened and often in acute physical pain. But she never gave in to self-pity or anger, and throughout her hospitalization she remained positive and upbeat, even inspirational. This little book is a collection of some of the words of wisdom she communicated from her locked-in body, one blink at a time.

"Jesus!" Karen said, almost scornfully. "Is that you? It makes you sound like . . . Mother Teresa, or someone."

"Who did this? Who made it?" I flicked through more of the pages, utterly astonished to see things I'd allegedly said.

When is a yawn not a yawn? When it's a miracle.

I'd a vague memory of blinking that out to Mannix Taylor. And:

Sometimes you get what you want and sometimes you get what you need and sometimes you get what you get.

The only clue I could find was the name of the printers. I Googled their number and said to the woman who answered the phone, "I know this sounds odd, but can you tell me what you do?"

"We're a private publishing company."

"What does that mean?"

"The clients give us their manuscripts; they choose the paper, the font, the size, the jacket illustration—everything is bespoke and to a very high quality—then we print it."

"And the client has to pay?"

"Yes."

"There's a book with my name on the cover but I didn't order it." I was afraid I'd have to cough up for this and it looked terrifyingly expensive.

"May I take your name? Stella Sweeney? Let me see." Clicking noises followed. "*One Blink at a Time*? The order was placed and paid for by a Dr. Mannix Taylor. He took delivery of fifty volumes in September of last year."

"When you say 'volumes' do you mean 'books?' "

"Yes."

"So why did I get them today?"

"I'm afraid I don't know. I suggest you take that up with Dr. Taylor."

"But I'm never speaking to him again."

"Perhaps you should revisit that decision," she said. "Because I can't help you any further."

"So will the books be in the shops?" I was a little excited.

"We're a private publishing house." She sounded prim, even defensive. "Our volumes are simply for our clients' personal pleasure."

"I see." For a second there I'd thought I'd written a real book. The tiniest shadow of disappointment passed over me, then it moved on.

"Thank you." I hung up. "Mannix Taylor is responsible," I said to Karen.

"Well! Who knew you were that good in bed?"

"I'm not. He got them done last September."

She stared hard at me. Her forehead would have furrowed if it hadn't been injected into cowed submission. "He must . . . *like* you. Why?"

"Because I'm positive and upbeat, even inspirational. Allegedly."

"I'm the inspirational one."

"I know. So . . . ?" I asked. "What should I do?"

"I see your point. The recycling will cost a fortune, now that they've started to weigh the bins. Could you . . . I don't know . . . keep them for birthday presents? Gradually offload them that way?"

"I meant, what should I do about him?"

Her mouth tightened. "Why are you asking me? You know what I think."

"But you said it yourself: he must like me."

"You've got two children. Your responsibility is to them."

"He told me he loved me."

"He doesn't even know you."

Karen insisted our mobiles were powered off when we were "doing" someone; it was professional-seeming, she said. But at twelve thirty, when Betsy and Jeffrey were on their lunch break at school, I didn't have a client, so I switched my phone on to give them a quick ring. This was my campaign to win them back—to offer as much time as they needed as well as regular, non-guilting reminders of my love.

I said a little prayer that their angry hearts might have softened and I could hardly believe it when Betsy answered. "Hi, Mom."

"Hi, sweetie! Just saying hello. How's your day going?"

"Good!"

"Did you have lunch?"

"Yes, Mom," she said gravely. "And I got dressed this morning, and put on my shoes."

"Very good! Hahaha! And you had breakfast?"

"Sorta. You know Dad. He's a little domestically challenged."

This was *not* the time to start slagging off Ryan. Proceed with caution, I counseled myself. Keep it neutral. "Okay, well, call me if you need anything, if you want help with your homework, anything. Day or night."

"Okay. Love you, Mom."

Love you! This was an enormous leap forward.

Buoyed by this, I immediately called Jeffrey.

Oookaaay. Less of a leap forward. He was still refusing to talk to me. As was Ryan.

But, ever hopeful, I took a quick look at my messages. And there were four voice mails. All from Mannix Taylor.

I darted a fearful look over my shoulder—Karen would go ballistic if she caught me listening to them. Then a strange calm descended. I was a grown woman. Who only had one life. I was going to hear what he had to say and I'd take the consequences.

I got a bit of a land when the phone then started to ring. And it was him: Mannix Taylor.

Confidently, I touched the green light. "Hello."

"Hello?" He sounded surprised. "Sorry, I wasn't expecting you to answer."

"Well, there you go."

"Did you get the books?"

"What's that all about?"

"Meet me and I'll tell you."

I had a think about it. "Meet you where? I'm not going to your apartment. I'm never going there again. And no, you can't come to my house, don't even ask."

"Well, how about—"

"Fibber Magee's for a pint and a toasted sandwich? No. Some fancy restaurant for an awkward conversation with all of the waiters earwigging? No. The Powerscourt Hotel where I'd bump into every person I've ever met? No."

He laughed softly. "There's a holiday cottage in Wicklow, on the coast. I own it with my sisters. It's only half an hour's drive from Ferrytown—and before you ask, Georgie hasn't been in years. She says it's boring."

"So it's okay to take me to a boring place?"

After a pause, he said, "You won't be bored."

"And I won't have to get a taxi home when you're done with me?"

Another long pause. "I won't be done with you."

Following Mannix's directions, I drove south with the rest of the evening rush-hour traffic. At Ashford I turned off the main road, then off a smaller road, then down a long, long boreen, passing fields of rough marram grass. Light was lingering in the evening sky—spring was coming.

I could smell the sea and I crested a hill and suddenly there it was, heaving and swelling below me, pewter colored in the oncoming night.

Down to the left, all alone, was an old, single-story farmhouse, lit with welcoming yellow lamps. That must be the place.

I drove through a gateway with dry-wall posts and up to a bright porch featuring some sun-bleached chairs and a couple of those eco-unfriendly heaters that everyone frowned on. (Although, to be honest, I never had any issue with them; I'd rather be warm.)

Mannix was in the yard, carrying an armload of logs.

He watched me as I parked and got out of the car.

"Hi." He smiled.

"Hi." I looked at him. Then I smiled too.

"Come in," he said. "It's cold out here."

Inside, everything was cozy in a rough-and-ready way. A fire was on the go in the grate, sending shadows jumping up the walls. Rugs were strewn across the wooden floor and two big shabby chenille couches sat facing each other. Fat cushions and throws in faded colors were dotted about the room.

"It'll be warm soon," he said. "The place heats up quickly."

He threw the logs into a box and walked under an archway, into the kitchen. On a long wooden table were two bottles of wine and an enormous bag from the Butler's Pantry.

"I got food," he said. "Dinner. I mean, I didn't make it. I picked it up. We just need to put it in the oven. Red or white?"

I hesitated. I didn't know how this was going to go. What if I decided to drive home? What if Betsy or Jeffrey needed me? "Red."

You will be punished.

I took a seat at the table and a glass of wine was put in front of me.

"I'll just sort out the white." He produced a bag of ice cubes and, with a tremendous rattle, emptied it into a metal ice bucket. "Jesus," he said. "What's wrong with the ice? Why's it so loud?"

Clearly he was as jumpy as me.

While he was jamming the bottle of white wine into the bucket I took the copy of *One Blink at a Time* out of my bag.

I waited until he had poured himself a glass of red and was seated opposite me.

"So!" I said, all business. "Tell me about this."

"Right!" he said, equally businesslike. "I was just giving your own words back to you. In the hospital, remember the conversations we had? When you blinked stuff and I wrote it down? Well, I kept the notebooks."

"Note*books*? Plural? How many?"

"Seven."

I found that astonishing. I'd never even noticed one notebook filling up and being replaced by another. All I'd been concerned with, at the time, was making myself understood.

"Why did you keep them?"

"Because . . . I thought you were brave."

Oh. I didn't know what to say. I hadn't been bred for praise.

"You didn't know how sick you were. You didn't know that almost no one thought you'd recover."

"God." Maybe it was a good job I *hadn't* known.

"And after we started doing the Wisdom of the Day thing? You said a lot that was wise."

"Ah no, I didn't," I said, automatically.

"I used to read them, when I knew Georgie was never going to have a baby and that she and I weren't going to make it, and they made me feel . . ." He shrugged. "You know? They made the . . . sorrow, if that's the right word, feel smaller."

"But why get them made into a book?"

"Because . . . I wanted to."

That was him in a nutshell: because he wanted to.

"Roland put the idea in my head," he said. "After he came out of rehab, he wrote a book about his dissolute life. No one would publish it, so he contacted these people. Then he realized that it mightn't be the best idea to put himself further into debt by publishing a book about owing a fortune. But it made me think about your stuff. It gave me something to focus on, choosing the paper and the script and all. I hoped I'd be able to give it to you sometime."

"Did you do it before or after you and Georgie had split up?"

"Before."

"That's not good."

"It's *not* good. Which is why it's no surprise that Georgie and I are getting divorced."

Okay. Next item of business. "Why didn't you come after me?" I asked. "The other night?"

"Because I didn't know what I'd done wrong. I'd been asleep and I'd just woken up. I was trying to show that I'm cool with you having kids, and the next thing a shoe is being thrown at my head." He leaned toward me and said, with intensity, "I got it wrong. I called and explained. I was sorry. I rang you eight times."

I nodded. He had.

"Why didn't *you* call *me*?" he asked.

I was startled. "Are you kidding?"

"No. I apologized. I held my hands up. There was nothing more I could do. So why didn't you ring me?"

Why didn't I ring him? "Because I have pride."

"A lot of it." He gave me a long, long look. "We're very different, you and I."

"Is that going to be a problem?"

"I don't know. Maybe."

A cracking noise made us both jump. It was the ice in the ice bucket melting and it broke the tension.

"Do you have a blindfold?" I asked, suddenly.

"For what?"

"I'm here . . . we might as well have fun."

"What do you . . . Why a blindfold?"

"I've never done it. I've never been tied up either."

"Haven't you?" All kinds of emotions were moving behind his eyes—caution and curiosity. And interest. "Ever?"

"Ryan was fairly . . . vanilla," I said.

Mannix laughed. "And you're not?"

"I don't know. I never bothered to find out. And now I want to."

He stood up and grasped my wrist. "Come on, then."

"What's the rush?" I grabbed my bag and he hurried me down a wooden-floored hallway.

"I'm afraid," he said, "that you'll change your mind."

He opened the door to a room and looked in, as if assessing it for its tying-up possibilities. I pushed the door further—it was a bedroom, which was lit by a dozen or so fat white candles. Flames flickered and reflected off the brass poles of the bed and the duvet was almost completely hidden by a thick layer of dark-red rose petals.

I didn't know whether to be offended or flattered. "You fancied your chances."

He looked like he was trying to come up with a plausible lie, then he shrugged and laughed. "Yeah. I did."

Hungrily, we kissed, and he steered me across the room. I fumbled at his shirt buttons and managed to open three, then the bed hit the back of my knees and I tumbled onto the mattress, pulling him on top of me. Petals flew everywhere and the smell of roses filled the air.

He straddled my hips and slid his hands over my fitted shirt, inserting his finger in the gaps between buttons and rubbing until, one by one, they popped open. I was wearing a black front-opening bra and slowly, almost experimentally, he snapped the clasp and my boobs spilled out, looking pearly white in the candlelight.

"God." He stopped in his tracks.

"Okay?" I could hardly breathe.

He nodded, his eyes gleaming. "Very okay."

Quickly he undid the last two buttons of his shirt and threw it off.

Then he whipped his belt through the loops of his jeans and pulled it taut between his two hands. He looked at me, as if he was trying to decide something.

Was he . . . ?

"You want to try?" With lightning speed, he turned me over, rolled up my skirt and flicked my bum with the tip of the belt. It hurt.

"Stop! I'm vanilla, I'm vanilla!" I was shrieking with excitement and glee, and he collapsed onto me, laughing his head off.

"Okay, we won't do that again." He pulled me to him, his eyes sparkling. "But you want to be tied up?"

"No. Yes. I don't know!"

"Right." He positioned me in the center of the bed, stretched my arms above my head, then wrapped his belt around my wrists and fastened it to a bar in the headboard. In the candlelight, he was a picture of concentration as he checked it was secure.

"Should we have a 'word?'" I was suddenly anxious. "If I want to stop?"

That made him laugh once more.

"Don't mock me." I felt wounded.

"I'm not. You're . . . sweet. Okay. How about 'No?'" He quirked an eyebrow. "Or 'Stop?'"

Uncertainly, I watched him.

"Just say, 'Stop, Mannix,'" he said. "And I'll stop."

He started to fold his shirt.

"What are you doing?"

"I don't have a blindfold handy," he said. "I'm improvising."

He kept doubling the shirt over on itself until it was an impressively neat strip.

"Okay?" He held it above my face.

I swallowed. "Okay."

He lay it across my eyes and fixed it in a knot, tight enough to generate a twinge of fear.

"Can you breathe?"

I nodded. Instead of roses, all I could smell was him.

I felt his hands working, easing my skirt off, followed by my knickers.

A door creaked open—I guessed it was the wardrobe—then something cool and silky was slid and knotted around one ankle; I was fairly sure it was a tie. There was a tug that went all the way to my hip socket, then I couldn't move my leg. The same happened on the other side and suddenly I was stretched and immobile. It was hardly a surprise, but yet it was. I gave an experimental pull on my hands and again felt that little thrill of fear. I'd asked for this and now I wasn't sure.

The room was silent. I couldn't hear him. Had he left? My anxiety went up a couple of notches. I could be abandoned in this remote house—no one knew I was here and . . .

Unexpectedly his weight pressed down on me and his breath was hot in my ear. "You will enjoy this," he whispered. "I promise you."

Afterward, Mannix removed the blindfold and untied me and my limbs fell heavily onto the petal-strewn bed. Stunned and floating in weightless bliss, I lay on my back and, for endless time, stared up at the ceiling, at the wooden beams . . .

"Mannix?" I eventually mumbled.

"Mmmm?"

"I read in a magazine about a swinging bed . . ."

He laughed softly. "A swinging bed?"

"Mmmmm. It's not for sleeping in, just for . . . you know?"

He rolled on top of me, so we were face to face. "For . . . you know?"

"Yes."

"You're full of surprises."

Languidly, I ran my hand along the taut muscles on the side of his body. "What do you do?"

" 'Do?' "

"To exercise."

"Swim."

"Let me guess. First thing in the morning. Fast lane in the pool. No one gets in your way. Forty laps."

He smiled, a little uncertainly. "Fifty. But people get in my way. I mean, I don't mind if they do . . . And sometimes I go sailing."

"You have a boat?"

"Rosa's husband, Jean-Marc, he has a sloop. He lets me take her out. I love the water."

I didn't; I was afraid of it. "I can't even swim."

"Why not?"

"I don't know. I never learned."

"I'll teach you."

"I don't want to learn."

That made him laugh. "So what do you 'do?'"

"Zumba."

"Really?"

"Well, I did it a couple of times. It's hard. Complicated steps. I don't really 'do' anything. So tell me things. Tell me about your nephews."

"I've four. Rosa's boys are Philippe, who'll be ten next month, and Claude, who's eight. And Hero has Bruce and Doug, also ten and eight. They're great fun. You know what boys are like—rough, uncomplicated . . ."

"Not always." I was thinking of Jeffrey. "Oh God!" It had suddenly struck me that I'd better call Betsy and Jeffrey. "What time is it?"

"When? Now?" Mannix stretched so he could see the old-fashioned ticking clock on the wooden bedside cabinet. "Ten past nine."

"Okay." I began to wriggle out from under him.

"Are you leaving?"

"Got to call my kids." I scooped my handbag up from the floor and into the bed.

"I'll give you some privacy."

"You don't have to."

He froze, half in and half out.

"If you promise to stay quiet."

"Of course." He seemed almost offended.

"It would upset them if they knew I was calling from . . . with you."

"Stella . . . I know."

I rummaged and found my phone. Jeffrey, as usual, didn't pick up. But Betsy answered.

"Everything okay, hun?" I asked.

"I kinda miss you, Mom."

Score! "I'm always here for you, sweetie," I said, lightly. "So what did you have for dinner?"

"Pizza."

"Great!"

Some shouting kicked off in the background. It sounded like it was Ryan.

"Everything all right?" I asked.

"Dad says you're to stop checking up on him. That he's been a parent as long as you have."

"Sorry, it's just—"

"Laters." She hung up.

"Okay?" Mannix was watching me.

I handed him my phone and he dropped it into my bag, and I said, "Make me feel better."

He looked into my eyes and took my hand. "My sweet Stella." He kissed my cracked knuckles with exquisite tenderness. Still holding eye contact, he moved his mouth up my arm and into the hollow of my elbow and I exhaled and let it happen.

I woke to the sound of the sea; the sun was starting to come up. Mannix was still sleeping so I slid out of bed and into the pajamas I'd brought, as if I'd been going to a Betsy-style sleepover.

I made tea, then wrapped myself in a blanket, got my copy of *One Blink at a Time* and went outside to the porch.

The day was cold but dry and I looked out to sea, past the marram grass and white sand, watching the sky fill with light. It was like living someone else's life, perhaps a woman from a Nicholas Sparks film. Just to see what it felt like, I wrapped both my hands around the mug, something I would never normally do. It was pleasant enough, at least initially, but you couldn't do it for too long, you'd burn your fingers.

Furtively, I opened *One Blink at a Time*. They were my words, but I barely knew this version of me. It was strange, and probably not healthy, to see myself via someone else's eyes.

I flicked through the pages and memories of my time in the hospital flooded back with each phrase I read.

"Stella?" It was Mannix, naked except for a towel around his waist.

"God! You gave me a fright."

"You gave *me* a fright. I thought you'd gone. Come back to bed."

"I'm awake now."

"That's what I mean. Come back to bed."

At work, Karen greeted me by saying, "You need to get this shit out of here." She meant the box of books. "I'm tripping over it. There isn't room."

"Okay, I'll offload them today."

She looked at me properly. "Jesus Christ! No need to ask what you were doing last night."

"Wha-at?" How did she know?

Her gaze moved to my wrist. "Is that blood? Are you bleeding?"

I followed her eyes. "It's a . . . rose petal." They'd got everywhere. Even though I'd had a shower and washed my hair, I'd be peeling them off me for days.

"Oh my God." She was almost whispering. "I can smell it. Roses. He did the rose-petal thing. You know there's a company that sells them? A big bag of petals, plucked from the stems? Don't go flattering yourself thinking he spent hours making them himself. All he had to do was tip the bag over the bed. It would have taken five seconds."

"Okay." I hadn't known but I wasn't getting into an argument.

"So?" she said. "Was it . . . sexy?"

I didn't know what to say. I was bursting to talk about it, but afraid of her judgment.

"Don't!" She held up her hand. "Don't tell me. Okay, tell me one thing. Was there bondage?"

I considered it. "Yes. A little."

Karen's face was a picture of conflicting emotions.

I wondered if I should show her the red mark on my bottom, but decided I couldn't be that mean.

I had no clients between ten thirty and noon, so I left the salon and distributed *One Blink at a Time* to nearby friends and family. I was trying to show everyone that Mannix Taylor was a good man who did good things.

Reactions to the book varied. Uncle Peter was bemused, but positive. "We'll find a lovely spot for it in the cabinet. Don't worry, there's a key; it'll be safe in there."

Zoe was impressed. "Wow." Her chin went wobbly and she had tears in her eyes. "That's one big sorry, in a different league from lilies and truffles. Maybe he's a good guy, Stella; maybe there are a few of them out there."

Mum was anxious. "Could you be sued? People who write books are always being sued."

Dad nearly burst with pride. "My own daughter. The author of a book."

"Dad, are you *crying*?"

"I am not."

But he was.

However, later in the day he rang and complained, "It doesn't have much of a story."

"Sorry, Dad."

"Are you going to show it to Ryan and the nippers?"

"I don't know." I'd been agonizing. Showing them the book might make things miles worse. But keeping it from them might also go down badly.

On Wednesday evening, Betsy rang me. "Mom? I saw the book? That Dr. Taylor did for you? Grandad showed us."

"Yes?" I was gripping the phone hard.

"It's like, really beautiful. He likes you, right?"

"Well . . ." I might as well be honest. "He seems to."

"Mom, could you buy us some food?"

"Like what?"

"Like granola and juice and bananas. Just stuff. *You* know. And loo roll. And I think we need a cleaner."

"I can come and clean."

"I don't think Dad would be comfortable with that."

"Oookay." The thing was, I wanted Ryan to fail as a sole parent. But I still wanted the kids getting proper food and wearing clean clothes and keeping up in school. So I needed to be supportive.

But not too supportive . . .

On Thursday morning, before work, I bought everything I thought the kids and Ryan might need. Praying that they had already left for the day, I rang the bell, and when there was no answer I let myself in. Their house was filthy. The kitchen, in particular—every surface was grimy and covered with crumbs and abandoned food. There were strange sticky spots on the floor and the bins were overflowing.

As I filled the fridge and set to disinfecting the worktops, I reflected that this was utter madness: *they* had left me, yet here I was doing their shopping and cleaning their house. But I knew that the time was fast approaching when it would all go belly-up for Ryan, and the kids would be mine again.

And I had to admit that I almost didn't want them back. Not yet. I wanted this time alone.

Except I wasn't alone. I was with Mannix.

Every day since Monday, as soon as I'd finished work, I drove out to the beach house, where he was waiting for me, the candles already lit, the wine already poured and the fridge full of lovely food that we mostly didn't eat. The minute I stepped through the door he was on me. We had so much sex that I was sore. We did it everywhere. He undressed me on a rug in front of the fire, then ran ice cubes around my nipples. He carried me outdoors, where, despite the astonishing cold, we tore into each other on the sand. One night, I woke in the darkness with such a longing that I stroked him until he was hard enough to be straddled— only when he was inside me, did he wake up.

Every morning, before we left for our jobs, we did it at least once.

Even so, by midday on Thursday, I was so horny that I didn't think I'd last until the evening, so in a gap between clients I drove home and rang him.

"Where are you?" I asked.

"At my clinic."

"Are you alone?"

"Why?"

"I'm not wearing any knickers."

"Oh, Christ," he groaned. "No, Stella."

"Yes, Stella. I'm lying on my bed."

"Don't tell me. You've never had phone sex before?"

"First time for everything. I'm touching myself, Mannix."

"Stella, I'm a fucking doctor! I have to see people. Don't do this to me."

"Go on," I whispered. "Are you hard yet?"

"Yes."

"Pretend I'm there. Pretend I've got you in my mouth. Pretend my tongue is . . ."

I kept up a steady stream of low talk as I listened to his breathing become faster and more ragged.

"Are you . . . touching yourself?" I asked.

"Yes." He hissed in an undertone.

"Are you . . . moving yourself?"

"Yes."

"Do it faster. Think of me, think of my mouth, think of my boobs." He moaned at that bit.

"Are you going to come?"

"Yes."

"When?"

"Soon."

"Go faster," I commanded.

I kept talking, until he made a noise halfway between a grunt and a whimper. "Oh Jesus," he whispered. "Oh God. Oh God."

I waited until his breathing slowed down. "Did you . . . ?"

"Yes."

"Really?" I squealed.

Phone sex! Me? Who knew!

I was getting by on maybe four hours' sleep a night but I was never tired. At some stage Dr. Quinn rang to say that my bloods had come back and everything was normal, but I already knew that: my chronic knackeredness had totally disappeared.

These few days were like a holiday from myself, and when Mannix and I weren't having sex, we lay in bed and talked—long, meandering rambles as we tried to catch up on two entire lives.

"So for five summers in a row I worked in a canning factory in Munich."

"Why didn't your dad pay your university fees?"

"He didn't have it. He paid the first term of the first year, then asked for the money back."

"God! Why?"

"Because he needed it."

"One day in hospital, you told me you became a doctor to please your dad. Is that true?"

"It was more to protect Roland. I thought Dad would leave him alone if I did it."

"But you like it?"

"Yeaaah . . . I probably haven't the best bedside manner—but you knew that. People expect miracles just because I've been to university, but I can't give them miracles and that makes me depressed. Working with stroke victims, like I do, or people with Parkinson's—at best, I help them manage their condition. I don't cure anyone."

"Right . . ."

"But you were different, Stella. There was a chance that one day you'd be fully cured, that you'd be my miracle. And you were."

I didn't know what to say. It was nice to be someone's miracle.

"Why be a neurologist?" I asked. "You could have been another kind of doctor?"

He laughed. "Because I'm squeamish. Really. I'd never have made a surgeon. And the other options? There was ophthalmology. Eyes. Eyeballs. The idea of working with them every day . . . Or brains . . . God . . . Or colons. I mean, would you?"

"So what would you have preferred to do with your life? Instead of being a doctor?"

"I don't know. I never had a 'thing.' I know it's not a *job*-job but I'd have liked to be a dad."

There. He'd said it—the issue we'd spent days deliberately skirting.

"And now, Mannix?" I asked, delicately. "Do you still want babies?" We had to face this head-on.

He sighed and shifted himself, so he could look me in the eyes. "That ship has sailed. After Georgie and I, all the disappointments . . . It went on for so long, so much hope, then so much loss. But I'm at peace with it." He sounded surprised. "I'm never at peace with anything. But, yeah, I'm at peace with it. I love my nephews. I see them a lot, we have fun, and it's enough. What about you?"

I was so mad about Mannix that the idea of a baby version of him gave me shivers; even the thought of being pregnant with his child gave me a powerful thrill.

But I knew the reality—babies were horribly hard work. Lots of women were having babies at my age and even later, but my maternal urges had been satisfied by the two children I already had.

"I don't think babies are going to be part of our story," I said.

"And that's okay," he said.

I fell silent. I was thinking about my children, about how I'd broken up their home, and how they'd never forgive me.

"They'll come back," Mannix said.

"The timing couldn't be worse. Only a few days after finding out Betsy is sleeping with her boyfriend . . . I should be there for her."

"You can't if she won't let you. And it's all going to be okay soon."

He was probably right. Relations between Ryan and the kids had deteriorated to the point where Jeffrey was now refusing to speak to Ryan.

"You know," I said, "I actually, genuinely, can't believe Betsy is sleeping with her boyfriend."

"But you were sleeping with your boyfriend at seventeen?"

"Of course! Were you at it at seventeen? Don't tell me. I don't even have to ask. You love it, don't you?" I said. "Sex."

He pushed himself up and gave me a look. "Yeah. I'm not going to lie. I . . . want you."

"And you want other people?" I needed some idea of how much of a player he was.

"What? You want a list?"

"The last person you had sex with? Before me? Was it your wife?"

"No."

That shut me up. I didn't know if I could handle knowing any more. Had there been lots?

"No," he said, reading my mind. "Anyway, you love it too."

It all came crashing down at eleven o'clock on Friday night with a phone call from Betsy.

"Come and get us. We're moving back in," she said.

"Right now?"

"Totally right now."

"Er . . . of course!" I shifted my naked body away from Mannix's.

"Dad has no sense of parental responsibility," Betsy said. "We've been late for school every day. And now he says he can't drive us to the places we need to go tomorrow. It's unacceptable."

"Is . . . ah . . . Jeffrey coming home too?" He still wasn't answering my calls.

"Yeah. But he's seriously peed-off with you and I'm not even joking."

"I'll be with you in forty-five minutes."

"Forty-five? Where *are* you?"

I hung up and rolled out of bed.

"Where are you going?" Mannix looked anxious, almost angry.

"Home."

"So what happens now?"

"I don't know."

"When will I see you?"

"I don't know."

As I drove up the dark, empty motorway toward Dublin, I was forced to confront thoughts that I'd kept boxed off all week. There was a right way to do things: a freshly separated mother of two proceeded with great caution with any new relationship. The man's existence was kept secret until the woman was certain that he was a decent, reliable type who was willing to make the effort with her children, and that this thing had the potential to last the distance . . .

I'd done it all wrong. But everything had been fast-tracked by Jeffrey's classmates spotting me with Mannix on the pier. And that unexpected, magical time in the holiday cottage had done for me.

Ryan opened his door wearing a sheepish smile. He was so relieved that the kids were leaving that he'd forgotten to be furious with me.

"So! Kids!" He waved from the door. "See you soon!"

"Whatevs." Betsy trundled her luggage to the car and got into the passenger seat.

In silence, Jeffrey hoisted his case into the boot, then got into the back of the car.

Ryan had already shut his front door.

"I'm saying this now," Betsy said, staring straight ahead. "And I don't mean it because, obvs, I'm like mad with him, but he's a really crap dad. Sorry for swearing."

"Saying 'crap' isn't swearing."

"Mom! Role model, please!"

When we got home and into the house, Betsy pulled me aside. "I'm totally fine, but you might want to try rebonding with . . ." She widened her eyes in the direction of the stairs that Jeffrey had disappeared up. "Go, Mom." She gave me a little smack on the bum—this was obviously my week for it—then she said, "Sorry! Total boundary invasion!"

For God's sake.

I gave it a few minutes then I went and knocked on Jeffrey's door. He was already in his pajamas and in bed.

"Can I sit down?"

"Go on, then." He sat up in bed and pulled the duvet to his chest. "Is Dr. Taylor your boyfriend?"

"I . . . ah, I don't know."

"You were having an affair," Jeffrey said. "That's why you and Dad split up."

"I wasn't having an affair." I could say that honestly.

"But what about that book? He did that ages ago."

"I wasn't having an affair." I was like a politician. "I hadn't heard from him in a long time, over a year."

"Does he have a wife?"

"He did, but they're getting divorced."

"Does he have kids?"

"No."

"So that's why he's with you. Because you have kids."

"It's not why."

"Do we have to meet him?"

"Would you like to?"

"We've met him. In the hospital."

"But that was long ago. Different."

"So he *is* your boyfriend?"

"Honestly, Jeffrey. I don't know."

"But you *should* know. You're the grown-up."

He was right. I should, but I didn't.

"You and Dad?" Jeffrey asked. "You're never getting back together?"

A million thoughts zipped through my head. In theory, *anything* was possible—but it would be really, really unlikely. "No." I settled for. "No."

"That's very sad . . ." A tear trickled down his face.

"Jeffrey." His grief was like a knife in my stomach. "I wish I could protect you from all pain, ever. I wish I could always tell you just happy things. This is a tough lesson for you to learn so young."

"You think Dr. Taylor likes you. Maybe he does. But he's not my dad. He can be your . . . boyfriend. But you can't make us into a new family."

"Okay." Even as I said the word, I realized I shouldn't make promises I couldn't keep.

"But if he's going to be your boyfriend, we should meet him."

I hadn't been expecting that. "You mean, you and Betsy?"

"And Grandma and Grandad. Auntie Karen, Uncle Enda, Auntie Zoe, everyone."

Jeffrey gave Mannix a cold stare. "My dad has a Mitsubishi pickup truck. It's the best car ever."

Jeffrey's opening salvo at his first meeting with Mannix wasn't exactly friendly.

"It's, ah, yeah, you're right." Mannix nodded vigorously and visibly forced his limbs to look loose and sprawly. "It's probably the best car ever. Pickups are . . . yeah . . . *great*."

"What car do you have?" Jeffrey asked.

I watched anxiously; a lot hinged on this.

"It's a . . . yeah, another Japanese car. Not as good as a Mitsubishi pickup but—"

"What is it?"

"A Mazda MX-5."

"That's a bit girlie." Jeffrey's scorn was savage.

"Technically, it *was* a girl's car," Mannix said. "My ex-wife—my soon-to-be ex-wife, Georgie—it was hers. She got a new car."

"What did she get?"

"An Audi A5. And she wanted me to take the Mazda."

"Why didn't you get a new car too?"

"Because, ah . . . the Audi cost a lot . . ."

"So she gets a new Audi and you get a secondhand Mazda? Man, you're lame."

Mannix eyed Jeffrey. He took a while before he spoke. "Sometimes it's easier to just give in. I'm sure, as a man who lives with women, you'll appreciate that."

Surprise whipped across Jeffrey's face. Suddenly he was realizing that he might have an ally in Mannix.

But later, when Mannix had gone home, I found Jeffrey sobbing in his bedroom. "If I like Dr. Taylor?" he choked. "Am I being mean to Dad?"

Over the next few weeks I introduced Mannix to my family and friends and their reactions varied. Karen was breezy and civil. Zoe didn't want to be charmed, but she was. Mum was nervous and giggly. Dad was chummy and tried to engage Mannix in book talk and was amazed that Mannix wasn't much of a reader. "But with all your education . . . ?"

"I'm more of a science person."

"But Stella is a great reader. What do you two have in common?"

Mannix and I flicked a glance at each other and it was as if a hidden voice had started whispering, *SexSexSex*.

Dad blushed and muttered something and hurried out of the room.

It was impossible to tell what Enda Mulreid thought of Mannix, because it was impossible to tell what Enda Mulreid thought of anyone. As Dad often said, "Plays his cards close to his chest, that fella." Then he always added, "Although he probably doesn't play cards at all. There might be a small chance he might start *enjoying* himself."

Betsy declared that she liked Mannix and that Tyler liked him too. "And Tyler's got like a great instinct for people," she said, earnestly. "Sometimes I feel really bad that you and Dad have split up. Sometimes I wish I could go back to being a kid and for us to be the way we were. But this is life. Like you said in your book, it can't all be bubbles and lollipops."

I nodded anxiously: could she really be as grounded as she sounded?

"She's in love," Mannix said. "Everything is hearts and bunny rabbits for her, right now."

"Okay . . ." Maybe it was as simple as that.

"You remember what that was like?" Mannix asked. "Being in love? I do. Because I'm in love—"

"Stop!"

He recoiled and said, "Oooookay."

"Don't say you're in love with me. You don't even know me. And I don't know you."

"We got to know each other in the hospital."

"A few blinked conversations? That counts for nothing. That's not the real world. I don't know the name for the feelings I have for you. The only thing I know for sure is that you scare me."

"How?" He sounded shocked.

"I'm terrified you're going to overwhelm me."

"I won't."

But it was already happening.

"Once upon a time, I loved Ryan and then I got sick and we didn't survive it. Once upon a time, you loved Georgie, then you couldn't have children and now you don't love her. That tells me something."

"And that is?"

"That you can't call something love until everything goes wrong and you manage to survive it. Love isn't hearts and flowers. And it's not good sex. Love is about loyalty. Endurance. Soldiering on, shoulder to shoulder. The snow blowing into your face. Your feet wrapped in rags. Your nose rotting with frostbite. Your—"

"Right, I get it. Bring on the disaster."

"I just mean—"

"Really, Stella, I get it. The ball's in your court now. I will never mention the word 'love' again until you do."

Mannix set up a reunion for Roland and me. As he came into the restaurant, togged out in an outlandishly patterned shirt and hip, thick-framed glasses, I felt a great wave of warm feeling. He already felt like an old, much-loved friend. We hurried toward each other and he swept me into a huge big squashy hug. "I've so much to thank you for," he said. "Going to rehab has been the saving of me."

"Oh, Roland, I did nothing! You're the one who went."

"You talked me into it."

"I didn't, Roland. You talked yourself into it."

Then it was time to meet Mannix's sisters. "It's my nephew's birthday. Philippe. He's ten. Just a family thing, Saturday afternoon. If you bring Betsy and Jeffrey, it'll be a nice, low-key way for them to meet. And to meet Roland too."

I drove us all there because Mannix was still driving Georgie's ex-two-seater.

On the journey, Mannix briefed Betsy on the people she was about to meet and she, very sweetly, put the details in her phone, so that she'd remember everyone's names.

Rosa and Jean-Marc lived in a McMansion in Churchtown, but as we drove through the gateway I saw that a stone lion on the left pillar had had its head knocked off. "Philippe and Claude did that with a cricket bat," Mannix said. "It always makes me laugh."

Rosa, a small, neat little creature, hurried down the hall to greet us. I recognized her top; I owned an identical one, and it had cost me eight euros. This was cheering.

"Hello, Stella, hello! I'm Rosa." She welcomed me with a hug.

"And I'm Hero." Another woman appeared behind Rosa and she too gave me a hug.

It was uncanny how similar they were. Rosa had dark hair, Hero had blond, but their faces and bodies, even the intonation of their voices, were identical.

"You're Betsy?" Rosa asked.

"Totally!" Betsy squealed and flung herself first into Rosa's arms, then Hero's.

Rosa and Hero seemed all set to move their hugging convoy onto Jeffrey, but one look from him had them backing away and giving Mannix a quick kiss.

"Come in, come in." Then Rosa said, to me, "Stella, we feel like we know you already."

"Mannix talked about you when you were ill," Hero explained.

I felt Mannix tense, then color flooded Hero's face.

"Not by name!" she said.

"Not by name, of course," Rosa said.

"Of course, not by name," Hero said. "Mannix is entirely professional."

"*Entirely* professional."

"As silent as the grave." That made both Rosa and Hero giggle.

"But he told us about your condition—"

"—and how courageous you were."

"Shut up," Mannix said.

"Let's get some drinks," Rosa said. "And we'll smooth over this faux pas."

In the kitchen, there was a big, lopsided cake that read: "Happy Birthday Phiilippe."

"Yeah, I know," Rosa said. "I did it last night. I'd had a few drinks. Wine, Stella? Or would you prefer gin?"

"Wine is fine."

"Betsy? A glass of wine?"

"Oh no. I totally don't drink. OJ for me."

"Jeffrey? A beer?"

"I'm only fifteen."

"Is that a yes or a no?"

Rosa dissolved into lighthearted laughter and Jeffrey said, very coldly, "It's illegal for me to drink."

He was going to be sixteen in six weeks' time *and* he already drank whenever I said he could, so either way it was a technicality. But it was an opportunity for Jeffrey to be rude and he wasn't going to pass it up.

"In that case, OJ it is!"

There was a clatter of feet at the back door and a small crowd of boys ran in. "Is it Uncle Roland?"

"Not yet. But it's Uncle Mannix."

The boys identified themselves as Mannix's four nephews: Philippe, Claude, Bruce and Doug. They all hugged Mannix, which I found touching, then Philippe tore open his present—the new season Chelsea kit. "Sick!" he said. "You're the best!"

The four boys had little interest in Betsy or me but they were very focused on Jeffrey. "What team do you support?" Philippe asked him.

"Team?" Jeffrey asked. "Football?"

"Or rugby . . ." Philippe was losing his nerve.

"I don't support any team. Group sports are for idiots."

I was mortified. "Jeffrey, please."

"Well, I know I'm only a girl!" Betsy declared. "But I totally love Chelsea! Come on, guys. Let's go out the back and kick some ball!"

"Will you come too?" Philippe humbly asked Jeffrey. "So we'll have even numbers?"

But Jeffrey ignored him.

"I'll come," Mannix said.

"Hurray!"

The husbands came in to say hello—Jean-Marc wasn't as good-looking as his name conjured up and Harry had quite a belly on him, but they were friendly and welcoming.

"Have some sausage rolls and things." Rosa thrust food at me. "And we'll have the birthday cake when Roland arrives."

A short time later, the nephews set up a clamor. "Here's Roland, here's Uncle Roland."

In he came, in an elaborately lapeled jacket and a faceful of smiles. His present to Philippe was the away kit for Chelsea and Philippe nearly combusted with the serendipity of it all. "Uncle Mannix gave me the home kit and you've given me the away kit! Isn't that lucky?"

"Amazing," Mannix said gravely.

"You'd nearly think we'd collaborated on it," Roland said. And he and Mannix exchanged a little smile that was so connected it almost shocked me.

"Hello, sir!" Roland advanced on Jeffrey. "I don't believe we've met."

"No . . ."

"It's a pleasure to meet you."

"You too."

I almost laughed. Before my eyes, Jeffrey was softening.

"And you must be Betsy?"

Betsy's eyes were out on stalks at Roland's hipster look, but she was polite and charming.

Then Roland turned his attention to me. "Stella." He gathered me to him in a huge hug, then he pulled back to inspect me. "Looking great, Stella. You get more beautiful every time I see you."

"You look great too, Roland."

"I do?" Sinuously he ran his hand over his belly. "Really?"

"Yes." And suddenly we were both doubled in two, yelping with laughter.

On the drive home, Betsy was wildly positive. "Those kids are super cute. Adorbs!"

"So what are they to us? Step-cousins?" Jeffrey was obsessed with this sort of thing.

"Friends, hopefully."

"In theory, they wouldn't be step-anythings unless Stella and I got married," Mannix said.

"That's not going to happen." Jeffrey glared.

Mannix opened his mouth. I flicked him a look and he clamped it shut again.

"Does Uncle Roland have a girlfriend?" Betsy asked.

"Don't call him that," Jeffrey snapped.

"Okay, does Roland have a girlfriend?" Betsy asked. "A special friend?"

"No special friend right now," Mannix said. "But even if he did, it wouldn't be a girl."

"He's gay?" Betsy said. "I am so totally cool with that."

I pulled up at the house and we all piled out.

"There's your girlie car," Jeffrey said to Mannix. "Off you go home."

"He's coming in," I said. "He's having dinner with us." I'd been gently but firmly trying to shoehorn Mannix into our lives.

"This is *our* weekend with *our* mom," Jeffrey said. "Next weekend we'll be with Dad and you two can do what you like." He swallowed at that bit. "But for now, good-bye."

He shooed Mannix with his hand. "Go on. We did what you asked: we met your nephews, who, incidentally, are a crowd of saps, we met your sisters and their drinking problems, and your so-fat-he's-going-to-die brother."

"Jeffrey!" I said.

"Go home. My sister and I have got places to go and we need our mom to drive us."

G eorgie wants to meet you."

"Mannix, I don't want to meet Georgie. I'm afraid of her."

"You've got to meet Georgie. If we're doing this thing properly, we've got to meet everyone."

So a table was booked at Dimants. For two.

"What do you mean, for two?" I asked Mannix, in a panic. "Why aren't you coming?"

"She wants to see you alone," Mannix said.

"We don't have to do everything she wants."

"We do. Meet her. You'll see."

The table was booked for eight o'clock, so I got there at eight o'clock.

"You're the first to arrive," the hostess said.

I sat at the table and the minutes ticked by, and at eighteen minutes past eight I decided to leave, just to protect the last few remnants of my self-respect.

Then I saw her.

Karen would say there's no such thing, but she was too thin. Even thinner than that time at the hospital. She was carrying a handbag the size of a Nissan Micra and was dressed entirely in black, except for a fascinating scarf-cum-necklace thing that featured a green stone.

She rushed toward me and kissed me on both cheeks, giving me a whiff of a strange, spicy perfume, then sat down opposite me, and although she was a bit sunken around the eye sockets, she was beautiful.

"Please don't scold me for being late," she said. "You know how it is. Traffic, parking . . ."

I, too, had engaged with traffic and parking and had managed to arrive on time but I already understood that different rules applied to Georgie.

She looked me straight in the eye and said, "You are not to feel guilty about Mannix."

"I . . ."

"Let me explain," she said. "We weren't good for each other, Mannix and I. He's a bit of a nightmare. And so am I."

I demurred, anxious to not give offense.

"I truly am," she insisted. "I'm moody and pessimistic and given to incredible darkness. I fly off the handle. I'm deeply sensitive."

I nodded, tentatively. This was my first time ever to meet someone who described themselves in such a fashion.

She was quite mesmerizing; she was very *long*. Everything about her—her limbs, her hair, her eyelashes, even her knuckles—was sort of stretched-looking. She had a mild touch of the Iggy Pops about her.

Unexpectedly she choked back a laugh. "I'm sorry," she said. "I can't stop looking at you and comparing us."

"Me too." And with that, we were friends.

"Your perfume is . . . ?" Then I understood. "It's a customized blend, isn't it?"

"Of course." She sounded surprised—as if it were really strange that a perfume *wouldn't* be bespoke. "There's a man in Antwerp. He's—no other word for it—an enchanter. You *must* come. His waiting list is about six years long, but say you're a friend of mine and he'll see you."

"So you go to Belgium a lot? On buying trips for your boutique?"

"Maybe five times a year."

"Your neck thing is beautiful," I said. "Is that one of your funny Belgian designers?"

Instantly she was unwinding it. "Have it," she said. "It's yours."

"No, really." I batted her away with my hands. "I wasn't trying to . . . Georgie, I'm begging you, please don't."

But there was no reasoning with her. She was up and out of her seat and was draping the scarf thing on my neck and rearranging my hair around it. Then she sat back down again to admire her handiwork. "See! Made for you. Like my husband."

"Sorry," I whispered.

"I'm joking! I don't care in the slightest. Really, Stella. Mannix and I were all wrong. I'm highly strung. Like a racehorse. Whereas you . . . you're . . . steady. You're sensible and—oh God, please don't take this the wrong way, Stella—you're solid. He needs someone like you." She studied me. "In your ordinary way, you really are very pretty."

I touched the neck thing. I was deeply miserable about this. I hated her thinking that I'd asked for it. I'd only been admiring the fecking yoke; I was only being *nice*.

"You could never be described as a classic beauty," she mused. "But you do have a lovely face."

"Was this very expensive?" I asked anxiously.

"It depends on what you call expensive. It's not like it needs to live in a safe. *Do* you have a safe? No? Well, then, don't bother, simply keep it in your jewelry box. Promise me you'll wear it lots. Every day. It's got jade for protection and I'm sensing you're going to need plenty."

Before I could get derailed by that, she said, "It's just I feel bad for what I said that Christmas night in the hospital. I implied that you weren't so all that. But at the time we were simply being cruel to each other, Mannix and I. I was losing my husband and . . . it hurt."

"It's okay," I said. "Anyway, I wasn't looking my best. I'd no makeup on and my roots hadn't been done in months."

"And at the time I was fucking my meditation instructor," she said. "Who was, quite frankly, a crashing bore. Spiritual people so often are, don't you find? I had no right to sneer at Mannix's romance. So how's it all going? I hear your son doesn't approve?"

"No."

"And you can't just say, 'Get used to it?'"

"He's my son—I've shattered his world and I've got to take care of his feelings."

"And what's going on with your ex? Is he helpful?"

"No." Suddenly I felt like crying.

Ryan and I had agreed that, to give the kids a sense of security, they lived with me during the school week. Every second weekend, they stayed with Ryan, and for those precious two days out of every fourteen, I got to see Mannix properly, to have sex with him, to go to bed with him and wake up with him.

"Sometimes Ryan flakes on the weekends he has custody," I said.

"So what happens when you can't see Mannix? How do you manage for sex?"

I blushed hot and red. Was this any of Georgie Dawson's business?

"God, I'm sorry, Stella," she said. "I should engage my brain before I speak."

But she had a point. Although we'd been seeing each other for more than two months now, Mannix and I were struggling with the limits on our time together. Now and again we cracked. There was that Wednesday I pretended to Karen that I had a dentist's appointment and I raced across town and met Mannix in his horrible, sleazy, single-guy's apartment for frenzied sex. There was another occasion when Mannix appeared when I was locking up the salon, and he said, "I know you've got to get home to your kids, but just give me ten minutes." And we sat in the empty salon and held hands, and I cried because I was worn out from wanting him and not being able to have him.

The chronic deprival was exhausting and the only thing worse was the carefully orchestrated, agonizingly awkward meetups when I tried to blend my two worlds.

Carefully, Georgie said, "I understand you have to take care of your son's sensibilities."

I began to prickle with unease.

"But," Georgie said, "take care of Mannix too."

This was a friendly warning, this was coming from a good place, but it scared me.

"And how about Roland?" she said. "Isn't he just the best? That's the sad thing about a breakup. You have to break up with the whole family."

"Do you miss them? Aren't you lonely?"

"I'm always lonely." Despite the desolate words, she sounded almost pleased with herself. "It's true, Stella. I am the loneliest woman on earth."

"I'll be your friend," I said, earnestly.

"You're already my friend," she said. "And I'm yours. However, I could have a million friends and it wouldn't stop the ache here." She put her hand on her solar plexus. "It's almost tangible. I feel like it's a black lump. Both a lump and a yawning emptiness. You know?"

"No."

I was fascinated. I'd never really met a depressed person before. Well, not one with such endless self-interest. And yet I really liked her.

"Maybe the three of us could live together," I said.

That made her laugh hard and wave her hand dismissively. "I'm so happy that I don't have to live with Mannix Taylor any longer." Quickly, she added, "No offense. He's great. You do know he's on antidepressants?"

"He said."

"But he's not depressed. It's just the way he is. A glass-half-empty guy. Sometimes he says he didn't get given a glass at all. But you're going to love his parents!"

"Am I?"

"They're such fun!"

"But what about the gambling and the paintings they can't afford and all that?"

She shrugged. "I know, I know. But it's only money, you know?"

No.

Hey. Work stuff. Wekend. Bummed to have missed
it. Ryan xoxo

Incredulous, I stared at my phone. It was five thirty on Friday evening, the kids were waiting outside the school gates, their bags packed, ready for Ryan to pick them up for the weekend, and he was canceling? *Again?*

Immediately I rang him and it went to voice mail. With fingers shaking with smacky rage I sent a text, telling him to pick up the next time I rang, or else the kids and I were coming to see him in person.

"Hey, Stella!"

"Ryan? *Ryan?*"

"Yeah. Crazy here. I'll be working through the weekend. Emergency."

He was lying; he'd never had a weekend emergency when he'd been married to me. The truth was that the kids bored him—when the four of us had lived together, Ryan could flit in and out whenever it suited him, but a whole forty-eight hours being the sole provider of attention and entertainment? He couldn't handle it.

"Ryan." I almost choked. "They're standing outside their school waiting for you."

"Too bad, eh?"

"It's not like you see them during the week."

"That's for their benefit. We agreed. Minimum disruption during the school week."

"So who's going to tell them you're not coming?"

"You."

"They're your children too," I hissed.

"You made this situation," he hissed back.

He was right. There was nothing I could say.

"What a pity," he said, "that you're going to have to miss your weekend riding your doctor boyfriend in the sand dunes in Wicklow, but, hey, shit happens."

He hung up and I couldn't catch my breath. I felt like my chest was caving in. Trying to manage Ryan and Jeffrey and Mannix was destroying me. I was constantly juggling situations, desperately trying to keep people happy, and the nearer every Friday got, the bigger my dread that Ryan would cancel. I could never relax, never be at ease in my own life, and I had no right to ask anyone to cut me some slack because I'd created this setup.

"Mannix, I can't see you. Ryan can't take the kids."

Silent tension flared on the phone.

"Mannix, talk to me, please."

"Stella," he said. "I'm forty-two years of age. I'm serious about this. I'm serious about you. I want to be with you twenty-four hours a day, instead of two nights in every fortnight and sometimes not even that. I'm lonely without you. I spend every night in a horrible rented flat, and you're four short miles away, sleeping on your own."

I said nothing. This was a familiar theme and there were times when I was afraid Mannix was going to give up on me.

"We're adults," he said. "We shouldn't have to live like this. You know how I feel about you but I don't know how much longer I can keep doing this weekend stuff."

Fear seized my heart. "Then you don't really care about me."

"You can't say that. This is real life where there are no blacks and whites. It's all just gray."

"But . . ."

"Good as you are at phone sex," he said, "this is starting to get old."

"Am I good at it?" I decided to focus on the positive.

"You're amazing," he said. "Why do you think I'm still around?"

D arling, I'm so sorry I'm late!" Georgie hurried across the restaurant to where Karen and I were waiting. "Blame it on Viagra." Georgie gave me a big hug. "Yes, I was with my new man, he'd taken two of his little blue pills of delight and the whole thing went on for an epoch." She groaned and rolled her eyes, then turned the spotlight of her smile on Karen. "Hi," she said. "I'm Georgie. And you must be Karen."

Karen nodded mutely. She had insisted on this meeting, had practically begged me for it, because she was fixated, to an almost unhealthy degree, on Georgie Dawson. She'd kept saying, in a mock-sad voice, "We really should be nice to 'the loneliest woman on earth.'"

"Honestly," Georgie pulled up a chair and exhaled heavily. "I thought he'd never come."

"I love your bag," Karen breathed.

"Thank you," Georgie said. "Afterward he asked me to lie in the bath and pretend to have drowned. Welshmen, believe me when I tell you this, they are *so* kinky."

"Kinkier than Mannix?" I asked, just to make her laugh.

"That little choirboy!" Her eyes blazed with mirth. "Oh, Stella, you are a hoot."

"Is it a Marni?" Karen was making pitiful stroking gestures toward Georgie's bag. "Can I touch it? I've never touched a real one."

"Haven't you? But you must have it." Instantly Georgie began emptying the contents of her handbag onto the table.

"No," I said, in alarm. "Georgie, no. She doesn't want it. Karen, tell Georgie you don't want it."

"Oh, there's my peridot earring," Georgie said. "I knew it would reappear." A pile of stuff began to mount up on the table—keys, a wallet, sunglasses, phone, gum, several thin silver bracelets, a small bottle of perfume, five or six lip glosses, a Sisley compact . . .

"There you go." Georgie gave the empty handbag to Karen.

"Oh, please." I buried my face in my hands.

"Stella, it's only stuff," Georgie said.

"That's right," Karen said, clutching the bag to her chest and looking like Gollum with the Ring. "It's only stuff."

"So how are you, sweet girl?" Georgie said to me.

Karen had called over a waiter and asked for a paper bag for Georgie's belongings.

"Can I apologize on behalf of my sister," I said.

"It's fine, it's fine." Georgie waved away my concerns. "Tell me how you are, Stella. How's your divorce going?"

"Not bad, actually," I said.

"Me too!"

We both burst out laughing.

It would be five years before Ryan and I were divorced; nevertheless our financial terms were surprisingly harmonious—probably because we owned so little: no stocks, no shares, no pension plan. Our home, with its mortgage, was transferred to me while Ryan got the Sandycove house and its negative equity. As Ryan earned so much more than I did, he agreed to cover all of Betsy and Jeffrey's maintenance, including school fees, until they were eighteen. Apart from that our financial affairs were completely severed.

What had proved less easy to agree was the care of Betsy and Jeffrey.

"We have to talk about custody." I'd eyeballed Ryan across my lawyer's desk.

"Custody," my lawyer repeated.

Ryan's lawyer jumped in immediately. "My client is entitled to see his children. It's generous enough that he permits you to have full access during the school weeks."

I sighed. "What I would like is for your client to stop bailing at the last minute on the weekends he's supposed to have the kids."

But apparently that couldn't be legally enforced.

Afterward, as we stood outside, Ryan said, "So that's our divorce underway. How do you feel? I feel awful sad."

I outstared him: he did *not* feel sad. "Ryan, I'm begging you. You have to keep your commitment to the kids on your weekends. And to take them away on holiday for a week when they break up from school."

"While you'll be doing what? Going down to your beach house with your neurologist?"

"He's not my neurologist anymore. And I'm entitled to a break. One week, Ryan, that's all I'm asking. I'll have them the entire summer."

"Grand," he muttered. "I'll organize something."

"In a different country," I said. "Not Ireland."

He took the kids to a tacky resort in Turkey, and he went out on the pull every night, having suddenly realized he was a single man, free to have sex with whomever he wanted. The kids spent their evenings confined to the tiny apartment, watching movies on their laptops, and their mornings waiting for Ryan to come home.

"It's unacceptable," Betsy said gravely, in one of her countless phone calls to me.

"What does Jeffrey think?" I was interested to hear his thoughts on Ryan's sex life, considering he had such strong views on mine.

"Jeffrey says Dad can do what he likes."

"Is that so? Because—"

Jeffrey grabbed the phone. "You started it. Dad wouldn't have any other girls if you hadn't cheated."

"I didn't cheat."

"He's making the best of a bad situation."

Somehow I knew that Ryan had said those very words to Jeffrey. But I couldn't afford to get too irate because I got my week in the beach house with Mannix.

One day, during that blissful week, Mannix said, "Could we get a dog?"

"When?"

"Not right now, obviously. But sometime in the future. I've always wanted a dog but Georgie wouldn't let me."

"I love dogs too." I was excited. "But Ryan hates them so I made myself forget how much I'd love one. What sort would we get?"

"A rescue dog?"

"Definitely. Maybe a collie."

"Can we call him Shep?"

"Absolutely! Shep it is."

"We'll walk the beach here, just you and me and Shep. We'll be a family. Promise me that one day, after your disaster has struck us and we've survived it, that that will happen."

"I promise."

"Really?"

"Maybe." Who knew? But it was nice to be optimistic.

As soon as Ryan got back to Ireland, he started canceling weekends again. He also produced a girlfriend, the first of many, all of them virtually identical. Every one of them broke up with him at the eight-week mark.

The first girl was called Maya—a twentysomething with stenciled eyebrows and eleven earrings.

Betsy disapproved of her. "Did you see her shoes? They're so high. Did she like steal them from a drag queen?"

"Just because you look like an Amish." Jeffrey had a massive crush on Maya. "She's pretty. She has a tattoo on her bum."

"She showed it to you?" It was time for me to be worried.

"She told me. A dolphin."

A dolphin? For the love of God. Would it have killed her to be a bit original?

And so the summer moved on and I lived in a state of constant dread, surviving on little parcels of time with Mannix and waiting for him to decide I wasn't worth the trouble.

Then came that otherwise ordinary day in late August. I'd finished work and had popped home to pick up the kids; we were going to Dundrum to buy stuff for their new school year, which was starting the following week.

"Come on." I stood at the front door and shook my keys. "Let's go."

"Have you seen this?" Betsy asked warily.

"Have I seen what?"

"This." The photo of Annabeth Browning, the drug-addict wife of the U.S. vice president, hiding out in a convent and reading the book I'd written.

One short phone call later established that Uncle Peter's sister's light-fingered friend was, in all likelihood, the reason that the book had shown up in D.C., and I was seized with fear. Which increased exponentially when the phone rang and it was Phyllis Teerlinck offering to represent me. When she hung up, the phone immediately rang again. I let it go to answerphone; this time it was a journalist calling. As soon as she finished speaking, the phone rang again. And again. And again.

It was like being under siege. We sat and watched the ringing phone until Betsy jumped up and pulled the wire from the wall and said, "We need Auntie Karen."

"No," Jeffrey said. "We need Dr. Taylor."

I was hugely surprised. Over four months since they'd first met, Jeffrey still bristled with hostility at the mere mention of Mannix's name.

"Ring him, Mom. He'll know what to do."

So I rang him. "Mannix. I need you."

"Oookaaay," he said, softly. "Just give me a moment to lock the door . . ." He thought I was ringing for phone sex. Our times together were so short and unpredictable that we took our chances where we could.

"No, not that. How soon can you get over here? I'll explain while you're driving."

I let Mannix into the house.

"There are photographers out in the street," he said.

"Oh my God!" I stuck my head out, then whipped it back in again. "What do they want?"

"Three Happy Meals and a Maltesers McFlurry."

I glared at him and he laughed. "Photos, I'm guessing."

"Mannix, it's not funny."

"I'm sorry. Hi, Betsy, hi, Jeffrey—is it okay if I close the curtains and blinds? Just until those people outside go away. So show me this magazine."

Jeffrey thrust it in front of him. "The woman who rang was called Phyllis Teerlinck," he said. "She wants to be Mom's literary agent. I Googled her. She's real. She has lots of authors. Mom knew about some of them. See." Jeffrey brought up Phyllis Teerlinck's Web site to show Mannix.

"Nice work," Mannix said. Jeffrey glowed a little.

"You know what I'm thinking?" Mannix said. "If one agent is interested—"

"Others must be also. That's what I thought," Jeffrey exclaimed.

"Really?" I was taken aback. "Why didn't you say so?"

"I was waiting to talk to Dr. . . . to Mannix about it."

"You want us to find out?" Mannix asked me.

I was caught up in excitement and fear and curiosity. "Okay."

Mannix started clicking at his iPad. "Let's try, say, five of the biggest U.S. agencies."

"Don't go to the big ones! Try some small, grateful ones."

"No!" Jeffrey said.

"He's right. You might as well go to the best. What have you got to lose? Okay, here's someone at William Morris who does self-help writers. Jeffrey, try cross-referencing the *New York Times* bestseller list with agencies. Focus on self-help writers. Where's my phone?" Mannix hit some buttons and listened. "Voice mail," he mouthed at me, then he spoke. "I'm calling on behalf of Stella Sweeney. She's written the book that Annabeth Browning is reading in this week's *People*. You've got thirty minutes to get back to me."

He ended the call and looked at me. "What?"

"Thirty minutes?"

"Right now, you've got a huge amount of power. We can play hardball too."

"Hardball?"

"Yeah. Hardball."

We dissolved into laughter that bordered on being out of control.

"I've another agency here," Jeffrey said. "Curtis Brown. They're big and they have some self-help authors."

"Nice work," Mannix said. "Do you want to call them?"

"Ah no," Jeffrey said, shyly. "You do it. I'll keep looking for agents."

So Jeffrey worked through the *New York Times* bestseller lists, finding self-help authors, and Googling until he'd found the agent's name and number, then Mannix placed calls and left the ultimatum: return the call in half an hour or lose the chance to be Stella Sweeney's agent.

The man at William Morris was the first to ring back and Mannix put him on speaker. "I appreciate you reaching out to me," the agent said. "But I need to pass. The association with Annabeth Browning is not something I'm comfortable with in the current moment."

"Thank you for your time."

It was mad, but I felt upset. Less than an hour earlier I'd never even considered that I wanted a literary agent, but now I felt rejected.

"Well, fuck him," Jeffrey said.

"Yeah," Betsy said. "Loser."

The agent at Curtis Brown didn't want me either: "The market is saturated with self-help books."

Gelfman Schneider also passed—the Annabeth Browning association again. Page Inc. wasn't taking on any new clients at present. And Tiffany Blitzer would prefer "to not coenmesh with Annabeth Browning, moving forward."

By the time Betsy plugged the landline back into the wall and Phyllis

Teerlinck rang again, I was feeling very chastened and all set to agree to anything she wanted.

"I hear you've been calling every agent in town," Phyllis said.

"Er . . . well—"

Mannix took the phone from my hand. "Ms. Teerlinck? Stella will speak to you in fifteen minutes."

To my shock, he disconnected the call and I stared at him. "Mannix!"

"I've had a quick look at her boilerplate client contract: her percentages are higher than the industry norm, her definition of 'intellectual property' is wide enough to almost include your shopping lists, she wants thirty percent on all film, television and audio-visual depictions, and she has an 'in perpetuity' clause that means that if you change agents, you still pay a commission to her as well as your new agent."

"Oh God." I didn't fully understand everything that Mannix was saying but I understood enough to have a sinking feeling. This wasn't real. No legitimate agents were interested in me. This whole episode was like getting one of those spammy e-mails that said you'd won a million euros, when they just wanted your bank details.

"Is she a bad agent?" Betsy asked.

"No," Mannix said. "She's obviously a very good one. Especially if she's as tough with publishers as she is with her own clients. But," he said to me, "I can get you better terms."

"I can do it on my own," I said.

But everyone knew I was a hopeless negotiator: I was famed for it. In work, Karen was responsible for all purchasing because I hadn't the brass neck to haggle for discounts.

"Let me do this for you," Mannix said.

"Why would you be any good at it?"

"I've had plenty of practice. I've cut a lot of deals to get Roland out of trouble."

"I say let Mannix do it," Jeffrey said.

"I totally do too," Betsy chimed in.

"Do you trust me?" Mannix asked.

Now *there* was a question. Not always. Not with everything.

"I will commit you to nothing," he said. "I'll make no promises on your behalf. But if you do decide to work with her, the conditions will be fairer."

"Let him do it, Mom," Jeffrey said.

"Do," Betsy said.

"Okay."

Betsy, Jeffrey and I holed up in the sitting room and watched *Modern Families* while Mannix established a command central at the kitchen table. Now and again, in the gaps between episodes, I could hear him saying stuff like, "Seventeen percent is killing me! I can't go higher than ten."

I'd never heard him sound so engaged about anything.

At some stage, Betsy tiptoed to the living-room window and took a sneaky look out. "They've gone, the photographers."

"Thank God." But there was a little part of me that was deflated. It was shocking how corruptible I was.

After four episodes of *Modern Families*, which meant he'd been on the phone for more than an hour and a half, Mannix hung up and made a triumphant appearance in the living room.

"Congratulations, you've got an agent."

"I do?"

"If you want one."

"What did she say?"

"She came down from thirty percent to seventeen on audio-visual rights, which means she really wants you—that's a lot of equity to give away. And on print she dropped from twenty-five to thirteen percent. I was prepared to go to fifteen."

"Well, that's . . . great."

"Still details to be ironed out, but it's small stuff. How would you feel about her coming here in the morning?"

"Coming where?"

"Here. Dublin. Ireland. This house."

"Wha-at? Why?"

"So she can sign you."

"God, she's in a hurry."

"She's had a preemptive offer from a U.S. publishing house. She needs a watertight contract with you before you can do a deal with them."

"You mean someone is offering money for the book?" I said, faintly.

"Yes."

"How much?" Jeffrey asked.

"A lot."

At 7 a.m. the next morning, Jeffrey and I were straightening up the sitting-room couch, where Mannix had slept, when we heard a car door slamming shut.

Jeffrey glanced out through the window. "She's here!"

Sure enough, a blocky woman, with short hair and a no-nonsense black skirt and jacket, was paying off a taxi driver. She looked like a Greek widow crossed with a bulldog.

"She's early," I said.

From upstairs came the sound of Betsy squealing, "She's here, she's here."

I went to the front door. "Phyllis?"

"You're Stella?" She rumbled her carry-on wheely bag up the tiny little path.

I didn't know whether to shake hands or offer a hug but she saved me the trouble.

"I don't do physical contact," she said. "Too many germs. I wave."

She raised her right hand and flashed the palm, like she was doing a single jazz hand. Feeling a bit foolish, I did the same.

"Let me take your bag."

"No." She practically shoved me away from it.

"Come into the house. This is my son, Jeffrey." Jeffrey was standing in the hall; he had put on a white shirt and a tie for the occasion. "No hand shaking, Jeffrey," I said. "Phyllis likes to wave."

Phyllis did her jazz hand and Jeffrey did the same. They looked like they were greeting each other in a science fiction film.

Betsy came bounding down the stairs like a golden Labrador, her hair still damp and fragrant from her shower. "Don't be so silly," she said. "I have totally *got* to hug you."

She draped herself all over Phyllis Teerlinck, who said, "If I get the flu, you get the blame and the doctor's bill."

"You are hilaire!" Betsy said.

"Would you like a lie-down?" I asked Phyllis.

She looked at me as if I were insane. "Get me some coffee and a place we can talk."

Then her focus moved past my face and over my shoulder—she'd seen something she liked: Mannix had emerged from the kitchen.

I turned to have a look—he was so sexy I could hardly believe he was mine.

"You must be Mannix," Phyllis said.

"Phyllis?" They checked each other out, like a pair of prizefighters about to enter the ring. "No physical contact, I hear?"

"I might make an exception for you." She was unexpectedly flirty. (And as Betsy said later, "I thought she was like totally lady gay.")

"Why don't you all go on into the sitting room?" Mannix said. "I'll make the coffee."

"Thank you." I was pitifully grateful. Mannix doing even the smallest domestic thing made my heart flutter. To see him boiling the kettle in my kitchen made me believe that there was a future where these things were normal.

In the sitting room, the table was set with plates and napkins. "Baked goods!" Phyllis said.

"Mannix got them." He'd gone out at 6 a.m. to the all-night garage and bought bag-loads of croissants and muffins.

"You mean you didn't bake them for me?"

"Well, I would have, but . . ." I hadn't baked in, like, ever.

"Mom," Betsy said, gently. "She's totally joking."

To my surprise, Phyllis Teerlinck didn't have a list of food allergies as long as her arm. She ate a muffin—"Damn, that's good." She ate a second, followed by a third, then she produced antiseptic hand wipes from her bag and wiped the crumbs off her mouth. "Where's that guy with the coffee?"

"I'm here." Mannix had appeared.

"You went to Costa Rica for the beans?"

Mannix surveyed the detritus on Phyllis's plate. "You eat fast."

"I do everything fast," Phyllis said. Again with that flirty overtone. "So let's parlay." To me, she said, "You want these kids here?"

"Anything I do affects them." I was mildly defiant. "Of course I want them in on this."

"Cool your jets, I only asked. So!" She produced a sheaf of paper from her bag which I guessed was a printout of my book and she waved it about. "We could go a long way with this. Drop ten pounds and you've got yourself an agent."

"What?!"

"Yeah, we need you a little thinner to make you promotable. TV adds ten pounds and all that blah."

"But—"

"Details, details." With a swipe of her arm, she dismissed my evident concerns. "Get yourself a personal trainer, it'll be all good."

"It will?" I didn't like the direction this was going in.

"Hey, *relax*, it'll be great. So first we need to fix the terms between you and me. You got the revisions?" She'd been e-mailing contract amendments until her plane had taken off. Mannix had printed out the final document and it sat in the middle of the table.

"You're good with the changes?" she asked.

"Um, yes, except you didn't deal with clause forty-three," I said.

"Which one is that?" Like she didn't know.

"Irish rights. I'd like to keep them."

She gave a sly laugh. "You're feeling sentimental and I'm feeling generous. Have them, have them."

She took the bundle of pages, crossed out clause forty-three, initialed it, then slid the contract and the pen toward me. "So sign it already."

I hesitated.

"It feels momentous?" Phyllis said. "Yeah, go on, take a moment. But it's not momentous. It's only stuff."

"You're a bit of a joy robber," Mannix said.

"Just keeping it real."

I scribbled my name at the bottom of the document and Phyllis said, "Congratulations, Stella Sweeney. Phyllis Teerlinck is your agent."

"Congratulations, Phyllis Teerlinck," Mannix said. "Stella Sweeney is your client."

"I like him," she said, to me. "He's good."

"I'm here all week," Mannix said. "Try the chicken."

"So, you said a publisher was interested . . . ?" I asked.

"Blisset Renown. You've heard of it? The publishing arm of Multi-MediaCorp? There's a deal on the table for twenty-four hours. They do not want a bidding war. This is a one-shot-only go."

"How much . . . ?"

Last night, on the phone, Phyllis had told Mannix it was "a lot," but she wouldn't name an actual sum and we'd spent a long time speculating about what "a lot" really meant.

"Subject to conditions," she said, "six figures."

Betsy gasped and I heard Jeffrey actually swallow.

"*Low* six figures," Phyllis said. "But I think I can get them up to a quarter of a million dollars. Life changing, right?"

"Cripes, yes." In a good year, I made forty grand.

"I could put it out to tender to all the big houses," Phyllis said. "But the Annabeth Browning factor is risky. She might be good for this book. She might blow it up in all our faces. Impossible to know. Think about it. And while you're thinking, tell me what's the relationship with you guys?" She meant Mannix and me. "Are you married?"

"Yes," Mannix said.

"Okay. Good."

"Oh! But not to Stella. To another person."

"Okay. Not good."

"Not bad either," I said, quickly. "We're both getting divorced."

"So what's the delay? Do it now."

"We can't," I said. "This is Ireland. You have to be living apart for five years. But we're as good as divorced. Ryan and I have agreed on everything—money, the kids, all of it. So have Mannix and Georgie. And we're all friends. Great friends. I mean, Ryan hasn't met Georgie yet, but he will love her. I mean, *I* love her and I should hate her, right? Fabulous-looking ex-wife, well, soon-to-be ex . . ." My voice trailed away.

"So what's it to be, guys?" Phyllis said. "Blisset Renown? Or you take a chance on the unknown?"

"I have to decide *now*?"

She leaned forward and said into my face, "Yes. Now."

"I need more time."

"You haven't *got* more time."

"Stop this," Mannix said. "You're bullying her."

"Tell me about the publisher," I said to Phyllis.

"His name is Bryce Bonesman."

"Is he nice?"

"Nice?" Phyllis sounded like she'd never heard the word before. "You want him to be nice? Yeah? Then he's nice. Maybe you should meet him." She had a little think. "What time is it in New York?"

"Three a.m.," Mannix said.

"Okay. Let me make a call." Phyllis hit a couple of buttons on her phone. "Bryce? Wake up. Uh-huh. Yeah. Yeah. She wants to know if you're nice. Okay. Yeah. Yeah. Gotcha."

She hung up and said to me, "Can you go to New York?"

"When?"

"What's today? Tuesday? Then Tuesday."

My head was reeling. "I haven't got the money to go to New York on a whim."

Phyllis was contemptuous. "You don't pay! Bryce Bonesman's guys pick up the tab. For everything." She waved her arm expansively. "The kids are invited."

Betsy and Jeffrey started squealing and jumping around the room.

"It's just for a day," Phyllis said. "You come back home tomorrow."

"And Mannix?" I asked. "Is he invited?"

Again, Phyllis looked contemptuous. "Of course Mannix. He made this happen. And he's your partner, right?"

Mannix and I looked at each other. "Right!"

Jeffrey abruptly stopped his squealing and jumping.

A long shiny car picked us up and Mrs. Next-Door-Who-Has-Never-Liked-Me nearly imploded under the weight of her own bile.

We were driven to an unfamiliar backwater of Dublin airport, where a fragrant charming lady led us down a glossy, glassy corridor into a room with art and couches and a full bar. Our luggage was ferried away and the fragrant lady took our passports and returned them a short time later, with luggage tags and boarding passes. "Your bags are checked through to JFK," she said.

Jeffrey was squinting at his boarding pass. "Are we checked in? We don't have to queue and that?"

"All done."

"Wow. Are we in business class?"

"No."

"Oh."

"You're in first class."

Ten minutes before the flight was due to leave, we were put into a black Mercedes—the most expensive Merc on the planet, if Jeffrey was to be believed—and driven about five meters to the plane. At the top of the steps, two female stewards greeted us by name: "Dr. Taylor, Mrs. Sweeney, Betsy, Jeffrey, welcome on board. Dr. Taylor, Mrs. Sweeney, can I offer you a glass of champagne?"

Mannix and I looked at each other, then started laughing a little wildly. "Sorry," Mannix said. "We're just a bit . . . We'd love some champagne."

"Come through to the first-class cabin and I'll bring the champagne in."

We stepped behind the magic curtain and Jeffrey said, "Wow! These seats are *huge*."

I wasn't a total stranger to luxury travel—at the height of the Celtic Tiger, Ryan and I had flown business class to Dubai. (The whole experience had been brash and blingy, but everyone was doing it at the time; we knew no better.) This, however, was in a different league. The seats were so enormous that there was only room for four abreast, two on each side of the aisle.

"Okay, Mom." Jeffrey suddenly took charge. "You go by the window. And I'll sit next to you. Then Betsy can go over here. And Mannix by the other window."

"But—" I wanted to sit next to Mannix. I wanted to drink champagne with him and experience every second of this together and . . .

Mannix watched me. Was I going to let Jeffrey do this?

"I want to sit next to Mannix," I said, weakly.

"And I want to sit next to you," Jeffrey said.

All of us froze in a tableau of tension. Even the steward, pushing through the curtain with her tray of champagne, paused halfway in and halfway out. Betsy had her eyes lowered, assuming her default setting that life was perfect, and Mannix and Jeffrey were both watching me. I was suddenly the center of attention and my guilt, always so easy to trigger, began flowing.

"I'll sit with Jeffrey."

Mannix flashed me an angry look and turned his back.

Jeffrey, smug and victorious, settled in beside me and spent the next seven hours making his seat whirr up and down, up and down, up and down. Far away, on the other side of the plane, Mannix made tight, polite conversation with my daughter.

At some stage I fell asleep and awoke just before we landed in JFK.

"Hi, Mom," Jeffrey said, chirpily.

"Hi." I felt muzzy-headed and I could hear Betsy laughing very, very loudly.

"You missed afternoon tea," Jeffrey said. "We got scones and stuff."

"Did you?" My tongue felt enormous.

The plane touched down, and as we stood up to leave, Betsy grasped me around the neck and gave me a hug that turned into a wrestling move. "Hey, Mom," she said. "Welcome to NEW YORK CITY!"

"Betsy?" This was far worse than her usual exuberance. "Are you . . . Oh my God, you're drunk?"

"Blame your boyfriend," she giggled.

Mannix shrugged. "Free champagne. What's a guy to do?"

The moment we stepped off the plane, we were hustled into a limo. "We need to get our bags," I said.

"They're being taken care of. They get their own limo."

I swallowed. "Right."

I'd been to New York a couple of times before, once with Ryan, long, long ago, before the kids, when we'd wandered the meat-packing district, looking for inspiration for his art. And again about five years back, on a shopping weekend with Karen. Both of those trips had been budget affairs and this was the complete opposite.

The limo took us to the Mandarin Oriental, to a suite on the fifty-second floor, with floor-to-ceiling windows and a view over the entirety of Central Park. There seemed to be endless rooms—dressing rooms, bathrooms, even a fully kitted-out kitchen. I wandered into a bedroom the size of a football pitch and Jeffrey appeared at my side. He scoped out the situation fast. "This is the master bedroom," he said. "You and Betsy can sleep here."

"No." My voice wavered.

"What?" He looked young and surprised and very angry.

I cleared my throat and forced myself to speak. "This is my room. Mine and Mannix's."

He glared at me with eyes of fire. He looked like he was considering saying something but eventually he set his mouth in a tight line and stalked away across the vast expanse of carpet, almost bumping into Mannix, who came reeling into the room, laughing in delight. "Stella, you should see the size of the flower arrangement they've sent! And . . . What's up?"

"Would you mind if Betsy and I slept in here?"

"And what? I'd stay in another bedroom? I would mind."

I looked at him, silently asking for mercy.

"Line in the sand," he said. "Got to happen sometime."

I lowered my head and I thought: I hate this. I hate it. It's so difficult. All I want is him. And for everyone to be happy. And for everyone to love everyone and for life to be simple.

"We won't have sex," he said, a little unpleasantly. "Would that make it easier?"

Before I could answer, the phone rang. It was Phyllis.

She had been on the same flight as us, but she'd been in coach. She'd told us that she always flew economy but charged the publisher for business class.

"Phyllis," I said. "You should see our suite!"

"Fancy? Yeah? Don't get too used to it; you're only staying one night."

"It must be costing a fortune."

"Nah. Blisset Renown put a lot of business their way; they'll have done some deal. And they sent flowers? They sent flowers. Bryce Bonesman's assistant will be over there tomorrow, soon as you've checked out, to take them home to her sad little apartment. So saddle up, he's looking for a meet."

"Who?"

"Bryce Bonesman."

"Now?" But we'd just got here.

"What? You thought you were here to have fun? You're not here to have fun. You and Mannix, a car will pick you up in thirty minutes. Look thin."

"Seriously?"

"Seriously. Look promotable. Wear Spanx. Smile a lot. And those kids of yours? A car is coming for them too. To do the sights, all that shit."

Bryce Bonesman was lanky, in his late sixties, and oozing sophisticated charm. He held my right hand and clasped my forearm and said, with great sincerity, "Thank you for coming."

"But thank *you*." I was flustered because he'd paid for the plane tickets and the magnificent hotel.

"And thank you, sir." Bryce moved his attention to Mannix.

"So they're here," Phyllis said to him. "It's great." She began moving down a corridor. "The usual place? Everyone in there?"

We followed her into a boardroom, where a small army of people was seated around a long table. Bryce introduced them all—there was Somebody Somebody who was vice president of marketing and Somebody Else who was vice president of sales. There was a vice president of publicity, a vice president of paperbacks, a vice president of digital . . .

"Sit by my side." Bryce helped me into a chair. "I'm not letting you out of my sight!"

The vice presidents laughed politely.

"So we love your book," Bryce Bonesman said. A cacophony of assent followed. "And we can make a great success of it."

"Thank you," I murmured.

"You know that publishing is dying on its feet?"

I hadn't known. "I'm sorry to hear that."

"Ease up a little," Phyllis said to him. "It's not your mom you're talking about."

"You've got a great backstory," Bryce said. "The Guillain-Barré thing. Mannix being your doctor. The stuff about your leaving your husband, that's going to be a little trickier to finesse. Is he a sex addict? A drunk?"

"No . . ." Suddenly I didn't like how this was going.

"Okay. You're still good friends with him? You all celebrate Thanksgiving together?"

"Well, we don't have Thanksgiving in Ireland. But we're good friends." Sort of.

"This is a once-in-a-lifetime chance for you, Stella. We're offering a sizable advance, but, if this works out, you could make a lot more money."

I could? "Thank you." My voice was barely audible because I was embarrassed to be considered so worthy.

Almost as a throwaway, he added, "Of course, we're going to need you to do a second book."

"Oh? Thank you!" I was profoundly flattered, then seized with terror: how the hell would I do that?

"Naturally, the offer is subject to conditions."

Which are?

"This book is not a slam dunk. You need to tour it and go on every talk show in the country. Grass-roots promotion, a lot of travel. We'll tour you possibly four times, starting early next year. Each tour lasting two to three weeks. We'll get you right out there in the boondocks. We want to make you a brand name."

I wasn't really sure what that meant, but I murmured, "Thank you."

"If you work hard, you could make it."

"I'm good at working hard." At least I was on solid ground with that.

"So you give up your job and base yourself here for at least a year. You go hard or go home."

I was surprised, almost shocked, then stricken with foreboding. I had already abandoned my children when I got sick and I couldn't do it again.

"But I have two kids," I said. "They're seventeen and sixteen, and they're still in school."

"We've got schools here. Excellent schools."

"You mean they could come with me?"

"Sure."

My head was whirling because I was almost obsessed with Betsy and Jeffrey's academic life. Betsy only had one more year of school to go, Jeffrey had two. What would moving to New York do to their studies?

But surely the schools here in New York would be better than the ones at home? And wouldn't the life experience of living in a different city stand to them? And, even if it was a disaster, it wasn't forever . . . ?

"The new semester is just about to start," Bryce said. "How about that for timing? And we can organize an apartment in a good neighborhood for you."

One of the vice presidents quietly said something to Bryce, and he replied, "Why, of course!"

To me, he said, "How does a ten-room duplex on the Upper West Side sound? With a housekeeper and driver and staff quarters. Our dear friends the Skogells are taking a year out in Asia, so their home is available."

"Yes, but—" Instinctively I knew that Betsy and Jeffrey would kill to live in New York—the bragging they'd do would be second to none. And that Ryan would—reluctantly, perhaps—agree to it, but where did Mannix fit in?

Phyllis stood up and announced, "We need the room."

Bryce Bonesman and his people got to their feet. I raised my eyebrows at Mannix—what the hell was going on? He messaged something with his eyes but, for once, I couldn't read him.

"A sidebar with my client," Phyllis said. "And you." She nodded at Mannix.

Everyone else filed out super fast; clearly they were used to this sort of thing.

To Mannix, Phyllis said, "Over there. Don't look. I want a moment with Stella."

In a low voice, she said to me, "I know what you're thinking. You're thinking about him." She flicked her eyes at Mannix, who had obediently turned away from us. "You're crazy in love; you don't want to be in a different country from him. But how about this? You need a person. An assistant, a manager, call him what you want. Someone running interference and taking care of business. There's going to be a lot of interfacing between Blisset Renown and you—travel stuff, promo logistics. He's good, your guy. He gets it. And before you even ask, I don't do that shit. I do great deals but I don't hold your hand."

"But Mannix has a job. Mannix is a *doctor*."

With contemptuous good humor, she said, "'My boyfriend, the doctor.' So why don't we ask 'the doctor' what the doctor wants?'"

"I'm thinking about it," he said.

"You weren't supposed to be listening."

"Well, there you go."

"Phyllis," I said, anxiously. "Bryce mentioned a second book."

"Yeah." She waved her hand dismissively. "Another collection of those wise, pithy bons mots, just the same as *One Blink*. You can do it in your sleep. First rule of publishing: if something works, just do it again, with a different title."

"And do you think they'll pay me the same amount?" I hardly dared to ask.

"Are you kidding me?" she said. "I could do the deal for your second book right now, this afternoon, and get you another quarter of a million dollars. But my gut—which is never wrong—says if we wait for the right moment, they'll pay you a shitload more."

It was her certainty, more than anything, that convinced me that a new life could be fashioned from the bizarre opportunity Annabeth Browning had given me. This was real.

To Mannix, I said, "Would you be willing to give up your job for a year?"

"For a year?" He went into some place in his head and I held my breath, hoping against hope. "Yeah," he said, slowly. "For a year, yes, I think I would."

I exhaled and felt almost euphoric.

"What about you?" he asked. "Are *you* okay giving up your job for a year?"

It was nice of him to ask but, to me, mine wasn't a "real" job, not like his.

"Perfectly okay," I said. "I'm in. A million percent." Life had suddenly revealed a solution to all my problems. Jeffrey would love to live in New York and if the price for that was me being with Mannix, he'd suck it up. I'd get to live with Mannix, to share his bed, night after night . . .

"Thank you, Mannix," I said. "Thank you."

This was the perfect moment to tell him I loved him. It had been worth waiting for.

"Mannix, I—"

"So this is done?" Phyllis interrupted. "We're good?"

Deflated, I nodded. I'd get another chance to tell Mannix I loved him.

Phyllis went to the door and called, "All of you, back in here."

When the various vice presidents had resumed their seats and the chair scraping and rearranging had finished, Phyllis stood at the head of the table and said, "You've got a deal."

"Terrific!" Bryce Bonesman said. "Terrific news."

Everyone was moving around and shaking hands and smiling and saying they were looking forward to working with me.

"You'll join my wife and me for dinner at eight p.m." Bryce Bonesman looked at his watch. "Which gives you time to view the Skogells' place and check out the neighborhood. I'll give Bunda Skogell a call, tell her to expect you."

"Thanks." I'd been hoping to go to Bloomingdales while I was still able to stand.

"And your kids tonight—Fatima will take them out on the town. Right, Fatima?" Fatima was one of the vice presidents and she looked a bit surprised at this news. "Take them to the Hard Rock, then to a show, but not *Book of Mormon*. Give them a good time but keep it clean."

He refocused on me. "Then go home tomorrow, shut your life down and get back here asap. We've got a lot of work to do!"

HER

"Have a Manhattan." Amity gave me a shallow glass from a silver salver held by a silent woman dressed all in black. "What better way to welcome you to Manhattan than with Manhattans, right?"

"Thank you." I was awed by Amity Bonesman's very high heels, her incongruously maternal air and her massive apartment, tastefully furnished with rugs and antiques.

"Oh, Manhattans." Bryce Bonesman had come into the room. "Amity always makes Manhattans when people are new in town. Hi there, Stella. Looking lovely. You too, young man." Bryce kissed me, then shook hands with Mannix. "Manhattans are a little bitter for my taste. I have a sweet tooth, but don't tell my dentist."

Mannix and I laughed dutifully.

"So!" Bryce raised his glass. "To Stella Sweeney and *One Blink at a Time*. Here's hoping it goes to the top of the *New York Times* bestseller list and stays there for a year!"

"Lovely, yes. Thank you." We drank from our bitter drinks.

"We've got a special guest for you tonight," Bryce said.

Oh really? I'd thought this was just a low-key dinner with my new publisher and his wife. I was half crazed with jet lag and adrenaline backwash and I didn't know how I'd handle any more hits to my system. But, obediently, I fixed a look of anticipation to my face.

"We're going to be joined by Laszlo Jellico."

Laszlo Jellico. I knew the name.

"Pulitzer Prize winner," Bryce prompted. "Great man of American letters."

"Of course," Mannix said.

"You've read him?" Bryce asked.

"Sure." Mannix was lying. Fair play. Far better than me at this sort of thing.

"I think my dad has read one of his books," I said. "*The First Casualty of War*, is that the name?"

"It *is*! This is the old guy with the bad back who worked on the docks from when he was a kid?"

"Er . . . yes."

Bryce Bonesman was probably the same age as Dad, but Blisset Renown seemed to have agreed upon a fiction that was my life—I came from a family of ill-educated, malnourished, soot-covered toilers, like the father and brothers in *Zoolander*.

"Laszlo will get a kick out of that. Be sure to tell him," Bryce ordered. To Amity, he said, "Laszlo's bringing a date."

"Oh wow. Who's it going to be tonight? Last time it was a Victoria's Secret model." She caught Mannix's expression. "Not really. But young. Really young and *really* hot."

She winked at me. "He'll like her."

"Hahaha." I had to pretend that I wasn't wildly jealous at the thought of Mannix finding another woman hot.

"The one before last got drunk out of her mind and sat on Laszlo's lap and fed him food like he had Alzheimer's. It was a stitch," Amity said, with an eye roll.

"We're also going to be joined by Arnold and Inga Ola," Bryce said. "Arnold's my colleague and my greatest rival. You met him this afternoon."

"In the boardroom?" Was he one of the vice presidents?

"We met him by the elevators as you were leaving."

"Oh!" I had a memory of a belligerent, toadlike man who'd said, "So you're Bryce's new baby."

"Was he sort of angry?" I asked.

"That's the guy!"

"She's a pistol," Amity said, about me.

"Arnold's really pissed that he didn't sign you. But he had his chance," Bryce said happily. "Phyllis gave him first look at your book and he said it was garbage. But as soon as I want you, so does he."

Mannix and I exchanged a flicker. *Keep smiling; keep smiling; whatever you do, keep smiling.*

"Speaking of whom!" Bryce said. "Here's Arnold and Inga."

Arnold—as belligerent and toadlike as I'd remembered—pushed toward me. "It's Bryce's new pet! And the tame boyfriend! Pleased to meet you, sir," he said to Mannix.

"We've already met."

Arnold ignored him. "So your little book has a publisher! How about that! And you're going on tour—the little Irish colleen charming the US of A with her sad little story about being paralyzed. I told my maid about you. She says she'll pray to the Mother Mary for you. She's from Columbia. Catholic, like you guys."

My face was flaming.

"And here you are in Brucie's well-appointed home. *And* he's booked Laszlo for tonight. You really must be important. He only books Laszlo when he really wants to impress."

"Laszlo is one of my dearest friends," Bryce said to me. "I've been his publisher for twenty-six years. I haven't 'booked' him."

"I'm starved," Arnold said. "Can we eat?"

"As soon as Laszlo gets here," Amity said.

"If we wait until that horse's ass shows, we won't get to eat at all," Arnold muttered. "Miss," he said to the anonymous woman holding the drinks tray, "can I get a bowl of raisin bran?"

"It's okay," Amity said. "He's here!"

In came Laszlo Jellico. He was tall and wide, like a petrol pump, with a big bushy beard and lots of leonine hair. "Friends, friends," he declared in a boomy voice. "Amity, my beloved one." He placed his hands on her breasts and squeezed. "Powerless to resist," he said. "Nothing beats the feel of real." He kissed all the men, calling them "my dear"; he refused the cocktails, demanded tea, then sent it away untouched; and he claimed to have been "quite transfixed" by my "sublime novel" when he obviously hadn't a notion who I was.

"And if I may introduce Gilda Ashley." His date was pink and golden and pretty, but, to my relief, she wasn't devastatingly sexy in the way of a Victoria's Secret model.

"What do you do, young lady?" Arnold asked, his tone of voice implying that she was a whore.

"I'm a nutritionist and personal trainer."

"Oh yeah? Where did you go to school?"

"University of Overgaard."

"Never heard of it."

Mannix and I exchanged a glance. *What a prick.*

"So you're Laszlo's nutritionist?" Arnold asked Gilda. "Whaddya feed him?"

She gave a melodious laugh. "Client confidentiality."

"So what would you feed me? I'd like the same diet as Laszlo Jellico, the genius."

"Maybe you should book a consultation?" Her voice was calm.

"Maybe I should. Gotta card?"

"No . . ."

"Course you've gotta card. Smart girl like you, smart enough to be working with Laszlo Jellico? Course you gotta card."

"I . . ." Gilda was flushed.

I watched, mortified for her. She probably did have a card but knew it would be bad manners to hand it out at a dinner party.

Salvation came from Mannix. "If she says she hasn't got a card, maybe she hasn't got a card."

Arnold gave him a fake surprised look. "Okay, farm boy. No need to get shirty."

"He's a neurologist," I said.

"Not in this city."

I opened my mouth to jump in and defend Mannix but he put a calming hand on my arm. With effort I turned away and found myself face to face with Arnold's wife, Inga. Without much interest she asked, "How are you enjoying New York City?"

Making a big effort to sound cheery, I said, "Loving it. I only got here this afternoon, but—"

Bryce overheard and said, "They're going to rent the Skogells' apartment."

"The Skogells' apartment?" Inga sounded surprised. "But you'll have your two kids with you, I hear. Where will you all *fit*?"

That was a slightly sore point—a "ten-room duplex on the Upper

West Side" sounded fabulous and enormous, but when my visit earlier this evening revealed that four of the ten rooms were bathrooms, it started to seem less impressive. Basically, the Skogells' apartment was a kitchen, a sitting room and three bedrooms. (The walk-in wardrobe counted as a room in realtor language. And the "staff quarters" was one shockingly small en-suite bedroom.)

"We're not used to much," I said, sweetly.

"It's a palace to us," Mannix said, deadpan. "An absolute palace."

"And in a beautiful part of the city," I said. "I can't believe that Dean & DeLuca will be my local grocery store." During our speedy walkabout of the neighborhood, Mannix and I had dropped in and I'd almost swooned at the freshly baked breads, the endangered-species apples and the handmade pasta. "When I was here with my sister five years ago, we were staying near the SoHo branch and every day we—"

"Dean & DeLuca?" Inga said. "My, the tourists do love it."

After a beat Mannix said, "We're quite the pair of rubes."

Inga gave him a sharp look. "Have you got a school for your kids? That's going to be a toughie. Most schools, there's a waiting list for the waiting list."

Almost triumphantly, I said, "Tomorrow morning at ten a.m., we're interviewing at Academy Manhattan."

"My. That's fast."

It was thanks to Bunda Skogell, who, perhaps sensing my disappointment over her less-than-fabulous apartment, had called in a favor. Her two kids went there and, in vague, delicate language, she implied that she had a certain amount of sway over the board of governors.

"It's a good school," Inga Ola said. "They do music, artwork, sports . . ."

"Exactly what I'm looking for. A similar ethos to their current school."

"Yeah," Inga said. "A good fit for the less academically gifted kid."

Much later, when we got back to the hotel, the kids were asleep in their separate rooms. I hadn't seen them since we'd left for the meeting with

Blisset Renown, hours and hours ago. "Should I wake them?" I whispered to Mannix.

"No."

"But all of this affects them. What if they don't want to live in New York?"

"Ssshh." His hand slid between my shoulders and the zipper of my dress whizzed down my back, the cold metal giving me a delicious shiver.

"You said you weren't going to have sex with me," I said.

"I lied."

His eyes were full of purpose. He steered me into our bedroom and kicked the door shut behind him, then flung me on the huge bed where, despite the presence of Jeffrey in the next bedroom, we had fierce, passionate sex. Afterward, as we lay in each other's arms, Mannix said, "That went well."

"What do you mean?" Sex with us always went well.

"I mean, Jeffrey didn't burst in, in a big black cape, singing the song from *The Omen*."

"Ah, Mannix . . ."

"Sorry. Will I turn out the light?"

"I'm so wired I feel like I'll never sleep again." I took a calming breath and was immediately seized by anxiety. "Mannix, Ryan is going to go bananas." I'd been saying this every chance I'd got, ever since I'd agreed to Bryce Bonesman's condition that I relocate to the USA. "I should have talked to him first. What if he won't let the kids move with us?"

"Then they stay in Ireland and live with him."

"But he can barely handle them two weekends a month."

"Exactly. Call him out on it."

"You're tough."

He shrugged. "I want this to work. I want this for us. Can we talk about me for a minute?" His tone was playful. "Tomorrow morning I have to impress Academy Manhattan with my daddy skills."

"You'll be great," I said. "You're great with your nephews." Fresh fear grasped me. "Mannix, are we doing the right thing? It's such a risk."

"I like risks."

I knew he did. And I also knew he wasn't stupid. If he was doing it, it couldn't really be that big a gamble.

"It was a weird night, wasn't it?" I said. "Arnold Ola and his horrible wife. And that Laszlo Jellico? It's like they'd hired someone to do magic tricks. But Gilda was a sweetie."

"Is Laszlo Jellico her boyfriend?"

"I hope not," I said. "She seems far too nice for him."

"Is this one unpasteurized? Aw? It's not?" The man pointing at a cheese behind the Dean & DeLuca glass counter seemed irked. "Then I don't want to know. So just show me the unpasteurized!"

I studied the man carefully; he wore a pair of smart-ish cords and a navy-blue polo-neck jumper in a strange, unpleasant-looking silky knit. He had a shiny bald head and looked the very picture of an Upper West Side intellectual. Also he was abrupt to the point of rudeness, which *again* was quintessential New Yorker behavior, so I was told. But, if Inga Ola was to be believed, he was just an eejit tourist visiting from Indiana.

The day had started with a lavish breakfast in our toweling robes in our suite in the Mandarin Oriental, then Mannix and I subjected Betsy and Jeffrey to a "serious talk."

I explained that I had a publishing deal conditional on me living in the United States.

"If your dad is okay with it—" I swallowed. "And we manage to get you into a good school, you would live in New York with me—"

The squealing and jumping started.

"—and Mannix," I finished. "If we do this, Mannix and I will be together. Living together. Think about it."

"It's totally fine with me," Betsy said.

"And you, Jeffrey?" I asked.

He wouldn't make eye contact—torn between wanting to live in New York and needing to demonstrate his disapproval. Eventually he said, "Yeah. Okay."

"Really?" I insisted. "You need to be sure about this, Jeffrey. Because once we make the decision, we can't unmake it."

He stared at the table, and after a long silence, he said, "I'm sure."

"Well, good. Thank you." I focused on Betsy. "What about you and Tyler?" They were still officially in love.

"He'll come visit," she chirped. He wouldn't, and we both knew it, but it didn't matter.

"So are you going to be rich?" Jeffrey mumbled.

"I don't know," I said. "It's . . . risky."

Everything was perilous and unknown. Who knew if the book would sell? Who knew how the kids would cope in the fastest city in the world? And who knew if Mannix and I would adapt from basically having an affair to living and working together 24/7?

Only one way to find out . . .

"Smarten yourselves up," I said. "But not too much. Academy Manhattan," I paused to quote from the promotional material that Bunda Skogell had given me, " 'celebrates the individualism of its students.' Betsy, don't brush your hair."

Thirty minutes later, we were getting the grand tour of Academy Manhattan's magnificent amenities. "Excellent," we murmured, at the swimming pool, the orchestra space, the glass-blowing room . . . "Excellent."

Then the real business began: the interviews. Three members of the board of governors interrogated us as a family unit to see if we were a good fit with the Academy ethos. Jeffrey was a bit surly but I desperately hoped that Betsy's sunniness would compensate. When the interview ended, Betsy and Jeffrey were taken to sit a slew of aptitude tests and I was subjected to a solo grilling with the governors. Their questions were fairly mild—what sort of parent would I describe myself as, that sort of thing—but when I was done, and it was Mannix's turn, my nerves were jangling.

"Good luck," I whispered to him.

"We'll be about thirty minutes," the nicest of the interview ladies told me. "Please avail yourself of the facilities in hospitality."

"Okay . . ." I tried to savor the comfort of the chair in the reception room but I was as jumpy as a cat as I focused on all the obstacles that might block this miracle opportunity—Jeffrey might deliberately fail the tests or Mannix mightn't make a convincing father figure without me at his side, feeding him his lines . . .

I stood up, wishing I could distract myself from the worry I'd try to think about nice things. Dean & DeLuca, for example . . . It was only a couple of blocks away; we'd passed it on the way here. When I remembered how Inga Ola had damned it as the haunt of hillbillies and hayseeds, I was slapped with shame. Then some fighting spirit rallied and I decided to go back and check—it was one small thing I could control in a life that had suddenly gone mad.

I didn't have much time so I hurried along the streets, and as soon as I passed through the store's doorway my heart lifted—the exuberant bunches of flowers, the architectural stacks of gem-colored fruit! Surely this wasn't simply another tourist attraction like, say, Woodbury Common? The silky-knit, unpasteurized-cheese man *certainly* seemed local.

In a bid to rescue my paradise from Inga Ola's judgment, I approached the silky-knit man and said, "Excuse me, sir, are you a native New Yorker?"

He stared at me from under hooded eyes. "What the hell?"

I had my answer. Rude, rude, delightfully rude: he was the real thing. "Thank you."

Feeling better, I went to stare at a sackful of coffee beans that had been passed through the digestive tract of an elephant. I'd read about this stuff—apparently it was more expensive per ounce than gold. I lingered, interested and repelled.

I would *die* if Dad could see me. He'd never had coffee in his life. ("Why would I, when I can have tea?") And certainly not coffee that had been processed by an elephant.

With some vague notion of buying presents for Mum and Karen, I moved on to the chocolate section and reached for a box at the same time as another woman did.

"Sorry." I backed off.

"No, you have them," the woman said.

That was when I realized I knew her: it was Gilda from last night.

"Heyyy!" She looked as pleased as punch to see me and I, too, felt great warmth toward her, so much so that, in less than five minutes, we agreed that she'd be my personal trainer when I returned to New York.

"The only thing is," I said. "I'm not sporty. Not one bit." I was afraid now. What had I let myself in for?

"We could try it for . . . say . . . a week? See if we're a good fit."

She gave me her card and reassured me that everything was going to be fine, which was nice to hear. "That's great," I said. "I'm so sorry but I'd better go."

"What's on for you today?"

"I pick up the kids and Mannix, collect our bags from the hotel, go to the airport. Fly home, tell everyone the news and start packing up my life."

"Wow. Big stuff. And Mannix? He's packing up his life too? He's relocating with you?"

"Yes," I said and let myself savor the thrill. "Mannix and I are doing this together."

We were sitting in the departure lounge in JFK when the news came that Betsy and Jeffrey had been accepted at Academy Manhattan. Betsy squealed and whooped and even Jeffrey seemed pleased.

"Wow." Mannix had paled a little. "We've got the school, the apartment, you've got the publishing deal . . . this is really happening. Time to start reassigning my patients for the next year."

Worried, I looked at him. "We don't have to do this."

"I want to. All the planets are in alignment," he said. "It's just . . . it's a big deal."

"I feel guilty about abandoning my clients when all I really do is paint their nails. So it must be much tougher for you."

He shook his head. "You can't do guilt when you're a doctor. You have to compartmentalize, it's the only way to survive. It's okay, Stella. It's only for a year. It's all good."

He reached for his phone and began clicking off e-mails.

I'd better start too. I had to speak to Ryan—I should have done it yesterday but I was afraid of the confrontation. And I had to work something out with Karen, perhaps see if someone could cover for me while I was away.

"Oh!" I'd remembered something. "While you were being interviewed this morning I did a quick visit to Dean & DeLuca and I bumped into Gilda."

"Gilda from last night? That was a coincidence."

"It was a sign—the planets *are* in alignment. When I come back, she's going to be my personal trainer. We're going to go running together. You can come too." Then I thought about it. "Or maybe not. She's a bit young and beautiful."

"*You're* young and beautiful."

"I'm not."

And even if I was, the world was full of young, beautiful women.

"Don't think that way." He read my thoughts. "You can trust me."

Could I? Well, I had no real choice but to believe him. Living any other way would just send me mad.

Back at home, as predicted, Ryan went berserk. "You can't take my kids away! To another country. Another *continent*."

"Okay. They can stay with you."

His lips twitched. "You mean . . ." He stumbled over his words. "Here? All the time?"

"For the next year or so. Until I know what's going to happen."

"You want me to stay here in crappy old Ireland, taking care of your children, while you and Mannix Taylor swank up and down Fifth Avenue?"

"They're your children too."

"No, no," he said, quickly. "Am I going to be the baddy who stops my kids living in New York City? No, it's a big opportunity for them."

I hid my smile. It was unattractive to gloat.

"So it's a good school you've found?"

"Similar to Quartley Daily but not as expensive."

This, Ryan grudgingly accepted as a good news story.

"And they can walk to school," I said. "It's only five blocks from the apartment."

"The 'apartment.'" Ryan couldn't hide his sneer. "Listen to you. And is Mannix really giving up his job?"

"Yep." I tried to sound breezy.

"But he's a *doctor*."

"It's only for a year . . ." I was thinking of getting a T-shirt printed with the words.

Everyone seemed outraged with Mannix, as if he had a duty to keep curing sick people. "Doesn't he feel guilty?" Ryan asked.

"He's good at compartmentalizing."

"I wouldn't go round boasting about that," Ryan said.

"Compartmentalizing can help you survive."

Ryan shook his head and smiled a small, mocking smile. "You keep telling yourself that and you'll be grand. So you're really getting a quarter of a million dollars? Do I get some of it?"

"Well . . ." I'd anticipated this question and Mannix had helped me prepare a reply. "You and I, Ryan, we've agreed our financial stuff . . ."

He shrugged; he'd only been chancing his arm. "You know it's not even that much, your massive advance? You used to make forty grand a year, Mannix about a hundred and fifty, right?"

"How do you know?" I knew Mannix's salary, but I'd never told Ryan.

"I've been . . . in touch with Georgie Dawson."

I stared at him. "Why?"

"Just keeping myself in the loop. Looking out for myself, seeing as no one else bothers. So, like I was saying, a quarter of a million dollars is only a bit more than a year of your current combined income. How are you and Mannix going to share it? You're going to give him a little bit of walking-around money every week, like he's your bitch? He won't go for that."

"This is none of your business, Ryan, but we've opened a joint account for our living expenses, rent and all the rest of it. Mannix didn't want any of the advance, but he deserves it: he made the book happen. And he's given up his job to work with me, so he should be paid."

"So you're sharing everything?"

"We still have the bank accounts from our current lives but we're opening a new joint account and from now on we're going to share everything."

"True love." Ryan pretended to wipe a tear from his eye. "Still, that money won't last long."

Defensively I said, "If things go well, we might make more. They've asked me to do a second book."

"As if that's going to work! This *One Blink at a Time* thing is a freak, a black swan. There are about eight million books published every year. There's an overwhelming chance that you're going to fail."

Okay, Ryan was jealous. He was the artistic one and this wasn't how things were meant to pan out. But I was the person who was moving to New York to live with the man of my dreams so I could afford to be magnanimous.

Not everyone was as mean-spirited as Ryan. When I asked Karen if I could take a year off, she suggested that she buy me out.

I was dumbstruck. I'd thought she was going to rage at me about how inconvenient it all was.

"You're over it," she said. "The whole salon thing."

She was right, and I was hit by a huge sense of relief.

"It's okay," she said. "I feel relieved too."

"It was always yours, really."

"Maybe. A couple of things," she said. "Good luck with your new life and all that, but don't sell your house."

"I wasn't planning to. I know this is a massive risk, Karen; I'm only burning a few teeny bridges."

"Good. Like, don't be stupid. Have a plan B. And a plan C."

Suddenly I felt queasy. "Karen, am I mad? Is it crazy? Giving up my job, moving my children across the world, Mannix taking a year off?" Nausea sloshed around in my stomach. "Karen, it's all just hitting me . . . I think, I think . . . I'm going into shock."

"Get a grip of yourself. This is a fecking miracle, like winning the lottery. Well, in a way. Not as much money as winning the lottery. But be *happy*."

I took a deep breath, then another one. "Listen, I'm going to sell my car. I've nowhere to put it."

"Leave it with me," she said, quickly. "I'll do it. Another thing—I hear you and Mannix Taylor are opening a joint bank account. I think you're crazy. I'd never let Enda Mulreid have a penny of mine. So, the money from your share of the salon, I'm putting it in a new account for you and just you. Call it your rainy day account, your running away account, whatever. One day you might be glad of it."

"But you just told me to be happy."

"Be happy *and* careful."

"Happy *and* careful," I repeated, a little sarcastically. "Okay, I must go, to tell Mum and Dad."

Mum and Dad claimed to be delighted for me, even if Mum didn't seem to fully understand what was happening. Dad, however, was painfully proud. "My own daughter, having a book published, in New York! I might come and visit."

"Do you even own a passport?"

"I can get one."

Next, I called on Zoe, who cried uncontrollably at the news, but she cried uncontrollably a lot these days.

"I'm sorry," she sniffed. "You deserve this. You went through hell when you were sick. Now something good has come of it. But I'll miss you."

"It's not forever."

"And while you're over there, I'll be able to visit and stay, rent free. Maybe I'll even move in with you, seeing as my life here has fallen to pieces."

"It'll improve."

"You think?"

"Of course." My phone rang. "It's Georgie," I said. "Do you mind if I take it?"

"Not at all." She waved me away and rubbed her face with a tissue.

"Darling!" Georgie declared. "I could die with joy for you! I lived in New York for a year when I was eighteen—I had an Italian boyfriend, GianLuca, a prince, I mean *literally* a prince, minor Italian royalty. Shedloads of them knocking around the world. Gorgeous man, not a penny to his name and crazy as a loon. Made me iron his shirts with vetivert linen water, and if I forgot he wouldn't screw me. Even today the smell of vetivert makes me weepy and horny."

I couldn't help laughing and Zoe stared at me woefully, hunched in on herself, clutching her tissue.

"Mannix tells me you leave next week?" Georgie said. "You're going to miss my separation party. I *so* wanted you both there. You couldn't change your dates just a teeny little bit?"

"I don't think so," I said, gently.

"Boo," she said. "Could you pop back for it? Simply jump on a plane?"

"No," I said. "You lovely nutter. But I'll see you before I leave. We can raise a glass of Prosecco to celebrate your separation then."

"Oh, darling. My bad. I always make everything about me. Congratulations on your book deal. Big kisses!" In a flurry of lip smacking, she ended the call.

"How do some people split up nicely?" Zoe asked. "I hate Brendan so much, I could spit. I wish every bad thing in the world to happen to him. I want him to go on holiday to Australia, and when he lands I want his father to die so he'll have to fly straight back home. I want him to get dick rot. You know, I Google diseases and wish them on him. There's this awful thing you can get in your anus, a bacteria that causes constant itching—"

I had to stop her. She could keep going in this vein for hours. Quickly, I said, "It wasn't always friendly with Mannix and Georgie."

"But it is now."

"Yep. Divorce paperwork filed, the house sold . . ."

"Negative equity?" Zoe asked hopefully.

"No debt. No money in it either. But a clean break."

Planets in alignment, just like Mannix had said.

Carmello twiddled a length of my hair around her finger and considered my reflection in the mirror. "You've great hair," she said.

"Thank you."

"With a proper cut, it could be really something."

"Er . . ."

Suddenly Ruben popped up at my side. "How much longer will you be?" He was nervy at the best of times but he sounded like he was going to start shrieking and not be able to stop.

"A bit more jhzuujhzing," Carmello said, languidly. "Then I'm ready for Annabeth."

But Annabeth Browning wasn't here. She'd been expected an hour and a half ago, and there was no sign of her.

"Ring her again," Ruben told his assistant.

"She's not answering."

"So text her, tweet her, friend her on Facebook, but find her!"

I was in a suite in the Carlyle Hotel, being readied for a five-page feature for *Redbook* magazine. Annabeth Browning had finally left the convent where she'd been hiding out and had moved home to live with her two children and her husband, the vice president of the United States. Everyone in the world wanted to interview her, but she'd agreed to an exclusive with *Redbook* and someone, somewhere—and I'd no idea who or how—had persuaded her to make the entire interview about how *One Blink at a Time* had "saved" her. Eventually the piece had morphed into "When Annabeth met Stella."

It was a big, big deal and both Annabeth and I would benefit. Annabeth would get her chance to say all the usual rehabilitation stuff ("I am stronger." "My marriage is stronger." "My faith in God is stronger.") and *One Blink at a Time* would get tons of publicity, just when I was doing my first tour to promote it.

People were milling about the suite—as well as Carmello, there was a makeup artist, a clothes stylist, a photographer, a features editor from *Redbook* and Ruben, my publicist from Blisset Renown. All the main players had brought assistants. I even had one myself—Mannix, who was wearing a dark suit and leaning against a wall, watching me and looking like he was in the CIA.

"Still no answer," Ruben's assistant said.

"So go down to the street and start looking for her. All of you! Go! You! Makeup girl. Go, go, go!"

Everyone stared at him.

"You!" He pointed at the photographer. "And . . . you . . ." He'd turned to scream at Mannix, but whatever he saw in Mannix's face made him step back in alarm.

Ruben's phone pinged. He looked at the message, and said, faintly, "Sweet Jesus."

"What is it?"

"Pack up, guys," Ruben screeched. "She's not coming."

"What? Why not?"

"Switch on the TV. Where's the TV? Try Fox News."

But it was on every channel. Annabeth had been arrested again. Just like the last time, she'd been driving erratically while banjoed out of her head on prescription drugs. A helpful passerby had filmed her taking a feeble swing at one of the officers.

"Looks like your book didn't cure her, after all," someone said.

Appalled, I stared at the screen. Poor Annabeth. What was this going to mean for her marriage, her children, her life?

Silently, everyone in the hotel suite began tidying away their stuff. As they left, they swerved around me, as if my bad luck might be contagious. A little later than everyone else, I realized that Annabeth's misfortune was also mine.

"Come on," Mannix said. "I'll take you home."

"Let's walk back." I felt dazed. "Some air might be good."

His phone rang. He looked at the screen and rejected the call.

"Who?" I asked. "Phyllis?"

"Not your concern."

It was definitely Phyllis.

He took my hand. "Let's go."

Late October and Manhattan was lovely—the temperature was mild, the trees were changing color and the shop windows were full of beautiful boots—but I was finding it difficult to appreciate it all.

"It's really bad, isn't it?" I said. "Annabeth relapsing?"

"Bad for Annabeth, sure. Bad for her family. But for you? It's just one publicity component. Ruben has lots of other stuff up his sleeve. Hey, was there something weird going on with his hair?"

I nodded. "He does that thing. Puts soot on his head to cover the baldness. Not actual soot, it's called Baldy-Be-Gone or something, but yeah, you weren't imagining it."

"I wonder what's for dinner?"

"I wonder." We both laughed, because we knew it would be Mexican. It was always Mexican.

When Bryce Bonesman had said we'd be getting a housekeeper and driver, I'd assumed he meant two separate people. But it was just the one person, a brooding Mexican woman called Esperanza. And there was no car; the Skogells had given theirs back to the dealer when they left for Asia.

Esperanza worked like a dog—she did all the shopping, the cleaning, the laundry, the cooking and she babysat in the evenings if Mannix and I went out. But she barely spoke and I wasn't sure if it was a language problem or a personality thing.

I tried making friends—on our first night, I invited her to join us for the dinner she had cooked, but she said, "No. No." And retreated to her woefully small living quarters, where she watched very loud Mexican soap operas. I felt uncomfortable about the her-and-us divide, but, as the days passed and more and more work was heaped on me, I got too tired to feel guilty.

"How am I going to spin Annabeth's relapse in my blog and Twitter feed?" I asked Mannix.

"Let's have dinner first and then we'll go to work on all of that."

As soon as we came in, Betsy and Jeffrey darted to the kitchen table. "Hurry," Jeffrey said. "We're starving."

No matter what else was going on, dinner with the kids was a fixed point in every day.

Esperanza—silent as the grave—served the chili and I murmured, "Thank you, thank you very much." She set a bowl of guacamole on the table and Mannix said, "Thank you, Esperanza." Then she set down a pot of refried beans and all four of us said, "Thank you."

"That looks delicious," Betsy said.

"Yes, delicious," Mannix said.

"Yes, delicious." I was sweating from the awkwardness.

Eventually Esperanza withdrew to her little room and her telly started bellowing in Spanish and I was able to relax.

"So?" I focused on the kids. "How was your day?"

"Great!" Betsy said.

"Yes, great!" Jeffrey echoed.

They were in high spirits—school was great, they were making friends and they loved being in New York. "It's like living in a movie," Jeffrey said.

My heart hopped with joy. Knowing that Jeffrey was happy took some of the poison out of my horrible afternoon.

"But I miss Dad," he said, quickly.

Right. "Of course you miss him," I said. "I mean, you were with him practically twenty-four hours a day, every day of the year. There's a lot to miss."

"Stella . . ." Mannix put his hand on my arm.

"Don't do that," Jeffrey said.

"What? Touch your mother?"

"Guys," Betsy said. "Let's be nice."

We ate in silence for about five minutes then Betsy said, "Are we all good? Because I have something to share."

"Oh?" I was instantly worried.

Betsy put her fork down and bowed her head. "Please don't be sad but Tyler and I have broken up. He's a great guy, he'll always be my first love, but it's impossible to sustain my schoolwork *and* give quality time to a transcontinental relationship." She raised her head and her eyes were shining with tears that I couldn't help feeling were a tad manufactured. "We did our best. We tried so damn hard—sorry for swearing! But we just couldn't make it work."

"Oh dear," I murmured.

"Are you okay?" Mannix asked.

"Sad, Mannix. Thank you for caring. Totally sad. He's still my best friend but we're transitioning to a new phase of our relationship, so I'm way sad."

"There're plenty more fish in the sea," I said.

"Mom!" She widened her eyes in horror. "It's like *decades* too soon. First I've got to mourn and honor my relationship with Tyler."

"Of course," I said quietly. "I'm sorry. I'm an idiot."

"You got that one right," Jeffrey said. "So are we done with this crappy dinner?"

"If you're okay to finish there, Betsy," I said.

"I'm okay," she said, in a near whisper. "I just needed you guys to know. You may find me crying or just staring sadly out of the window and I need you to know that it's not you, it's me, simply working through this."

"You're very brave," Mannix said. "And please know we're all here for you."

"I appreciate that."

"Right, then," Mannix said to me. "Let's get to work."

"Who made you the boss of her?" Jeffrey said.

"I did," I said.

"But you're always working. You never stop."

"Because there's a lot to do." I was sick of explaining this to him.

Bryce Bonesman wanted fast-track changes to *One Blink at a Time*. "You have to rewrite a lot of the book. Some of those sayings just don't cut it. And some, they belong to other people, right? So we have copyright issues."

Basically, they needed twenty-five original inspirational sayings and they needed them by mid-November in order to publish in March. "I wish we could publish in January," Bryce said regretfully. "No one publishes in January, it's a wasteland—you could have the market all to yourself. But we don't have time to turn it around."

Every evening, Mannix and I went through the notebooks he'd kept of our conversations in the hospital and so far we'd polished and finessed nineteen extra sayings that Bryce Bonesman had deemed acceptable. But we still had six to go and our deadline was two short weeks away. It was a lot harder than I'd ever realized to be wise.

What made it more difficult was that Bryce had told me that my second book was to be "more of the same." "Exactly like your first book, but with new material, obviously."

So I was in a constant bind between wanting to give all my good sayings to *One Blink at a Time* but also needing to hold some good stuff back for the second book.

Mannix and I withdrew to our bedroom, which also doubled as our office.

"That call you got after the photo shoot?" I asked. "Was it from Phyllis? She's canceled tomorrow's meeting?"

Mannix hesitated. He tried to protect me from bad news. "Yes," he said.

True to her promise, there was no day-to-day contact with Phyllis. All she cared about was the optimum moment to do the best deal for my second as-yet-unwritten book with Blisset Renown. So when she'd heard about my upcoming interview with Annabeth Browning for *Redbook*, she decided it would be ideal to have a meeting with Bryce and his team on the morning after. "They'll be high as kites and in we go, boom! We walk out with half a million dollars."

"Another time will come," I said. "So how bad is the fallout from poor Annabeth's relapse?"

"The public isn't making any connection with you."

"But . . . ?"

"Sorry, baby. There's an e-mail from Ruben saying four of the glossies have canceled the pieces you've written."

Ruben had made me do countless articles for the monthly magazines—some big, some small, everything from my first kiss to my favorite tree to the lipstick that saved my life—to be run in the April editions. The April editions—which were published in March, to coincide with my first tour—were about to be put to bed, so I'd been killing myself to get everything written in time.

"Okay." I took a moment to feel the loss. "What's done is done. So today's blog? Should I say that we're praying for Annabeth? They love that holy stuff here."

"I think you should distance yourself from her."

"That sounds a bit . . . brutal."

"It's a brutal country. No one wants to be associated with failure. You saw what they were all like today at the photo shoot."

Mannix's phone rang. "It's Ruben."

"Great news!" Ruben yelled. Even though he was talking to Mannix, I heard everything.

Some Midwest magazine called *Ladies Day* wanted me to write an article about my illness. "I know," Ruben said. "You've never heard of it. But it's massive in the heartland. Readership of eight million. They need fifteen hundred words by midnight."

"Midnight?" I said. "Today's midnight? Mannix, give me the phone. Hi, Ruben, Stella here, have you any advice on how I should handle the Annabeth story in my blog?"

"Annabeth who? That's how you handle it."

He went away. Mannix crafted some words, meant to have been written by me, for the blog and I started work on the piece for *Ladies Day*. Everything to do with my book happened at high speed, and I always felt like I was lagging far behind.

Both Mannix and I were clattering away at our laptops when the doorbell rang and jolted us from our concentration.

"Gilda," Mannix said.

"It's ten p.m. already?" Gilda came three nights a week to do Pilates with me.

"You too tired? Will I cancel?"

"No, it's okay."

"Look at you." Mannix laughed. "All lit up by your girl crush. Should I be jealous?"

"Should *I* be jealous?"

But I wasn't worried that Mannix fancied Gilda. It's not that I was naive—a bass note of low-level watchfulness hummed constantly in me—but there just wasn't any spark between them. They were civil and friendly, and that was about it.

Jeffrey shouted, "Gilda's here." Jeffrey, on the other hand, was mad about her.

Gilda stuck her head around the door. She was all smiley and rosy. "Hey, Mannix. All set, Stella?"

"Just coming."

I had my Pilates lesson in the hallway because there wasn't any other room to do it in. But Gilda had said, "Some of my clients have a private gym in their own home and they don't work as hard as you."

We started and it was tough, like it always was. Halfway through a hundred pelvic thrusts, tumbling noises came from Betsy's bedroom— clearly something had fallen, I was guessing it was one of her shelves— and she started yelling for Mannix. He came out of our bedroom and cut through the hallway.

"Sorry about this," he said, and for a moment he stood over me, his legs outside mine. He looked down and silently he mouthed, "I want to fuck you so hard."

Between the squeezing of my lady center I'd been doing and the look in his eyes, I was afraid I was going to orgasm there and then.

"Can't persuade you to do Pilates too?" Gilda said, in her melodious voice.

She was still in pelvic-thrust mode. Her hips were raised and her region was angled toward him. It was almost as if her voice had come from down there. He flicked the quickest, quickest look at it, then colored slightly and went off to see to Betsy.

After Gilda left, I took my laptop into the family room to continue work.

"Come to bed," Mannix said.

"I can't. I've to finish this."

"Come to bed," he said. "That's an order."

But I was too anxious to laugh. "Soon."

When I finally e-mailed the article and climbed into bed, Mannix was asleep. Sometimes when this happened, his arm would snake across the bed and he'd pull me to him, but this night it didn't.

At seven the next morning, Mannix and I were still asleep when the doorbell rang.

"Fuck's sake," Mannix mumbled. "Oh, it's Gilda. Time for your run." He woke up a little. "You still haven't found out if Laszlo Jellico is her boyfriend."

"She's mentioned him once or twice." I was pulling on my running clothes. "But I don't know if she's, you know, at it with him. I don't think she is. Go back to sleep."

"Me? I have responsibilities, including persuading your charming son to get out of bed."

My heart sank. Sometimes this was so very difficult.

"I'll be home in forty-five minutes. Thank you for getting the kids up."

"Whatever. Find out!" Mannix called after me. "Is she or isn't she?"

Down in the street, Gilda was doing her stretches. She wore a pink hoodie and a pink hat and looked so cute that it made me laugh. "You look like you're about twelve."

"I wish! I'm thirty-two years of age."

Thirty-two. I'd always been curious but hadn't known how to ask.

Going for broke, I asked, "And do you have a boyfriend?"

"I'm not dating right now."

I had a little think. I gathered she meant "No," but they arranged words differently in New York.

"Yourself and Laszlo Jellico . . . ?" I prompted.

"We had a thing. Nothing serious. Relationships are hard."

"I know."

She gave me a look. "Not for you."

"Yes for me, sometimes."

"But Mannix . . . ?"

I hesitated. "My son hates him. And we're very different, Mannix and I. We were brought up differently, we think differently." It was a huge relief to say this to someone who wouldn't judge me, who hadn't known the old me, the one who was married to Ryan.

"But you seem crazy about each other," Gilda said.

"We have a . . . spark." I was mortified, but this was my fault; I'd started this conversation. "You know, the physical thing. Sometimes, the rest of it can be difficult."

I got back from the run to find Mannix trying to get the kids out to school, so when Ruben rang I picked up. Usually Mannix dealt with Ruben's torrent of demands and fed them back to me in a more manageable form; however, he was locked in some standoff with Jeffrey over something that was totally inconsequential but that mattered to both of them.

"Great news!" Ruben declared. I had already learned to mistrust that phrase and I would eventually come to loathe it. "*Ladies Day* loves your piece."

"That's great."

"But they need some rewrites. About your faith. How prayer and your faith saved you."

"You mean faith in God? But I don't really have a faith in God."

"So make it up. You're a writer. They need it by this afternoon."

"But my author photo is being done this afternoon."

"So you've got all morning."

"Any news on Annabeth? How's she doing?"

"Like I said, Annabeth who? I've got a list of other smaller pieces for you. The *Sacramento Sunshine* want five hundred words on your favorite star sign, the *Coral Springs Social* want an original recipe from you, with an emphasis on low cholesterol—"

The phone was taken from my hand by Mannix. He mouthed, "Don't talk to him," then left the room.

Mannix was suspicious of Ruben. He didn't like his scatter-gun approach to my publicity. He said there was no structure to it, no targeted demographic, that I was simply providing filler for countless local newspapers and exhausting myself in the process.

A few minutes later Mannix was back. "Do the *Ladies Day* piece," he said. "It's actually got a decent readership. Unlike those other pamphlets that Ruben is plugging. And don't talk to Ruben, that's my job. Right, I'm going for a swim."

Every morning Mannix went to a nearby pool and powered through fifty laps, slapping the water like it had insulted his mother. "I'll be back in an hour."

I labored over the *Ladies Day* piece, trying to bump up my faith in God, but I couldn't bring myself to actively lie: that was wrong and potentially dangerous. Although I didn't believe in God, I was still afraid of Him.

During the daytime, Mannix set up office in the family room while I stayed in the bedroom, bent over my laptop. Now and again, through the wall, I could hear Mannix's voice murmuring on the phone, and it still had the power to thrill me. All I had to do was stand up and take my clothes off and in thirty seconds I could be having sex with him. But we had work to do. Sometimes I made coffee and left one for him by his door, but I didn't speak to him; that was what we'd agreed, the only way we'd get anything done.

At the moment Mannix had a side project on the go; he'd dropped one or two hints about it but I knew not to push him until he was ready to tell me. It was coming up to one o'clock when he burst into the bedroom and announced, "Thirty grand."

"What is?"

"Your advance from Harp Publishing. To publish *One Blink at a Time* in Ireland."

"Oh my God."

It had been my idea to keep the Irish rights out of the deal with Phyllis. I was just being patriotic. But a few weeks ago Mannix had realized that those rights could be sold. He'd asked me if he could try to land an Irish publisher and, apparently, he just had.

"They're really reputable. They've published a couple of Man Booker winners."

"Are you serious? Dad will be so happy. Jesus, Mannix. Thirty grand."

"Their initial offer was fifteen hundred euros. I got them up to thirty thousand." He couldn't hide his pride. "And because there's no Phyllis, there's no agent percentage."

"*You're* the agent. You've agented this. Mannix, you're an actual agent! Oh, Mannix, I'm so impressed."

"How impressed?"

I glanced at the clock. We needed to be quick. "*This* impressed!" I declared, putting the palm of my hand on his chest and shoving him onto the bed.

He was easy to undress—a T-shirt, a pair of sweats, they were off in seconds. His musky smell made my body open like a flower.

I lowered myself onto him and moved in sinuous figures of eight above him, squeezing myself tight and moving him with me. It was still a novelty, this control over my own body. He kept trying to speed up and I kept placing my hand on his abdomen and saying, "Slow down."

Eventually he flipped me over and the weight of his pelvis on mine triggered an immediate orgasm.

"Not yet," I begged. "Wait. One more."

"I can't," he gasped, and convulsed into me. "I'm sorry," he whispered into my hair.

I stroked the back of his head. "Testosterone boy. All fired up from doing your deal. God, I've never met anyone who loves sex as much as you."

"You love it too. You're having a long-overdue sexual awakening and you're just using me."

"Really?"

He shrugged. "Maybe."

At the studio for my author photo, the stylist brought along a case of stunning Jimmy Choos, which Berri, the art director, instantly nixed. "All wrong," he yelled. "You've got to look momsy."

I slid my feet into a pair of super-high, pointy-toed, bling-encrusted beauties and Mannix grabbed his phone and took a shot.

"Don't tweet that!" Berri said.

"Too late," Mannix said and we both laughed.

"I'm the art director! I'm the boss here! And you two need to take this seriously!"

"She looks great in those shoes," Mannix told Berri. "Why make her into something she's not?"

"This!" Berri pointed at Mannix and got the attention of everyone in the room. "This right here is why we don't encourage boyfriends on author shoots." To Mannix, he said, "You don't get it. It's not who you think Stella is: it's who we decide she is. And we decide she's cozy and safe. It's how her book will sell."

Quietly, Mannix said to me, "I'll buy you those shoes."

The stylist overheard. "I can do you a fifty percent discount."

"In that case, I'll buy her two pairs."

The three of us dissolved into giggles, which earned us cold looks from the photographer and Berri. But the problem was that this shoot was way too similar to four or five other photo shoots I'd already done, including yesterday's shoot-that-never-happened with Annabeth in the Carlyle.

Admittedly, each time, I'd had a different hairdresser, a different photographer and a different art director, with a different brief, but it was the same me with the same face. The waste of time and resources made the whole process seem silly.

We got home just in time for dinner with the kids. They were chatty and so obviously happy that it was balm to my soul. After the shoot today and the awful photos in which they made me look like a ninety-three-year-old great-grandmother, I'd wondered if I'd made an appalling mistake, uprooting us all and bringing us to this strange country.

When dinner finished, Mannix said, "Put on your new shoes and let's go out for a martini."

Regretfully, I shook my head. "We'll do it when we've delivered all twenty-five of Bryce Bonesman's wise sayings. Until then, we've got to keep working. Sorry, baby. Hey, any e-mails from Ruben?"

"No."

"Can I ring him? I just want to know if the *Ladies Day* piece was okay. I put a lot of work into it."

Mannix sighed. "I'll ring him. I'll put him on speaker."

"Hi, Ruben," I called across the room. "Was the *Ladies Day* piece okay?"

"Lemme see my e-mails. *Ladies Day, Ladies Day* . . . Right, here we are. No. They didn't like it. *Que sera*, right?"

"None of it?" I asked.

"None of it."

"So that's it?" I couldn't quite believe it.

"That's it. Junked. Onward and upward."

October ended and we hurtled on through November. Every day was insanely busy.

Mannix and I got our twenty-five new sayings in just ahead of Bryce's deadline, then I started media training with a consultant called Fletch. We did dozens upon dozens of fake TV interviews in which no matter what I was asked—what age were my kids, what was in my bucket list—I answered with "*One Blink at a Time*."

"Seriously," Fletch said. "Saying the title of your book every ten seconds is optimal."

I was given detailed points on posture, ankle crossing, head placement. Even the correct height of shoe to get the most upright angle for my body.

"And you need some jabs."

"Jabs?" I thought he meant inoculations.

"You know, filler in your lips, Botox around the eyes. Nothing major. Nothing surgical. I know a good guy."

Mannix opposed it furiously. "It'll ruin your face."

Until now I'd resisted injectables because Karen wrought such disaster on the faces she "treated," but I couldn't help wondering how I'd look if a proper person got their hands on me. So I went to Fletch's guy, who lured me in with his "less is more" approach and who sent me away looking a little fresher and brighter but not much different. A complete contrast to the poor creatures who staggered out of Honey Day Spa after Karen's ministrations, often looking like they'd had a stroke.

In fact, the improvements to my face were so subtle that Mannix didn't even notice until I told him, and then he got angry. "You can do anything you like," he said. "But don't do it behind my back."

"Sorry," I said. But I wasn't. I was really very, very pleased with my perkified face.

However, despite my jabs and all the Pilates and running I'd been doing, Fletch deemed that I still wasn't TV ready. "Watch yourself on the monitor," he said. "See how round your torso looks."

My cheeks flamed with shame.

"Hey, you're okay in real life," he said. "But this is our job. We've got to fix this before the great American public sees it. Get yourself a nutritionist."

"I already have one," I said.

"Who?"

"Gilda Ashley."

"Oh?"

"You know her?" I asked.

"Just the name. So this is great, you have a nutritionist. Get her to turn you into a carborexic. No carbs like, ever. You don't even look at bread. If you accidentally see a pastry, repeat this mantra in your head: *May you be well, may you be happy, may you be free from suffering.*"

"Is the mantra for me or the pastry?"

"The pastry. It can't be part of your life but you don't wish it ill, right?"

"Right."

"If you say it often enough, you'll find that your attitude genuinely changes to one of love and compassion."

"Okay."

Funnily enough, I'd always heard it was Los Angeles that was full of nutters, not New York. Well, we live and learn.

So Gilda got total control of my diet. Every morning she delivered a chill container with my food for the day. For breakfast I got a strange green juice including, among other things, kale and cayenne pepper.

"Midmorning, if you get really hungry—and I mean *really* hungry—you can eat this." She gave me a little Tupperware box.

"What is it?"

"A brazil nut."

I looked in at it. It rumbled around in the box, seeming so small that it made me laugh and laugh and soon Gilda was laughing too.

"I know," she said. "It's a bit sad looking, right?"

"What would Laszlo Jellico have said if you gave him one of these?"

I changed my voice to a pompous boom: "This is no good to me, Gilda my dear. Bring me Amity Bonesman's boobies! Let me suckle on them awhile."

Gilda was still laughing—sort of—but she'd gone pink.

"I'm sorry!" I clapped a hand over my mouth.

"That's okay," she said, a little coldly.

I smiled, uncertainly. "I'm sorry, Gilda."

I realized I was afraid of losing her. She was the closest thing I had to a girlfriend in New York. I missed Karen and Zoe, and I was working too hard to have time to make any other women friends.

"It's okay." Gilda smiled. "We're good."

S tarting with Thanksgiving at the end of November, New York turned into party season. Blisset Renown had their Happy Holidays shindig on 10 December. But they held it in their offices because, as everyone kept telling me, "publishing was dying on its feet" and it would be unseemly to spend a fortune on a big blowout.

I was making awkward small talk with two production editors when something sharp was poked into my bum. I turned around. It was Phyllis Teerlinck, whom I literally had not clapped eycs on since the day she'd done my book deal, all that time ago in August. "Hey there," she said, wielding the pen that she'd stuck into me. "My God, what have they done? They've 'New Yorked' you! Shiny and skinny!"

"Lovely to see you, Phyllis."

"No touching!" She repelled my protoembrace by showing me the palm of her hand. "I hate these things. Everyone kissing everyone else's asses. Hey there, girls." She addressed the two women I'd been talking to. "I'm just picking up some cupcakes for my cats. Yeah, I'm the crazy lady who lives alone with her cats. Give me that tray." She decanted a tray of pastel-iced mini cupcakes into a large Tupperware container, which she then put into a small wheely bag. "So, Stella, where's that sexy man of yours?"

"Over there."

Standing nearby, leaning against some shelves, Mannix was talking to Gilda. Gilda said something that made him laugh.

"Great teeth," Phyllis said. "Very white. Who's that little popsicle he's talking to?"

"Her name is Gilda Ashley."

"Oh yeah? Why's she here?"

"She asked if she could come. And . . . why not?"

"You trust Mannix with her?"

To amuse Phyllis, I shook my head. "Nooooo."

Phyllis laughed. "Wise, Stella."

As if he felt our scrutiny, Mannix looked at me and mouthed, "Okay?"

I nodded. Yes, okay.

Then he noticed Phyllis and he came over, trailing Gilda with him.

"I hear you did a deal," Phyllis said to Mannix. "With a teeny-tiny Irish publishing house. Good for you! Let's hope I haven't accidentally omitted any other territories from our contract, right? You'd make a good agent."

Mannix inclined his head graciously. "Coming from you, that's quite a compliment. So will we see you in the new year?"

"What? You want me to take you two out for a fancy lunch on my dime? When Stella's written her second book and the time is right, I'll do a new deal and make you a lot of money. Until then, happy holidays!"

She noodled her way through the guests, then lifted a tray of cupcakes from the hands of a surprised-looking intern and emptied it into one of her boxes.

"She's your agent?" Gilda said. "My God, she's . . . *horrible*."

On 21 December, Mannix, Betsy, Jeffrey and I flew to Ireland for Christmas. It was all a bit weird because we had nowhere to live. My house had tenants in it and Mannix had no home at all. There wasn't enough room in Mum and Dad's for the four of us. Turbo capable as Karen was, I didn't think it was fair to land us all on top of her and her two young children. Rosa's house was full because Mannix's parents had come from France. Hero and her family had had to downsize to a two-bedroom box when Harry had been made redundant from his banking job, so there was no space there either.

In the end, Betsy and Jeffrey stayed with Ryan, Mannix stayed in Roland's little apartment and I shuttled between both places.

I was anxious about meeting Mannix's parents, Norbit and Hebe and, as it transpired, I was right to be. Despite their reputation for being high-spirited and jolly, they clearly didn't think I was good enough for Mannix. His mum eyed me coldly and treated me to a limp handshake.

"So you're the one," she said. Then she noticed Georgie, who had shown up at this Taylor family get-together, and she gasped, "Darling Georgie. Angel girl. Let me smother you in kisses."

Mannix's dad didn't even bother shaking hands with me, just scampered around Georgie, like a dog wagging his tail, trying to get in to lick her. I swallowed down my hurt and decided to be adult about this. But it agitated the suspicion I always carried, that I was a gate-crasher in Mannix's world.

Norbit and Hebe weren't the only ones who took issue with me. Ryan, also, was quite horrible—nothing new there. One night he came home, totally scuttered, and said, "There she is. The woman who stole my life."

"Stop it, Ryan; you're jarred."

"It should have been me," he said. "It was all over the papers here when you got your deal with Harp! And it's only going to get worse when your shitty little book comes out. You'll be on the telly and all. From now on I refuse to call you Stella. You are known to me as The Woman Who Stole My Life."

The following morning, he said, "I remember what I said last night. And I'm not sorry."

"Grand. I'm going out to see Zoe. She's nice to me."

But Zoe told me she was "on the turn." "I'm moving from sad to bitter."

"Ah, don't," I said.

"But I want to. I even have a mantra: *Every day, in every way, I am becoming bitterer and bitterer.*"

Not everything in Ireland was unpleasant—Karen and I had a great night out with Georgie. And I was really pleased to catch up with Roland. He was still decked out in his gaudy threads but had lost a bit of weight.

"I know!" he said, wobbling his still-enormous tummy. "Skinny, right? You're worried? You think I have a wasting condition?"

He made me laugh so much.

"I've been doing the Nordic walking," he said, with pride. "Soon I'll look like Kate Moss."

Back in New York, Gilda scolded me for gaining six pounds in Ireland. "We'll put you on a juice fast. Ten days to start with and then we'll review it."

Ten days!

The juice fast was horribly difficult. It wasn't simply that I was always hungry, but I found myself crying a lot. Three feet of snow fell in New York that January, bitter winds blew in straight from the frozen north and I was always cold and always weepy. Except for now and again when I found myself white-hot with rage, usually over something ridiculously small.

Gilda was kind but immovable. "All those pieces of pie you ate in Ireland? Now it's payback time."

One particularly miserable morning, it all became too much. The snowflakes were blowing in vicious flurries outside the window and I felt shaky and weak. Then the phone rang and a posh woman's voice said, "May I speak with Mannix?"

"He's out at the moment. He's at the swimming pool. This is Stella. Is that Hebe . . . er . . . Mannix's mum?"

"This is she. Please inform my son that I called. I trust you can do that?"

Then she hung up. Dumbfounded, I stood staring at the handset. I didn't want to let myself cry, but there was no one in the apartment to see, so I gave in. However, when Gilda arrived, I was still sobbing.

"Sweetie, what's wrong?" She was full of concern.

"Nothing, it's nothing." I wiped my face. "It's just Mannix's mum. She rang a little while ago and she talked to me like I was a . . . sneaky servant, a dishonest lowlife, and it scares me."

"But she lives in France, right?" Gilda said. "You never have to see her."

"But what if Mannix thinks the same way? Like subconsciously?"

Gilda rolled her eyes.

"Really," I said. "You don't understand. You just think we're all Irish, that we're all the same, but Mannix and I come from different worlds. We don't have much in common."

"Looks to me like you've got plenty in common."

"You mean . . . the sex?" My red face went even redder. Okay, admittedly, that was lovely. "But what if that's all we have? We'll only get so far on that. Gilda, could we please not do our run today? I'm too upset. My legs feel like jelly."

Sympathetically, she shook her head. "My job is to make you run. Your job depends on you doing it."

I put on my running gear, and out in the street the wind hit my face like slaps from a cruel hand. As I ran, I cried, and the tears froze on my cheeks, and I thought: I'm not able for this life. I'm not tough enough. Only hard people survive in this city, people with abnormal self-belief and drive and inner strength.

H appy birthday," Mannix whispered in my ear.

I opened my eyes, blinking to wake myself up.

"Champagne?" I said. "In bed? For breakfast?"

"It's a special day."

I sat up and sipped from the glass.

"Are you ready for your gift?" Mannix produced a miniature black carrier bag, which looked sheeny and expensive.

"Is it a puppy?" I asked.

He laughed.

"Will I open it?" I undid the bag's ribbons and found a small black box within. That, too, had ribbons and I undid them slowly. Inside the box was a black velvet pouch and I emptied its contents into the palm of my hand. Out tumbled a pair of silver earrings, set with stones that glowed with a clear, intense fire.

"Are they . . . diamonds?" I was awestruck. "Oh my God, they are!"

I owned no proper jewelry. My engagement ring from Ryan had cost about a tenner.

"This is awkward but, just so you know," Mannix said, "I paid for them, you know . . ." Out of a different bank account, not from our joint account.

"Is this how you thought your life would be at forty?" Mannix asked.

I could hardly speak. I was living in New York, with this beautiful man, and in four days' time I started my first book tour of the USA. I couldn't believe how lucky I was.

This was the moment to tell Mannix that I loved him. The words rushed into my mouth, but I swallowed them back—they would sound as if they'd been prompted by the gift of expensive jewelry, which was a whole world of wrong.

*   *   *

Gilda's birthday gift to me was two tickets to a Justin Timberlake concert, because I'd always had a thing for him. To make things extra great, Gilda gave me a one-day-only free pass on chocolate, ice cream and wine because she said that I'd dance it off. We went together to the gig and I adored every second: I shrieked every time Justin thrust his hips and wept buckets during "Cry Me a River" and danced so much in an overadrenalized state that my hurty-hurty high heels caused me no pain whatsoever. As we made our way home, me in a state of almost ecstatic happiness, Gilda observed, "We need to do this sort of thing more often. You don't have enough fun in your life. Have you ever been to the ballet? To *Swan Lake*?"

"No, and to be honest, Gilda, it doesn't sound like much fun to me."

"Oh, but you're wrong, Stella, it's absolutely beautiful. It's . . . transcendent. I'll get tickets. I think you'd love it."

"Okay."

And, to my great surprise, I did.

A nd then it was time to start the book tour . . .

At *Good Morning Cleveland*, the makeup woman found me a challenge. "Your eyebrows, what am I supposed to do with them?"

"What's wrong?"

"They're just . . . *awful*."

How productive I was! Only 8:30 a.m. and I'd already been up for three hours, flown five hundred miles and had my eyebrows insulted.

"I can color them in," she said, "but you need to not pluck them."

That was interesting, because one of yesterday's makeup people in—where had it been? Des Moines?—had told me they were far too bushy. But I didn't have the energy to go to bat on behalf of my eyebrows.

The feel of the soft makeup pencil on my forehead was lovely. I'd just close my eyes for a moment and . . .

"Stella?"

I jerked awake; I was looking into a young woman's face. "Power nap!" I said, thickly.

But there was nothing power-y about it—I could feel drool on my chin and I hadn't a clue where I was.

"I'm Chickie," the woman said. "You're in Cleveland, Ohio, and you need to wake up; you're on TV in seven minutes."

"How long was I out?"

"Thirty seconds," Mannix said.

"You're Mannix," Chickie said. "And you're going to need some base."

"Excuse me?" Mannix said.

"We need you on the show with Stella. We need to focus on, like, do you feel emasculated working for her?"

"*With* me," I said, for what felt like the millionth time. "He works *with* me."

This kept happening everywhere we went on this book tour. The media were obsessed with Mannix, and their questions always went one of two ways: how could I live with myself, having entirely emasculated a man? Or how did it feel, being a traitor to feminism by ceding management of my career to my fiendishly clever, controlling partner?

"We need to talk to him," Chickie persisted.

"No," Mannix said.

"See!" I said. "Not emasculated at all."

But Chickie had her orders. "We need him in this slot."

"You don't *need* my ugly mug on TV," Mannix said.

"You're cute." Chickie seemed confused. "Like, for an old guy. I mean, old*er* guy. Hey, I didn't mean . . . I need—"

"Stella is the star. You need her."

"But—"

"I *need* to not go on your show."

Chickie glared at him for the longest time, then stomped away, speaking rapidly into her headset.

"I need people to stop saying they 'need' stuff." Mannix watched her disappear. Regretfully, he said to me, "Sorry, baby."

It was okay. I guessed we'd got away with it.

But we hadn't. As a punishment, the host didn't give details of my midmorning book signing, so no one came. But maybe no one would have come anyway. I was quickly learning that the whole book-signing business was impossible to predict. I'd assumed that it would be difficult to scare up a crowd in the bigger cities because they had so much more choice and that people would be more likely to come out in droves in the backwaters, but it didn't always work that way.

Anyway, whatever the reason, Cleveland didn't love me and I was too tired to care. It was nice to not have to talk to dozens of people, to not have to say the same thing again and again. Mind you, it was hard sitting upright, a smile fixed to my face. There was a very real danger that I was going to nod off and crash headlong onto the table.

For eleven days now, I'd been on the road promoting *One Blink at a Time*. There hadn't been one day off. If you drew the route of the tour on a map of the USA and saw how often I was doubling back on myself, you'd laugh.

But I kept reminding myself of what Gilda had told me: I was lucky. *I'm lucky,* I told myself. *I'm lucky, I'm lucky, I'm lucky.* I was so tired I could barely dress myself, but I was living the dream.

In fact, if it hadn't been for the wardrobe plan Gilda had done for me, I really *wouldn't* have been able to dress myself. However, it worked like clockwork.

Although you can't factor in the entirely unexpected . . .

Later that same day, in Cleveland, Ohio, at a charity lunch, a drunken eejit slopped half a glass of red wine onto my light blue suede stilettos, the shoes that were in shot in nearly every TV appearance I did.

All credit to me, I managed to not bite him. Baring my teeth in a rictus smile, I poured white wine on the shoes, then doused them with salt and kept on smiling even though nothing lifted the stains. Smiling, smiling, smiling. All fine, yes, thank you, only shoes, hahaha, no, no need for the dry-cleaning bill, anyway you can't dry-clean shoes, you drunken old cretin, if you would just leave me alone now, please stop apologizing, please stop making me make you feel okay about it, I must go now, wonderful time, yes, thank you, yes, at least I have feet, true enough for you, but now I must go to a private place and scream.

Back in the hotel room, Mannix said cautiously, "You *do* have other shoes." No fool, he knew this was the wrong sort of thing to say to a woman.

"I haven't!" Tearily, I held up a pair of black boots. "Can I wear these with skirts? No. Or these?" I held up a pair of Uggs, then a pair of trainers. "No. No."

"What about these?" Mannix produced some blingy sky-high platforms.

"They're for evening, for gala dinner events. These shoes . . ." I held up the ruined pair. "They were perfect for daytime, for bare legs, for wearing with skirts. They were pretty, they were glamorous, they were even comfortable! And now they're ruined. I know I'm overreacting but they were the *very linchpin* of this book tour!"

"The very linchpin?" Mannix repeated and looked at me.

"The very linchpin and don't make me laugh."

He could always defuse a situation. For a few blissful moments, before we had to start work again, we lay side by side on the bed.

"Can't we get another pair?" he asked.

"They're from Kate Spade. We're in Hicksville, Ohio. They won't have Kate Spade here."

"I thought Kate Spade was over," he said.

"They've had a reboot. And you shouldn't know about things like that. Be a man."

He rolled over on top of me and looked into my face. "Be a man?"

I stared at him for a moment. The mood between us changed and thickened.

There wasn't time. But I didn't care. "Be quick," I said, tearing off my knickers.

He *was* quick. Just about. His moans were still dying off when the phone jangled.

"Jesus," Mannix groaned.

It was the front desk, telling me that a journalist was waiting in the lobby. "Thanks," I gasped. "I'll be right down."

"Stay a minute." Mannix tried holding onto my hips.

"I can't." I wrenched myself free of him. "While I'm out, will you see if you can do something about my shoes?"

"What if I try spilling more red wine on them and pretend it's a feature? A Jackson Pollock look."

"Okay . . ." It was worth a try. I pulled on a pair of jeans and boots that were all wrong for Cleveland and all wrong for an interview, but I had no choice.

"If that doesn't work we'll just cancel the rest of the tour," Mannix said.

"Grand. I'll be back in half an hour."

Mannix's Jackson Pollock spatters didn't work; they just looked like red wine stains, more of them. Then he'd tried cleaning the stains off with makeup wipes, but they gave the shoes alopecia. While I clattered out my blog, Mannix tried to order a replacement pair of shoes from Kate Spade in New York.

"You can overnight to Cleveland, Ohio? But we're flying to Tucson at five p.m. today. We leave Tucson at seven a.m. tomorrow. You can't guarantee they'll get there by then . . . ? Okay, tomorrow we'll be in San Diego between nine thirty a.m. and four p.m. But we don't have an address, we'll be moving around. Tomorrow night? Seattle. Great." After he'd given all his details, he hung up. "Okay, an identical pair of shoes will be waiting for you in Seattle."

I couldn't wear jeans and boots tomorrow in San Diego. I'd melt. I'd have to go out and try to find a temporary pair of shoes here in Cleveland but I had three back-to-back interviews to do.

"I'll go," Mannix said.

He returned with a pair of light blue shoes: they were patent not suede; they were round-toed, not pointy-toed; the heels were clumpy rather than curved and skinny. They looked plastic and cheap and horrible.

"Nearly identical?" Mannix sounded pleased with himself.

Rage—terrible, awful rage—rose up in me. Fucking *men*. They were so *stupid*. They hadn't a fucking *clue*.

Something somewhere told me that I was being irrational, so I swallowed down the fury and reminded myself that these crappy shoes were only for one day.

As it happened, that wasn't true. The Kate Spade shoes didn't make it to Seattle until we'd left. They were then dispatched to San Francisco to meet us there, but once again they arrived too late. They were probably still out there, to this day, in the great landmass of America, trailing in my wake, like a Grateful Dead fan.

While I was trying to make peace with the cheap-looking shoes, my phone rang. It was Gilda—and I wavered about answering. All through the tour, Gilda had continued my personal training by phone. She knew my schedule, so she factored in a run every day and Pilates every other day.

"Hey, Gilda," I said. "I've got my gear on, my earpiece in and I'm ready to go."

"Great!"

I lay on my back on the floor of the hotel room and breathed a little heavily. "Okay, I'm outside in the street now. I'm running. I'm at twelve-minute pace."

"Pick it up," she said. "Ten-minute miles. Keep that pace for fifteen minutes."

"Okay." I huffed and puffed, while Mannix quietly looked at me and shook his head and smiled.

Gilda spoke encouraging words into my ear and I made myself gasp for breath.

"Turn back now," she said. "But do the next mile in eight minutes."

I panted into the mouthpiece until Gilda said, "Slow it down to ten. Now twelve. Stay steady at twelve until you get back to the hotel. How's your food?"

"Good," I wheezed. "I ate the chicken and the green beans at the charity lunch. No bread. No rice. No dessert."

"And now you're flying to Tucson for a charity dinner. Same rules apply: no matter what they put on your plate, no carbs. Ever! Especially no sugar. I'll call you in the morning at five thirty a.m. Tucson time. Four-mile run before you go to the airport. Do your stretches now. You did good."

"Thanks, Gilda." I hung up and remained lying on the floor.

"You know," Mannix said. "This is crazy. Just tell her you're too tired to do it."

"I can't. She'd be . . . disappointed in me. Come on, we have to go to the airport."

The flight to Tucson was delayed by three hours and Mannix and I made good progress on our his-and-hers ulcers.

"It's a charity dinner," I said, my face in my hands. "All those people have paid for their tickets. They're expecting me to show up to talk to them."

Once we'd landed in Tucson and run to catch a taxi, I tried to wriggle into my evening dress and accidentally kicked the driver in the head. I was still apologizing when we drew up outside the hotel, where a deputation of hysterical committee members was watching out for me. "Hello," I said. "Sorry for—"

"Come on. This way." They bundled me onto the stage without a chance to catch my breath.

Immediately I knew it was a tough crowd. Sometimes the energy is with you and sometimes it isn't. I'd kept these people waiting and they were wounded, so as soon as I finished telling my story, the hostile questioning started.

"My husband got Guillain-Barré Syndrome . . ."

I nodded sympathetically.

". . . and he died."

"Oh dear," I murmured. "I'm so sorry."

"He was a good person, probably better than you. How come he died and you didn't?"

"Well, I survived because I was given a tracheotomy and put on a respirator in time."

"He got a tracheotomy too. Did he get the wrong kind?"

"Well, er . . ."

"Why does God let people die? What's up with God's plan?"

She stared at me, waiting for an answer. I was even less of an expert on God's plan than I was on effective tracheotomies.

"God's ways are mysterious," I eventually managed. "Any other questions?"

A Tucson matron with astonishing hair took the roving mic and cleared her throat. "Do you think they'll make a movie of your book? And if so, who would you like to play you?"

"Kathy Bates," I said.

A confused murmuring broke out at this. "Kathy Bates?" I heard them turn to each other and say. "But she's a brunette."

I'd forgotten the Americans didn't do self-deprecation.

"I mean Charlize Theron," I said quickly. "Or Cameron Diaz." I was racking my brain for blond movie stars. "I see a lady over there has her hand up. What's your question, please?"

"How do I get to be famous?"

"You could murder someone," I heard myself say.

A shocked *Oooooh* moved through the room. Aghast, I said, "I'm very sorry! I shouldn't have said that. It's just the tiredness—" *And* I'd been unsympathetic to the woman whose husband had died. This exhausting process had sapped me of my compassion. "I've been on the road for eleven days and—"

The mic was grabbed from me by one of the committee ladies. "Thank you, Stella Sweeney." She paused to allow some desultory applause and a couple of boos. "Stella will be signing her book in the auditorium."

The line was a short one. Nevertheless, I was on nutter alert. The nutters always hung around until the end. The nutters didn't queue up with the rest of the people and let themselves get conveyor-belted along.

Tonight, as a special treat, there was a nutter-off with two alpha nutters squaring up to each other. One, a perky lady nutter; the other, a bloke, an anger-management-problem nutter.

"You first," Perky Lady Nutter said, sweeping her hand in a gracious inviting manner to the man.

"No, you."

"No, you."

"Look, bitch, I'm letting you ahead of—"

As he was led away, he threw some pages at me. "It's my book. Critique it! Call me!"

Perky Lady Nutter leaned too close and said gaily, "I'm going to take *you* for cocktails in a great bar I know, and you're going to tell *me* your secret formula for writing a bestseller."

"That's so nice of you," I said. "But I've got to be on a plane in about six hours to . . ." Where the hell was it tomorrow? "San Diego," I said.

"Oh yeah?" She narrowed her eyes at me. "I bought your book! I recommended it to my friends. You bitch! All I'm asking for—"

"Thank you." I stood up and smiled around blindly. "Thank you, you've all been lovely. Tucson, yes, lovely. All of you here, lovely. But I must go now."

I grabbed an abandoned glass of wine from a table, downed it in one, took off my shoes and said, "Mannix, shall we?"

We got a taxi to our hotel, where I lay on the floor of our room in front of the minibar and poured M&Ms into my mouth and intoned over and over again, "Chocolate, chocolate, I fucking love chocolate."

R uben wants to talk to you." Mannix held the phone at me.

I widened my eyes and shook my head: I didn't want to talk to Ruben. I'd got back from the book tour two days previously and had spent the entire time in bed, almost unable to speak.

"It's okay," Mannix said, quietly. "It's good."

I took the phone.

"I have some incredible news," Ruben said, tantalizingly. "Are you ready? Okay! *One Blink at a Time* has charted. Number thirty-nine in the *New York Times* bestsellers. Meanwhile, Bryce needs to get you guys in for a posttour debrief. We'll see you Friday, at eleven. Bryce can take you for lunch afterward."

I lay back on the pillow, light-headed with relief.

Hot on the heels of Ruben's call came a flurry of congratulations from six or seven of the vice presidents.

Next to get in touch was Phyllis. "Number thirty-nine?" she said. "My cats could get to number thirty-nine."

Before the meeting, Gilda came to the apartment and blow-dried my hair—it turned out that as a teenager she'd had a Saturday job in a salon and had "picked up the basics."

"Is there anything you can't do?" I asked, as she twirled the brush through my hair.

She laughed. "My rocket science is a little spotty." Then she frowned. "You're not planning to wear that dress?"

"Er, yes." It was a really pretty one from Anthropologie; Gilda had helped me choose it.

"Not today," she said. "Sorry, Stella, but today you need to look tough." She began flipping through items in my wardrobe and brought out a sharply tailored suit. "Wear this," she said. "This is the right thing."

"Okay," I said.

At Blisset Renown, Mannix and I were herded to the boardroom table, where a small army of vice presidents was waiting. I'd expected to see Phyllis—she'd been copied in on the e-mails—but there was no sign of her.

"Welcome, everyone." Bryce strode into the room and took his place at the head of the table. "Let's get going."

It seemed we were starting without Phyllis.

"Great work, everybody, on *One Blink at a Time*," Bryce said. "Special thanks to Ruben and his team for the excellent coverage he got. And, of course, we're all thrilled that the book charted. So this is a good time to reflect and see where we are. We don't yet have final numbers from Barnes & Noble and online retailers, but we have hard information from the independents and we can extrapolate from there. For that I'm going to hand over to our colleague Vice President of Sales Thoreson Gribble."

Thoreson, an enormous-chested man in a snow-white shirt, sent a blinding flash of teeth around the room. "So the book charted, which is terrific news. However, we didn't get the optimal sales liftoff we would have preferred." He referred to his iPad. "We're guessing the Annabeth Browning association scared folks away. But the signs are hopeful. For example, sixty-four copies sold in one independent in Boulder, Colorado, driven by a rave review on *WoowooForYou*."

I realized I was holding my breath.

"Vermont also showed strong sales," Thoreson said. "Maple Books in Burlington sold thirty-three copies in a single week, driven by a lone bookseller who describes herself as 'passionate' about *One Blink at a Time*." Another blaze of Thoreson's gnashers. "So high five for that—"

"That's great, Thoreson," Bryce interrupted smoothly. "Stella and Mannix, you guys can read the full report at your leisure. To summarize, this is a marathon not a sprint. We've had an encouraging start and the plan is to build aggressively on this solid foundation. Could we have seen more encouraging results from the first tour? Hell, yeah. But basically it's all good."

"Thank you," I murmured, a little anxiously.

"There are many pockets of support for you out there, so our math-whizz Bathsheba Radice's cost-benefit algorithm indicates there's value in two more tours."

"Okay, but——" Mannix said.

"Here's the plan," Bryce said. "Another tour in July, when people are starting their vacations. Then we'll go again mid-November, to catch the holiday-gifting market. By the start of the new year we'll have had an avalanche of sales. Have your new book ready February first and we'll publish July."

He shoved his chair back and stood up. "Terrific to see you guys."

He was leaving? I'd thought we were going for lunch.

I stumbled to my feet and Bryce was shaking my hand and patting my shoulder, already halfway out of the room. "Stay well, Stella."

It was the middle of April and spring had arrived, seemingly overnight. The sun was shining, there was even a bit of heat in it. Mannix and I came home via Central Park, where hundreds of Day-Glo yellow daffodils lined our route. Despite being bum-rushed by Bryce, it was impossible to not feel hopeful.

Back at the apartment, I texted Gilda to let her know I was home and ready for my daily run. Fifteen minutes later, she arrived at my front door.

"So they didn't take you for lunch?" she asked.

"No . . ."

"Ah . . . Oookay. So! How's your crazy agent? What did she steal today?"

"She didn't come."

"Wooah! She just left you hanging in an important meeting? She doesn't do much for her ten percent."

Phyllis actually got thirteen percent but I still felt I had to say, "She's not the hand-holding type."

"Hey, none of my business. So, Stella, let's get out there and speed up your metabolism!"

"Be careful with her," Mannix said.

"Yeah, yeah." Gilda flicked her eyes upward. "Precious cargo, I know."

We went down in the elevator and stepped out into the sunshine.

"He's so nice to you," Gilda said.

"Ah, you know, he . . . Ah yeah, he is."

"Okay, get those arms pumping, get that heart beating."

"So are you . . . er . . . dating at the moment?"

It was strange, my relationship with Gilda. We were instinctively intimate, but because I paid her, some boundaries had to be observed.

"Kissing my frogs, kissing my frogs."

"You'll meet some lovely man," I said, encouragingly.

"Well, I'm sure as hell not putting up with some asshole." Her tone was clipped. "I'm holding out for a dreamy guy like Mannix."

I'm holding out for a dreamy guy like Mannix. Her words repeated in my head and—surprised and rattled—I turned to look at her. I'd always thought she was pretty but, unexpectedly, she appeared like a queen. A beautiful queen with the power to take Mannix away from me. My mouth fell open and I retreated from her.

She lurched toward me and grabbed my arm. Her eyes looked shocked and bright blue. "Oh my God," she said. "That came out all wrong. I know what you're thinking! But don't think it!"

I didn't need to speak; I knew my fear was all over my face.

"Stella, you and me, we work together, but it's more than that. We're friends. I'm so loyal to you. I would *never* hurt you."

I still couldn't speak.

"I'm not saying another girl's guy is always off-limits." She spoke fast. "No matter how good a person you want to be, if there's a spark, there's a spark, right?"

I tried to nod, but I couldn't.

"If a guy's relationship isn't doing well and you feel you and him could have something going on, then . . . maybe I would. But even if I didn't have this you-me loyalty thing, Mannix is crazy in love with you. I was just having a pity party for poor little Gilda. I was jealous. Not of you having Mannix," she added quickly. "Just wishing I could stop meeting assholes and start meeting nice guys."

"Okay."

We ran for three miles. But I still felt rattled.

As soon as I got home, I went straight to the living room.

"Mannix?"

"Ummm?" He was transfixed by something on his screen.

"Do you fancy Gilda?"

He turned to me. He looked surprised. "No," he said. "I don't fancy Gilda."

"But she's young and beautiful."

"The world is full of young and beautiful women. What's going on?"

"A long time ago I asked if the last person you slept with before me was Georgie and you said no." I couldn't *believe* I hadn't pestered him about it since. "Who was she?"

He was silent for a while. "Just a girl. I met her at a party. Georgie and I had already split up and I was living in that apartment you loved so much. It was a one-night thing."

I was so jealous I felt like throwing up. " 'Just a girl,' " I repeated. "That's a respectful way to speak about a woman you had sex with."

"What would you like me to say? That she was a stunner, a twenty-four-year-old yoga instructor with massive boobs?"

I pounced. "Was she?"

"I can't win. Look, I don't know what age she was. At the time, I was crippled with loneliness. And so was she, I'm guessing. I felt worse the next morning. And I think she did too."

"What was her name?"

"It doesn't matter. I'm not telling you because I don't want you to obsess. I hate that you don't trust me."

"I don't trust you."

"Well, *I* trust me. And look at it this way—you let me share your home with your eighteen-year-old daughter. Clearly you trust me with her. Stella, I'm not throwing any stones, but you're the one who left your husband for another man."

"Ryan and I had already split up." I stopped talking because I was lying. "Do you think Gilda acts flirty with you?"

"She's flirty with everyone. It's her . . . thing . . . you know, her modus operandi, her way of getting through the world."

"I know what 'modus operandi' means."

He laughed. "I know you do. Here's how it is: I was with Georgie for a long time and I didn't cheat. Things got messy at the end and both of us did stuff we're not proud of. I'm not perfect, Stella. I've made mistakes . . ."

I stared at him and he stared back at me and I had no idea what he was thinking. At times I found him impossible to read, like I didn't know him at all.

"We need to talk," he said.

My heart started beating faster.

"It's good news," he added, quickly.

"Oh?"

"*One Blink at a Time* is number four in the Irish bestsellers list."

"What?" I was extremely surprised. "How?"

"It was published last week. A lot of the articles you've written for publication here have made their way there. Even that one for *Ladies Day*."

"Really? Well, great." This was fantastic to hear, but my mood was a few seconds behind the facts.

"They've invited you on a publicity trip next month, but you're wrecked. On the other hand, you'd get to visit home and see everyone, and there wouldn't be any stress about whom we stay with because Harp would pay for a hotel."

"What sort of hotel?" I was dubious. We'd stayed in more than our share of grim, soundproof-free lodgings on the Blisset Renown tour.

"Any hotel we like."

"The Merrion?" I gasped. "They'd pay for the Merrion? Oh my God. Say yes."

He laughed. "And the schedule from Harp? They're asking for less work in a week than Blisset Renown did in a day. They want just one TV appearance—on *Saturday Night In*."

"Could I get on it?"

"They'd kill to have you," Mannix said. "I've had a deluge of e-mails from them."

"Could Dad meet Maurice McNice?"

"I didn't know he liked him."

"Oh he doesn't, he hates him. But he'd love a chance to tell him. Keep talking."

"Harp wants just one press interview and one book signing."

"And that's it?"

"There's one other thing . . . Lots of the radio stations are looking for an interview. But, as a favor to me, I'm asking if you'd go on Ned Mount."

Ned Mount had been a rock star before he'd been a broadcaster—he'd been in a band called the Big Event—and everyone loved him.

"I'd . . . ah . . . you know, like to meet him . . ." Mannix said.

"You would? Well, grand." I was distracted by my phone ringing. "It's Ryan. I'd better answer it. Hey there, Ryan."

"Hey there, Life Stealer."

I sighed. "What can I do for you?"

"I hear you're coming to Ireland to publicize your joke of a book."

"How do you know? Nothing is agreed—"

"There's something you can do for me, Stella—arrange for me to meet Ned Mount. Seeing that you've taken my entire life, you can consider this a small reparation, a chance to salve your conscience just a smidge."

"Okay."

As soon as I disconnected, my phone rang again. "Karen?"

"You're coming to Ireland? Nice that I discover it on the radio."

"It's not even decided!"

"Whatevs. That's not why I'm ringing. Something weird's after happening. You know Enda Mulreid?"

"Your husband? Er . . . I do." I mouthed, "WTF?" at Mannix.

"He wants to talk to you. The next voice you hear will be his."

After some crackling and throat clearing, Enda Mulreid's voice came on the line. "Hello, Stella."

"Hi, Enda."

"Stella, this doesn't sit well with me but I am asking a favor from you."

"Oh?"

"Yes. Well, *indeed* you might say 'oh' in an interrogatory fashion. I am behaving extremely out of character and you are, doubtless, surprised. My request is this: if you're going on the Ned Mount show, may I accompany you? I'm a 'long-term' fan. The Big Event was the 'soundtrack' to my 'youth.' However, it is necessary to state that I could never repay the favor by dint of my position in An Garda Síochána. To give an example, if you got caught breaking the speed limit, I could not intervene to quash the charge. You would simply have to 'suck it up.'"

"Enda, if I'm going on Ned Mount, and it's okay with him, you're welcome to come and there will be no expectation of anything in return."

"Perhaps I could get you a gift set from the Body Shop?"

"No need, Enda, no need."

I hung up and said to Mannix, "The Ned Mount show? We're going to have to hire a bus."

In the flurry of preparing for Ireland, the weirdness with Gilda got washed away. There was just one moment, the day following our exchange, when I opened the door to her for our Pilates class and we eyed each other warily.

"Hey, about yesterday—" she said.

"Please, Gilda, I overreacted—"

"No, I'm an idiot. I should've thought things through."

"I'm too sensitive about Mannix. Come in. I'm sorry."

"I'm sorry too." She stepped into the hall.

"I'm sorrier."

"I'm the sorriest."

"No, I am."

We both had a little laugh and, all of a sudden, things were okay again. As Mannix had said, the world was full of young and beautiful women. If I regarded them all as threats I'd be utterly destroyed.

"Just know," she said. "I'm devoted to you."

I realized I truly believed her. Even though I paid her, Gilda was my friend and more. She gave me her optimism and enthusiasm and she provided solutions to problems that were way beyond her remit. She demonstrated over and over again how much she cared about me.

"Everything is fine," I said. "We're good."

"Phew. So what about your trip to Ireland? How great is that? I can style your clothes for it."

"Well, I'm only going for a week and I'm just visiting Dublin and the weather will be consistent, as in consistently awful, but . . . Oh sorry, Gilda, that sounded ungrateful. Thanks, it would be great if you did my clothes."

"So!" Ned Mount twinkled at me. "Did you pray a lot when you were in the bed in the hospital?"

"Of course I did." I stared into his shrewd, intelligent eyes. "The way I pray before I look at my credit card bill!"

Ned Mount laughed, I laughed, the production staff laughed and the twenty or so men who had insisted on accompanying me to the radio interview, and who were watching avidly through the soundproofed glass, they too laughed.

"You were very brave," Ned Mount said.

"Ah, I wasn't," I said. "Shur, you just get on with things."

"We've been flooded with positive tweets and e-mails," he said. "I'll just read a few out. 'Stella Sweeney is a very brave woman.' 'I had a stroke last year and Stella's story gives me hope that I'll get better.' 'I'm loving Stella's humble, no-nonsense attitude. We could do with a few more like her in this country of whingers and bellyachers.' There are literally hundreds more like that," Ned Mount said. "And I have to say I echo the sentiments."

"Thank you," I murmured, mortified. "Thank you."

"So that's Stella Sweeney, listeners. Her book, which I'm sure you already know about, is called *One Blink at a Time* and she'll be signing copies at three o'clock on Saturday in Eason's, O'Connell Street. I'll be back after this break."

He took off his headphones and said, "Thanks, that was great."

"Thank *you*. And thanks——" I flicked a glance at Mannix, Ryan, Enda, even Roland and Uncle Peter, who were all pressing up against the glass wearing clamoring, beseeching looks—"for coming out and saying hello to my friends."

"No bother." Ned Mount stood up. "And well done again. I don't know how you endured that time in the hospital. You must be very special."

"I'm not. I'm off-the-scale ordinary." My face blazed with heat.

"Now, brace yourself," I said, as he opened the door and the mob of men descended on him. I couldn't stop smiling as I watched Enda Mulreid earnestly trying to convey to Ned Mount what the Big Event had meant to him—apparently he had lost his virginity to "Jump Off a Cliff." That was something I *didn't* need to know.

Other than hearing unwanted details about Enda Mulreid's sex life, this trip had been wonderful. Everywhere I went, people turned up in droves and I was celebrated for surviving. One of the reviews called me "the Accidental Guru." "You give us hope," I kept being told. "Your story gives us hope."

I went on *Saturday Night In*, where Maurice McNice described me as "the woman who's been taking America by storm," which was far from the truth, but for a while I joined in with the fiction and agreed that yes, it felt lovely to be a success.

Mannix and I stayed in the Merrion, where I ate and drank what I wanted and the only exercise I did was clinking wineglasses with Mannix. For a week I pretended Gilda didn't exist.

Of course it wasn't all positive. One newspaper ran a scathing review, headlined: "The poor man's Paulo Coelho? More like, the bankrupt woman's." And one of the more vicious lines said, "It took me longer to read this book than it took the author to write it."

Then my appearance on Maurice McNice was savaged by a TV journalist called William Fairey, who said, "Yet another self-pitying woman uses her 'sad' story to try to flog a couple of her rubbish books to other self-pitying women."

Roland—who had come to see Mannix and me in the hotel—took one look at it and laughed. "William Fairey is a bitter prick. He's failed at everything except being bitter. He is so beneath you, Stella. He's beneath all of us. He's beyond contempt."

In May, Georgie breezed through New York for a couple of days, en route to Peru.

"Why's she going there?" Karen asked me, over the phone.

"To 'find herself.' "

"Feck's sake," Karen said. "The rest of us have to 'find' ourselves in the borough we were born and brought up in, but posh girls like her can only find themselves by traveling to another continent and doing yoga on hilltops at dawn. Will she be gone for long?"

"Indefinitely, she says."

"So who's running her boutique?"

"The woman who's been managing it."

"Well, if Georgie ever needs any help," Karen strove to sound like she didn't really care, "ever needs anyone to cast an eye over the figures or anything, I could always do it."

"Grand."

"How do I look, Mom? Mannix?" Betsy asked.

She stood in the living-room doorway, wearing a minty-green satin ball gown, with workman's boots and an XL lumberjack shirt. Her hair was wild and uncombed and she'd drawn wobbly lines of thick black eye pencil right up to her hairline. But nothing could stop her being beautiful.

"You look fabulous, sweetheart," I said.

"You absolutely do," Mannix echoed. "Happy prom."

The bell rang and Betsy said, "The guys are here!"

Academy Manhattan's prom was as touchy-feely as the rest of its ethos: the pupils were "encouraged" to embrace a simple night, with no limos, no corsages, no coupling-up. A neighborhood Tyrolean restaurant had been filled with long tables and there was no seating plan, so everyone could pile in and no one would feel left out. Apparently, the Prom Queen was a boy.

"Come down to wave me off," Betsy said. "Take lots of photos for Dad."

Idling curbside in the late May sunset was an orange VW camper van which had been hired for the night. It was filled with teenagers, both boys and girls. The side door rattled open and I clicked off shot after shot. From what I could see, only one person had bothered with a tux—a stout girl, with slicked-back hair and vampiric eyes and lips.

"Get in, Betsy, get in!" Arms reached out to grab her and she tumbled in, and, amid squealing and shrieking, the van drove away.

Mannix watched them go, a wistful look on his face.

"Are you going to cry again?" I asked him.

Betsy had had her high-school graduation ceremony earlier that day, which Mannix had attended because Ryan said he couldn't afford the flight. As Betsy stood on the stage and accepted her rolled-up parchment and smiled shyly and with pride, I was sure I saw a little tear in Mannix's eye.

He denied it, of course, but it was at times like that that I was reminded of how he'd once longed for kids of his own.

"Shep," I said to him, as we watched the VW van shoot off down the street. "You, me and Shep, walking on the beach. Focus on Shep."

"Okay," he said. "Shep."

Shep had become our security-blanket word, our comfort word.

We went back upstairs to the apartment and I said, "I'm just going to send some photos to Ryan. Then he's going to Skype me and go mad about Betsy's nonglammy outfit."

"Fuck him," Mannix said. "She looked great."

"I'd say he'll be on in less than five minutes."

"I give it three."

Mannix won. In two minutes, fifty-eight seconds, Ryan's furious face appeared on screen. "It was her prom!" he yelled. "What the hell was she wearing?"

"She's finding her look. Let it happen."

"And what did her yearbook say?"

I swallowed. This was going to be tough. "She was voted 'Pupil most likely to be happy.'"

As expected, Ryan went berserk. "This is a disgrace!" he raged from across the Atlantic. "This is practically an insult. Who the hell wants to be happy? What about successful? Rich? Powerful?"

"Is happy so bad?"

"Is she still at that nanny lark?"

Betsy had caused massive upset some weeks back when she'd outlined her future plans by saying she wanted to be a nanny.

"That's not a career," I'd said.

"Oh really?" She'd shown an uncharacteristic flash of steel. "Whose life is it, exactly?"

"Betsy, you need to go to third-level education."

"Let's face it, Mom, I'm not the brightest, I mean not academically."

"You are bright! You're fluent in Spanish and Japanese. And you're extremely gifted at art and design, your teacher says so. This is my fault," I'd said. "We arrived too late in the USA to start prepping you for an Ivy League school. We should have come a year earlier."

"Mom, are you tripping? Even if that made any sense—*Ivy League?* I'll never be that person."

I couldn't get a read on Betsy. She was so out of step with the rest of her generation and, indeed, the entire Western world—she lacked the desire that everyone burned with, to find a job that paid shedloads.

I'd spent most of my life worrying about her future—hers and Jeffrey's. Even while I'd been paralyzed in hospital I'd devoted a huge amount of time to praying that Ryan was supervising their homework properly. But Betsy herself didn't seem bothered. It wasn't that she was lazy, just abnormally laid back.

I flip-flopped between being worried sick about her and wondering if there was anything wrong with actually being content with one's life.

"She's knocked the nanny thing on the head," I told Ryan. "She says now she wants to be an art therapist."

"Art?" he barked.

Ryan had the weirdest attitude to either of the kids showing any aptitude for art. I couldn't decide if he wanted to be the only artist in the family. Or if he despised art because he'd failed at it.

"Art therapy," I said. "It's a different thing." I spoke soothingly, because I had another piece of unpleasant news to deliver. "She interviewed well at a couple of liberal-arts universities. But first she's taking a year off."

"To do fecking what?"

"Well . . ."

"Oh no. She's not coming here, is she?"

"Ryan, you're her dad. She misses you, she misses home. Anyway, it'll be just a short visit. Then she's going to Asia for three months. Five others from her class are going. It'll be fine."

"Sweet suffering Jesus," he muttered. "And that other eejit is just as bad."

That other eejit being poor Jeffrey.

It was true that Jeffrey hadn't really found his groove, academically speaking. It had been established that he wasn't "mathematically minded." But he wasn't exactly excelling in the more artsy subjects either. At Ryan's insistence, we'd steered him toward what Ryan called the "more manly" subjects, like economics and business, but that hadn't taken off either. There was a short spell when he had shown an almost uncanny aptitude for Mandarin, but that had proved to be a disappointing blip.

"I gave them everything," Ryan said. "Ungrateful little fuckers. This is your fault," he said. "Just say it for me."

"This is my fault. There's one thing you'll like," I said. "Jeffrey's made a rich friend. He's been invited to their place in Nantucket for a month."

"How rich?"

"Someone said his dad owns half of Illinois."

There really wasn't anything negative Ryan could say about that, no matter what angle he came at it from, so, after a curt farewell, he hung up.

Mannix swished his glass of wine. "I'm getting shades of impertinence."

"Insolence, I'd call it," Roland said, smacking his lips.

I stuck my nose in my glass and said, "Could I be getting the tiniest hint of . . . actual *rudeness?*"

Mannix and I were on holiday with Roland in the wine country in northern California.

In early June, Betsy had departed on her trip to Asia via Ireland, and Jeffrey had gone to Nantucket with his rich new friend. All of a sudden, Mannix and I were alone in New York.

"It's weird here without them," Mannix said.

"I know. But it's a good chance to start the second book."

"Why don't we go on holiday?" Mannix said. "Just for a week?"

"No way." I was adamant. I kept a beady eye on our money. A quarter of a million dollars had sounded huge—it *was* huge—but our rent and taxes and the day-to-day costs of living in New York were crippling. All kinds of unexpected expenses had popped up—like hiring a nanny to take care of the kids while I was on tour—and the advance was eroding much more quickly than I'd anticipated.

"You've had a tough year," Mannix said. "You've worked so hard; you need a rest."

"I know, but . . ."

"How would you feel about going someplace with Roland?"

"Roland?" I practically shrieked. "Where's Roland going to get money for a holiday from?"

"He's just brokered the sale of an office block and he's paid off a big lump of his debts. He says there are a couple of other things in the pipeline. And he's been behaving so well, going to his Debtors Anonymous meetings . . ."

I chewed my lip.

"Just for a week," Mannix repeated.

"I'm agreeing to nothing, but where would we go?"

"Wherever you like." He shrugged. "The wine country in California?"

"Would it be nice?" I asked, suspiciously.

"I'd say it would be wonderful."

And, oh God, I was so tempted.

"Okay." I squeezed my eyes shut. "Okay. Do it. Let's do it!"

It all came together very quickly. We met Roland in San Francisco and hired a car and drove north, stopping off at vineyards and artisanal food makers during the days and every evening staying at "inns," which were in actuality five-star hotels but with chintz. They had stables and Michelin-starred restaurants and private wineries.

It was blissful—the sunshine, the daily drives through beautiful countryside and the pleasure of seeing Mannix so happy.

Roland was part of some secretive foodie online collective—each morning he input his GPS coordinates and we were given magical mystery-tour directions to the location of some remote baker who ground his own flour by hand, or a duo of brothers who used some extraordinary technique for smoking bacon.

I wasn't a foodie. I didn't care if bread came from a massive factory or from an ancient water mill, but each adventure was great fun. Roland was a delight, always positive, always good company, but not one of those abrasive entertainers who needed constant attention.

Every night, at the chintzy inns, we had elaborate tasting menus, where Mannix and Roland tried to push me out of my comfort zone.

"I can't believe you've never had oysters!" they exclaimed on the first night.

"Or pigeon," I said. "Or quail's eggs. And I'm not starting now."

They tried to tempt me with tiny amounts on their forks but I wouldn't budge, especially on the pigeon, so instead they decided to educate me in wine.

"Swirl it." Mannix gave me a massive round glass. "Take a few moments and see what comes to you."

"It smells like wine," I said. "Red wine, if you want me to be really specific."

"Close your eyes," Roland said. "Swish it around and say what it makes you think of."

"Okay." I swirled for a few seconds, then inhaled. "Missing teeth."

"What?"

"I'm serious. A ruined smile. It could have been beautiful but . . . it failed . . ."

I opened my eyes. Both men were still and startled, frozen in a stare. Their postures and expressions were identical—even though Roland was five stone overweight and Mannix as lean as a wolf, you'd know they were brothers.

Mannix reached for his glass and swirled and coughed back the wine. "She's right. There's a terrible sadness in it."

"That's just you," Roland said.

"It's not. I've never been happier. Try some yourself."

"Jesus." Roland rinsed a swig around his mouth. "You're completely right, Stella. I'm getting top notes of loneliness and an aftertaste of dread."

"Dashed dreams," I said.

"Faded beauty."

"Punctured tires," Mannix said. "All four of them. Slashed deliberately."

Suddenly we were in convulsions, and it seemed like we spent the entire week laughing that way.

Every glass of wine we drank became a competition for the most elaborate and unlikely descriptions.

"I'm getting shades of shoe leather."

"And wobbly table legs."

"Graffiti."

"Ambition."

"A bus driver's jacket."

"Appendicitis."

"A soupçon of sulfur."

"Flotsam."

"And jetsam?"

"Noooo . . . Yes! The jetsam is coming through now."

"Gilda will kill me," I said, after yet another five-course dinner.

"The diet resumes next week," Roland said. "Eat up."

"Are you still doing the Nordic walking?" I asked, a little tentatively.

"No." He was solemn. "I had to knock it on the head when I broke the machine and they barred me from the gym."

I snorted with involuntary laughter.

In fairness, he looked like he'd abandoned all exercise. The svelte-ish figure he'd showcased last Christmas was no more. And at the Meadowstone Ranch and Inn, when the stableboys saw Roland waddling toward them, they seemed distinctly anxious.

"Did you see their expressions?" Roland asked. "Even the horses looked worried."

Tears of laughter were streaming down my face.

"I'm starting with a new personal trainer when I get back to Ireland." He raised his glass. "But for now, we're here, in this beautiful place, having this wonderful food and wine, and we are going to enjoy it."

Later on, as we got ready for bed, Mannix said, "You're in love with my brother."

"Of course I am," I said. "How could anyone not be? He's fabulous."

It was the best holiday of my life and when we said good-bye to Roland at San Francisco airport, it was hard work to not cry: the holiday was over; I should have started writing my second book and I'd done nothing; and in two weeks I was starting another book tour.

"It's okay." Mannix squeezed my hand. "Think of Shep. You, me and Shep walking the beach. In the meantime, this tour won't be as bad as the last time."

And it wasn't. The starts weren't so early, the schedules weren't so packed and I got every sixth day off.

M annix and I gathered at the boardroom table with Bryce Bonesman and some of the vice presidents. The turnout was considerably down from the last debrief we'd had and, once again, there was no sign of Phyllis.

"Welcome, everyone," Bryce said. "A couple of folk couldn't be with us today because it's vacation season. So *One Blink at a Time* didn't chart this time round."

"I'm very sorry," I said.

"It's too bad," Bryce said. "But we're guessing it's due to the time of year; a whole bunch more books are published in July than in March."

"Sorry," I repeated.

"Our vice president of sales, Thoreson Gribble, couldn't be with us at this moment but his report will be e-mailed to everyone," Bryce said. "Bottom line, we remain tentatively hopeful. Enough to suggest you release the Skogells' apartment. They're staying on in Asia for another year. You tour again in November and that's when all our hard work will come together. Who knows, we could be looking at a *New York Times* bestseller for the holidays? Right?"

"Right! And I'm on schedule to deliver my second book in February." Well, I'd made a start on it. "I've got a great title." I forced myself to speak with confidence. "I'm calling it 'Right Here, Right Now.' I think it will chime with mindfulness and the Power of Now and all that fashionable stuff."

With monumental effort I injected positivity into my voice: "It's going to be even better than *One Blink at a Time*!"

"Terrific," Bryce said. "I look forward to reading it."

Down in the street, the August heat and humidity hit us like a blow. Immediately Mannix and I launched into talk.

"I'll take another year off work," Mannix said.

"But—"

"It's okay. I've been thinking about everything and we can't just abandon ship now."

"Are you sure?" I felt guilty and miserable.

"But if we're going to lease the Skogells' apartment for another year, we need to know where we are, moneywise. We need to talk to Phyllis—"

"How long since one of us has actually spoken to her?"

Ages. Neither of us could remember the last time.

"But," Mannix said, "it's different now. We need to make decisions and you need a new contract."

As soon as we got home we rang Phyllis and put her on speaker.

She picked up directly. "Yep?" She sounded slurpy, like she was eating noodles.

"Hi, Phyllis, it's Stella. Stella Sweeney."

"I know." It was definitely noodles. "You think I'd answer my phone without knowing who you were. What's up?"

"We just had a meeting with Bryce," I said. "He's really gung ho." Well, he wasn't exactly but I'd learned that around here it was normal to put a wildly positive spin on everything. "So we were wondering, Mannix and I, if you'd talk to Bryce about doing a new contract for the second book?"

"No."

"Phyllis, I'm sorry, but Mannix and I, we need to get our financial stuff in place."

She laughed. "You're cute! You think this is about you! This isn't about you. This is about me and my reputation. Mexican standoff, baby. This is not the time to blink."

"But—"

"Hey, I'm not saying I don't feel for you. You don't know if you should sign a lease for another year, you don't know if you should keep your kid here in school. But now is not the moment to go to Blisset Renown to make a new deal. Maybe if you'd charted this time round . . ." A meaningful and unpleasant pause followed.

"Look," she said. "Bryce is touring you again in the fall. He's still spending money and committing resources to you. That's a good sign. He hasn't given up on you. But nothing happens until after the tour."

"So what should we do?"

"You do what you have to do—go home to Ireland or stay here— but regarding a new deal, we wait this thing out. I'll know when the time is right. And that time is not now."

"Phyllis, I—" But I was talking to the air; she'd hung up.

"Oh!" I turned to Mannix.

He looked as shocked as I felt.

"What should we do?" My mind was whirling.

Mannix took a deep breath. "Let's look at the issues." He sounded like it was an effort for him to stay calm. "Highest on the list is Jeffrey and his education—it was a big deal for him to be yanked out of school in Ireland and parachuted into a new one in New York. He's done his best to settle in here *and* he's about to start his all-important final year at school—we can't disrupt him at this sensitive time."

"Thank you," I said. "Thank you for making Jeffrey a priority."

"It's okay."

"Other factors?" I said. "I don't have a job to go back to and there are tenants in the house in Dublin, so we'd have nowhere to live."

"And all my patients have been reassigned. It would take a while to build up a new practice."

After some anxious silence, Mannix said, "Let's look at things another way: we have enough money to live here for one more year."

"If we're careful. And we *will* be careful," I said, fiercely. "No more holidays. No more Gilda. No more anything. But oh God, Mannix, what if we find out in February that they don't want another book from me? What if *One Blink* hasn't sold enough? They're not going to want a second one just like it. I must make this new one better than the first. Jesus." I buried my face in my hands. I hated financial insecurity more than anything.

"We can't think that way. And Bryce was hopeful at that meeting," Mannix reminded me.

"*Tentatively* hopeful."

"Hopeful enough to tour you again in November. I think we have to stay. Come on, Stella, let's decide to be positive. Let's simply decide to not worry."

"Have you had a personality transplant?"

But Mannix was right. We'd burned too many bridges. We'd invested too much emotionally and too much financially in everything here in New York. The door to our old life had closed over more completely than we'd expected. We couldn't go back.

Suddenly the summer had ended and it was September and Jeffrey was back at school, doing his final year.

I broke the news to Gilda that I couldn't afford to pay her any longer, but she was adamant that we still run together four times a week. "We're friends, right?" she said.

"Yes, but . . ."

"I like to run and I prefer to have company."

I wavered, then gave in. "Okay, thank you. But if I ever get the chance to pay you back in any way, I will."

"Like I said, we're friends."

Betsy returned from Asia and couldn't get a job doing anything. Until, like a miracle, Gilda somehow secured her an internship in an art gallery. The job was unpaid, but it was vaguely in keeping with Betsy's plans to study art therapy, so my worry eased.

The owner of the gallery was a cadaverous, black-clad man called Joss Wootten. According to Google he was sixty-eight, and it took me a while—longer than everyone else—to realize that he was Gilda's boyfriend.

"Jeez, Mom," Betsy said. "How else do you think I got the internship?"

"Cripes," I muttered. What was it with Gilda and the old blokes? Carefully I broached the subject of what attracted her to Joss.

"He's so interesting," she said dreamily.

"Like Laszlo Jellico?" I asked, desperate to understand. "Was he interesting?"

Her face went blank. "He was the wrong sort of interesting."

"Right," I said. "Sorry." I knew not to go there again.

I was making progress with the second book, which was exactly the same sort of thing as *One Blink at a Time*. Every conversation I had, I concentrated till my head hurt, desperately hoping to hear words of everyday wisdom. I rang Dad a lot and kept urging him to remember what Granny Locke used to say. I had about thirty sayings that worked and I needed to get to sixty.

Ruben still kept me very busy—every day I had to do a blog and tweet a wise and comforting platitude, but it was tricky because anything decent I came up with I wanted to save for the second book. Then Ruben made me start on Instagram. "Do cashmere and coziness," he said. "Pictures of sunrises and babies' hands."

That kind of stuff wasn't really me—I'd prefer to do beautiful shoes and pretty nails—but Ruben said, "It's not who you are, it's who we decide you are."

Salvation came from Gilda, who said, "I'll do it. And your Twitter stuff too. And your blog, if you want."

"But—"

"I know. You can't pay me. That's okay."

I wrestled with the rights and wrongs of the situation, then I gave in, because I simply couldn't cope with the torrent of Ruben's demands.

"Someday, somehow, your goodness will make its way back to you."

"Oh, please." She waved away my gratitude. "It's nothing."

Ruben's demand for written articles remained relentless. And there wasn't a hospital, a school or a physical rehab place in the tristate area (basically anywhere that it didn't cost money to send me) to which I wasn't dispatched, to do a speech.

It was around the end of October that Betsy met Chad. He'd come into the gallery and brazenly said he'd buy an installation if she would go out with him.

I was shocked and worried: he seemed all wrong for Betsy. He was far too old—only five years younger than me—far too mercenary and far too cynical.

He was a lawyer and corporate to the bone. He worked twelve-hour days and lived a life of suits and limos and dark expensive restaurants.

"What is it you like about him, sweetie?" I asked, cautiously. "He makes you laugh? He makes you feel safe?"

"Oh no." She shivered. "He *thrills* me."

I stared at her, mildly horrified.

"I know," she said. "I'm totally not his type. But he's going through his kooky-girl phase."

"What about you?"

"And I'm going through my older lawyer-guy phase. It's all good!"

I lifted a pile of leggings, searching for my makeup palette. Gilda had assembled a bespoke kit that had all the eyeshadow, blush, concealer and lip gloss I'd need for my three-week tour, but I couldn't find it. Clothes were everywhere, strewn on the bed, on the dresser and in the suitcase on the floor. I took a look in a drawer. It wasn't in there. It would want to turn up soon; we were leaving tomorrow. Maybe I'd left it in another room.

I raced into the living room, where Mannix was, and said, "Have you seen my—?"

Immediately I knew something was terribly wrong. He was sitting at his desk, his head in his hands.

"Mannix? Sweetie?"

He turned to me. His face was gray. "Roland's had a stroke."

I rushed to his side. "How do you know?"

"Hero just called. She doesn't know exact details but she says it's serious." He picked up the phone. "I'm calling Rosemary Rozelaar. Apparently he's under her care."

Jesus. Small world.

"Rosemary?" Mannix said. "Bring me up to speed." He scribbled lines back and forth onto his jotter until eventually the page tore. "CT scan? MRI? Ptosis? Loss of consciousness? *Complete?* How long? Fuck. Ischemic cascade?"

I didn't understand most of the words. All I knew about strokes was a horrible television ad that went on about FAST—it made the point that a stroke victim had to get treatment quickly to ensure any kind of decent outcome.

Mannix hung up. "He's had an ischemic stroke, followed by an ischemic cascade."

I hadn't a clue what that meant but I let him talk.

"How fast did he get to hospital?" I asked.

"Not fast enough. Not in the first three hours, which are the critical ones. His heart rhythm is abnormal, which suggests atrial fibrillations."

"What does that mean?"

"It means . . ." The doctor in him was trying to talk to the civilian in me. "It means he might have a heart attack. But even without that complication, he's in a coma. Whatever happens in the next three days is what counts."

"How do you mean?"

"If there's no indication of normal brainstem activity, he's not going to survive."

I was appalled; but this wasn't my tragedy, this was my time to be strong.

"Okay." I took charge. "We're going to Ireland. I'll look up the flight times."

"We can't. You can't cancel your tour."

"And you can't not go to Ireland."

We stared at each other, paralyzed by the novelty of our situation. We had no road map, no idea how to behave.

"Go to Ireland," I said. "And take care of your brother. I'll go on the tour. I'll be fine."

I was thinking that maybe Betsy would come with me. That was, if I could persuade her to leave Chad's side. She was practically living in his downtown apartment and we hardly saw her these days.

It was then that the doorbell rang. It was Gilda, dropping off some drapey cashmere things that were part of the wardrobe plan she'd done.

"I've got blue, which would work really well with your hair, but I saw this russet and I thought—What's happened?"

"Mannix's brother has had a stroke. It's serious. We've got to get Mannix back to Dublin as soon as possible."

"And you?" Gilda asked. "Are you still going on the tour?"

"It's fine," I said. "I'm going to ask Betsy to come with me."

"I'll come," Gilda said. "I'll be your assistant."

"Gilda, that's really nice, but I don't have the money to pay you."

"Let me talk to Bryce."

"Gilda. It's for three weeks. Eighteen-hour days—"

"Let me talk to Bryce."

"Okay. But—"

"Don't worry," Gilda said to Mannix. "I'll take care of her."

"Have you got Bryce's cell?" I asked.

"Yeah. From when I was seeing Laszlo."

"Oh. Okay . . ."

I'd just said good-bye to Mannix at Newark airport when Gilda rang.

"Blisset Renown is paying me. It's handled."

"How?"

"It just is."

N othing." Mannix's voice echoed on the line. "Absolutely no response."

"Stay hopeful," I said. "There's still time." It was two days since Roland had had his stroke.

"Mum and Dad have arrived from France."

I swallowed hard. If Roland's parents had shown up, things must be really serious.

"We're doing another MRI later today," Mannix said. "Maybe some brainstem activity will show up."

"Fingers crossed," I said.

"I miss you," he said.

"I miss you too."

I wanted to tell him I loved him, but to say it now, on the phone and in these circumstances, would just sound like pity.

I'd put so much importance on saying the words that I'd painted myself into a corner. I'd told myself too often that the situation had to be right, and I realized now that the situation would never be perfect.

"How's it going with you?" he asked. "I hear Gilda is actually making you exercise. You can't just lie on the floor and breathe heavily into the phone, like you did on the other two tours."

"How do you know that?"

"She rang, to give me a progress report. Listen, Stella, if you're not able for the running as well as all the work, just tell her. So what city are you in now?"

"Baltimore, I think. We're just about to go to a charity dinner."

"Call me when you get back, before you go to sleep."

"I will. And promise me you'll try to be positive."

"I promise."

In every conversation I had with Mannix, I forced myself to sound upbeat, but I felt sick with worry.

What if Roland died? I was full of grief at the thought of a world without Roland. He was such a special person . . . but a special person with a lot of debts. Someone was going to have to pay them. My selfish thoughts were fleeting, but they shamed me.

And what would it do to Mannix if Roland didn't make it? How would he cope with the death of the person he loved the most?

Even if Roland didn't die, his recovery was going to be lengthy and expensive. How were we going to manage that?

Maybe someone should have suggested to Roland that being massively overweight wasn't a good idea. But when you knew how funny and clever and sweet he was, it would have been like kicking a puppy. And God knows, he'd tried his best. He'd been working with a personal trainer since he'd got back from his holiday in California.

I sighed, then slid on my high heels, picked up my evening bag and knocked on the door that connected my room to Gilda's. After a second, I stepped inside.

"Oh!" She was working on her laptop and quickly she shut it.

"Sorry." I stopped short. "I knocked. I thought you heard."

"Oh . . . okay."

"Sorry," I repeated, backing toward the door. "I'll just . . . Let me know whenever you're ready."

I wondered why she was being so secretive, but she was entitled to a life.

"No, Stella, wait," she said. "I'm just being stupid. There's a . . . sort of project I've been working on. If I show you, promise you won't laugh."

"Of course I won't laugh." But I would have said anything because I was dying to know what was going on.

She hit refresh and a page of color burst into life. It said: *Your Best Self: A Woman's Optimum Health from Ten to One Hundred* by Gilda Ashley.

"Oh my God, it's a book." I was astonished.

"It's just something I've been playing around with . . ."

"Can I look?"

"Sure." She gave me the laptop and I scrolled through the pages.

Each chapter focused on a decade in a woman's life, the correct food and exercise, the changes in physique to expect and the best ways to embrace age-specific ailments. Every decade had its own beautifully colored background and information was dotted about the pages in friendly bullet points or pretty little sidebars.

The layout was great. No page was overcrowded with text and the fonts changed as the decades advanced, starting off cartoon-y for the teens and becoming more elegant for the thirties, forties and fifties, then bigger and easier to read for the sixties onward.

"It's brilliant," I said.

"It's getting there," she said bashfully. "But it's still missing something."

"It's great," I insisted.

Its simplicity was what made it so perfect—people were put off by hefty tomes with dense text. This was accessible and informative and, with its beautiful colors and deftly placed illustrations, it felt fundamentally optimistic.

"The graphics are amazing," I said.

She squirmed. "Joss helped me with them a little. Well, a *lot*."

"How long have you been working on it?"

"Oh forever . . . at least a year. But it's only really come together since I met Joss. Hey, Stella, do you mind?"

And I had to admit that I *did* feel rattled. Partly because she'd kept it secret from me. But I was just being childish. *And* mean-spirited—why shouldn't Gilda write a book? This wasn't a zero-sum game, where only a limited number of people were allowed to be writers. After all, it was ridiculous good fortune that *I'd* got a book deal.

"I don't mind," I made myself say. "Gilda, this is good enough to be published. Would you like me to show it to Phyllis?"

"Phyllis? The crazy lady who won't do physical contact and who steals cupcakes for her cats? I'm good, thanks."

We both started laughing but I couldn't sustain it for long.

"Gilda?" I asked, tentatively. "You've met other literary agents, yes?" I was trying to allude to her time with Laszlo Jellico, without causing upset. "Are they all as tough as Phyllis?"

"Are you kidding me? She's insane. Eccentric, I get; that can be fun and a lot of agents are a little cuckoo. But she's horrible. You were unlucky because you had to make a quick decision. If you'd had more time, you could have interviewed several agents and picked somebody nice."

"Mannix says I don't have to like her. That it's just business."

"Good point," she said. "But can I tell you what's so crazy?"

"Okay," I said, nervously.

"Mannix would make a great agent."

On the third day of his coma, there was a flicker of response from Roland's brainstem. But any celebrations were premature. "There's a ninety percent chance that he's not going to survive," Mannix told me. "And if he does, it'll be a long road back."

Gilda and I soldiered on through the book tour—Chicago, Baltimore, Denver, Tallahassee . . . On the fifth day I had to stop exercising. "I'll die, Gilda. I'm sorry, but I will."

I did my interviews and talks and book signings on autopilot. Gilda was a godsend. Over and over again, she reminded me where I was and what I was doing there.

I missed Mannix terribly; but whenever I got to speak to him, he was barely present. Now and again he tried to connect with me by saying something like, "Gilda said there was a good turnout last night." But his heart wasn't in it.

Over eleven days Roland went into cardiac arrest three times. Each time, he was expected to die, but miraculously he hung on.

The tour ended. Gilda and I came back to New York and I wanted to go immediately to Ireland to be with Mannix, but Jeffrey needed me more. Esperanza and a nanny had taken care of him while I'd been on tour and to fly off again so soon would be like an abandonment. I toyed with taking him out of school two weeks before term ended, and both of us going to Ireland, but it would be wrong to interrupt his education.

Whenever Mannix could spare the time away from the hospital, he Skyped me. I tried to be positive and lighthearted. "Think of Shep, Mannix. You, me and Shep, playing on the beach." But I could never make him smile; his worry had made him unreachable.

Betsy fluttered in and out of our lives, bringing us gifts of strange things like ribbon-wrapped boxes of marrons glacés. "Chad's opened an account in my name at Bergdorf Goodman," she said. "I've got two personal shoppers. I'm being totally reimaged—right down to my underwear."

"Betsy!" I was appalled. "You're not a doll—"

"Mom." She gave me a woman-to-woman look. "I'm an adult. And I'm having fun."

"You're only eighteen."

"Eighteen is grown-up."

"These things are disgusting." Jeffrey had abandoned his marron glacé. "They're like chickpeas."

"I think they *are* chickpeas," Betsy said. "Like, sweet ones."

I could have wept. All that money on her expensive education for her to become a rich man's toy and to think that chestnuts were chickpeas.

At the Blisset Renown Happy Holidays party, I bumped into Phyllis. "Where's Mannix?" she asked.

"Not here."

"Oh yeah?"

"He's in Ireland."

"Oh yeah?"

I refused to expand any further. Phyllis had had plenty of opportunities to stay current with my life and she hadn't bothered.

"I hear your Betsy is running around town with a man twice her age."

"How do you know *that*?"

She winked at me. "And how's that angry kid of yours? Jeffrey?"

I sighed and gave in. "Still angry."

"I see from my diary you're due to deliver your second book to Blisset Renown on February first. You going to make it?"

"I am."

"It's good?"

Was it? Well, I'd tried my hardest. "Yes, it's good."

"Well, step up your game," she said. "Make it great."

"Happy holidays, Phyllis." I moved off. I was looking for Ruben and I found him by a platter of seviche.

"Ruben?"

"Yeah?"

"I was wondering . . . you know . . . any news on the charts?"

"Yeah. Too bad."

"*One Blink* didn't chart?"

"Not this time round. Hey, it happens."

"I'm sorry." I felt crippled with guilt.

I couldn't tell Mannix, he had far too much to worry about, but later I rang Gilda and she was shocked. "*You* asked Ruben? *You?* Stella, never ask that question. If your book had charted, believe me, twenty different people would be calling you, every one of them taking the credit."

The day Academy Manhattan closed for the Christmas break, I went to Ireland with Betsy and Jeffrey.

The kids stayed with Ryan and I stayed in Roland's flat with Mannix. But he was hardly ever there; he was practically living at the hospital.

Mannix had said that Roland had made progress, but the first time I visited him, I was shocked. He was conscious, his right eye was open but his left side was paralyzed and a constant stream of drool poured from the left side of his mouth.

"Hi, sweetheart," I whispered and tiptoed toward him. "You've had us all very worried."

Carefully I picked my way through all the cords and wires connected up to him, so I could kiss his forehead.

A sound came from Roland, like a weak howl. It was so pathetic and strange, it scared me.

"Answer him," Mannix said, almost impatiently.

"But—" What had he said?

"He says you look beautiful."

"I do?" Forcing cheer into my voice, I said, "Thanks very much. In fairness, I've seen you looking better."

Roland howled again and I looked at Mannix.

"He's asking how your tour went."

"Well!" I took a seat and tried to produce entertaining anecdotes, but this was horrific. I knew myself how hellish it was to be unable to speak and it must be far, far tougher for a person as articulate as Roland.

I tried not to show my discomfort. But I was having flashbacks to my time in the hospital and I was *certain* that Roland was deeply shamed by his condition.

"He's delighted to see you," Mannix insisted.

For every one of the ten days I was in Ireland I sat with Roland and told him stories. When I'd get to the end of the tale, he'd let out one of his terrible howls and the only person who could make sense of them was Mannix.

Rosemary Rozelaar was Roland's neurologist but she'd clearly ceded all control to Mannix, who was in his element, moving around Roland's bed day and night, studying printouts and brain scans.

Mannix's parents were still in Ireland and appeared sporadically at the hospital. They always seemed to be just coming from a party or on their way to one, and they brought gin in a flask to Roland's bedside and drank it from white plastic cups.

I never stopped being aware of Roland's debts; they wore away at my thoughts like a stone in a shoe. Over the past couple of years he'd repaid a lot, but he still owed thousands upon thousands and there was no chance that he'd be working again for a long, long time.

I wanted to bring it up, because ultimately it would surely affect Mannix and me, but I didn't want to add to Mannix's worries.

Eventually he addressed it. One rare morning in bed, when he didn't jump up and go immediately to the hospital, he said, "We're going to have to talk about money."

"Who? Us?"

"What? No, about Roland's debts. Me, Rosa and Hero. And Mum and Dad, for all the good they'll be. We've been in denial, but we need some sort of family conference. The problem is, every one of us is broke."

"But when I deliver the new book in February . . ."

"We can't use your money to pay my brother's debts."

"But it's *our* money. Yours and mine."

He shook his head. "Let's not go there. Let's see what else we can come up with. Okay, I'm going to jump in the shower."

He was halfway across the room when his phone, which he'd left on the bedside locker, rang. He sighed. "Who is it?"

I picked it up and looked at the screen. "Oh? It's Gilda."

"Don't bother answering."

"What's she ringing for?"

"Just asking about Roland."

Oh. Okay.

Two days before Academy Manhattan reopened after the break, Betsy, Jeffrey and I were due to return to New York.

"I can't leave here," Mannix said to me. "Not yet. Not until he's stabilized."

"Take as long as you need." I wanted to be with Mannix; I missed his presence, his advice, everything about him, but I was trying to be a bigger, more generous person.

Mannix took us to the airport and the thought of going back to New York without him was suddenly overwhelming. I loved him. I loved him so much it hurt, and I knew I had to tell him. I should have told him long ago.

In the post-holiday mayhem of the departure hall, Mannix shoved our trolley through the throngs to our check-in desk.

"Get in the queue, kids," I said to Betsy and Jeffrey, then shunted Mannix to one side.

"Mannix," I said.

"Yeah."

"I—"

His phone started to ring. He looked at it. "I'd better take this."

"Rosa?" he said. "Right. Okay. But *be* there. See you then."

"Everything all right?" I asked.

"Rosa's trying to weasel out of the talk about Roland's money. Or lack of. I'd better get going. Safe flight. Ring me when you land."

He kissed me briefly on the mouth, then turned away and was instantly swallowed up by the crowds. I was frozen to the spot, stricken with terror that our moment had been and gone. That somehow the best bit had already happened, while I'd been waiting to get there, and now we were on the downward slope.

January in New York was snowy and very quiet. The promotion for *One Blink at a Time* had finally finished and my days were strangely peaceful. Apart from going to the movies about once a week with Gilda, I had no social life. I worked on *Right Here, Right Now* and the highpoint of each day was a call or a Skype from Mannix. It seemed that Roland's condition was starting to settle. I always wanted to ask Mannix when he was coming back, but I managed not to. Nor did I ask about Roland's finances. I knew they'd had their family discussion and if Mannix was too stressed to talk about the outcome, I'd go along with it.

In the last week in January, I got an unexpected phone call from Phyllis. "How's the new book?"

"Finished, really. I'm just playing around with it."

"Why don't you come see me? Today. Bring the pages."

"Okay." I might as well. I was doing nothing else.

When I walked into Phyllis's office, the first thing she said was, "Where's Mannix?"

"In Ireland."

"What? Again?"

"No. Still."

"Ooooooh." It was information that she hadn't had and I didn't feel like telling her the whole story. "What's going on with you guys?" she asked.

"Just . . ." I shrugged. "Stuff."

"Oh yeah? Stuff?" She stared at me hard but I wouldn't give in.

"So you wanted to see my new book." I handed over the printout.

"Yeah. I'm hearing things on the bush telegraph and they're making me twitchy."

Instantly I was filled with alarm.

I watched as she studied the first nine or ten pages, then she started flicking and speed-reading, and before she'd reached the end, she said, "No."

"What?"

"Sorry, honey, this won't do." Her kindness was what was really worrying. "*One Blink at a Time* didn't work. You cost them money. You need something different. They won't buy this."

"But it's exactly what Bryce told me to write."

"Things were different then. Now we're eighteen months on and *One Blink at a Time* has bombed—"

"It's bombed?" No one had told me. "It's actually bombed?"

"Yeah. Bombed. You thought no one was calling because they're all on a diet and grouchy? No one's been calling because they're so embarrassed for you. They will not publish a *One Blink at a Time* reboot."

"Can't we wait and see what they say?"

"No way. You never bring them something they're sure to reject. Bottom line, Stella: I will not agent this book. Go away and come up with something else, fast."

Like what? I wasn't a writer; I wasn't a creative person. I was just someone who'd got lucky. *Once.* All I could offer was more of the same.

"You were rich, successful and in love," Phyllis said. "Now? Your career has tanked and I don't know what's up with that man of yours but it's not looking so good. You've a lot of material there!"

She shrugged. "You want more? Your teenage son hates you. Your daughter is wasting her life. You're the wrong side of forty. Menopause is racing toward you down the track. How much better does this get?"

I moved my lips but no words came out.

"You were wise once," Phyllis said. "Whatever you wrote in *One Blink at a Time*, it touched people. Try it again, with these new challenges." She was on her feet and trying to move me toward the door. "I need you out of here. I've got clients to see."

In desperation, I clung to my chair. "Phyllis?" I was pleading. "Do you believe in me?"

"You want self-esteem? Go to a shrink."

She ousted me into the snowy street, then called later that afternoon.

"You've got until March first. I promised Bryce 'new and exciting.' Don't let me down."

I was in bits. I didn't know what to do. It was impossible for me to come up with a new book. But one thing was certain: I couldn't tell Mannix. He had enough on his plate.

The thought of having no income made me feel like I was falling through endless space. Mannix and I had always known that giving up our jobs and moving to New York was a risk. But we'd never contemplated the exact details of how it could go wrong—and where it would leave us financially. From what Bryce had said at that first meeting, I'd assumed I'd have a career that would last some years, one that would guarantee us security indefinitely.

For two days, I got through the hours, frozen with fear. Gilda noticed I was being weird but I fobbed her off. I was too frightened to talk about what had happened. If I talked about it, it made it real.

Then—in one of those jokes that God likes to play on us—Mannix rang to say he was coming back to New York the following day. "Roland's out of danger and there isn't really anything more I can do for him."

"Great," I said.

"Aren't you glad?"

"I'm thrilled."

"You don't sound it."

"I am, of course I am, Mannix. You know I am. See you tomorrow."

In desperation, I rang Gilda and I told her everything that had happened, every single word that Phyllis had said to me.

"Hang tight," she said. "I'm on my way over right now."

Half an hour later, she arrived, her cheeks pink from the cold. She was wearing a white furry hat, white furry boots and a white duvet coat. She was dusted with snowflakes, some even on her eyelashes.

"Wow, it's cold out there. Hey, Jeffrey!"

Jeffrey came to hug her. Even Esperanza stuck her head around her door and said, "Madam, you look like a princess from a fairy story."

"I'll take that, Esperanza." Gilda smiled and Esperanza retreated.

"Where can we talk?" Gilda unpeeled her layers of outdoor clothing.

"Come into the bedroom."

"Okay. Shut the door. Stella, I'm going to propose something here. If you don't like it, you forget I said it and we never refer to it again."

"Go on . . ." But I already knew what she was going to say.

"We collaborate."

"Say more."

"We merge our two books—"

"Right."

"—and create an all-bases-covered go-to guide for all ailments, physical and spiritual, for every woman who wants to live her best life."

God, she was inspiring. "Yes!"

"We're a good fit, Stella, you and I. Always were. Kismet."

"We could even call the book that—'Kismet!'"

"Sure! Or how about: 'Your Best Self?'"

"Maybe we don't have to decide on the name just yet."

"But this is real?" she asked. "This is actually happening?"

"Yes!" I was overjoyed, almost queasy with relief.

"There is just one thing. I don't want Phyllis as my agent."

"Oh, Gilda." I was instantly sobered. "I signed a contract with her when all this first started. She has to be my agent."

"Not if we're both the authors. Obviously your name would be *huge* on the jacket and mine would be teeny tiny, but legally, under these circumstances, you can step away from her."

"I don't know . . ."

"Hey, look. She was the right agent for your first book; she put you on the map, got you a deal. But you don't need her now. Why pay her ten percent when she does nothing?"

"But *who* would be our agent?"

She looked at me like I'd lost it. "Mannix, of course. It's so obvious." And in a way it was.

"Look at that great deal he got for you with that Irish publishing house."

"Can we talk to Mannix about it?" I asked.

"Sure! He's back tomorrow. I say we give him twenty-four hours to get over the jet lag then we both go at him." She giggled. "He'll be powerless to resist."

"She blew it." Gilda made an impassioned plea for bypassing Phyllis. "She should have done the second deal as soon as you got the first one. But she thought if she waited she'd get more. She was greedy."

Mannix and I exchanged a look: by cutting Phyllis out, weren't we also being greedy?

"You're just being smart," Gilda said.

"I don't know . . ." Mannix said. "I feel loyal to Phyllis."

"So do I," I said.

"It's not about loyalty," Gilda said. "It's just business. She's still Stella's agent for anything published under her own name. Always supposing you can get her support. But, guys, here are the facts: she's refusing to agent Stella's second book. And you're hurting for money."

And that was what everything came down to: money.

Almost all of the first advance had been spent. Not on fast cars and champagne, just on the daily demands of a city as expensive as New York.

"You need to live," Gilda said to Mannix. "And there are Roland's debts . . ."

I looked at her in confusion: did she know how much Roland owed? Because I didn't. Perhaps she was just talking in general terms.

After a lengthy silence, Mannix said, "If this is our best chance to keep earning a living, then I'll do it."

"Great! Ten percent to you. Stella and I split the rest fifty-fifty?"

"Sure."

Mannix sounded so weary that I said, "I thought you liked the bit of agenting you've done."

"I did. I do."

"Who tells Phyllis?" Gilda asked.

After a silence, Mannix said, "I will."

"Do it now," Gilda said. "Let's get that put to bed."

Obediently Mannix picked up his phone and Gilda scrambled to her feet. "Jeez," she said, almost gleefully, "this is one conversation I don't want to hear. Come on, Stella, let's have some wine."

A few minutes later, Mannix came into the kitchen and I gave him a glass.

"So . . . ?" I asked.

He took a mouthful of wine.

"How did she take it?" Gilda asked.

"As well as you might expect."

"That bad?" I said. "Cripes."

Mannix shrugged. He didn't seem to care.

G ilda and I spent the next month merging the two books, matching the appropriate sayings with each chapter. Gilda had broken up with Joss Wootten so we took the project to a young enthusiastic graphic artist called Noah. It was delicate, challenging work, much more so than I'd imagined—it involved cutting some of Gilda's text and shoe-horning mine in. We had to do it over and over again until the blend felt natural and we put in such long hours staring at computer screens that I nearly went blind.

But it was important to get it right. I was scared now, really really scared, because this was my last chance.

Mannix had let Bryce Bonesman know that he was now the agent for the book; he promised him "new and exciting" and said it would be ready by the start of March.

On a Thursday night, on the second-last day in February, at around nine o'clock, Gilda said, "I think that's it. I don't think we can make it any more beautiful."

"Print it?" Noah said.

I took a deep breath. "Okay," I said. "Print it."

We watched the glossy pages flop from the printer and we assembled two copies of our beautiful book, one for each of us.

The awkward matter of a title still hadn't been resolved. Gilda wanted to call it: "Your Best Self"; I preferred: "Right Here, Right Now." So I suggested we leave the final decision to Blisset Renown.

"Should we e-mail it to Bryce?" I asked.

"The files are too big," Noah said. "The download would take forever."

"Why don't you deliver it in person to him tomorrow morning?" Gilda said to me.

"Why don't we both?"

"You're the main author. You should do it."

"Okay. If you're sure."

We gave each other a congratulatory hug, thanked Noah and left.

Down in the street, I asked Gilda if she was getting the subway.

"No. I'm going to visit a friend." Instinctively I knew it was one of her interesting older blokes and I didn't want to pry.

"So let's put you in a cab." She had her hand out and a taxi had already pulled over.

At home, Mannix mustered an enthusiastic response to the pages, but I could see it was an effort. I'd been increasingly worried about him since he'd come back from Ireland. Though he'd always joked about being a glass-half-empty kind of person, I wondered if he was having a bout of actual depression, triggered by the shock of Roland's stroke. He'd stopped going swimming, his smiles were rare and he never seemed to be fully present.

"Everything's going to be okay," I told him. "Everything's going to be great."

The next morning, I hurried over to Blisset Renown and gave the book to Bryce's assistant. She promised she'd give it to him as soon as he came in.

Back at the apartment, shortly after eleven o'clock, Mannix's phone started to ring.

"It's Bryce," he said.

"He must have got the book!" I said.

Mannix grabbed the phone and put it on speaker. "Hey, Bryce."

"Mannix, sir? Congratulations! You couldn't have picked a better project to launch your U.S. career."

"Thank you."

"I need to brainstorm with sales, marketing, digital, the whole team, and pull together a consummate vision. But we need to get you guys in for a meeting asap. Does tomorrow morning work?"

The following morning, at Blisset Renown, Ruben met Mannix and me as we came out of the elevator and we followed him down the hallway.

I'd assumed we'd be going to the boardroom but instead, to my surprise, we were diverted to Bryce's office. Gilda and Bryce were already there, sitting behind Bryce's desk. They were deep in chat.

A slew of colorful pages—the new book—was strewn in front of them.

"Mannix, Stella, take a seat," Bryce said.

"We're having the meeting here?" I asked. "Just the four of us?" What about all the vice presidents?

"Take a seat," Bryce repeated and I felt a prickle of unease.

I pulled up a chair so I was sitting facing Bryce. Mannix sat beside me and Gilda remained where she was.

"So," Bryce said. "Everyone here, we love the new book."

I felt almost ecstatic with relief.

"The thing is, Stella," Bryce continued. "We don't love you."

I thought I was hearing things. I stared at him, waiting for some kind of punch line.

"Yes." Bryce sounded regretful. "This is real. We don't love you."

Looking for clues, I turned to Mannix: he was watching Bryce with intense focus.

"You're not working," Bryce said to me. "We've sent you out there, into every corner of the United States. *Three* times. We've spent a lot of money. Ruben got you plenty of inches and the book just didn't sell. Not in the way we projected it would."

He tapped the pages of the new book. "But this . . . This we can make work."

Mannix spoke up. "But Stella's sayings are in there."

Bryce shook his head ruefully. "They're coming right back out again and her name is coming off the title credits. She will have no part of this book."

"But Stella's sayings are what make this book work," Mannix said.

Again came that regretful head shake from Bryce. "Gilda's got plenty of sayings of her own, and they're all better than Stella's. We're going to start fresh with Gilda. She's got a great concept, she's got wow presence and everyone's going to love her."

"So what about the things I wrote?" I already knew the answer but couldn't stop myself from asking.

"You're not hearing me," Bryce said. "Yeah, I know, you're in shock and that transitioning to the new normal will be painful. So here it is in plain English: there will be no second book for you. It's over, Stella."

"And you're going to publish Gilda's book?" I asked. "Without me?"

"That's it. We've been watching Gilda for a while; we love her work on your blog and Twitter."

Mannix spoke. "How much are you offering for Gilda's book?"

"Now you're talking like an agent," Bryce said, admiringly. "That's what I want to hear."

"One moment," Mannix said. "I need to talk to Stella. I can't just—"

"You don't need to speak with Stella," Bryce shut him down. "You need to speak with your client—and that's Gilda. Let's start a dialogue."

"A dialogue?" I asked.

"You know what?" Bryce looked at me with pity. "You guys have a lot to discuss. Why don't you leave now? Take some time. Process what's happened here this morning. And you and I, sir," he addressed Mannix. "We'll talk later."

Bryce stood up. "Go." He hurried us from the room with sweeps of his hands.

I looked at Mannix, he looked at me. I didn't recognize the look in his eyes and I didn't know what to do.

"Go," Bryce repeated. "But remember! It's all good!"

I had no memory of going down in the elevator. Suddenly I found myself standing outside in the street with Mannix and Gilda.

"So I don't have a book deal any longer?" I asked.

"No," Gilda said.

"And you do? But how is this going to work?" I sounded almost slurred. "Who's your agent?"

She shrugged, as if she couldn't believe my stupidity. "Mannix."

"Mannix?" I looked up at him. "Really?"

"Stella," he said. "We're in a bad way financially, we need the money–"

"So what becomes of me?" I asked.

"You can be my assistant," Gilda said. "You can do my Twitter account, my Instagram, my blog. You can come on tour with me, if Mannix can't."

"Mannix is going on tour with you?"

"Stella, you weren't expecting this," Gilda said. "I get that. But let's be grown-ups here. Try thinking of it like we've all just swapped roles. Well, nearly." She flashed a tender glance at Mannix. "Mannix can stay being Mannix. But you're me. And I'm . . ." She cocked her head to one side and smiled a wide, happy smile. "Well, I guess I'm you."

ME

Wednesday, 11 June

10:10

"My house!" Ryan wails. "My car! My business, my money—it's all gone! Why did you let me do it?"

"I tried. Jeffrey tried." I could weep with frustration. "But you wouldn't listen."

"I've nowhere to live. You've got to let me move in with you."

"No, Ryan."

"Do you know where I slept last night? In a hostel for homeless men. It was bad, Stella. Beyond bad."

"Did they . . . did someone try to . . . ?"

"No one tried to bugger me, if that's what you're asking. They just . . . mocked me. Men with nothing except beards and lice, they *scorned* me."

It's less than two days since Ryan's karma stunt and already all interest has melted away. People just wanted to see if he'd go through with his lunatic project and, now that he has, the machine has moved on, looking for the next freak. No one is saying now that Ryan is creating Spiritual Art. They just think he's a total fool.

Worse, they seem to be taking some sort of perverse pleasure in proving him wrong—no one is giving him anything.

With creeping dread, I remember what Karen said the other day—that I'm a soft touch and that, if I'm not careful, I'll end up with Ryan in my bed. Karen is always right. Everything she has predicted so far with this karma business has come true.

But I don't want to end up with Ryan in my bed! Ryan and me, it was a million years ago. I can barely remember it, never mind consider rekindling it.

"Please, Ryan. I don't want to come downstairs every morning and find you lounging around in your jocks on my couch. It's too . . . *studenty*."

"You're supposed to be a good person," he says. "It's how you make your living."

"I don't make any living at the moment. Why don't you talk to a lawyer?" I suggest. "See if you can get back some of the things you gave away. Say that you weren't in your right mind when you did it. Because you weren't."

"You know," he says, speculatively, "this was *my* house."

"Don't you dare," I say, suddenly afraid. "That was all sorted out. Very *fairly*. You agreed, I agreed, everyone agreed. We *agreed*, Ryan!"

"Maybe I wasn't in my right mind then, either. Maybe I was unhinged with grief."

"And maybe I wasn't in my right mind the day I married you!" My face is hot and I'm finding it hard to breathe.

But fighting with Ryan isn't going to achieve anything. "Sorry," I say. "I'm very . . ." What am I? Stressed? Afraid? Sad? Tired? ". . . hungry. I'm very hungry, Ryan. To be honest, I'm hungry a lot of the time, and it makes me cranky. I'm very difficult to live with. Look, what about Clarissa? I'm sure she'll help you."

"That Clarissa . . ." Ryan shakes his head. "She's changed all the codes and I can't get into the office. She's emptied the business bank account. I suppose she must have set up a new one. She's vicious."

This isn't exactly a surprise, but it's a blow.

"Look," he says, "could I sleep in with Jeffrey?"

"No!" Jeffrey yells from an upstairs room.

"No," I say.

"What am I to do, Stella?" He fixes me with pleading brown eyes. "I have nowhere to go. I have no one to help me. Please let me stay here."

"Okay." I mean, what else can I do? "You can sleep in my office. For a while."

"How long is a while?"

"Nine days."

"Why nine?"

"Eight, then, if you'd prefer."

"Where am I going to keep my things?"

"You haven't *got* any things. And Ryan, understand this: I *need* to work." I felt panicky at the thought of tripping over my ex-husband lying on a futon in my office every morning. "As soon as I come into that office you need to get up and get out."

"Where will I go every day?"

"The zoo," I say, on impulse. "We'll buy you a season ticket. It'll be nice, with the baby elephants and all. You'll like it."

03:07

I awake.

It's still dark outside, but something has happened.

It takes a moment to realize what it is: I am not alone in my bed. I have been joined by a man. A man with an erection, which he is pressing into my back.

"Ryan?" I whisper.

"Stella," Ryan whispers back. "Are you awake?"

"No."

"Stella." He strokes my shoulder and presses his erection harder into my back. "I was thinking . . ."

"You have got to be fucking kidding me." I'm still whispering but in a shrieky sort of way. "Get out."

"Ah, come on, Stella—"

"Get out. Out of my bed and out of my room and out of my house."

Nothing happens for a moment, then I see the ghostly flash of his naked body as he scuttles toward the door, bent protectively over his erection, like an arthritic crab.

For the love of God. How did I end up in bed with Ryan? How has my life doubled around on itself and deposited me back where I started?

L et's get you in out of the cold." Gilda took my arm. "Mannix, you go home. We'll catch up later."

Mannix hesitated.

"Go," Gilda said. "Really. Stella and I need to talk. I'll make everything okay."

Gently, Gilda led me into the front lobby of Blisset Renown. Mannix was still out in the street, looking uncertain.

The security guard seemed surprised to see us back so soon after surrendering our visitors' tags.

"We're good," Gilda said to him. "We don't need passes. This won't take long."

Through the glass door, I saw that Mannix had gone.

"It's okay," Gilda said to me, reassuringly. "It's all okay."

I was reeling with confusion. Why did she keep telling me things were okay when I knew they weren't?

"Everything's the same as before," she said. "Except this time, well, I guess I'm the star."

She was so confident, so very sure of herself.

"Today with Bryce?" I asked. "Did it 'just happen?' Or you had it planned?"

She went pink, then giggled. "You got me. It's been in the works a little while."

"How long?"

She twisted coyly. "You know . . . a while."

How long was "a while?"

My memory scooted back over all that had happened and, suddenly, every event of the past eighteen months stacked one on top of the other, collapsing neatly into one realization. "Oh my God." My face flooded with heat. "That morning I bumped into you in Dean & DeLuca? That wasn't an accident?"

She looked as gleeful as a naughty child. "Okay, it wasn't. I paid attention the night before. I knew you were going to the Academy Manhattan and I thought there was a chance I might bump into you at Dean & DeLuca. I thought we could be . . . friends."

"Friends?" My voice was faint.

"Don't look at me that way! I've been your friend. I've kept you skinny. I've styled your tours. I've even blow-dried your hair."

"But . . ."

"Is it my fault that your book bombed and they don't want another?"

"No, but . . ."

"I have talent," she said. "Do you know how it hurts to have your stuff turned down again and again? You want me to walk away from this opportunity because it's with the people who don't want to publish you?"

"No—"

"We've all got to survive, right?"

She was making it sound like I was a willing participant in every strange thing that had happened today.

"This is simply business," she said.

"What about you and Mannix?" What was going on?

She flushed even pinker. "Okay, that's not business. Well, not *just* business. Mannix and I have become close. Yeah, it's grown over the last few months. A connection that wasn't there before."

"But you told me—"

"—that I wouldn't go after your guy. I meant it. But he's not your guy anymore. You and Mannix have been winding down for a while. You and he were all about the sex, and when did that last happen?"

I was speechless and horrified—it was true that Mannix and I hadn't had sex since before Roland's stroke. But I'd been putting it down to the fact that I'd been working such long hours.

"He's my agent now. And, I guess, my manager," Gilda said. "He'll be doing the stuff he used to do for you. He'll be spending all his time with me."

"I thought you only liked older men."

"Are you kidding? They make me sick to my stomach. I've . . . hung out with them because they've been, you know, helpful. But I want Mannix."

"What does Mannix say?"

She lowered her eyes. "I know you're hurting." She looked up and held me in her blue gaze. "Ask him to walk away from me and I promise you he won't."

"But has anything happened between you?"

"This is difficult for you, Stella." She patted my arm. "It'll get easier."

"Has anything actually happened?"

"Stella, this is difficult for you. But he wants this too."

"Ruben?"

"Stella? I'm not even meant to be talking to you."

"I need a favor—Laszlo Jellico's number."

He hesitated.

"You owe me," I said.

"Okay." He rattled the number off. "You didn't get it from me, right?"

Immediately I rang Laszlo Jellico and, to my surprise, he answered. I thought I'd be shunted to voice mail.

"Mr. Jellico? My name is Stella Sweeney. We met once, in Bryce Bonesman's apartment. I wonder if I could speak to you about Gilda Ashley."

After a long pause, he said, "There's a coffee shop on the corner of Park and Sixty-ninth. I'll be there in half an hour."

"Okay. See you then."

I walked across town and found Laszlo Jellico's coffee shop. I'd been at the table for about five minutes when he arrived. He didn't look as big and bushy as he had that long-ago night in Bryce's apartment. I stood up and signaled to him and he came over.

"I'm Stella Sweeney," I said.

"I remember you." His voice wasn't as boomy as I recalled. He sat down opposite me. "So? Gilda Ashley?"

"Thank you for meeting me. Can I ask where you first met her?"

"At a cocktail party."

"So . . . ? You clicked? You asked for her number?"

"No. We barely exchanged two words. But the very next day, when I was taking my dogs to the dog park, I bumped into her in the street just outside my apartment. Serendipitous, right?"

"Right."

"I thought it incongruous," he said. "Because she was from a different part of town. But she was—"

"—visiting a client." I finished the sentence for him.

He chuckled coldly. "She got you too, eh? She popped up in my path and, boy, was she surprised! If her current career doesn't work out, she could always turn to acting."

"So what happened?"

"I found her to be charming and somehow it was agreed that she do over my diet. Then she overheard me grouching about my paperwork and she offered her assistance. Very quickly she made herself . . . indispensable."

I was thinking back to that morning in Dean & DeLuca. I'd been so grateful for a friendly face in this big fast city. It was to Gilda's credit how quickly she'd made herself vitally important to me also.

"We got on famously until she produced a collection of pages . . ." Laszlo waved his hand in the air. "I hardly know how to describe it— lists and symptoms and simplistic solutions to women's health problems. She insisted it was a book. It was not a book. She wanted my help in getting it published. But it was entirely without merit. I couldn't advocate it. Shortly after I refused my endorsement, she withdrew her . . . friendship. I gave her no further thought until suddenly she was being squired around town by that old fraud Joss Wootten. He made a contemptible attempt to taunt me because he was—if I remember his words correctly—'banging' my girl. And in the midst of his swaggering, he alluded to his tremendous good fortune in having had a chance meeting with Gilda in his dentist's waiting room, no less."

I had a flash of terror mixed with something close to admiration for Gilda.

"I became—a little late in the day—mistrustful. I did a small piece of background research and . . ." He shrugged. "And nothing. The University of Overgaard exists. It's an online school but there's nothing wrong with that. She got her piece of paper. Her qualifications as a nutritionist and personal trainer are real. Then today I heard that my old friend Bryce Bonesman plans to publish a book by her. And this book consists of—how did I describe it?—'lists and symptoms and simplistic solutions to women's health problems.'"

I nodded.

"She had her eye on the prize," Laszlo Jellico said. "And now she's got it. She played me but I probably wasn't the first guy and I doubt I'll be the last. Speaking of which," he added. "I hear your husband is agenting her."

"He's not my husband."

"Right. And he's not ever going to be. Not if Gilda wants him."

"Gilda wants him." I was afraid I might faint.

Laszlo Jellico shook his head. "So Gilda's going to get him. I'm sorry, kid."

As I made my way home, waves of panic washed over me as I contemplated the reality that I'd lost Mannix. Mixed with the horror was humiliation, as I relived, again and again, the conversation in Bryce's office. *We don't love you, Stella. There will be no second book for you, Stella.*

There had been multiple betrayals—from Bryce, from Gilda and, worst of all, from Mannix. Why hadn't he stood up and pounded the table and said he wouldn't tolerate a book written only by Gilda?

By the time I reached the apartment, I was so overwhelmed I thought my head would burst.

Mannix was in the living room, in front of his computer. He jumped to his feet. "Where have you been? I've rung a thousand times."

Breathless with anguish, I asked, "Are you really Gilda's agent?"

"You know I am."

"And her manager?"

"I don't know. I guess so. If I'm paid to do it."

"How could you?" I was so wounded by his treachery that I could barely breathe. "You should be in my corner. Did you know she was going to pull that stunt today with Bryce?"

"Of course I didn't. I was as shocked as you were. But . . . Stella, please look at me." He tried to grasp me by the shoulders but I stepped away from him. "Neither of us has any income. She's all we've got."

"I don't want you working with her."

"Stella," he beseeched me fervently. "We've no other option."

"Has anything happened with you and her?"

"No."

"She said you've become close."

He paused. "Maybe we're closer than we once were."

I went cold with fear. That was enough to confirm all the doubts and questions she'd stirred up.

"Stella, I'm just trying to be honest."

"Mannix." I fixed him in my gaze. "I'm begging you to walk away from Gilda. She's not what she seems. I met Laszlo Jellico. He says she uses people."

"Well, he would, wouldn't he?"

"Why?"

"Because Gilda left him and he was in bits. He's been a prick to her ever since."

"That's not what happened. Gilda showed him her book and—Hey! What do you know about it?"

"She told me."

"When?"

"Sometime." He thought about it. "On the phone. Probably when I was in Ireland."

"What? You had lovely chats where you confided in each other?"

"You're making it sound . . ."

"Oh God." I choked. I was done for. Gilda's beauty and her absolute certainty that she'd get what she wanted—I had no chance against that combination.

"Mannix, she's stolen my life."

"She hasn't stolen me."

"She has. You just don't know it yet."

He compressed his mouth into a tight line.

"Mannix," I said. "I know what you're like."

"I'm not *like* anything."

"You are. You're led by your dick."

He recoiled. He looked sickened. "Have you ever trusted me?"

"No. And I was right not to. We're too different, you and I. We were a mistake right from the start."

"That's what you think?" He bit the words out. I realized he was very, very angry.

"Yes." Well, I was angry too.

"Really?"

"Yes."

"Then I'd better leave."

"Then you'd better."

"Really? Because if you tell me to go, I'll go."

"Go."

He looked at me, his expression bitter. "You never told me you loved me. So I guess you never did."

"The time was never right."

"It's certainly not right now, is it?"

"No."

He made his way into our bedroom and pulled a small suitcase out from a cupboard. I watched as he threw some clothes into it. I was waiting for him to stop but he went into the bathroom and emerged with a razor and a toothbrush, which he added to his stuff.

"Don't forget your medication." I lunged for his bedside drawer, found a card of tablets and chucked them into the case.

Silently he zipped it shut and went into the hall, where he put on his coat. Even as he opened the front door, I thought he'd call a halt, but he kept going. The door slammed behind him and then he was gone.

That night, he didn't come back and it was like living in a bad dream. I was tormented by thoughts that he was with Gilda, but I wouldn't ring him. I'd always had to work hard to resist being annihilated by the force of his personality and this was more true now than ever. I held on to my pride like it was a shield—so long as I had it, I still existed.

At around six in the morning, he called me. "Baby." He sounded wretched. "Can I come home?"

I had to reach deep into myself for strength. "Are you still Gilda's agent?"

"Yes."

"Then no, you can't."

He called again at 10 a.m. and we had a near-identical conversation. It happened several times over the next two days. I didn't know where he was living, but I couldn't bear to discover it was with Gilda, so I didn't ask. I could have got some clue about what he was doing by checking our bank account—to see if he was withdrawing cash or debiting costs to a hotel—but I was too afraid to look.

I told no one what was happening because if nobody knew, then it wasn't real.

But Jeffrey began to notice. "Mom, what's going on with you and Mannix?"

Guilt flamed through me.

"Have you and Mannix broken up?" he asked.

I flinched at the words. "I don't know. We're having a . . . disagreement. He's staying someplace else for a few days."

"It's something to do with Gilda?" Jeffrey asked.

I froze—how did he know? What had he seen?

"I just noticed that Gilda isn't around either." He gave me an anxious look. "But everything's going to be okay?"

"Hopefully."

I still had a sliver of faith that, if I waited long enough, things would somehow right themselves spontaneously. But the hours ticked by and, hollow-eyed, I lurched from room to room, unable to settle to anything.

I had no one to confide in. I couldn't ring Karen—she'd tell me that this had always been in the cards and that I shouldn't be surprised. I couldn't ring Zoe—she'd start crying and telling me that all men were bastards. And I couldn't ring my best friend in New York because she was Gilda.

I wondered what advice I'd give to someone else in my position. I realized I'd probably tell her that she should fight for him.

But the only way to fight for Mannix was to keep delivering ultimatums.

The next time he rang, I repeated what I'd said in every other conversation: "Mannix, I'm begging you. Please stop being Gilda's agent."

"I can't not be her agent." His tone was urgent. "Our money's running out, Stella, and this is the only chance we have."

"Mannix, you're not hearing me: if you're her agent, we have *no* chance. We might as well call it a day right now."

"Be careful of what you're saying."

"I'm only saying the facts." I was scared to death. "You have to get away from her."

"Or?"

"Or else we're finished."

"Right."

He hung up.

I sat staring at the phone, then I saw that Jeffrey was in the room. Shame drenched me. He shouldn't be hearing stuff like this. He was too vulnerable; his short life had already been subjected to too much upheaval.

"Hey, Mom." He tried to sound chirpy. "Let's go out for a pizza."

"Okay."

We went to a neighborhood Italian place and we both made an effort to be cheery and I felt a bit more hopeful when we returned.

We were taking off our hats and scarfs by the coat stand in the hall when I noticed something not right—Mannix's heavy boots were gone. They usually stood by the front door with the other winter shoes and there was a faint outline of them on the carpet. But they were gone.

Breathless, I ran into the bedroom and threw open the wardrobe; Mannix's side was empty.

"Oh my God." I was gasping for breath.

Followed by Jeffrey, I raced around the apartment—Mannix's computer was gone; his sports bag was gone; his chargers were gone. With each fresh realization, it was like being punched in the stomach.

With fumbling fingers I opened the safe: I couldn't find his passport. I scrabbled through all the documents and papers and still couldn't find it, and finally I admitted the truth: he was gone. Properly gone.

I ran and knocked on Esperanza's door. "Did you see Mannix? Did he come here while Jeffrey and I were out?"

But Esperanza was conveniently blind and deaf. "I see nobody, madam."

I threw myself on my bed and curled into a ball. "He's gone." Tears began to pour down my face. "I can't believe it."

"You told him to go, Mom," Jeffrey said.

"He wasn't supposed to do it."

I curled in on myself even tighter and I howled like a child, then I caught a glimpse of Jeffrey's terrified face. Instantly I choked back my grief. "I'm okay." I sounded like an animal trying to speak. My face was drenched with tears. "Sorry, Jeffrey." I sat up. "I don't mean to scare you. I'm okay, I'm okay, I'm okay."

Jeffrey was making a call. "Betsy, it's Mom. She's not so good."

The following morning, Jeffrey sidled into my bedroom.

"Sweetie." I sat up in bed. "I'm sorry about yesterday."

Betsy had come over, with a Xanax she'd purloined from Chad; she'd made me take it. After a while I'd calmed down and eventually I'd fallen asleep.

"Mom, can we go home?" Jeffrey asked.

"What do you mean?"

"Home to Ireland?"

"No, sweetie. You're in school here. You've got to finish that."

"But I hate it. I hate the other kids. All they talk about is money and how rich their dads are. I don't want to go to that school anymore."

"What are you saying? You want to . . . drop out?"

"Not drop out. Just give it up for this year. Start again in September at my old school in Ireland."

I went silent for a long time. This was catastrophic. Everything was crashing down around me.

"Are you on drugs?" I asked.

"No. I just hate my school." Then he admitted, "I sort of hate New York."

"I thought you loved it."

"In the beginning. But the people here, they're not like us, they're too tough. And Betsy's not coming back to us. She's all grown-up now. She's gone."

"I'm sorry, Jeffrey." I was consumed with remorse. "I've been a terrible mother to you."

"Not everything was your fault. But I want to go home."

"Would you like to live with your dad?"

"Not really. But I will, if that's my only choice. Think about things, Mom. You have no book deal and Mannix and you have broken up— you've no reason to stay in New York."

Silently I contemplated the bitter truth of his words.

"How do you know I've no book deal?"

"Betsy told me. She said everybody knows. So can we go home?"

"Okay," I said. "We'll go home."

"Both of us?"

"Both of us."

"Do you mean it?"

Did I mean it? I was moving into very dangerous territory—I couldn't mess Jeffrey around. If I said we were going back to Ireland, then we really *were* going back to Ireland. It was like deciding to board a fast train knowing I wouldn't be able to get off.

"Yes," I said. "I mean it. We won't be able to move back into our old house right away. We'll have to give the tenants a month's notice."

"That's okay. I'll stay with Dad. And you can stay with Auntie Karen."

I rang Mannix, who answered immediately. "Baby?"

"You can move back into the apartment."

"What are you saying?" He sounded hopeful.

"Jeffrey and I are leaving New York. We're going back to Ireland."

"You're leaving New York?" He was shocked. "When?"

"Two days' time."

"Really. Right." He couldn't hide his anger. "Well, good luck with that."

"Thanks."

He'd already hung up.

Two days later, Jeffrey and I landed in Dublin, our New York dream over. For a few weeks, Jeffrey lived with Ryan and I stayed with Karen. When our old house became free, we moved in. Jeffrey took up yoga with a vengeance and I threw myself at carbs, reigniting my love affair with them.

Jeffrey and I were living on the money that Karen had paid for my share in Honey Day Spa, but it was only a matter of time before it ran out and I had to get a job. Somewhere along the line, motivated by desperation, I decided I'd try to write another book.

I never let myself think about Mannix because that was the only way I'd survive. I wasn't going to honor our relationship, or mourn it, or any of the things that Betsy would have advised. What I had to do was get past it. A clean break, I kept telling myself. *Clean.* My time with him had to be parceled up and put away in a crate in my memory, never to be opened.

My resolve stayed strong except when I heard his voice—and this happened every week to ten days because, to my surprise—shock, even—he'd taken to leaving voice mails on my phone. We never actually spoke; he just left short messages in an anguished voice. *"Please talk to me." "You were wrong." "I can't sleep without you." "I miss you."*

Sometimes I was strong enough to delete them without listening, but sometimes I played them, and when I did, it took days to recover my equilibrium. My curiosity was always ignited—an awful, self-lacerating urge to know exactly what was happening with him and Gilda—and it was a terrible struggle to stay away from Google.

The one link with Mannix that I couldn't break was with Roland. I didn't visit him, I didn't even call him, but I kept an eye on him via his carer, whom Mum had once upon a time worked with. In entirely inappropriate, yet very Irish, breaches of confidence, she reported to Mum, who funneled news back to me that Roland was recovering well.

Thursday, 12 June

07:41

I awake. I was dreaming about Mannix. But although my face is wet with tears, I'm in a strange mood: reflective, almost accepting of all that has happened.

For the first time I understand what went wrong for us—our foundation had been unsound. There hadn't been enough trust—the fact that I wouldn't say I loved him told me that I'd always expected things would end badly.

Then, on top of our rickety base, too many bad things had happened, too close together—Roland's stroke, chronic money worries, the failure of a shared dream—and we weren't strong enough to withstand it.

Perhaps one day in the far-off future, when I'm about eighty-nine, I might look back and say, "When I was a young-ish woman I fell in love with an intense charismatic man. He was way out of my league and when it ended it nearly killed me, but every woman should experience that sort of love once in their lives. Only once, mind, you mightn't survive a second bout. A bit like dengue fever, that way."

I sit up in bed—at least Ryan isn't here with me, so I've plenty to be grateful for. The nerve of him, though, the colossal *nerve*!

I find him in the living room, putting on his shoes. Guiltily he looks up and cries out, "Don't say a word."

"I will," I splutter. "I fecking *will* say a word."

"It was an accident," he says, talking over me.

"You got into bed with me!"

"Because I was uncomfortable and lonely."

"You were looking for sex!"

"Your trouble, Stella Sweeney, is you're too quick to judge. No wonder your relationships never work."

The blood drains from my face. Ryan looks shifty: he knows he's gone too far. But, still, he styles it out.

"Have I hit a nerve?" he asks. "But I'm only saying what's true. Like, see the way you just jumped straight to the worst conclusion with Mannix and that Gilda."

I flinch. Even hearing Mannix's name is like being slapped.

"Mannix was a good guy," Ryan says.

"Really?" I'm stunned. Ryan never had a pleasant word to say for Mannix. "You've changed your mind."

"Because I'm adaptable. Because I give people a second chance."

"Based on what information have you changed your mind?"

"The same information that you have. I'm going out to buy a phone," Ryan says. "So I can get my life back. Jeffrey wouldn't give me any money. He's already gone, to yoga, he said. That's not right, Stella, that's not normal, a young man like him—"

"Here." I thrust fifty euro at Ryan. "Take it. Anything to get rid of you."

"Bitter Stella." Ryan shakes his head sadly. "So, so bitter."

And away he goes, leaving me alone with my thoughts.

He's wrong about one thing: I'm not bitter. I don't hate Gilda. In a way I almost understand her—she'd only been doing what she had to do. Okay, I'm not looking forward to her book coming out and having to see her on telly and in magazines, being young and beautiful and with Mannix. I wish I could fast-forward through that part of things and be safe on the far side, but I'm not bitter.

A thought worms its way into my head: had I been too quick to judge Mannix? He'd sworn that he had no feelings for Gilda but I'd been so hysterical with fear that I hadn't been able to hear him. Even Gilda had never insisted that something was actually going on; she'd simply suggested that it probably would, if I got out of the picture.

I'd always been afraid that Mannix would wound me, so when it seemed as if it was actually happening, I was quick to believe it was real—I was expecting to be hurt and humiliated and I gave in before the fight ever started.

I don't want to think this way. Less than an hour ago, I felt like I was making my peace with everything and now it's all stirred up again.

But the questions won't stop asking themselves—what if I *had* been wrong about Mannix and Gilda?

But there's no point in agonizing. I made my choice and there is no going back.

Right, I'd better do some work.

08:32

I stare at the screen.

08:53

I'm still staring at the screen. I'm about to make a decision. Right, I've made it! I am officially junking this writing business. It's not going to work, not ever.

I'm going to be a beautician again. I'd liked it, I wasn't bad at it and there's a living to be made. I'll retrain, learn all the new stuff . . . and there's Karen on the phone.

"Guess what?" She sounds a bit giddy. "I see from Facebook that the loneliest woman on earth is home from South America."

"Who? Georgie Dawson?"

"Back from her travels. Come to spread her largesse among us stumpy peasants."

"Great! That's really great. Listen, Karen, I'm stopping pretending to write a book and I'm going to retrain as a beautician and learn all the new things."

"The book writing is going that badly, is it?"

"It's not going at all."

"That's a shame," she says. "No more going on the radio with Ned Mount?"

"No."

"Ah, well. It was fun while it lasted. I'll do a little research, find out what course is the best for you."

"Okay, thanks. And I'll call Georgie."

I rang the old mobile number I had for Georgie—and she answered. "Stella!"

"Hello! Are you back?"

"Yes. Back, like, literally twenty minutes ago. Well, two days ago. So *what's* going on with Ryan?"

"Oh, Georgie, where do I start?"

"You must come and see me," she says. "Come to dinner tonight. I'm living in Ballsbridge—a friend of a friend had a spare house, you know how it is?"

"No, not at all, but it doesn't matter."

"Darling, I'm just going to get this out of the way: I know about you and Mannix being over. I'm very sorry. How are you doing?"

"I'm fine." I swallow. "Maybe not exactly fine, but I will be one day."

"Absolutely. It reminds of when I was twenty and living in Salzburg and having a *terribly* sexy affair with a much older man, a count. An actual real count who lived in an actual schloss. He wore black leather knee boots, I kid you not! Married, of course. With children, even grandchildren. I just adored him, Stella, and when he broke up with me I ran out into the snow—naked!—and waited to die. Then the Bundespolizei arrived and one of them was so *hot* and we began this *incredibly* passionate thing and the old count showed up with a Luger—Oh, I *am* sorry, Stella, I'm doing it again, making everything about me. What I'm trying to say is that you'll meet another man. And You. Will. Love. Again. You will! See you tonight. Eight thirty. I'll text you the address."

She hangs up. She's wrong: I will never love another man. But I have my lady friends. They will suffice . . . and hold on, there's someone at the front door.

To my astonishment, standing on my front step is Ireland's most popular broadcaster, Ned Mount.

"Ned, hi . . . Are you looking for Ryan?"

"No," he says, smiling at me with his shrewd, intelligent eyes. "I'm looking for you."

19:34

Karen comes over to help me get ready to visit Georgie.

"This isn't necessary," I protest.

"It *is* necessary. You're representing all of us when you go to see her. Here, try on this top and let's brush your hair out, so it's smooth and shiny. I must say, you're looking well, Stella. You've lost a few pounds."

"I don't know how. I haven't stuck to the carb-free thing. Well, I guess I *have* been sticking to it, in between the binges."

"And the anxiety you're having about Ryan. If I've said it once, I've said it a thousand times: anxiety is the fat girl's best friend. Not that you were exactly fat," she says. "Just . . . you know."

19:54

The doorbell rings. "Who's that?" Karen asks suspiciously.

"Probably Ryan home from the zoo."

"You haven't given him a house key?"

"No."

"Good."

It is indeed Ryan and there's an air of barely contained excitement about him. "I'm not staying," he says. "Great changes are afoot. Firstly, I've found a person to take me in."

"Who's that?"

"Zoe."

"*My* friend Zoe?" I ask.

"And *my* friend Zoe," he says. "She's my friend too. Her little bitches of daughters have gone away for the summer and she's got two spare bedrooms."

"And what other great changes are afoot?"

"It looks like I'll be getting my own house back. The charity realized that it doesn't look good for them to benefit by making someone homeless, right?" He really *is* in high spirits. "I'll do some fund-raising stuff for them . . . we're all pals! And there's a good chance I'll get my business back from Clarissa. I told her that I was going to found a new company called Ryan Sweeney Bathrooms, which would take away her business, and that she was better off working with me than cutting me out."

"And you came up with all these solutions yourself?" Karen asks Ryan.

"Yeah," he says, confidently. "Pretty much."

"Really?"

"Okay. Maybe I've had an adviser, but basically it's all down to me."

20:36

Georgie's friend-of-a-friend's house is in a gorgeous little mews off the most expensive road in Ireland. She really is a class act. No parking, mind. The narrow lane is jam-packed with high-end cars. I squash my little Toyota into a space and refuse to be intimidated.

Georgie flings open her front door. Her hair is long and loose and she looks tanned and yoga-ish. I'm extraordinarily happy to see her and I reflect that if a friendship with Georgie is the only legacy from my time with Mannix, it's not so bad.

"You look great," she cries, throwing her arms around me.

"So do you."

"No, darling, no. I'm so *wrinkly*. All that sun. I'm going to have a jaw lift. I should have had it in Lima, but I was too loved up. Twenty-six-year-old bodybuilder. Ended badly." Her eyes are sparkling. "For him! He wept when I left."

"While I think of it, Georgie, Ned Mount is trying to get in touch with you. He called at my house today—he knows we're friends—and left a number."

"He did? What a sweet man. We met on a plane a few days ago. Mmmm, there was a bit of a spark! I'll call him. So, come in, come into the kitchen. As you can see, it's all very bijou here, but so cozy."

There's someone already in the kitchen, sitting at the table, and

I'm momentarily irritated. Then, to my profound shock, I realize that the person is Mannix.

"Surprise," Georgie says.

Mannix looks stunned. About as stunned as I feel.

He glances from Georgie to me, then back again. "Georgie, what's going on?"

"You two need to talk," she says.

"No, no, we don't." I'm trying to get to the door. I need to get away. Clean break. Clean break. The only way I can do this is by a clean break.

Georgie blocks my path. "You do. Stella, Mannix didn't do anything wrong. There was nothing going on with him and Gilda."

I'm finding it difficult to breathe. "How do you know?"

"I breezed through New York for a week on my way home from Peru and we arranged to meet. I spoke very firmly to her. I think she was quite frightened of me. Yes, she had a thing for Mannix." Georgie shrugs. "Each to their own. Hey, I'm joking!"

Because I'm fond of her I summon up a reluctant smile.

"Come and sit down, sweetie." Gently, Georgie coaxes me, until I'm sitting at the table, opposite Mannix. She puts a glass of wine in front of me. "Don't be so scared."

I bow my head. I can't look him in the eye; it's too intense, just too much.

"Gilda messed with your head, darling. She needed you to think that she and Mannix were having a thing. But they weren't. Were you, Mannix?"

He clears his throat. "No."

"Ever?"

"Never."

Tentatively I lift my head and look into Mannix's face. Energy flames between us.

"Never," he repeats, his gray eyes locked onto mine.

"So there you are." Georgie beams. "You both need to understand what happened. You were in a very messy situation. Roland was potentially dying and everyone was devastated. When I heard, I wept.

We were all terribly upset—although, Mannix, you know I've always thought that you're *too* attached to Roland. But you're not my husband so it's not my problem." She beams again. "You were running out of money, which you both worry too much about. You should be more like me—I never fret and something always comes along."

Mannix gives her a look and she snorts with laughter.

"Stella." Georgie becomes serious. "Mannix thought he was doing the right thing for you when he said he'd be Gilda's agent. He was panicking; he wanted to take care of you financially and this was the only way he knew how. But you jumped to the worst interpretation, and, to be frank, I don't *really* believe you have such a low opinion of Mannix, I just think you were afraid. You have that working-class chippiness thing," she muses. "You think he's too arrogant and he thinks you're too proud. You two *do* have communication issues . . ." Her voice trails away, then she collects herself and says, brightly, "But you'll sort it out. Okay, I'm leaving now. The place is yours."

"You're going?"

"Just for tonight." She swings her handbag onto her elegantly bony shoulder—a very beautiful handbag, I can't help but notice. Perhaps I should tell her I like it; she'd probably give it to me—Oh, hold on, she's speaking again. More advice.

"One final thing: Gilda's book will be published at some stage. Maybe it'll be a success, maybe it won't, but you have to wish her well. There's a wonderful ritual I suggest—write her a letter and let it *all out*. All your jealousy and resentment—everything! Then burn the page and ask the universe—or God, or Buddha, or whoever you like—to remove the bad feelings and leave the good. You could do it together, you and Mannix. It would be a wonderful way to cleanse and rebond. Okay, I'm gone."

The front door shuts and Mannix and I are alone in the house.

We watch each other warily.

After a silence, he says, "She did that letter ritual when we were married and she set the bedroom curtains on fire."

I laugh nervously. "I'm not really a ritual person."

"Neither am I."

"I know."

Startled, we look at each other, shocked by the flash of our old familiarity. Then my mood darkens.

"What's going on?" I ask. "Are you still Gilda's agent?"

He seems surprised. "No . . . Don't you know? I called, I left messages."

"I'm sorry." I clear my throat. "I didn't listen to them. I couldn't . . ."

"I stopped being her agent the day you told me you were leaving New York. There was no longer any point. I'd only been doing it for you."

"Really? So how is she?"

"I've no idea."

"Honestly?" I look hard at him. "Aren't you even a bit curious about her? Don't you run into her in New York?"

"I don't live in New York."

I'm hugely surprised. "Where do you live?"

"Here. Dublin. I'm building up my practice again. It'll take a while but . . . I like being a doctor."

Something has just occurred to me, some piece of information that's slid home. "A mysterious friend has been helping Ryan today— is that you?"

"Yes."

"Why?"

"To help you."

"Why would you do that?"

"Because you're everything to me."

That silences me.

He takes my hand across the table. "It was always you. It was always only you."

The touch of his skin makes tears start in my eyes. I thought I'd never again hold his hand.

". . . I can't sleep without you," he says. "I never sleep. Please come back."

"It's too late for us," I say. "I've made my peace with it."

"Well, I haven't. I love you."

"I did love you. I'm sorry I never told you at the time. Now I'd better go." I stand up.

"Don't." Sounding panicked, he gets to his feet. "Please don't go."

"Thank you, Mannix. My time with you was wonderful and thrilling and beautiful. I'll never forget it and I'll always be glad it happened." I give him a quick peck on the mouth and go outside and find my car.

I sit behind my steering wheel and wonder which is the best way to Ferrytown from here. Then I think, Am I completely insane? Mannix is in there, Mannix who says he still loves me, Mannix who didn't cheat on me, Mannix who wants us to try again.

I switch off the engine and get out of my car and go back to the house. Mannix opens the door. He looks wrecked.

"I'm sorry," I say, helplessly. "I wasn't thinking straight. I'm thinking straight now. I love you."

He pulls me into the house. "And I love you too."

A Year Later

I cradle the baby in my arms and stare down into her tiny little face. "She's got my eyes."

"She's got *my* eyes," Ryan says.

"Guys," Betsy says. "She's four weeks old. It's too soon for her to have anyone's eyes. Anyway, she totally looks like Chad."

Kilda makes a mewling noise, then another and it looks like she's going to launch into full-blown crying.

"Betsy," I say, anxiously.

"I'll take her," Chad says. He gathers the tiny bundle into his chest and immediately Kilda quiets.

Dad watches this with keen interest. "You've a good way with her, haven't you, son?" He sounds a tad suspicious. "We had our doubts about you. Weren't sure you'd be father material, but all credit to you, gameball!"

"Gameball," Mum agrees.

"Thanks," Chad says.

"No bother. Well!" Dad smiles around at us, all crowded into the front room of the beach house. "This is a fitting entrée to the world for my first great-grandchild. "Entrée being a French word. Hold on . . ." He pauses, then taps himself on the chest and emits a robust belch. "This fizzy stuff is giving me the gawks. Have you any Smithwicks?"

"Jeffrey," I say. "Get Grandad some working-class ale. There are a few bottles in the kitchen."

Jeffrey obediently gets to his feet and Mum says, "While you're in there, could I have a cup of tea?"

"Sure, anyone else want anything?"

"Can I have some cake?" Roland asks.

"Noooooo!" a chorus of voices calls out.

"Don't, love," Mum says to him. "You worked so hard to lose all that weight, you don't want to start piling it on again."

"Oh, all right." A little glumly, he toes the rug with his pink and orange trainer.

"Why don't you have a coconut water?" Jeffrey suggests.

"Okay!" And instantly Roland is back to being cheery again.

"And maybe you'd tell us a story," Mum says. "Tell us about the time you met Michelle Obama. Chad would like that, him being American."

"And then," Ryan glances meaningfully at Zoe, "we'd better get going."

"Yes." Zoe giggles. "We'd better."

Riding. Nonstop riding. Last year, when Ryan moved into Zoe's house, something big had ignited between them. Even after he managed to win back his house and his business, they remained together.

Over at the door, Karen is staring out at the waves. "Doesn't it ever get to you?" she says. "All that . . . water?"

I laugh. "I love it."

"I couldn't live here," she says. "I don't know how you do it. I'm not a rural person. Am I, Enda?"

"You're a city girl." Enda looks at her with solid admiration. "You're *my* city girl."

"Christ, Enda." Karen's look is scathing. "Whatever it is you're drinking, go easy on it."

Clark and Mathilde come thumping down the hallway and into the room. "Hey!" Clark yells. "What's that funny swinging bed in the end bedroom?"

I color slightly. "Just a bed."

"Do you and Uncle Mannix sleep in it?"

". . . No." I flick a look at Mannix.

"No." Mannix clears his throat.

We're telling the truth. We do very little sleeping in it.

Karen watches me and Mannix closely, then rolls her eyes. "I suppose we'd better get moving too. But before we go, Stella . . ." She crosses the room to me and says, almost without moving her lips, "I need a word."

She pulls me into a corner. "Look, I didn't know if I should tell you or not but there was something in one of the British papers today. About—"

"—Gilda and her book," I finish for her.

"Oh, you know? You saw it? Are you okay about it?"

"Well . . ."

Over the past year Mannix and I have had many discussions about how we might feel when Gilda's book is published. "If we're bitter," I'd concluded, "it would be like holding a hot coal in our hands—we're the ones who'd get hurt."

Today, when it finally happened, as I saw the photo of Gilda's pretty smiling face and read the positive review of her book, my hands were shaking and my heart was beating way too fast. I showed the page to Mannix and I said, "Can we wish her well?"

"Is that how you feel?" he asked.

"It's the way I want to feel," I said.

"Very worthy." Mannix gave a little laugh. "But also remember," he said, "that she really, really, really doesn't matter."

The last of our visitors leaves around seven o'clock. We wave the cars away up the boreen, up through the dunes and over the hill, until it's just Mannix and me.

"Where's Shep gone?" Mannix asks.

"Running around in the field, the last I saw of him."

"Come on, we'll all go for a walk."

Mannix whistles for Shep and, after a moment, he comes bounding over the hill, his black tail waving behind him like a plume.

The three of us are alone on the beach. The evening sun casts a golden glow and the waves deposit a stick on the shiny sand, right at my feet. Shep barks and jumps with excitement.

"A gift from the gods!" I say. "I'll throw it for Shep. The two of you, go ahead a little bit."

Mannix and Shep walk on a few meters. I throw the stick and it accidentally hits Mannix.

"Ow!" he yelps.

I double over, laughing. "It was the breeze, blame the breeze."

"I forgive you." Mannix comes back and pulls me to him and Shep noses himself between the two of us.

This is my life now.

Acknowledgments

Thank you to Louise Moore, the best publisher in the world, for her unwavering faith in me and this book. Thank you to Celine Kelly for editing me with such verve and insight. Thank you to Clare Parkinson for the painstaking, meticulous copyediting. Thank you to Anna Derkacz, Maxine Hitchcock, Tim Broughton, Nick Lowndes, Lee Motley, Liz Smith, Joe Yule, Katie Sheldrake and all the team at Michael Joseph. I feel very lucky to be working with such brilliant people.

Thank you to my legendary agent, Jonathan Lloyd, and everyone at Curtis Brown for believing in my books and taking such beautiful care of them.

Thank you to my friends who read the book as it was written and who advised and encouraged me: Bernice Barrington, Caron Freeborn, Ella Griffin, Gwen Hollingsworth, Cathy Kelly, Caitríona Keyes, Mammy Keyes, Rita-Anne Keyes, Mags McLoughlin, Ken Murphy, Hilly Reynolds, Anne Marie Scanlon and Rebecca Turner.

Special thanks to Kate Beaufoy, who held my hand every step of the way, and Shirley Baines and Jenny Boland, whose runaway enthusiasm let me know I was on the right path.

Thank you to Paul Rolles, who made a generous donation to Action Against Hunger to have his name included as a character.

In order to understand Guillain-Barré Syndrome, I read *Bed Number Ten* by Sue Baier and Mary Zimmeth Schomaker, *The Darkness Is Not Dark* by Regina R. Roth and *No Laughing Matter* by Joseph Heller and Speed Vogel.

Thank you to the wonderful Elena and Mihaela Manta at Pretty Nails, Pretty Face, who inspired me to write about a beauty salon—although I need hardly state that Pretty Nails, Pretty Face is nothing like Honey Day Spa!

Finally, thank you to my beloved husband and best friend, Tony, for all the encouragement, help, support and belief in me—there are no words to adequately express my gratitude.

AVAILABLE FROM PENGUIN BOOKS

The Mystery of Mercy Close

Helen Walsh's private investigator business has dried up, until a lucrative missing-persons case falls into her lap. Playing by her own rules, Helen is drawn into a dark and glamorous world, where her own worst enemy is her own head and where increasingly the only person she feels connected to is Wayne Diffney, the missing man she has never even met.

The Brightest Star in the Sky

Seven neighbors lives become entangled when a sassy and prescient spirit descends on 66 Star Street to radically transform at least one person's life in the Dublin town house. With the comic appeal of Nick Hornby's novels and delicious drama akin to Jane Green, *The Brightest Star in the Sky* will keep readers guessing, laughing, gasping, and in tears until the very last page.

Saved by Cake
Over 80 Ways to Bake Yourself Happy

Refreshingly honest and wickedly funny, *Saved by Cake* shines with Marian Keyes' inimitable charm. Written in Keyes' signature style, her take on baking is extremely accessible and full of fun. Her simple and delicious recipes, with step-by-step instructions and stunning photography, are guaranteed to tempt even the most jaded palate.